STARSHIP'S MAGE

CHIMERA'S FALL

BOOK SIXTEEN
OF THE STARSHIP'S MAGE SERIES

Faolan's Pen Publishing
22 King St. S, Suite 300
Waterloo, Ontario
N2J 1N8 Canada

For paperback sales information, visit faolanspen.com. For special events, release alerts, and more books from the author, visit glynnstewart.com.

A record of this book is available from Library and Archives Canada.

ISBN 978-1-989674-69-7 (Trade Paperback)
ISBN 978-1-989674-70-3 (Amazon Paperback)
ISBN 978-1-989674-68-0 (Ebook)

1 2 3 4 5 6 7 8 9 10

STARSHIP'S MAGE

CHIMERA'S FALL

BOOK SIXTEEN
OF THE STARSHIP'S MAGE SERIES

GLYNN STEWART

FAOLAN'S PEN
PUBLISHING
faolanspen.com

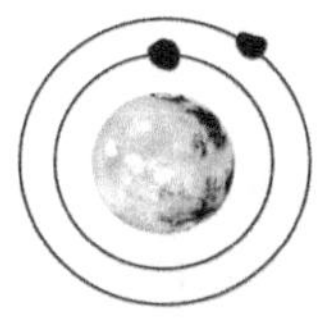

CHAPTER 1

THERE WERE STEREOTYPES AND STANDARDS about what type of coffee hard-bitten, war-winning, senior military officers like Admirals were supposed to drink. The coconut vanilla latte sitting on the desk of Mage-Admiral Jane Alexander, Crown Princess of Mars and the victor of the UnArcana Rebellions, didn't live up to any of them.

It wasn't black. The coconut milk was sourced from a specific plantation on the continent of Magna Madagasca on the planet Dracon in the Sigma Draconis System. It wasn't bitter. The vanilla beans were sourced from a second plantation on the same continent, as were the coffee beans.

Jane owned all three plantations, guaranteeing them security against any market fluctuations so long as she could get her exact latte reliably. It was a continuing comfort, a support that had held her through an ugly civil war.

The latte was far too frail a shield against the reality being laid out in her meeting.

"The evacuation of an entire star system's population is mind-boggling," General Akuchi Kamau pointed out, as if the commanding officer of the Royal Martian Marine Corps was the only person who saw the problem in front of them.

"How many people are even *in* the Chimera System?" the Black officer asked.

"Just under a billion humans, who constitute roughly forty-five percent of the population," a large and muscular redheaded man replied. Ambassador Connor O'Hannagain was on Garuda, the habitable planet of the Chimera System, acting as the representative of the Mage-Queen of Mars and her Protectorate to the Dual Republics of human and alien occupants of that system.

"Give or take, two-point-two billion people," he concluded. "The reezh are the majority of the population. I've forwarded files on their life-support needs, but they look quite comparable to me."

"The reezh, at least, should be safe if the Kazh takes the planet, shouldn't they?" The questioner was José Kumiega, the Protectorate's Minister of the Economy. A dark-skinned non-binary economist from the Epsilon Eridani System, Kumiega was far from Jane's favorite member of her niece's cabinet.

"Given the costs and scale of an evacuation of two billion individuals, it seems that committing our resources to this project was somewhat injudicious, Ambassador."

Jane was about to say something, but she saw the woman in charge of the meeting lean forward and held her tongue.

The various participants in the meeting were scattered across the entirety of known space. O'Hannagain was in Chimera itself, the center of the problem, over a hundred light-years beyond regular human space. Jane was in the Exeter System, the official border of the Protectorate, gathering ships to support Chimera against the threat.

The Ministers were mostly in the Sol System, rarely far from Mars itself and the capital at Olympus Mons. The quantum-entanglement Link allowed them to speak to each other live, a conference that would never have been possible with the old magical forms of interstellar communication.

That meant that everyone could see the sharp green eyes of Kiera Michelle Alexander, the Mage-Queen of Mars and Protector of Humanity, as she leveled her glare on Minister Kumiega.

"Ambassador O'Hannagain acted exactly as We would have wished him to," she told them. The Royal *We* was very clear. "The Reezh Kazh was not aware that Chimera still existed until *Our* traitors went poking around sleeping dogs.

"Now they have attacked the system once, and We do not have the resources to stand against the fleets the Kazh appear to have available.

Evacuation is a reasonable request. We will do *everything* the Protectorate can to assist the Dual Republics in moving their population to safety."

And that, Jane was certain, was that.

"Minister Kumiega," she said, inserting herself into the conversation. "Is there an actual *problem* with the objective?"

They gave her a surprisingly grateful look.

"I perhaps spoke inappropriately," they conceded. "But yes, there is. Frankly, we don't have the passenger lift to move two billion people. There are, approximately, thirty-two thousand civilian jump ships in the Protectorate. Of those, less than four thousand are designed primarily for the purpose of carrying passengers."

Any jump ship required at least one Mage. Only a Mage could teleport a ship between stars, using the runic jump matrix that amplified their magic. The limited supply of such Mages was the real restriction on the number of ships in human space. Those thirty-two thousand ships employed roughly a hundred thousand Jump Mages—nearly ten percent of *all* human Mages.

"Forty-two percent of our civilian-passenger traffic travels aboard freighters and cargo transports," Kumiega explained. "The size necessary to provide rotational pseudogravity means that such ships often have excess volume to work with. A three-megaton freighter carrying two hundred passengers, however, isn't going to help us evacuate Chimera—especially as her cargo is designed to be loaded in pods, so she does not even have empty volumes we can retrofit.

"I will have to have my staff review the exact numbers, but given the usual characteristics of our passenger-liner fleet, I would estimate that those transports have a total carriage capacity of perhaps forty million. Assuming we commandeered them all immediately, that would require fifty-five flights, minimum, to evacuate the Chimeran population."

Kumiega looked almost distressed, and Jane felt a moment of discomfort for her willingness to dismiss their concern. She'd known they probably had a real one, but they were prone to stating the obvious.

"I am not certain of the flight times involved for such flights," they admitted, "but pulling our entire passenger transport fleet away from their usual routes for over a year would have drastic effects on certain parts of our economy."

"I can speak to the flight times," Jane noted. She'd been going over those numbers in excruciating detail the last few days. She had a single dreadnought, *Mjolnir*, at Base Deveraux, already vastly distant from Sol. Chimera was even farther out—and the enemy, the church ruling the remnants of the reezh's ancient empire, were thankfully even farther. Tasked to fight the war across those empty stars, she'd been staring at the maps for weeks.

"From Chimera to the closest of our new worlds in the Mackenzie/Exeter region is roughly a hundred light-years," she reminded everyone. "Base Deveraux at Exeter is incapable of handling significant amounts of civilians; there's no habitable planet here.

"I would suggest sending the evacuees to Mackenzie itself and distributing from there. Everyone in the region is likely to step up to help gladly—their own occupation by the First Legion is all too recent.

"For a liner with three Jump Mages without military training, we are looking at nine light-years per day and a roughly thirteen-day flight to Mackenzie," she concluded. "Including loading and offloading, a minimum of thirty days for a round trip."

And fifty-five trips, as Kumiega had pointed out. Almost five *years* to evacuate the population with just the civilian transport. Of course...

"Any civilian transport we can commandeer will be a useful adjunct to the evacuation effort," she continued. "But it can only be an adjunct. As the Minister noted, those ships are already busy."

Jane met her niece's gaze and raised an eyebrow slightly. A silent question: *Do you want me to take the lead on this?*

Baked into that question was whether or not Kiera Alexander saw the answer Jane did—but given that it was the young Mage-Queen who had mandated the creation of the transports that would solve their problem, she suspected so.

An equally slight nod came back. *Go ahead.*

"As much as possible, the transportation must fall on the Protectorate," Jane concluded, looking around the virtual room. "While warships will be needed to guard the convoys, we will be moving as many of those as we can manage into Chimera itself."

"Of course." There were two Generals sitting at the table, though the primly gaunt and silver-haired Pádraigín Alserda was perfectly fine with her service's status as the juniormost of the Protectorate's three military arms.

The Protectorate Guard had been born out of the need for forces capable of securing and occupying planets during the UnArcana Rebellions. It had been Kiera's idea, with its original strength drawn by requesting that every world in the Protectorate transfer a full division from its planetary army.

"We've done a lot of work since the Rebellion to expand the Guard's transport capability," Alserda continued. "We now have sixty *Bushido*-class transports, specially built units intended to carry a corps of fifty thousand soldiers and support personnel, plus heavy equipment."

"The Marine Corps has forty of the same vessels," Kamau said slowly, the Marine sounding displeased at the concept of the Guard and the Corps sharing the same ships.

Probably because Alserda had caught Jane's meaning first and so it sounded like the Corps had the *Guard's* ships rather than the other way around.

"A hundred ships that can carry fifty thousand people," Jane concluded. "Enough lift for five million people, each ship crewed by three Mages."

Few, if any, of those Mages would be up to the standards the Royal Martian Navy expected of their own Jump Mages. Still, like the civilian Jump Mages, they could jump a ship every eight hours each. Nine light-years a day was respectable.

"That gives us a start, then," O'Hannagain said. "We'll need as many of those civilian ships as we can get, too. Even at forty-five million a trip, this is going to take longer than I expect the enemy to leave us."

"A *Bushido* is designed to carry a Marine or Guard *corps*, Ambassador," Kamau pointed out. "That's not just fifty thousand people. It's also over ten thousand vehicles, mobile repair sites, munitions... We will have to consult with the engineers, but I am confident we will be able to double if not *triple* the capacity of those ships for civilian transport."

"We won't want to send them out empty, though," Alserda added. "If we are unlikely to fully evacuate Chimera, I believe we will best serve Her Majesty's plan by deploying our own troops to lay the ground for a network of resistance to Kazh occupation."

She gestured to Kamau.

"I believe that would, traditionally, fall into the hands of the RMMC," she conceded without his even raising the point. "The Guard will provide any resources or support needed, of course, but I feel that a mission this important should be led by the senior ground combat service."

Alserda, Jane reflected, was clearly used to the game.

"If your staffs can get mine a plan for moving all of the transports to Exeter, I'll make certain we have escorts to take them out to Chimera," Jane promised. "Battleship Task Group *Righteous Guardian of Liberty* should arrive within two weeks, Mage–Vice Admiral Janet Adamant commanding."

Jane hadn't intended to give Admiral Adamant her last ship as her new flagship. The Mage–Vice Admiral had been in the same place as *Righteous Guardian* when she'd needed a capital ship she could tear free to reinforce the RMN ships in Chimera.

Adamant's "Battleship Task Group" was *Righteous Guardian* and two cruisers. They didn't have the mobile logistics in place to move her own dreadnought flagship, *Mjolnir*, up to Chimera yet.

"Make it happen," Prince-Chancellor Damien Montgomery said firmly. The Protectorate's head of government was a dark-haired man as intense as he was small, but everyone in the room knew that he spoke for the Mage-Queen.

"We will," Jane promised—echoed before she'd even finished speaking by General Kamau.

Mars would not abandon Chimera. Their Queen had decided that, and the Royal Martian Navy and Marines would make certain of it.

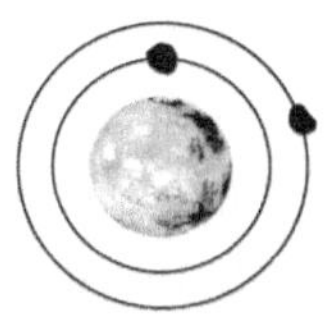

CHAPTER 2

THE HOLOGRAMS AND SCREENS FOLDED AWAY, and Kiera Alexander closed her eyes for several long moments, gathering her thoughts and strength. She was reasonably sure she was doing the right thing, but the resources of her Kingdom and Protectorate seemed far smaller than they'd appeared a few weeks earlier.

Vast as her Navy was, numerous as the Guard and Marines were, immense as the industrial might entailed by over a hundred star systems was, Kiera feared they weren't up to the task she'd set them.

Her gloom was rudely interrupted by a warm furry body arriving on her lap with a confused "merp?!" She opened her eyes to see a familiar black cat with a white stripe across his left ear look up at her—and at the man who'd just dropped Zagreus into her lap.

"You looked like you needed a distraction," Barry Carpentier told her. Despite hair nearly as dark as Zagreus's fur, the Royal Boyfriend was as pale as only someone who'd grown up on Tau Ceti's second habitable planet could be.

Tau Ceti *f* was a chill and stormy world, barely warm enough for humans and notorious for lacking enough sunlight for a decent tan. Add in that Barry had spent much of his life indoors or on ships—he'd been a professional shuttle thief before accidentally saving her life—and Kiera had seen few paler humans.

"You're not wrong," she conceded, reaching down to scratch the cat behind his ears. Zagreus had taken being bodily plopped onto a monarch's lap with confusion but also hadn't left while she spoke. He now leaned in to her hand and purred loudly.

Zagreus was of the third generation of the carefully managed and cared-for family of mostly black cats descended from Persephone, the kitten Kiera had acquired for Damien Montgomery as a therapy animal after he'd been crippled in her father's service.

Persephone herself was barely separable from Damien and his children, but her kittens and her kittens' kittens were sufficiently integrated into the Royal Family that Kiera was worried the Royal Geneticists were going to start genegineering them along with the royals themselves.

"How much did you hear?" she asked. Barry hadn't been supposed to be in the meeting but was cleared for most things by the necessity of living in her back pocket.

"What, between reestablishing the Roman Empire before Islam is founded?" he replied with an innocent small and meaningful tap on his eyebrow. Her boyfriend had an implant in his brow ridge that projected a small screen into his eye. Most people who had the uncommon cybernetic used it for business and calls.

He used it to play video games. Currently, a political simulator of Europe in the second half of the first millennium, from what Kiera understood.

"The day you can only focus on your video games is the day you *stop playing them*," she pointed out. She understood that Barry found focusing on one thing at a time actively difficult, but she also found that his *divided* focus allowed him to remember and understand things better than a lot of people giving their full attention.

"Zagreus and I came in around when the Crown Princess managed to both lecture and support Minister Kumiega in the same sentence," he admitted. "I need to take lessons from that woman."

He grinned at her.

"You don't. You did well, if you were worried. No high horses today."

Kiera met the grin with a glare that lacked any real force. The situation in Chimera had nearly triggered a constitutional crisis when her Parliament had felt she'd failed to keep them in the loop. She'd aggravated the situation, she had to admit, by getting up on a high horse until Barry had hauled her back down.

She loved him for his support—*and* for his willingness to argue with her.

"Thank you," she told him. "Just why *were* you and Zagreus in here?"

Barry had blanket authorization to go anywhere in the Royal Apartments, but he usually didn't interrupt her meetings.

"Zagreus was scratching at the door to get in. I wasn't sure if you could hear him, but I also knew he'd be better behaved *inside* than *outside.*"

The cat took that moment to rotate three times around Kiera's lap and settle down, leaning even harder into her hand. Like most of the Royal Cats, he was extremely well behaved but also very, very, *very* smart.

Smart enough to make Kiera wonder if the Royal Geneticists had *already* started poking at her pets.

"Then you heard most of the situation anyway. Your thoughts?"

Barry wasn't quite sure what to make of himself yet, she knew. He didn't want to just be the kept man of the Mage-Queen of Mars, but the Royal Boyfriend definitely couldn't be a thief anymore—and was too visible to be a spy, which was about the only legitimate use of his skills.

Still, he was smart and perceptive—and had a very different point of view from the military commanders and politicians that often surrounded her.

"It's what we have to do," he said quietly. "The task is impossible. We cannot evacuate two billion people in time, but we have to try."

"Four hundred warships and a hundred troop transports, plus another hundred logistics ships," Kiera totaled aloud. "That's every military ship we have, every hull we can move. Against the Kazh, it looks like nothing— but they only have a few systems."

"Which means this is a question of how hard we fight," Barry countered, refusing to accept the despair Kiera was fighting. "We know they have at least three systems. Odds are that out of the surviving Primes, there's, what, five aligned with them? Maybe six?

"So, they have the resources of six Core Worlds plus the Nine itself. We have *twelve* Core Worlds, plus Sol. Plus almost forty MidWorlds and over sixty Fringe Worlds—and that's *ignoring* Chimera and the Independent UnArcana Worlds."

He snorted.

"And despite the complete lack of sympathy and understanding I have for the so-called 'Free Worlds,' I do not for one moment believe they will stand aside if humanity is truly threatened.

"Six hundred military ships is all humanity has *needed*. Or, more accurately, it's all the *Protectorate* has needed. The only reason Damien isn't raising the blind spot is because warships won't change what's needed right now."

Kiera paused for a moment in thought, until Zagreus headbutted her hand and the pieces fell together.

At the start of the UnArcana Rebellion, the Republic had managed to put the Royal Martian Navy badly on the back foot with a series of Pearl Harbor–esque raids and attacks that had wrecked communications and fleet bases across the entire border. Their early successes, however, had come to an end at the Ardennes System.

Not at the hands of the Royal Martian Navy—though there had been plenty of RMN ships present—but at the hands of a fleet assembled from half a dozen system militias that had answered Damien Montgomery's call for help.

The system militias didn't have the fully unrestricted amplifiers that made RMN warships so terrifying in the hands of their Mage-Captains, but they had jump matrices, missiles and battle lasers. And, across the hundred and seventeen star systems of the Protectorate, potentially had *more* jump ships than the RMN's Act of Parliament–mandated four hundred.

"If any of them have transports, we scooped them up when we put together the Guard," she admitted. "We paid for them, but I'm not sure the Guard gave them *back* when they were done with them."

"But you'll want to make sure High Command and the Crown Princess keep them in mind," her boyfriend told her. "That's five hundred and twenty, per the numbers in my last bit of research, jump warships that the RMN can call in for backup.

"Even the Core Worlds don't have anything bigger than cruisers, but those are cruisers and destroyers that can fill gaps back home while the Navy fights this war."

Kiera nodded slowly. Her main hobby was building models of spaceships, which meant she might have a better idea of what the individual *ships* available to the system militias were. While many of them used the semi-standard destroyer and cruiser designs—often Core World–built—others went for different designs. Many were smaller than destroyers, but the "frigate" that fell between the two Navy types was common enough.

"They'll help and they'll *want* to help," Kiera agreed. "I'll put out a call, through Parliament I think, for them to contribute any transports they have."

"Never make the same mistake twice, right?" Barry murmured.

"I try not to," she said. "Those ships belong to the system governments. We have some rights to commandeer the warships, but that's pretty limited and explicitly *just* the warships."

She shrugged.

"But like you said about the UnArcana Worlds, no one is going to stand aside when this many people are in danger."

"Speaking of the UnArcana Worlds, though, there's another blind spot your meeting seemed to have," Barry noted quietly. "I've been poking around a few things as I try to decide what to do with myself—spending a bit of time with Minister Kumiega's analysts, truthfully, so I knew what his numbers were going to look like when I walked in here."

"So, *that's* why you figured I was going to need a cat," Kiera realized triumphantly. She'd doubted he'd just happened to wander by and see Zagreus trying to get into her office.

"Honestly, no, that happened much as I described," he said with a chuckle. "I was talking to them... yesterday? Maybe the day before? Time is a fuzzy thing for me; sorry."

"Speaking of blind spots," she said. "You've never missed an appointment, but sorting out what day you had a conversation is beyond you."

"I have a *computer* to make sure I make appointments," he said plaintively. "But yes, you are missing something, and it is orbiting Charon with an answer to your question."

For the first time in that conversation, Kiera didn't have enough pieces in her head to put together the puzzle he was putting down. She knew, without any false humility, that she was extraordinarily intelligent and impossibly magically powerful—the first result of careful genetic engineering and the second the result of the Runes of Power she'd inscribed on her own flesh.

The same careful genetic engineering had made certain she would share her father's Rune Wright gift, the talent to read the flow of magic. Most human Mages worked with the Martian Runic script, a script they now knew had been taken from the reezh. Rune Wrights could shape runes to match the true flow of energy.

It was the key to wielding the star-system-scale amplifier built into Olympus Mons, an impenetrable defense for Sol. A defense that it seemed the reezh homeworlds shared... and Chimera, sadly, didn't.

"There is almost nothing at Charon," she finally said. "Just a few scientific research outposts."

Barry eyed her and sighed.

"I assume someone *told* you what they did with the leftover RIN ships, right?" he pointed out.

"Probably," Kiera admitted, wracking her brain. She knew that a number of Republic Interstellar Navy warships had been captured intact over the course of the war. All of them had used the brains of murdered Mages—many of them teenagers—as a faux-technological jump drive.

All of those victims had been removed. Most had been euthanized before the Protectorate had realized that they hadn't actually been brain-dead, merely in a very deep medical coma.

The Prometheans, as the awake survivors were called, were in a special rehabilitation-and-care facility on Phobos, Mars's larger moon. The ships themselves...

"I don't remember," she conceded. "Charon?"

"Charon," Barry confirmed. "I got distracted trying to sort out just how many jump ships we had after some of the early discussions around working with Chimera and tried to track down everything. The RIN ships don't really count, but I did end up tracking down where they were.

"Don't ask me where the name came from, but apparently it's called the Rat Graveyard," he said. "Every ship we captured of the Republic Interstellar Navy—and, most importantly right now, *every jump transport of the Republic Space Assault Force.*"

Kiera saw his point immediately. Except.

"I don't know as much about the RSAF's transports as I should," she admitted. "By the time Dad died, the invasions were mostly going the other way. They came up dealing with the First Legion out at Mackenzie and Exeter, but transports weren't a major deal there, either."

"May I?" Barry asked, gesturing to her desk and its concealed holo-projector.

"Go ahead."

He didn't do anything visibly but the projector came to life, showing a ship that had an all-too-familiar profile. Most people using their wrist-comp to assume control of a desk system would need to actually *touch* the thing, but Barry's eye implant had more uses than just games.

At first glance, the ship looked like an RIN battleship. All Republic ships had been built on one of two standardized cylinder hulls. Both hulls were five hundred meters long, but the newer ships had a hundred-and-seventy-five-meter diameter versus the one-fifty of the older designs.

Like the battleships, the transport was made up of two one-hundred-seventy-five-meter cylinders linked together along the long side. On closer examination, it had a version of the linking central deck of an RIN carrier, but where a carrier's deck was a hundred meters across and roughly eighty meters tall, this ship's connecting section was barely forty meters high and twenty meters between the two hulls.

"The *Saladin*-class planetary invasion ship," Barry said calmly. "Carries basically no long-range weaponry, so I'm guessing the RIN had to clear the way to orbit, but they were designed so *one ship* carried enough hardware and personnel to seize one of our worlds."

The program he was using to display the ship was Kiera's, so she knew where to look for the information she needed. The *Saladins* might lack offensive weaponry, but they had the full defensive suite of the similarly sized battleships and carriers.

They had also carried what the RASF had classed as a "Planetary Invasion Army." Twenty-five divisions, organized in five corps of a *hundred thousand* troops apiece. Kiera had known that the Republic had successfully invaded several Protectorate worlds they'd been forced to liberate, but the sheer scale of that task had never truly sunk in.

One *Saladin* carried half a million soldiers, plus enough heavy gear to fight a war and take control of an entire planet. That had ranged from tanks to aircraft to satellite systems.

"I'm guessing we stripped most of the gear out," she noted.

"I didn't dig too hard, but we can find out," he agreed. "Anything that's left we might as well take to Chimera, honestly. We certainly haven't used it in five years."

"How many of them?" Kiera asked. "Of the *Saladin*s at Charon, I mean."

"Twenty-five. To match the speed of the other ships we're sending, they'd need four Prometheans each."

And the obvious flaw in Barry's suggestion stole Kiera's stab of hope. There was transport, right there in Sol, for almost thirteen million people. Probably more like twenty-five, if they could augment the life support, as was being planned for the RMMC and Guard ships.

That would make a vast difference in the timetable for evacuating Chimera—but there was *no way* anyone in the Protectorate was going to ask the Prometheans at Phobos to link themselves back into warships.

"We could... No," she cut herself off. "We already know that a ship rigged with a Prometheus Drive doesn't have a jump matrix a regular Mage can access. They need Prometheans. That's why they're sitting at Charon, Barry. Because they're useless except as analysis projects and scrap—and no one's managed to plan out scrapping them yet."

They'd been brought to Sol using the Prometheus Drive, bringing both the ships and their captive brains to the greatest concentration of knowledge and magic in human space. Having removed those murdered and captive Mages, the ships would never leave again.

"They're useless *without Prometheans*," he countered. "There are two hundred and thirty-six Prometheans at Phobos, Kiera. They've all been awake for at least two years at this point. Just... sitting in a virtual reality, getting counseling and playing video games with no actual needs anywhere."

There was something in his tone that made Kiera want to shiver. She gave him a level gaze as Zagreus stood up in her lap and mewled at Barry. With a chuckle, he leaned forward and scratched behind the cat's ears.

"Yes, they went through something awful," he told her. "But we can't treat them with kid gloves forever, my love. And they are human. Given a chance to help, some of them will."

"I don't think you understand how horrified we all still are over their existence," she said grimly.

"That's a *you* problem, not a them problem," he countered. "They *need* the chance to make decisions for themselves. You can't take that away from them and wrap them in cotton until they die from old age. That would be as wrong as leaving them in those comas.

"I want to *ask*, Kiera. We're not drafting them. We're not forcing them. I want to tell them what's going on, what's at stake, and ask them to help save two billion lives.

"If they volunteer, are their caretakers really going to stop them?"

Kiera snorted, considering some of the doctors, Mages and soldiers she knew were involved in the Phobos Special Rehabilitation Facility.

"They might try, but I'll back any volunteer," she promised.

"Then we have to ask. Because while we won't make them do any-thing... we need them."

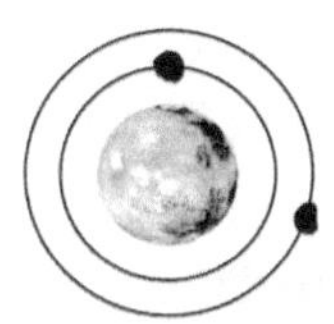

CHAPTER 3

MAGE-CAPTAIN ROSLYN CHAMBERS didn't know who the building had belonged to before. It was a small office building, just within ambitious walking distance of the Legislature Building of the Dual Republics of Chimera in Twin Sphinx.

Whatever signage had marked the government department or business that had owned the conveniently located structure was gone. The only replacement was a hastily printed sign declaring this the Embassy of the Protectorate of the Kingdom of Mars, flanked on either side of the name by a surprisingly decent rendition of the crowned mountain.

Anyone who missed the sign would have known what the building was by the presence of the two exosuited Martian Marines. There were exosuits on the planet, of course, but those were built on the model used by the Republic of Faith and Reason deserters who now formed the Chimera Space Navy.

The Martian design was noticeably different. The pair of Marines following in the redheaded Mage's wake weren't as heavily armored as their comrades at the door, but some silent exchange passed between the four soldiers as Roslyn stepped up to the embassy.

"You're not expected, sir," the senior Marine told her. "The Ambassador is in; his staff will be able to check in with him for you."

The woman paused.

"Can I get an ID confirmation, sir?" she asked, almost apologetically. There was no way any Martian Marine or spacer on Garuda, Chimera's habitable planet, didn't know who Roslyn Chambers was. If nothing else, there were only two living human beings authorized to wear the sapphire pin marking her as a three-time holder of the Medal of Valor.

"Of course." It was the Marine's job to make sure that the Ambassador was safe. Roslyn would be stunned if there wasn't a Protectorate Secret Service Agent positioned at one of the windows above her with a sniper rifle.

Her wrist-comp interfaced with the Marine's scanner and confirmed that Roslyn's genecode matched that on file.

"Head on in, sir," the guard instructed. "I'll need to confirm IDs on your companions as well, of course."

"I'll wait on them for the moment," Roslyn said. She gestured to the two women behind her. "This is Master Chief Petty Officer Precious Kovalyow, my aide, and Chief Steward Tajana Baars, my steward."

It took the Marine only a few moments to confirm the identity of the two noncommissioned officers, along with their Marine escort, and wave them all through.

The embassy interior was exactly what Roslyn had expected. Now she was inside, it had clearly been a government office of some kind. There was a front reception—currently occupied by an attractive dark-haired man in a Protectorate Secret Service uniform—and open spaces showing a mix of cubicles, meeting rooms and offices.

Very few of those spaces were occupied. Ambassador O'Hannagain hadn't brought many people to Chimera with him, but they were setting to their task with a will.

A longer-term relationship had been expected to take more time. Now, though, it looked like Chimera and its Dual Republics might not *have* much time.

"It's a delight to see you, Mage-Captain. How can I and the Embassy assist the Royal Martian Navy?" Connor O'Hannagain asked when Roslyn entered his office.

The space had clearly been the pride and joy of whichever bureaucrat had run this building. The personal touches had been stripped away, but quality wooden wainscotting covered the lower half of the walls, and a diffuser filled the air with a pleasant scent Roslyn couldn't quite place.

The furniture was new and somewhat basic, but whoever had acquired it had made sure that it matched both itself and the room. It was just a desk, a trio of chairs and some shelves, though, and gave the place a distinct *not-quite-finished* feel to it.

"The question is more the other way around, actually," she told him. O'Hannagain had his sharp edges, but he was the Protectorate's Ambassador and seemed to be quite good at his job.

"The other Mage-Captains and I find ourselves in the difficult situation of, well, having more Captains than starships."

Her *Thorn* was dead, a crippled wreck towed back into Garudan orbit. The explorer cruiser had never been meant to fight in the central scrum of a battle, but what choice had they had? Against the Reezh Kazh's opening reconnaissance in force, failure could have meant the death of everyone on Garuda.

"Since I'm hardly asking one of my fellows to give up their vessel, we realized that the Embassy here on Garuda was going to be in desperate need of a military attaché." She shrugged. She wasn't entirely certain what such an attaché would do normally, but she could see the need for a military officer to act as interface for O'Hannagain.

"If you're prepared to have me, sir, I am available to take up that posting until the Navy has a better use for me," she concluded.

O'Hannagain studied her intensely for a few silent seconds, then nodded slowly.

"We're all recreating much of this from half-forgotten history textbooks," he admitted. "I suspect you and your fellow Captains are correct, but tell me: what do *you* envisage a military attaché doing?"

"We have no real formal job description for such a role," she agreed. "I have a few thoughts, of course."

"Of course." He gestured for her to carry on, though they were interrupted by Baars knocking on the door.

"Sir, Ambassador," the steward greeted them. "Forgive the interruption, but there was some confusion as to where the coffee stocks were living. Then no one had any idea when Mr. O'Hannagain had last got a coffee, so I took the liberty of preparing cups for you both."

In less than ten minutes, Roslyn judged, her steward had not-so-accidentally taken over whatever setup the embassy had so far for catering and food management and produced two cups of coffee along with a carafe and a tray.

The tray looked like it belonged in the cheapest cafeteria on the most run-down base on the most forgotten planet in the Protectorate, but the coffee smelled surprisingly good.

When neither of the office's occupants objected, Baars swept in, swiftly cleared a portion of O'Hannagain's desk and laid out the coffee. A small bowl held packages of sugar, creamer, and two sachets of the microground spices used for Tau Cetan café masala.

"Thank you, Chief," Roslyn told Baars as she took her own coffee—already spiced to her tastes.

"I'll leave you two to the work," the NCO replied, saluting Roslyn and slipping out of the room.

O'Hannagain chuckled.

"If you come with her, I might be sold on your subordinate alone," he said wryly.

"Subordinates, sir," Roslyn replied. "While we've found plenty for *Thorn*'s crew to be doing, I can definitely source personnel if we need them. No matter what, though, I'll have Chief Baars and Chief Kovalyow as my personal staff.

"I suspect that they will have the embassy in somewhat more order rather quickly, though I don't know how your civilians will take it," she admitted.

"Right now, Roslyn—may I still call you Roslyn?—nobody in this building has a *damn* clue what we're doing. My aide, Zahid Kootenay, is extremely competent, but he is just one man." He shrugged massively. "Fourteen staff, six Secret Service. Your Mage-Captain Morales was kind enough to assign me a dozen Marines to back up Agent Sarvesh Ansel and his people, but it's not enough people to run a real embassy."

Mage-Captain Deepa Morales was the senior RMN officer in the system, with the death of the Battleship Task Group commander, Mage-Commodore Banderas, with his flagship and staff.

"You can call me Roslyn... Connor. And I'm guessing we don't have the hands for a wartime embassy that needs to coordinate a full planetary evacuation," Roslyn said. He'd told her to call him Connor before the attack, but when she'd found out how hard he needed to push the Dual Republics, she'd responded harshly.

Correctly, in her opinion, but they did seem to be on the same side. Whatever price O'Hannagain had needed had been paid—in the aftermath of the Kazh attack, the Dual Republics were in no position to argue.

And Mars wasn't going to leave them now, either. Too many RMN ships and people had died in this system for them to leave the Chimerans to their enemies.

"Exactly. If your Master Chief Kovalyow can put her head together with Mr. Kootenay, we might find some organization around here," O'Hannagain told her.

One of the things he was telling her, though, was that he knew more than he liked to pretend. Roslyn hadn't used Precious Kovalyow's full rank. O'Hannagain had.

"As for my own role, I see much of it as providing you with advice and understanding when it comes to the military side of matters," she told him. "As we move forward with the evacuation, I will probably bring in more RMN people to help with that, but my main duty will be supporting you and acting as an interface between you and the military: ours and Chimera's."

"I am extremely familiar with politics and economics," he noted. "But you are correct that I am out of my depth with military matters. Within my area, I will admit few equals, but outside of it, I know when to accept my limits.

"Let's start with the basics, shall we? Brief me on the status of our military assets here in Chimera, please, Roslyn."

Roslyn had expected that and took a sip of her coffee as she mustered her thoughts.

"The Royal Martian Navy has two cruisers and six destroyers in the Chimera System at this moment," she began. "While *Thorn* remains in Chimeran orbit, she is neither combat- nor jump-capable, hence our decision to move her crew to the surface to support the locals as best as we can."

What she wasn't telling O'Hannagain was that she'd set the scuttling charges herself. If they held Chimera long enough, the explorer cruiser could potentially be repaired or at least salvaged. The moment it looked like they *couldn't* hold Chimera, Mage-Captain Morales would send the command that would vaporize Roslyn's first cruiser command in a blast of antimatter fire.

"The Chimeran Space Navy's losses in the battle were horrific," she said, the words still a major understatement. "The carrier *Chimera* herself remains intact and mostly undamaged, but they only have enough gunships left to fill her decks if they strip every other base around Garuda.

"My understanding is that they are doing that, but reorganizing squadrons takes time. The two cruisers of the Ifrit Squadron are on their way to Garuda, but they lack Prometheans for their jump matrices and are still two days out."

"Weren't there gunships at Ifrit as well?" O'Hannagain asked. "Would it be worth transferring those to Garuda's bases?"

Ifrit was the inner gas giant of the Chimera System, a hot gas giant that was also the innermost planet of the entire star system. It anchored Chimera's hydrogen-extraction industry and had been under heavy guard for that reason alone... or so the Chimerans had told them.

"Have the Dyad come clean to you about what's in orbit of Ifrit?" Roslyn asked.

"All I've really heard is that it's very important to the system economy," he said. "On the other hand, since we're *aware* of the Ifrit Accelerator, I haven't exactly pushed them on it."

The Ifrit Accelerator Ring was an immense project, a space-station particle accelerator that encircled the entire gas giant. Once online, it would allow Chimera to produce enough antimatter to arm their ships and fuel their industry.

"They haven't said anything official to us, either," she confirmed. "But they did leave all two hundred gunships there to protect the Ring. The *Andreas*-class cruisers will be here to protect Garuda, but the Accelerator is key to their long-term economic and military plans."

"When the *Andreas*es get here, what are we at in total?"

"Two RMN cruisers and six RMN escort destroyers on our side. A carrier, battleship and three cruisers on their side." She shrugged. "Two hundred and fifty gunships, soon to be based on *Chimera*. We're providing antimatter supplies to arm their missiles, but they only have so many weapons to begin with."

Mages could transmute matter to antimatter with ease, allowing for the power-dense fuel to be used in vast quantities. The Chimerans hadn't expected to have antimatter in sufficient quantity for a while yet—but they *also* hadn't expected to use up their entire existing inventory of missiles plus a supply brought by the Protectorate.

"I know they had missile-production lines. How bad is it, Roslyn?"

"Bad. *Scharnhorst* is the focus of their repair and fabrication capability right now," she warned. "Four weeks to get her back online. Maybe even six. By then, they'll be up to maybe two hundred missiles a day."

"You're the military woman," O'Hannagain concluded. "Is *bad* the summary of our entire situation here?"

"That is why Wang requested the evacuation, Connor," Roslyn reminded him. "The RMN ships have refilled magazines from our colliers, but we're repairing our damage out of onboard resources. That's why we had to write off *Thorn*.

"Mage–Vice Admiral Adamant is due in three weeks. The only reason we can even do that is because the logistics support that she needs is already here and, well, we don't have a battleship to supply anymore."

Righteous Guardian of Liberty was one of the oldest battleships still in the fleet, dating back to when the RMN had only kept twelve of the big ships in commission at a time. Fully ten million tons lighter and carrying fifty fewer missile launchers than the *Peace* class, she was still four times the size of the cruisers they had left.

"And the evacuation ships?"

"You know as well as I do," she said grimly. "There aren't enough ships in the entire Protectorate to move two billion people, Connor. They're going to move every stone to find what ships they can, but my guess is that we're going to be seeing troop transports first."

"Four thousand ships," O'Hannagain told her. When she looked at him blankly, he sighed. "Passenger liners, nonmilitary personnel transports, the like. There are about four thousand ships that are primarily passenger liners in the Protectorate. *Someone* should have a briefing paper put together on our lift capacity by now."

"That's on the political side, I suspect," she said. "I know we have troop transports, I presumed we had passenger liners, and there are the colony ships. The last might be useful if we can grab them."

The specialist colony ships were designed to carry a million people with enough gear to set up a new settlement at the destination. Roslyn wasn't sure how many of them existed, but she would guess less than ten. The Protectorate only saw a new planet settled every few years, after all.

"I'll poke at the Government," O'Hannagain agreed, the capital *G* clear. "For your part, make sure that Mage-Captain Morales knows that I and my people are prepared to provide any assistance we can."

He grinned.

"As my military attaché, of course, sourcing said assistance will probably fall on you."

"I can tell you right now that the biggest thing we need is to make sure the logistics structure is in place to handle *Righteous Guardian of Liberty* when she arrives," Roslyn told him. "If we can handle a battleship, we can handle cruisers and destroyers. Mage-Admiral Alexander won't be arriving until she has enough *mobile* support in place to handle her dreadnoughts."

"What if Chimera can put together something that can handle them?" her new not-quite-boss asked.

"Then Alexander can be here in ten days, possibly less," she replied. "But a *Mjolnir*-class dreadnought requires roughly ten thousand tons of hydrogen and a hundred tons of antimatter *per day* just to sit in orbit. They're hundred-million-ton warships, Connor. The scale of that is difficult to grasp until you've seen one."

He smiled thinly.

"I *have* seen them, Roslyn," he pointed out. "And the colony ships you mentioned, which are around the same size.

"Consider yourself hired as the attaché," he continued. "Your first task is to find yourself and your two NCOs offices around here—you three have somewhere to sleep, right?"

"I honestly have no idea," Roslyn admitted. "Getting into the loop with you seemed more important. I slept on *Mole* last night."

The big Ambassador sighed.

"So, that's your *second* task," he instructed. "If we're going to lean on the RMN for staff—and I don't see another choice—we'll want somewhere safe for them all to sleep that's reasonably nearby."

Any humor faded as he met her gaze.

"After that, I need you to talk to Admiral Wang and whichever Dyad Minister you can reach," he told her. "We need to get moving on a proper evacuation plan. We're going to have some warning of when we're getting evacuation ships, but the last thing we're going to be able to afford is confusion when they get here.

"I don't think anyone believes we're getting everyone out before it's too late. But we will, as the hills of Tara are green, get out everyone we can."

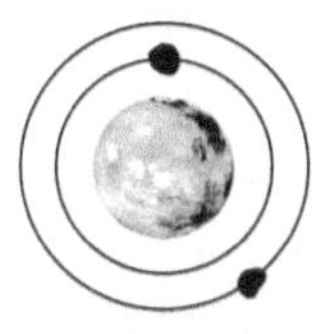

CHAPTER 4

"I CANNOT IN GOOD CONSCIENCE AGREE TO THIS plan, Your Majesty."

It was fortunate, in Kiera's opinion, that Dr. Jessica Starling didn't *have* to agree with the plan to ask the Prometheans to once again strap on starships to save lives. The good doctor answered to the Mountain, which meant that Kiera could override the woman and do whatever she wanted.

Still, the Mage-Queen had spent her formative years with Damien Montgomery as her Regent. She'd learned then that there was a time and a place for running roughshod over the opposition—and a time for convincing people to at least stand aside, if not agree.

A lesson that the whole mess around Chimera had only reinforced. Part of that reinforcement had been by Barry, of course, which was part of why her boyfriend was at her side as they followed Dr. Starling through the administration section of the Phobos Special Rehabilitation Facility.

This was his idea, so she was going to make sure he wore both the credit and the blame alongside her.

Starling tapped her palm to a secure door lock and opened her office. Like most Rehab Facility's spaces, it was carved out of the Phobos rock with only the barest attempt to disguise the bare stone.

The administrator's office had even less concealment than the rest of the underground structure. Where most of the halls they'd passed through to get there had white paneling covering whatever wiring and conduits had been run along the tunnels, Dr. Starling's office was bare stone.

It had been sharpened by either laser or magic and polished to a near-mirror sheen that allowed a single light to illuminate the entire space magnificently.

"The patients in this facility have undergone what I can only describe as *the* most traumatic experience a human being can endure," Starling told her guests as she pulled chairs together.

She did not, Kiera noted, attempt to sit behind her desk. Starling laid out three chairs facing each other in front of the desk and took one of them.

"My patients no longer have bodies," the doctor concluded grimly. "And part of that atrocity was that they were forced to act as engines for these ships. The very ships you want them to serve aboard again."

"We're not asking them to serve as engines," Barry pointed out. "We're asking them to serve as *Ship's Mages*—with the rights, privileges, and *pay grade* entailed in that."

"Including a significant upscale to account for the fact that nobody else can jump these ships," Kiera added. "I've spoken with the senior officers of the RMN Logistics Bureau. They will provide non-Mage commanders for the ships, but the Prometheans will be ship's officers."

"I understand that the offer you want to make is more than fair, Your Majesty," Starling conceded. She sighed. "But even the name you use speaks to the problem. These are *Prometheus Drive* ships, and you are looking for the component needed to make them work.

"If I could get away from the term *Promethean*, I would. It ties our patients unavoidably to the machine the atrocity was meant to fuel. Surely, you understand why putting them *back* into that monstrosity is a problem?"

"Doctor, I am the Mage-Queen of Mars," Kiera said quietly. "I now know that every human Mage owes their existence to a project intended solely to provide brains to something like the Prometheus Drive."

The Reezh Kazh called them *Engines of Sacred Sacrifice*. Every evidence suggested that the reezh who had worked on Mars had done so without the approval of the old Reezh Ida empire—at the very least, the Kazh appeared to have no records of the project.

And while the Reezh Kazh, the central Church of the Nine, wasn't the Ida, it had been the central administration of that old state before it had expanded to absorb its remains.

If the Kazh didn't know about Earth, the Ida hadn't known. And if they *did* know, Kiera suspected that the millions of human Mages would have been all too tempting for the old empire trapped in its cold war with its first colonies.

"I will do just about anything to prevent the Kazh succeeding at their plan," Kiera told Starling. "Including asking your patients to once more link themselves into the Prometheus Interface. I am, however, *asking*. If they all refuse, they all refuse. I will not press."

"Merely by asking, you press, Your Majesty," the doctor replied. "Their psyches are fragile. Even years of counseling and every resource we can muster can only do so much against the knowledge that they were murdered and turned into *spare parts*."

Barry reached over to squeeze Kiera's hand before she responded, and the Queen remained silent. He leaned forward and met Jessica Starling's gaze with a frankness that surprised Kiera.

Her boyfriend wasn't a big fan of eye contact. He clearly thought this was important.

Though it probably helped that Jessica Starling was easy on the eyes. She shared the same slimly attractive build as Kiera, though Starling was taller, with pitch-black hair along with her faded brown Martian coloring.

"What would you have them do, Doctor?" Barry asked. "They need to be *human* again. Believe me when I say that just sitting around, playing video games and talking to counselors, isn't going to get them there. Boredom can kill as thoroughly as bullets—and it's all the more dangerous because you don't even realize it happened until it's too late."

He clearly spoke from experience, though Kiera was *reasonably* sure he wasn't speaking about his current situation. She was going to have to prod on that later—she'd always suspected, though, that Barry had kept stealing shuttles long after he'd no longer needed the money!

"From a clinical perspective, I agree with you completely, Mr. Carpentier," Starling told him. "But we have only begun to unpack the level of psychological harm our patients have undergone. Our textbooks and history and sciences do not cover someone having their brain physically removed from their body."

"You don't think they're ready?" Kiera asked.

"I don't." Starling met Kiera's gaze levelly, clearly prepared to defy her Queen. She knew what the consequences of that could be—the Special Rehabilitation Facility wasn't even a military hospital, though there were Marines guarding it.

It fell directly under Kiera's authority. Starling could resign in protest, but all that would do was make Kiera think twice. Which she'd already done.

"Who decides that?"

Kiera glanced over at Barry. Her boyfriend had his own gaze locked on Starling still, and there was an intensity to his expression that she'd only seen a few times. Usually when calling her out on her own bullshit.

"I don't understand," Starling said, confused.

"Who decides when the Prometheans are ready?" he expanded. "When they're healthy enough, healed enough, to even admit to them that the outside world exists? Is wrapping them in packing material for the rest of their lives *enough*?

"*They are human*," he repeated, his tone fierce. "The last thing you can do is take that from them, Dr. Starling. If they become merely patients, just victims, then how are we treating them any better than the Republic?

"Tell me, Doctor, can they even access the *news* in the virtual utopia you've locked them in?"

"Of course they can," she snapped. "What kind of hospital do you think we're running here?"

Barry snorted.

"I'm glad; I was starting to wonder," he admitted. "So, they know what's going on in the Protectorate?"

"They do. This isn't some lotus-eater machine we've trapped them in, Mr. Carpentier," Starling told him, her anger clear. "Yes, a lot of it does, as you put it, boil down to *playing video games*, but they have access to news feeds and even limited access to the planetary datanet."

"They're probably checking the news feeds as much as anyone else," Kiera said wryly. "Just because any citizen of the Protectorate has access to near-complete information on what's going on across a hundred and twenty-plus star systems doesn't mean they even know what's going on in the city next door!"

"They're watching the news about Chimera quite closely," Starling admitted slowly. "We do not censor their news feeds, but we keep an eye on what they're following. We... had an argument about the news about active Prometheans in Chimera, but the decision was made to..."

"Trust them?" Barry finished as she trailed off. "To let them make their own assessments of what they can handle?"

Starling sighed.

"Yes."

"Let us make the pitch, Dr. Starling," Barry asked. "They deserve the right to know that they can make a difference. We will face this challenge without them if we must, but if a few of your patients are more ready than you think, they could save millions of lives.

"Don't you think they have the right to *know* that? We'll do everything we can not to pressure them, but it really should be their choice.

"Not yours."

Kiera could write a list of reasons why she loved Barry Carpentier as long as her arm, but she realized that she would have been adding several more that day, watching him passionately argue for people he'd never met to have control of their own fates.

"I suppose," Starling said, her voice very quiet. "You have to understand: I am responsible for these people and so many of them are still *children* chronologically. I don't want to send them into another war. They didn't volunteer for the last one."

"Doctor, you have my word," Kiera told the other woman. "No one has any intention of letting our volunteers anywhere near the actual *war*. We need them to get people out of the line of fire.

"Nothing more."

Starling exhaled sharply, then nodded.

"Then let's go make your pitch," she told them. "I'll have something set up."

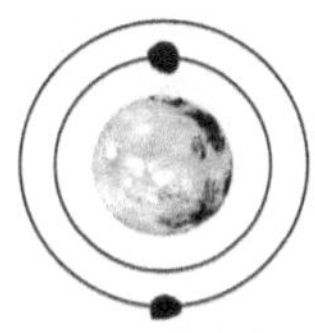

CHAPTER 5

STARLING LED THEM INTO an auditorium-style chamber that it took Kiera a moment to realize was much smaller than the impression it gave. Even in the twenty-fifth century, few wallscreens were built to *this* level of fidelity.

"We do most of our communicating with the patients either in our offices or specific treatment rooms," Starling told them. "But sometimes, it's necessary to make announcements to all of them, and we want to keep most of our communication with them as close to face-to-face as possible."

"I appreciate your cooperation and support, Doctor," Kiera told the other woman. "I understand wanting to protect these people. We owe them that, at the very minimum."

The doctor nodded grimly, then gestured to a spot for the chairs being brought in. A quartet of young men—with the type of musculature that told Kiera, at least, that they were Marines most of the time—hauled in a trio of comfortable-looking seats and set them up facing the empty virtual seats.

"I should warn you now," Starling said quietly. "And I probably should have mentioned it earlier. We have grounds to believe that at least some of the patients have made the Facility's computer network something of their own personal playground.

"With you being, well, as important as you are, there's a decent chance that they listened in on our conversation in my office."

"Fair enough," Kiera forced herself to say calmly. And it *was* fair enough. The problem was that Starling *should* have told her. That was a security risk she and her escort should have been aware of.

Even there, in a Royal facility surrounded by military reservations, red-exosuited Mages of the Royal Guard were only on the other side of the door. No one was taking risks with her safety, but occasionally, people like Starling forgot that the Queen's confidentiality was almost as important as her safety.

In *this* case, she'd let it slide. She had to.

"We're bringing the audience functions online now," Starling warned. The walls shimmered, then returned to their perfect fidelity—but now many of the seats were filled.

There were more seats than there were Prometheans on Phobos, but Kiera had long since mastered the skill of judging a crowd's size at a glance. Of the two hundred and thirty-six Prometheans in the Phobos Special Rehabilitation Facility, only two hundred and five had shown up.

Which was probably at least two hundred more than she deserved.

"My friends," Starling greeted them. "Today I have the honor of introducing important guests: Her Majesty, Kiera Alexander, and her companion, Barry Carpentier. They want to talk to you about the war out in Chimera and a mission they believe you can help with.

"I want to make very clear, right now, that while I have an obligation to let Her Majesty speak, my first obligation is always to you. If you feel you are done listening, I can end this presentation. None of you are obliged to do *anything*."

The crowd was eerily silent. Kiera was used to judging an audience at least partially by the unconscious noises they made, but the virtual avatars didn't make those sounds.

She nodded to Dr. Starling. She hadn't agreed to let the doctor cut the audience short if the Prometheans disagreed—but she *would* have. The other woman needed to be better at laying out her conditions in advance, Kiera reflected, but they were where they were.

"First, I owe you all an apology," she told the Prometheans. That definitely surprised Starling, but she ignored it and charged forward.

Like most of her speeches, she spoke from the heart.

"This is the first time I have set foot in the Special Rehabilitation Facility, and it is when I want something from you," she confessed. "I should have come here sooner, to assure you that you were not forgotten, and that the Mountain acknowledges the debt owed for our failure to protect you."

She was trying to get a feel for the audience, and the silence was nerve-wracking. There was no question in her mind, though, that the Prometheans were doing it on purpose.

"So, before I even get into what I came here to ask about, I want to hear from you," she told them. "Dr. Starling seems to have your best interests at heart, but I understand that is not always enough. If there is anything you need, anything that could make your lives or your recoveries easier, let me know. If there is anything *wrong*... please let me know."

Kiera waited. While the Prometheans might be hooked up to computers that gave them distinct advantages in mental processing, they were still human. It took time for them to make decisions—and just as she was certain the silence was intentional, she was certain they were having entire conversations she couldn't hear.

One of the virtual avatars rose from their seat and was suddenly standing in front of the rest. While the crowd of avatars mostly registered as a crowd, now that the avatar was near full-size, Kiera realized that this one wasn't human.

A red-furred fox had been stretched into the mold of a human woman, with exaggerated hips and breasts. Piercing green eyes met Kiera's and the fox-woman smiled, showing far too many teeth.

Kiera doubted the Promethean meant to intimidate, but she suspected the mind behind the fox had expected her to be perturbed. Except that Kiera had met several people who had undergone sufficient cosmetic surgery to look like the avatar in person—if not *quite* so exaggerated.

"I am Mikayla Spencer," the Promethean greeted her. "My fellows have elected me to speak for us today. That seemed... easier than trying to balance two hundred voices."

"I understand, Miz Spencer," Kiera allowed. "You are all speaking through the network, I presume?"

"We are. Dr. Starling can confirm the others have elected me, if you wish," Spencer told her.

Kiera glanced over at the administrator, who was studying her wrist-comp. She looked up to meet Kiera's gaze and nodded.

"I believed you anyway, Miz Spencer, since I imagine your fellows would find ways to make their disagreement clear," she told the young woman. "While I suspect my wrist-comp would resist whatever intrusion techniques your troublemakers have developed, I imagine that it would be far too easy for one of them to simply turn off the screens in this room.

"You have my full attention. If there is anything the Mountain can do for you, we will."

"You can get Dr. Starling and her people to stop choking on the word *Promethean*," Spencer said with a giggle.

"What?" Starling asked.

"All of you. Every time one of us uses the word, you wince," the Promethean told her doctor. "It might be derived from the horror that forged us, Doctor, but we *choose* that name. We need one for all of us, and we picked that one.

"If it doesn't bother *us*, it shouldn't bother you!"

"She's got you there, Doctor," Barry said with a chuckle.

"So you do, Mikayla," Starling conceded. "We will... try."

"I, for one, find *patient* even more dehumanizing," Spencer warned. "We know what we are. The more you dance around it, the more it feels like we're having our metaphorical faces rubbed in it."

Kiera waited for a few seconds. Starling had given up the point, but Spencer seemed tempted to belabor it.

"Is that all, Miz Spencer?" she asked. "While my resources are not infinite, they are large. Is there anything you need?"

"We have basically an infinite library of entertainment and educational materials," Spencer told her. "We don't need physical comforts, and we don't sleep as much as we did before."

The fox sighed.

"I follow the research projects around us as closely as I can," she admitted. "You're a long way from being able to give us bodies. If we can't walk free, this is as comfortable a place to be stuck as any, I suppose."

Kiera glanced over at Barry.

"It's a dual problem," he told her, confirming her suspicion that he'd have researched it before they arrived. "First, that we don't *build* human-iform robots outside of specialized applications. We have the tech and some teams fiddling with it, but the other problem is that the Prometheus Interface is the size of a personal truck.

"Engineering that down into something that can go into a mobile platform is proving difficult, especially with the life-support needs."

"Your boyfriend summarizes it well," Spencer agreed. "He's almost as smart as he is cute, isn't he?"

Kiera had a strong suspicion about Mikayla Spencer's biological age, one that suggested she was probably too young for Barry's twenty-five.

"He is," she agreed genially. "It's why I keep him around. He's the one who came up with the idea we want to talk to you all about."

"About Chimera?" Spencer asked. "We know there are Prometheans out there, working with the CSN. It's strange, to us, to think of our kin volunteering to stay aboard warships, but what I've heard says the Chimerans are nicer about it than the First Legion."

The First Legion had woken up their Prometheans because they needed the force multiplier. They'd been careful, even brutal when they thought it needed, to keep their Prometheans loyal.

There were people in the Phobos Facility who had served on Legion warships, but even the ones who had bought in to the Legion's indoctrination hadn't *volunteered*.

"Admiral Wang gave the Prometheans in his fleet choices," Kiera confirmed. It was something of a relief that Spencer had practically demanded they use the term her government used for the disembodied Mages. They had picked up the term from a Legion Promethean who had turned her coat to help them save tens of thousands of prisoners forced into labor camps—though unfortunately, Sharon Deveraux had died saving those prisoners in the end.

Since the Chimeran Prometheans had come up with the same term independently, she could see why Spencer and her colleagues were fine with using it.

"They could stay aboard the ships, treated as respected members of the crew; they could transfer to the surface, where he and the Chimeran government would do everything they could to take care of them; or... they could choose mercy. Euthanasia."

There was no point sugarcoating the last option. It had been offered to every Promethean in the Phobos Rehab Facility—and as many of their fellows had taken it as remained.

"Admiral Wang has never actually told us how many Prometheans are on Garuda, only that there *are* some," she admitted. "He is extraordinarily protective of them, a virtue I commend both him and Dr. Starling for."

Kiera would have to quietly raise that point with the Mage-Captains on Garuda. Possibly off the record, with Roslyn Chambers. They suffered the downsides of having a personal friendship; she may as well get the advantages of it.

The Prometheans should be high on the list for evacuation... but they also potentially should be offered the same chance to volunteer as the people on Phobos.

"Others remained in his fleet," she concluded. "Two died aboard their ship in the Battle of Chimera, fighting in defense of their adopted home-world. If you wish, I can make arrangements for you to speak with the Prometheans of the CSN."

There was a pause, likely filled with silent conversation between the trapped Mages.

"We would like that," Spencer confirmed. "We are beginning to build a culture and community of our own. We will not last forever, but we should all stand as one. I am not certain what it might feel like to fight for a world that accepted us as people instead of machines."

"You could know." Barry's words were soft. They weren't what Kiera would have said, and he glanced over at her apologetically. "That's what we want to ask of you."

"Not to fight," Kiera corrected. "But..."

She sighed.

"It is an open secret, though I hope still held to the government and military, that we do not expect to be able to hold Chimera against the

Reezh Kazh," she told the Prometheans. "So many of the RMN's ships are tied down with duties we cannot pull them away from, and the enemy appears to have vast resources.

"We can match those resources, given time. But if they mobilize their resources with any speed at all, we will be forced to concede Chimera."

For the first time, the virtual avatars reacted. Whatever silent conversation was in the background was joined by audible questions, coming from enough sources that Kiera couldn't make out anything specific.

"Please, my friends," Spencer said. "You chose me to speak. Let me?"

Her fellows quieted.

"Some of us wondered," the fox-woman avatar admitted. "Two dreadnoughts at Mars. One at Legatus. Three on patrol and two in refit. Correct?"

The Protectorate had a very free press and tried to be extremely transparent as a government. It wasn't a surprise that someone could lay out the status of the eight *Mjolnir*-class dreadnoughts. She hadn't expected it from the Prometheans, but she was realizing that Starling hadn't understated the degree of access and curiosity they had.

This could be either easier or harder than she'd expected.

"The two doing courtesy visits through the MidWorlds are now on their way to Chimera, but yes," Kiera confirmed. "It will take time for us to break free the others. There is a purpose for their locations, after all."

And while it would probably be easier to pull free the dreadnoughts and battleships than the cruisers and destroyers, the bigger ships needed a lot more logistics support. Logistics support that had been allowed to atrophy since the end of the Rebellion, even with the First Legion conflict.

"We are evacuating Chimera," she concluded. "It is not a fast or easy process, with over two billion souls to move and our passenger shipping, like our warships, already engaged.

"But Barry here saw an option no one else really did," Kiera said, gesturing to her boyfriend. "We captured the invasion transports of the Republic Space Assault Force intact. Twenty-five of them, each capable of carrying half a million soldiers.

"But they require Prometheans, not Mages. If we are going to use them to evacuate people from Chimera, we will need volunteers prepared to once again be placed inside Prometheus Interfaces and use their magic to carry starships across the void."

Kiera waited to let them think that over for a while. The silent conversation continued for at least a minute before the fox avatar leading the conversation nodded once and met her gaze again.

"We have questions," Spencer told her. "Are you willing to answer?"

"Anything," Kiera replied. "Well, anything relevant, I suppose."

"You obviously don't expect us to go back to sleep," the Promethean said firmly. "What would the position involved look like?"

"You would act as traditional Ship's Mages," she told them. "Third in the chain of command, with complete authority over the jump. We will need four Prometheans per ship, but we would class you as co-equal senior officers alongside the Executive Officers and Chief Engineers we find for the ships.

"You will be paid as specialist Ship's Mages, as befitting the fact that you are the only people who can jump these particular ships, plus danger pay, as we are sending you into a war zone." Kiera wasn't going to sugarcoat that. "We will do everything in our power to make certain you are kept away from the fighting, but this is not a mission where I can guarantee safety."

"What happens if none of us volunteer?"

"Nothing." Kiera met Spencer's virtual gaze and hoped that all of the Prometheans could see the truth in her eyes. "We are *asking* you to volunteer—but it is a voluntary mission. There will be no pressure, no privileges withdrawn for refusing, nothing.

"If no one volunteers, we may attempt to refit the transports for a regular jump matrix, but most likely, the ships will sit idle."

And they'd get twenty million or so fewer people out with each evacuation convoy, but Kiera wasn't going to guilt-trip the Prometheans. She refused.

"The invasion transports are armed and carried military equipment. Will we be expected to transport weapons or use the ships' armaments?"

"We are still inventorying what equipment is left aboard the transports," Kiera said. "Our intention is to deliver it all to Chimera to assist in their defense. We're not removing the weapons installed on the *Saladins* because they are almost entirely a defensive suite.

"A Navy contingent will be carried on each ship to operate the defenses. We hope not to need them, but with over half a million innocents aboard, we cannot ignore a means of protecting them.

"If transporting weapons is a problem for some of you and not others, we can transship cargo before leaving Sol," Kiera offered. "I cannot justify removing the defenses from the ships."

"I appreciate your honesty, Your Majesty," Spencer told her. "How many evacuation flights do you expect to get out of Chimera before it falls?"

"We don't know. It could be as few as one or as many as twenty," the young Queen admitted. "We're confident we'll get at least one. While the Kazh's home system is half the distance from Chimera that Sol is, we have the Link, and we have no evidence of FTL communication on their part."

"That means each ship that you find Prometheans for will save at least half a million people and potentially ten million people from hostile occupation?" Spencer asked.

"Possibly more." Kiera didn't have solid numbers. There was a work crew from the Jovian Yards going through *Saladin* herself at that moment, assessing what they could do if the Prometheans signed on. Just the *possibility* of those volunteers had mobilized almost a thousand people to start tearing through the mothballed transports.

"You said, in your speech to the Parliament, that the reezh were the origin of the Prometheus Interface," the fox avatar noted. "Are you sure of that?"

"We are," Kiera confirmed grimly. "Much of the proof was lost in the problems with Nemesis, but I can provide you with the files we have. They call them *Engines of Sacred Sacrifice*, and part of the tribute worlds like Chimera gave to their empire was in *minds*—young Mages to be sacrificed as you were."

The rest of the Prometheans had been content to let Spencer lead as they had agreed, but now a second avatar appeared next to the fox-woman. This one took a more regular form, of a young man with dark stubble on his cheeks and shaven head.

"You're asking leading questions to get the arguments out of her, Mikayla," he growled.

"Would you rather not know these things, William?" Spencer demanded.

A chill ran down Kiera's spine as she realized who the other Promethean was. He turned to face her, and she recognized his clothing as an RIN uniform without insignia.

"I am William Connors," he introduced himself flatly. "Once of *Battlemaster*."

The first Awakened Promethean the First Legion had fielded. If a regular Mage had accomplished all that Connors had done for the Legion, he'd have been a war hero. Instead, even awake, he'd simply been a machine to his masters.

But he'd been well indoctrinated. He'd survived the destruction of his ship thanks to an RMN rescue party—they'd pulled five hundred people and two Prometheans from *Battlemaster*'s wreckage—but Kiera knew that he'd been a problem there on Phobos for a while.

"I know you've had an even harder time than most, Mr. Connors," Kiera told him. "And I am as willing to answer your questions as Ms. Spencer's."

"I have but one. If the Kazh take Chimera, are they likely to seek out the Mages on the planet and subject them to what was done to us?" he demanded.

"We cannot be certain," Kiera admitted. "We believe they didn't know that the people they were identifying as *channelers* for their engines were actually Mages, but they most definitely could identify them.

"Whether either of those things is still true, the evidence from the Battle of Chimera does suggest that they are using Prometheus Drive equivalents rather than Mages for most of their ships," she continued.

"I *believe*, but I have no basis beyond belief and fear, that the Kazh will subject much of Chimera's population to testing. Anyone who registers will likely be sacrificed to expand their fleet."

"Both increasing the Kazh's threat to the Protectorate and murdering innocents," Connors said flatly. "I am done asking questions, Mikayla. If you want to equivocate and debate, go ahead, but for all the flaws of what I was and what the Republic and Legion made of me, *I was a soldier.*

"I volunteer, Your Majesty. I will gladly carry arms to a world under threat, and I will be delighted to host Navy personnel tasked to protect the innocents I take in my charge."

There was a pause as another silent conversation flickered through the background, then Spencer shrugged.

"We will need to discuss and debate, as William notes," she said. "I can ask questions for us all, but I cannot speak a decision for us all. Each of us will decide on their own."

"That is all I can ask," Kiera said. "Those of you who choose to volunteer should talk to Dr. Starling. It will be at least a few days before the ships are ready for even the most basic of occupation, but the sooner we are moving, the better.

"We will honor your choices, whether to stay and continue to heal or to join us to save others," she assured them. "I am grateful for any of you who volunteer."

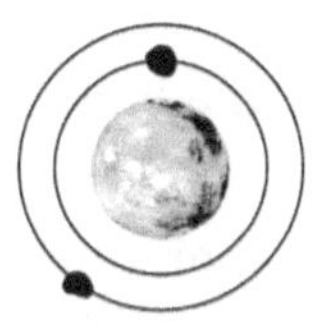

CHAPTER 6

ROSLYN HAD BEEN ABOARD ADMIRAL Emerson Wang's flagship and in his home in the Duchy of the Blue River, the region he administered in the aristocratic structure the Eastern Republic used for some things but not others.

She had never visited his office in the capital of Twin Sphinxes. It was part of the Chimera Space Navy's military headquarters, the Triangle. Three heavily armored buildings, wider than they were tall, surrounded a beautifully manicured courtyard—all of it covering an underground bunker, according to the diagrams she now had access to.

Security was visible everywhere, with an even mix of human soldiers and reezh troops with their double-jointed limbs and armored frills. Unlike anywhere else she'd been on Garuda, there were Chimeran exosuited soldiers as well. Those, she understood, were all human—the locals only had the suits from the armories of Wang's ships.

"Is this security normal?" she asked her guide, a CSN Lieutenant Commander of roughly her own age.

"No," the other woman admitted. "We raised security pretty heavily after your Nemesis friends came through, but this is another level again."

The Chimeran shook her head.

"No one is quite sure what's coming, Captain Chambers," she said. "We have to make sure we're ready for it."

"I won't argue with that," Roslyn agreed.

The Triangle was large enough that it took almost ten minutes from her identity being verified at the north gate to her knocking on the door of Wang's office at the top of the south building.

"Enter."

Even if she hadn't had an appointment, that same ten-minute delay would have allowed Wang to be ready for her. The door slid open at his command, allowing her into a space that strongly resembled the Dyad Ministers' offices in the Legislature Building.

A floor-to-ceiling window took up one wall. A small seating area was marked out with comfortable-looking seats, and an impressively sized and carved wooden desk was placed off to the right, with a decorative folding screen shading Wang's displays from the sun.

There were shelves along the walls perpendicular to the window, but most of them were empty. A hologram of the Dual Republics flag hung above one empty shelf, and a few others had books, but the overall effect was of a space that had been designed to uplift its occupant's stature... and that said occupant had barely used.

"Join me, Mage-Captain," Wang instructed her, gesturing her to the seating area. There was a small table amongst the four chairs, all of it collected on a mid-sized rug in a style she didn't recognize.

"Coffee?"

"When an Admiral is threatening to pour you coffee with his own hands, no wise woman says no," Roslyn replied, recognizing that there was no one else in the room.

The Chimeran officer chuckled and picked up the carafe. Wang was a heavyset man of Mongolian extraction, with heavy epicanthic folds to his eyes and the jowls of a man of enthusiastic appetite.

"Not a bad rule, Mage-Captain," he agreed. "I even had my people source a small shaker of Tau Cetan coffee spice mix, which I am going to ask you to apply yourself."

"Fair enough." Roslyn took a small sip of the coffee before doing so, judging the flavor. Her home system of Tau Ceti had seen a unique blend of French and Indian cultures that had, among other things, produced such wonders as escargot rogan josh and café masala.

The coffee was decent, and she added a thoughtful dash of the spices before taking a second sip and relaxing to the taste and smell of cinnamon and cardamon.

"I'm here as much as Ambassador O'Hannagain's attaché as for the RMN ourselves, sir," she told Wang. "Though the difference is mostly going to be irrelevant. Wearing either hat, I will likely be your main contact with the RMN until Mage–Vice Admiral Adamant arrives."

"An arrival I look forward to, though I hope she is wise enough to keep you in place," the Chimeran murmured. That was all Wang would or could say about the fact that the *last* new RMN senior officer had removed Roslyn from the diplomatic-relations aspect of the mission with haste.

"Admiral Adamant will only be bringing three more ships," Roslyn warned. "While *Righteous Guardian of Liberty* has been updated and refitted since the Rebellion, she is one of our oldest battleships. Her escorts are more modern, two *Honorific*-class battlecruisers.

"Combined with the ships we already have, we hope she will be enough to keep Chimera secure from whatever follow-up scouting forces the Kazh sends."

"But you can't be certain," Wang said. It wasn't a question. "Nor are we in position to provide the logistics support your dreadnoughts need."

"No, sir. Mage-Admiral Alexander is arranging that support as we speak, but it will take longer than we would like." Roslyn knew the CSN's commander knew as much about all of that as she did, but making *certain* he was on the same page was now part of her job.

Wang sipped his coffee, and she waited for him to speak. There were things she was there to ask him about, but she wasn't going to push the senior Admiral of the system she was tasked to protect.

"I can do the math on the evacuation, you know," he finally said, his voice grim. "What do we have as a plan so far?"

"The Guard and Marine Corps have put their transport fleet in play," Roslyn told him. "Negotiations are ongoing for civilian transport, but a number of ships have already been committed.

"We are estimating that the first evacuation convoy will arrive roughly a week after Admiral Adamant. We should know the estimated carrying capacity at least ten days before that, potentially sooner."

"We will need to minimize delays here in Chimera. The more information we have in advance, the easier it will be to make that happen," he told her.

"Will ten days be enough, ser?" she asked. "On the low end, we're looking at five million people. Potentially a lot more, depending on what kinds of refits we can manage."

"That's what we're working on. I have a few people I'm going to need you to meet. We're setting up an official government agency, the Evacuation Commission, headed by Abdul Karim. You've met him, I presume?"

The grandiosely named Abdul Aziz Fikri Karim was the First Secretary to the Eastern Dyad Minister, the leader of the human half of the Dual Republics. If nothing else, Karim had the unquestioned trust and backing of both Dyad Ministers.

"I have met Mr. Karim. He seems a good choice."

"He is," Wang confirmed. "He knows more about all the various bits and pieces of societies on this planet than anyone else, I think. His second, Shozha, was the head of what we'd call *human resources* for the Western Republic."

And since the Western Republic was ninety-nine percent reezh, its government wouldn't have a *human* resources department.

"Their mandate is to prepare for the evacuation?" Roslyn guessed.

"Exactly. They've been granted broad authority with the full backing of the Dyad Legislature and Ministers, plus the CSN. We will be ready to move our people aboard as soon as your ships arrive."

"We will make sure we bring as many ships as we can find, sir," she promised. She took a large gulp of her coffee.

"You've been advised, I hope, that the ships will not be arriving empty?"

"I'm not convinced of the value of bringing *more* people into what we have already accepted is a trap," Wang replied, "but yes."

"If we can evacuate everyone, we'll bring our troops out," Roslyn countered. "But since we don't think we will manage that, we owe it to the people we're leaving behind to fight for them. The last information I have is that we're loading a joint Guard–Marine Corps Army Group, roughly two hundred thousand troops, onto the transports we're bringing out.

"Plus the hardware for a lot more than that."

"Which makes sense, I know; I just don't like it," Wang admitted. "We're already preparing to set up caches of our own gear. It's going to be a hard sell to my people, though. If we're going to fight, why run, after all?"

"Because we need to save what we can of your people."

"Like the Reezh Ida Lachai." His tone was dry, almost bitter. The CSN's commander clearly knew the price that had been demanded for Mars's help.

"Regardless of what we may desire or plan, it makes sense to evacuate the Lachai and her library," Roslyn said gently.

The Reezh Ida Lachai had been the Chimeran equivalent to the Keepers on Mars: an organization tasked to preserve the memory of an enemy they hoped had forgotten about them.

Unlike the Keepers, the Lachai had struggled to maintain any legacy of magic on Chimera. In the end, only one "true" Lachai, the Mage Razhkah, had survived to see the Protectorate arrive on Mars.

But their records and archives represented a significant chunk of the magical knowledge available to the old Reezh Ida—and, given the haphazard nature of humanity's magical knowledge, a priceless prize for the Protectorate.

Something neither nation could see fall into the hands of the Reezh Kazh.

"I understand. I've already given the orders to have people help Razhkah pack," Wang conceded. "She's probably more accepting of the deal Ambassador O'Hannagain extracted than I am."

"At this point, sir, there was no question that Mars would fight for you," Roslyn said. "Not with RMN spacers dead at the Kazh's hands. But the Lachai's archives might make the difference between winning or losing this war."

"We are now allies, and I have placed my faith in your Queen's word that my people will be protected," Wang said grimly. "I must plan for the moment, for the battle and the evacuation to come.

"The Kazh will not give us much time, if any. As soon as they learn of what happened here, they will send more ships. The only question, I suppose, is if they send a small group of scouts to learn what happened to the last fleet—or a fleet even more powerful than that one."

Roslyn shivered at the thought, emptying her coffee cup to warm herself against it.

"The only good news is that they're a hundred and eighty light-years away," she said. "At least twenty days each way, so we shouldn't see any response for twice that. Another thirty-ish days."

"Assuming they have no form of faster-than-light communication. We saw no signs that suggested a Link, but we both know their magic is more advanced than yours."

The only magical long-range communication known to humans was the Runic Transceiver Array, an immense runic artefact that could only transmit a single Mage's voice at a time. An RTA was too large to fit on a ship, which was why the Protectorate had adopted the Link they'd acquired from the Republic so broadly and quickly.

"That's the question mark, I know," Roslyn admitted. "And unfortunately, we have no way to find out. We have to project, and calculate, and move things as fast as we can."

And hope that was enough.

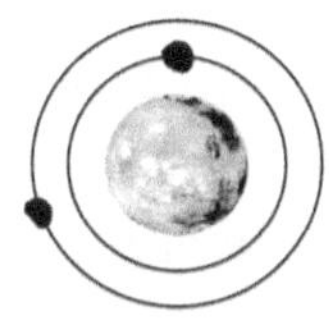

CHAPTER 7

"SECRETARY KARIM, DIRECTOR SHOZHA," Roslyn greeted the two senior members of the Evacuation Commission as she took her seat. She didn't know the other half dozen humans and reezh around the table, but she knew who was in charge today.

Karim was the only one still standing as he gestured the rest to their seats. He was a pudgy and somewhat balding man wearing a toga-like garment. It seemed poorly designed for Garuda's vicious winds to Roslyn's eyes, but she'd seen him handle it calmly in a near-gale, so it couldn't be too bad.

Plus, it was a common-enough clothing choice in the Chimeran capital city.

"Thank you for joining us, Mage-Captain Chambers," Karim told her. "We have a lot of work to do if we're going to get our people to safety. With your presence, I believe we have every key constituency involved in our task represented.

"To make sure everyone is on the same page, I'd like to fill you in on where we stand with the organization," he continued. "Then you can let us know if you have any information we haven't considered yet."

"Of course, Secretary."

Karim nodded, his gaze drifting off into the distance for a few moments.

"We are in the process of bringing on a team of two hundred and seven analysts and clerks," he began. "The goal is that once we receive confirmation of the number of seats available in a given convoy, we can have people contacted and moving well in advance."

"As the potential scale of the convoys expands, we will likely need to rapidly expand that number," Shozha noted in the gravelly tones common to all reezh Roslyn had met, "but we want to train up those two hundred as an initial seed. They will train the others, who will train others."

"Our current low-end estimate of the seats in the first convoy is five million," Roslyn warned. "I imagine that is more contacts than two hundred clerks can handle."

"Hence the plan for rapid expansion," Karim agreed. "We are currently collating and reconciling our medical care, official identification, vehicle registration, and tax filing databases to create a complete list of our citizens and means of contacting them.

"Our primary form of selection will be by lottery. We will weight the criteria toward children and make certain families are kept together, but near-pure randomness seems to be the most equitable option available to us," he concluded.

"Any given candidate will have the right to decline transport," Shozha said. "We will not force any individuals onto transport ships. The thought would be impossible for my people."

Roslyn nodded. She'd seen the art in the Dyad's Joint Museum, showing the tribute ships taking the youth of Chimera away—some to be murdered for Engines of Sacred Sacrifice, others to be forced into the military service of the Reezh Ida.

Regardless of the task, those taken away had never returned. No Chimeran government could force their people onto transports against their will. Too many memories and histories spoke against it.

"There are some things that will need to be moved to the front of the queue," she noted quietly. "Histories and archives—the Reezh Ida Lachai's, yes, but not just theirs. The stories and history of your world must be preserved.

"I dislike that the best way to do so is to move the records elsewhere, but that is the reality we face."

"It is," Shozha confirmed. "We have a list of personnel associated with the Lachai, along with other major scientific and historical institutions, that will be loaded onto the first transports—along with the families of our military personnel.

"The total is just over one hundred thousand people. A convoy of five million passengers will require us to randomly select millions upon millions of people. Creating that structure is the absolute priority."

Roslyn nodded and leaned backward. There was no arguing that—especially since everything she had seen said that five million was the *minimum*. Some of the estimates she'd seen were twenty, even thirty, million seats on the first convoy.

She had more hope for that in the *second* evac convoy. The first would be whatever could be gathered up and sent immediately, mostly from the Core Worlds. There might be an earlier convoy, but the first real evacuation flight wouldn't be until a few days before they were expecting the Kazh to investigate the loss of their fleet.

"That structure will then be scalable," Karim said quietly. "Any ship that makes it here will be loaded with people selected by the same rules. We will be as able to handle evacuating five thousand as five million."

"We might have issues evacuating five thousand," Roslyn warned. "There's going to be a lot of panic and fear once everything is moving."

"We know." Karim looked around the table and spread his hands. "It is *our* job here at the Commission to minimize that panic by having clear plans, communication, and organization. So long as it is within our power, no one will be left behind."

"And Mars stands ready to assist," she promised. Karim's comment about scalability had planted a thought in her mind. She'd have to talk to Morales about it. "From as large as the ships we are sending to as small as providing as much information in advance as possible, we will do everything we can.

"I have a number of hats I'm balancing at this moment, but I am quite certain that the Commission is the most important of them. If you will permit, I believe we would be well served if I were to sit in on at least one meeting a day of the Evacuation Commission, to make certain that you are updated on what we are doing and vice versa."

She could already see that this job was going to involve more meetings than she wanted—but with this many lives on the line, she'd tolerate a lot more than a few meetings!

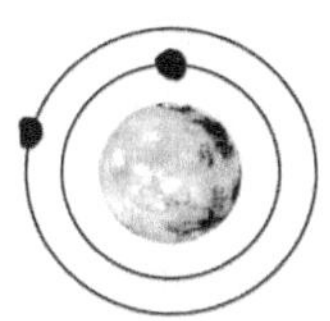

CHAPTER 8

TWO DREADNOUGHTS ORBITED the gas giant of Exeter-I at a distance large enough to make the orbits a matter of calculation near-invisible to the naked eye. *Excalibur* was the long-expected new arrival, giving Jane Alexander a core of firepower unseen since the UnArcana Rebellions.

Six battleships completed that core, flanked by a dozen cruisers. A mere ten destroyers were interspersed through the walls of metal, a shortfall that Jane knew should be made up shortly.

All of that mass of metal was basically trapped in the Exeter System, as far as the conflict in front of her was concerned. The problem was obvious to a trained eye, though Jane knew many civilians would have been overawed by the sheer mass of her fleet.

There were exactly *two* RMN support transports in Exeter. Base Deveraux had massive logistics facilities, but all of the shipping to support those facilities had been loaned to BTG Romana and was already in Chimera.

"Do we have an update on the logistics convoy?" she asked her Chief of Staff.

Commodore Peta Soból was a dark-haired woman from the MidWorld of Xanth, her eyes a sharp emerald green that contrasted with her Slavic coloring. She looked awkward at the question.

"I haven't seen an update since our meeting yesterday," she admitted. "I haven't had an opportunity to chase them down. It's been... busy."

Jane took a sip of her coffee to buy herself time. Soból wasn't making excuses. It had just taken them ten minutes to go through all of the major tasks that the Commodore had handled in the twenty-four hours since their previous evening meeting.

"If nothing has changed, that means we'll have the first ships in a week, correct?" she asked.

"Yes, sir," Soból confirmed. "Three weeks after that before we truly have enough support to deploy both dreadnoughts forward."

By which point, Jane silently thanked whatever deity was listening, Janet Adamant would be in the system. One old battleship might not make all of the difference, but it was more than nothing.

"Put checking in on our logistics at the top of your list going forward," Jane instructed gently. "Right now, I have enough firepower to fight a war but not enough fuel to put it where it needs to be."

"Yes, sir. We... do have a line on more reinforcements, too."

"I hadn't heard that," Jane admitted. "What have we got?"

"The Nia Kriti fleet base made some kind of deal no one wants to investigate too closely and broke free the entire Eleventh Cruiser Squadron," Soból explained. "Six *Honorific*-class ships left Nia Kriti this morning. Running at full speed, we expect them in twenty-four days."

Nia Kriti had been reinforced before the Rebellion to keep watch on the Republic of Faith and Reason. The opening attacks had successfully seized the system, though the Republic hadn't held it for long.

Most of the infrastructure had survived, and the base there remained significant. Jane had already claimed two of their three battleships—and it seemed they'd left with friends.

"That leaves Mage-Admiral Hammond with only one cruiser squadron to back up *Pax Atlantica* in Nia Kriti," she noted. "Any comment in the reports of why he feels he can spare half his cruiser strength?"

"I am not sure, sir," Soból admitted.

"Suspicions?" Jane prodded. Her Chief of Staff was solid, dependable, reliable, sensible and a few other words ending in *-ible*. She was not, sadly, particularly imaginative. Solid and dependable had made Soból a calmly rising presence in the staff officer corps, but it occasionally made conversations feel like pulling teeth.

"Nia Kriti and the surrounding MidWorlds built their militia strengths up after being liberated during the Rebellion," Soból noted. "While none of them have cruisers, there are twenty-four Tau Ceti–built export destroyers present in Mage-Admiral Hammond's region of responsibility.

"If he is coordinating with the militias to provide hulls for patrols, that could allow him to draw down his numbers. We have no official policy supporting such an action, though."

"Yet," Jane murmured. "There's a few documents rattling around the Parliament that will get us there, at which point I hope George will admit what he's been up to so we can commend him for it."

"Yes, sir," Soból said. "With those additions, we have confirmed that we will have another battleship, four cruisers and four destroyers arriving this week. Two battleships and eight destroyers the next week, then another four each of cruisers and destroyers. The Nia Kriti ships are our farthest confirmed detachment, bringing two more battleships and six more cruisers."

Which would bring Second Fleet to two dreadnoughts, eleven battleships, twenty-two cruisers and twenty-two destroyers by the point she expected to have enough logistics to move the whole fleet up to Chimera.

"That does give us some options. The next thing I need you to get from Command is a timeline on the evacuation convoys," she told Soból. "We should be able to detach a cruiser squadron, at the very least, to cover their trip to Chimera."

"There are some... oddities in the timelines I'm getting, sir," her subordinate warned. "We've confirmed we're getting at least eighty of the *Bushidos* over the next ten days, but I've been asked to set up logistics for an unknown number of transports in the forty-to-sixty-megaton range, minimum ten."

"We're getting the colony ships, then," Jane concluded. "That's good news."

"Sir... I checked. There's only sixteen colony ships in the *entire Protectorate*," Soból pointed out. "And half of them are *bigger* than that. Everyone at High Command is being very quiet about what ships we're talking about, only that we should expect them in twenty days."

Jane took that in with a nod and another sip of her coffee. *Twenty days* didn't tell her much—for a "fast" freighter like most passenger ships with three civilian Jump Mages, that was almost two hundred light-years. Even from Exeter, that covered most of the Protectorate... but if she presumed the ships still needed to be prepped wherever they were, that led to an interesting conclusion.

"They're coming from Earth." She shook her head. "It doesn't matter. We'll get details once Command has them"—or Kiera did; Jane wasn't above leaning on her niece if people were playing secrecy games—"and we'll work with them then. We'll send the *Bushido*s in once we have those eighty, and prep for a second wave when the big girls arrive ten days after that.

"Having two convoys looping every thirty days and spreading potential targets out seems useful to me."

"I agree, sir. Can we spare the ships? We're going to be critically short on destroyers."

"We are," she agreed. "Which is why we'll be sending cruisers instead. Overkill, maybe, but our *primary* purpose until the *Lancelot*s commission is to evacuate Chimera."

The *Lancelot*s were the next-generation dreadnoughts being built in Sol and Tau Ceti. Ten were almost complete, six months away from being deployable. Only slightly larger than the *Mjolnir*s, they had comparable offensive firepower but were even more survivable.

The timing of the conflict with the Kazh was lucky in some ways. In a year, the Protectorate would have had a more technologically advanced fleet but not a *bigger* one, as the plans called for the *Fidelity*-class battleships and their smaller siblings to replace old ships on a one-for-one basis.

Now the older ships would remain in commission as the new ships came online. Jane wasn't sure how they were going to find crews and Mages for the hundred-odd starships commissioning over the next year, but that, thankfully, wasn't her job.

Her job was to use them to their best potential.

CHAPTER 9

WHEN THE MESSAGE CAME IN from Dr. Starling, Kiera had to sit on a rather immature urge to put it aside until Barry got back from his appointments. She could justify it from a work perspective, of course—just because she wasn't in meetings this afternoon didn't mean she wasn't overloaded and busy. Just the summaries of the reports that had landed in her inbox that day were easily two hours of reading, and if something required a decision, she'd have to read in more detail.

But if enough Prometheans had volunteered, there were wheels she needed to get turning. Barry wouldn't be back until much later in the day—he was interviewing with professors for the complicated custom university program that he was assembling around himself.

Olympus City University had won out over every other university on Mars by the simple measures of being the best economic institute in the Solar System, if not the Protectorate, and offering Barry the opportunity to earn a master's alongside his regular degree.

Kiera suspected that when the dust settled, her boyfriend would walk out of the program with a PhD and the stunned respect of the OCU Economics Department. If he was half as good an economist as he'd been a shuttle thief, he was going to be very pleased with himself and very useful to Kiera.

That wasn't why he was doing it or why Kiera was encouraging him to find a new path that didn't involve high-end technical crime. Barry needed to find his own way in the universe rather than being a satellite of his girlfriend, even if said girlfriend was the Mage-Queen of Mars.

As did the Prometheans. Kiera sighed and opened Starling's message.

Sixty-two. The number sprang out of the text as she skimmed it, years of practice letting her narrow on to the key points of a page in moments.

Sixty-two Prometheans had volunteered, including both William Connors and Mikayla Spencer. Kiera didn't know any of the other sixty names, though Starling had been helpful enough to include context.

Four others, like Connors, had been Awakened Prometheans in the service of the First Legion. Some of the others had been on Legion ships but, like most of the residents of the Phobos Facility, had first regained consciousness in Sol.

It was more of them than Kiera had dared hope. It was an awkward number, leaving her with two extra Prometheans, but she wasn't going to let any of the volunteers go unused.

She had the contact information for the man leading the Charon work parties up within a moment, relaying through the Link for a live conversation with the cruiser hosting them.

"Is Commodore Okorie available?" she asked the sallow Lieutenant Commander who answered—presumably the senior officer's aide or secretary.

"Your Majesty! I will get him on the line immediately," the junior officer almost squeaked before vanishing from the screen, his image replaced by the rotating rocket-on-crowned-mountain-and-planet of the Royal Martian Navy.

Commodore Chinedu Okorie was part of the RMN's Logistics Bureau, the oft-underestimated collection of officers and ships that made certain the Navy had missiles, fuel, food and people wherever they ended up.

He was also almost as dark-skinned as his uniform, a pitch-black Nigerian coloring that only made his broad smile more obvious.

"Your Majesty, how may the engineers and water-haulers serve you today?" he asked.

"If you're hauling water out at Charon, I have questions," Kiera told him. "Your review of the *Saladins* is progressing, I hope? We have numbers on our volunteers."

"Excellent," Okorie said, drawing out the syllables. "I have divided our efforts in the interests of accelerating the availability of the ships in the best state.

"Four of the vessels, including *Saladin* herself, were assessed as in workable condition on initial scans. Survey parties confirmed this, and we have been focusing on getting those four online.

"I expect them all to be ready to deploy by morning OMT," he concluded. "We have been surveying the rest of the ships in, well, order by how much deployable hardware the manifests list them as carrying.

"We have started repair work on two ships, but survey work is continuing, and we have only set foot, if I am honest, on about sixteen of the vessels."

"Thank you, Commodore," she told him. "Conveniently, sixteen is how many we're going to need. We have sixty-two volunteers. You will need to coordinate with Dr. Starling to arrange transport out to the ships as they become capable of handling Prometheans safely."

"Of course. A large portion of the work we are doing is to make certain that the new officers will have extensive access to the ship's systems—duplicating what the First Legion did with their Awakened Prometheans but with even more flexibility and access for the Mage in question."

It was a fascinating word choice, Kiera noted, that Okorie easily referred to the Prometheans as *Mages*. It was true and important, but it also showed that he was seeing them as *people*, not *hardware*.

"You will need more people," she guessed. "And crews for the ships?"

"I have spoken with the Reserve Administration Center on Mars already," Okorie confirmed. "By poaching Logistics officers and spacers from various facilities in Sol and backfilling them with reservists, I can assemble full crews for—sixteen ships, you said?—within twenty-four hours.

"Those crews will do much of the repair work themselves, which will accelerate affairs."

He shrugged and grinned again.

"We could bring the volunteers aboard the first six ships tomorrow," he promised. "The other ten, the day after. The entire flotilla should be able to move within sixty hours."

Kiera blinked.

"That is faster than I had dared hope, Commodore," she admitted.

"The difficult we do immediately; the impossible takes a little longer," he told her, clearly quoting something. "This barely even qualifies as *difficult.* These are sturdy ships that never even had battle damage. The only real damage is where the Prometheans were removed, and given how much work we are doing in those sections, that is almost helpful."

"Thank you," Kiera told him. "With the refits, how many people are we going to get on those ships?"

"A lot of work will be done en route, but we're loading prefabricated modules into the cargo space to enable it," Okorie said. "My understanding is that we aren't putting any soldiers on these ships?"

"No. Whatever hardware is on them, we'll deliver to Chimera and let them use as they see fit, but once that's off, those ships will be dedicated evacuation ships."

"It's a *lot* of hardware, Your Majesty. None of the ships were carrying more than a half-complement of equipment when they were surrendered, but they are *planetary invasion ships.*"

"None of it's compatible with our people's training or munitions," she reminded him. "Where the CSN has a number of people with that training and has the capacity to manufacture the munitions."

The Logistics Commodore snorted.

"They're not going to need to make more once we make the delivery," he said—at which point Kiera started to grasp just how much *a lot of hardware* was. "I'd have to double-check the manifests and our own counts, but we're going to be delivering just over two thousand suborbital/atmosphere interceptors and half a million *missiles*, alone, for said interceptors.

"As an example."

"Which doesn't make them any more useful to *us*," Kiera repeated. "But makes our gift of glorified scrap metal look very impressive to our new friends, I suppose."

He laughed.

"As you say, Your Majesty. I will make certain the crews have the manuals to check over the gear on our way. We're going to be quite busy on our journey."

"*We*, Commodore?" Kiera asked.

"Unless you or High Command have someone else in mind, I believe I make the most sense to command the convoy, Your Majesty," he said calmly. "Either way, I will need to accompany the convoy to supervise the en-route fitting-out."

"I am not aware of any alternative plan," she conceded. She didn't think anyone had been planning on Okorie taking command, but no one had yet picked a flag officer to command the massive transports.

"You may consider that command granted," she decided after a momentary double-check of her files. "Official paperwork will follow through Admiral Medici, of course."

She paused, making sure to meet Okorie's gaze and hold it for a few moments.

"How many people are those ships going to carry?" she repeated.

"A million," he said flatly. "We might need to pick up some more prefab modules from Exeter or even Chimera to be certain everyone has a bed and a shower, but we'll be able to carry a million people on each of those ships.

"Then between you and our volunteers, you are going to be saving at least sixteen million lives," Kiera told him, still holding his gaze. "They will be your utmost priority, Commodore. Their lives are going to rest in your hands.

"Can you handle that?"

There was a long silence.

"My family left Africa during ethnic violence in the twentieth century," Okorie said, his tone sad. "We returned in the mid-twenty-first, only to be driven out *again*. We then joined the Mars colony, only to be conquered and oppressed by the Eugenicists.

"I exist because men and women in uniforms much like mine risked—and, in some cases, *gave*—their lives so my ancestors could get to safety. I would dishonor their memories and betray my daughters' faith if I were to refuse to make the same effort.

"So, yes, Your Majesty. I will handle it. We will save every life we can. You have my word."

The second set of wheels Kiera needed to get turning were a more-complicated set. They still required the Link—even Dr. Starling on Phobos was far enough away that the FTL communicator was useful—but the distance from Mars to Charon was nothing compared to the distance from the Solar System to Chimera.

"Master Chief Kovalyow," Kiera greeted Precious Kovalyow when Chambers' senior NCO answered the call. "Is Mage-Captain Chambers available?"

"Last time I checked, Your Majesty, the only acceptable answer to the *Mage-Queen* asking that question was *Yes, Your Majesty*," Kovalyow said. "She is in her office, probably looking at the kinds of spreadsheets that make sane people cry.

"I'll check and connect you."

There was a certain degree of lèse-majesté that Kiera would tolerate from most people. The amount allowed to the RMN was higher still—and she had accepted before even becoming Queen that the rules for the senior noncommissioned officers of the Protectorate's Navy were a very different thing again.

Even beyond that, though, Kovalyow helped keep Roslyn Chambers sane. Kiera would forgive far more than an amusing bit of snark for the woman taking on that monumental task.

"Your Majesty." Chambers looked exhausted, her red hair ever so slightly less perfectly braided than Kiera would expect, and her uniform jacket hung over the back of her chair.

"Did I miss the audience?" Kiera replied. "This is more than a bit of work, but it's not official. You can call me by my damned name."

"Fair enough, Kiera," her friend allowed. "Long day."

"*Spreadsheets to make sane people cry?*"

"Yeah. The kind that calculate how many people we're likely to get off this planet before it's invaded."

Kiera winced. Kovalyow's comment hadn't been as much of a joke as she thought.

"How bad does it look?" she asked.

"It's been eleven days since the attack," Chambers noted. "The first evacuation convoy is expected to leave Exeter in eight days, with eighty

*Bushido*s and some civilian shipping, still to be determined. Given fundamentally civilian Jump Mages and jump schedules, they'll arrive eleven days after that.

"Thirty days after the destruction of the Kazh fleet. We know that several warships of the strike fleet escaped, but we have no idea of how many Mages or Promethean-equivalents they carry," the officer warned. "We also don't know if they have FTL communicators, though the Ida tech base we have records on didn't include such a thing."

Kiera waited silently, allowing her friend to lay out the numbers.

"One hundred and eighty light-years from here to the Nine. Assuming they are running the equivalent to our civilian jump sequence—the best Prometheans can handle, in our experience—that's twenty days.

"Assuming five days for them to debrief and assemble a new strike fleet, that fleet could be here forty-five days after the attack. Thirty-four days from now—and before the evacuation convoy could return for a second pickup.

"If they deploy the way I expect, well." Chambers shook her head. "We'll have Adamant and her battleship here, but in their position, I'd send twice as many ships as last time. We'll be overrun and we'll only get one evacuation flight out."

Kiera nodded.

"I have some good news on that front," she told her friend. "There will be a second convoy of ships assembling at Exeter. My math is still rough, but I would expect them to reach Chimera in thirty to thirty-two days.

"Their carrying capacity will *significantly* exceed that of the first convoy."

Chambers looked at her with the expression that told Kiera she was playing too many games.

"There are only twenty troop transports left in the Protectorate, which are the only ships I've been advised are arriving on that timetable," the Mage-Captain said flatly. "And I understand they'll be at least partially loaded."

"Ten divisions of Marines, fifteen of the Guard," Kiera confirmed. "That's why they've been delayed behind the other ships. I believe they're going to require some refit work in Chimera, but it should be quick?"

"Not my area, but I believe so. But even doubling their troop lift, that's only eight million in the first wave and two in the second. Against two *billion* people. And two million isn't *significantly more* than eight, Kiera."

"The second flotilla will have more civilian ships," Kiera pointed out. "At least two hundred ships, average lift five thousand apiece. Another million souls. That's what we've managed to contract and pull away already—the current plan is to feed whatever ships we can get our hands on to Mackenzie to join up with the two convoys as they come in, possibly adding as much as a million seats to each loop."

"That's good news."

"The Derry Colony Expedition Corporation also turns out to have friends in high places," the Queen continued. "I'm not normally a fan of corporate joint ventures turning out to know any level of state secret, but when it means that the Board of Directors volunteers to put *six colony ships* at our immediate disposal, I will bite my damn tongue and thank them very prettily.

"That's another six million in passenger lift. We need to come up with extra Mages for them, and they might not make it to Exeter for the second convoy. If they don't, they'll rendezvous with the first convoy at Mackenzie in thirty-three days."

She saw Chambers sigh in relief, then shake her head.

"If they miss the second convoy, they may not get a chance for round two with the first," she warned. "The first loop back to Chimera won't be complete until fifteen days after I expect their attack to arrive."

"You can't hold them?" Kiera asked.

"It depends on what they send," Chambers replied. "They sent enough ships last time that they very nearly overran BTG Romana, Kiera, and we had more and better ships than we're going to have once BTG Righteous Guardian is here.

"Like I said, in their place, I'd send more. Anyone we don't get off in the first trips by the two convoys isn't getting out."

"I'll remind people of that when we look at what it will take to get the colony transports there," Kiera promised. "But the second convoy will have a *minimum* of eighteen million seats, Roslyn. Even if we don't get the colony ships."

"Kiera, this isn't the time for false hope," her friend growled.

"It's not false. Sixty-two Prometheans volunteered to take up Ship's Mage duties on the planetary invasion ships of the Republic," Kiera said quickly. "That's fifteen ships that can be there with the second convoy, most of them carrying at least half of their military hardware loadout at the same time.

"They'll provide a massive amount of military materiel for the Chimerans *and* I have been promised they are easily refitted to carry a million people each. They were designed for half a million troops, including heavy armor, after all."

Roslyn Chambers was silent, staring at Kiera, then tapped something on a keyboard the Queen couldn't see.

"We still might only get one flight," she said softly. "But that's a lot more people out than it looked like before. It's still a lot of nightmares on this ledger, Kiera."

"I know." Kiera couldn't say more than that. The task she'd set her Navy—and her friend—was impossible. She *knew* that. But what choice did she have?

"I need something from you with that, though," she said grimly. "We have enough Prometheans to get fifteen ships to ten light-years a day. But one ship is only going to have two Mages aboard, and we can't backfill with regular Mages on Prometheus-Drive ships.

"I need two more Prometheans, Roslyn, and I've already shaken the one tree that hides them in the Protectorate. I absolutely will *not* lean on the ones that didn't feel they could volunteer for this. That leaves only one potential source of the last two."

"I'm not certain Wang will want to give up the Prometheans left on his warships. Not only are they key to any chance of us carrying this battle, but he is also extraordinarily protective of them."

"And rightly so," Kiera said. "All we can do is ask. How many are left in his fleet?"

"Seven, technically, but two are out-system."

"Roslyn, there were over fifty Prometheans in Emerson Wang's defecting ships," the Queen pointed out. "I one hundred percent believe that he gave his Prometheans a choice and only nine of them chose to serve on his ships. But especially now that I've talked to *our* Prometheans?

"Some of them chose somewhere in between. There are civilian Prometheans in the Chimera System, Roslyn. We need to know where they are—so we can evacuate them first, if nothing else!

"But if two of them are prepared to volunteer to crew one of the *Saladins*, we can load them on a courier or some such and rush them back to rendezvous with our slowpoke. Otherwise, that last ship won't arrive in Chimera until the *second* round of pickups."

The pickups Roslyn Chambers clearly wasn't convinced were going to happen.

"I... will talk to Admiral Wang," she promised.

"That's all we can do," Kiera agreed. "Though... two of his Prometheans are out of the system? Where are they?"

That sounded familiar, but it wasn't something she'd committed to her prodigious memory.

"Before Banderas and BTG Romana arrived, the Dyad sent a diplomatic mission to one of the Primes. We reported it," Chambers noted.

"You did; it just slipped my mind," Kiera said grimly. "We should have heard back now, shouldn't we?"

"With only two Prometheans aboard, *Barracuda* can only make five light-years a day," Chambers noted slowly. "It's a three-hundred-and-fifty-light-year round-trip, so seventy days. Another thirty days or so, I think, assuming that they somehow forge an alliance in hours instead of days."

"I take it we didn't lend them a Link."

"We would have needed to send our people with them to operate it, and they were doing everything they could to make sure there were no humans aboard *Barracuda*." Chambers sighed. "It made sense, but in hindsight, I wish we'd done so anyway. Now I'm expecting them around when I'm expecting the Kazh."

"I suppose that offers the chance of some reezh cavalry coming in to save the day?"

"Much as I would love that, I suspect we'd need to tell *Barracuda* how bad things had become before they would even ask for that. They're under strict orders not to reveal exactly which minor colony system survived the Burning."

"So... talk to Wang on that mission as well," Kiera instructed. "I know I'm laying a lot on you, my friend. I wish I could promise a better reward than defeat, retreat and a new job."

"Too many lives are at risk for us to do anything else. What purpose is your Protectorate if we don't protect people?"

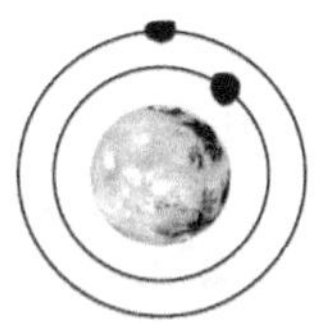

CHAPTER 10

CONNOR O'HANNAGAIN WASN'T THE FIRST HUMAN in the secret archives beneath the Joint Museum in Twin Sphinxes. *That* had been the Nemesis operative known as Kay and his team of killers, when their paranoia had led them to decide that Chimera's open friendliness hid something dark.

Local Chimeran humans had been allowed into the place since then, he believed, but he knew that he was the first Martian to have been invited under the Museum.

The elevator down into the archives was no longer concealed, letting him out into a broad, open space with cubicles and archives on either side of a pathway leading toward the elevators leading deeper into the mound.

He wasn't sure how many different layers there were to the "hill" next to the Legislature Building that held the Joint Museum. Each of them was a radiation-containment dome, built over the wreck of the last Reezh Ida tribute ship to ever visit the system.

Something about the reactor on the saucer-like ship had gone very, very wrong and the ship was effectively *still* actively melting down hundreds of years later. That ship had, until recently, held a near-complete copy of the Ida's own military archives.

But Nemesis had stolen that and wrecked Chimera's trust in the Protectorate. That Connor had been invited down into the underground archives was a sign that his work was fixing that relationship, but he understood how close it had been.

"This way, Ambassador," his escort told him. The young reezh woman wore the dark-red uniform of the Western Republic's federal constabulary, like the armed guards he saw scattered through the archive.

As she led the way, he realized he was specifically being taken past a section of the archive that had been left untouched after Nemesis's visit. There were visible bullet holes still scattered through the cavernous space, but a chunk of desks and storage had been left shattered and burned, just off the main thoroughfare.

The only new things added to the wreckage were a series of photographs of individual reezh, and small piles of colored rocks. His escort stopped in front of the impromptu shrine, taking a moment to show her respect, and Connor joined her in a moment of silence.

The rocks were hand-painted, he realized. Some were more roughly done than others, and he suspected they filled the same role that flowers would for humans.

"This should never have happened," he murmured.

"Did you know them?" his escort asked, then stopped as if she couldn't believe what she'd said.

"No. It doesn't matter. They were *ours*, traitors and murderers, but *our* criminals to deal with. This should not have happened."

Connor chose his words with care. His initial comment had been a rare moment of impulse, but his explanation was as picked as any of his speeches. He couldn't read reezh well, but he had his suspicions about the constable the Reezh Ida Lachai had selected to escort him in.

"My brother was a researcher here," she said quietly, confirming his thoughts as she gestured to one of the photos. "Your people shot him dead. He was unarmed—had never carried a weapon in his life."

The Protectorate had officially taken what responsibility they could for Kay's massacre. That meant that Connor didn't need to dance around the topic as he might have earlier in his time on Garuda.

"Kent Riley and his people were scum who betrayed not only our nation but even the cause they were supposed to serve," Connor said grimly. "They were *intended* to be like the Lachai, holding knowledge until it was needed. Instead, they became... this."

He shook his head.

"We cannot undo what was done here," he told her. "We will do everything in our power to protect Chimera, and we *did* bring these people to justice, but none of that undoes their crimes.

"It's just all we can do."

The young woman looked at him with the large multi-faceted eyes above the armored brow ridges of her people. Her protected lower eyes were still focused on her brother's picture.

"We should move on," she finally said.

"You can stay here, Tollo," a new voice interjected.

Connor turned and was utterly unsurprised to see Razhkah had quietly come up behind them while they were speaking. The leader of the Reezh Ida Lachai—technically, in fact, *the* Reezh Ida Lachai, as he understood it—was one of the oldest reezh he'd met. Her skin was faded to a smooth tone close to white marble, and three of her eyes were focused on Tollo, Connor's escort.

Her upper left eye stared blankly off into space, the dark facets long clouded into uselessness with some reezh version of cataracts that had likely resisted easy treatment.

"Lachai Razhkah, I—"

"You stopped to mourn your brother and to show the Ambassador the shrine," Razhkah interrupted. "I approve. I can lead O'Hannagain the rest of the way. I am not yet completely decrepit, Tollo."

"I believe the Lachai is safe from me here," Connor promised. "You can stay for a while; we will find you before I go."

That was all the gentle push the constable needed, and she let her focus return to the picture of her brother. For his part, Connor bowed slightly to the old reezh Mage and waved for her to lead the way.

Razhkah did so with a will, causing him to heavily reassess how "decrepit" the old reezh was. He was a large, muscular man who made a point of working out and staying extremely fit, but he had to consciously lengthen his stride to keep up with her.

They didn't have far to go. He doubted the plain office she led him into was her normal working space, though he could have been wrong.

Like everything else in the underground archive, it had been furnished with plain but sturdy furniture that was either military surplus or bought from the people who supplied Chimera's armed forces.

The Lachai took a seat behind the desk without a word, and Connor waited politely for her to say something.

"Sit down, Ambassador," she instructed. "You're tall enough I can't see you with my lower eyes without twisting in a way my bones won't take anymore."

He chuckled and obeyed. She didn't offer him refreshment, but he'd half-expected that. He was an invited guest there, but the Lachai couldn't be particularly happy with him.

"How proceeds the packing?" he asked. He hadn't seen any sign of the archives being packed up in the offices outside, but the plan was for everything down there to be on the first transport out.

"Slowly and carefully," Razhkah said sharply. "There is a great deal of research stored down here, Ambassador, including entire databases stored in systems that can be quite temperamental. I believe you are aware of how the Ida maintained technological control of the colonies?"

"Key parts were restricted in where they were manufactured," Connor summarized. He suspected it was more complicated than that, since mere *parts* could probably be improvised somewhere, but it seemed a useful summary.

"Fundamentally correct. Much of our old technology relies on complex long-chain molecules acting as superconductors and holographic storage and similar such key components." She stared past him for a moment. "What was left of those materials has been solely in the care of the Lachai for a long time. We ran out... ten Garudan years ago."

Almost forty Terran standard years.

"You were using them for computers, I take it?" he asked.

"We were. We transferred what data we could and established makeshift solutions to keep the systems we needed operational. There is a thriving subculture among my people around finding ways to get old Ida tech operational.

"It was from that subculture, we believe, that your Nemesis found the information necessary for stealing the Last Ship's computer core to be useful to them."

"How badly does that hurt your archives?"

"We had mostly complete copies of the Last Ship's systems," Razhkah said. "But accessing the core was always a difficult task, given the radiation level, and, well, we didn't need most of the records there.

"Outside of the data on the last few years of the Reezh Ida, we already possessed much of the information stored there. It was of value to Nemesis, I am sure, but the Lachai had the records elsewhere."

"That is better news than I had hoped," Connor admitted. "We understood that the loss of the Last Ship's computers might limit how much information was available."

"The information you seek on the magic of the Reezh Ida is more limited than you may hope," she warned. "But we have more-detailed history and maps and such of the Ida than Nemesis stole."

"Which makes it all the more important that we get it all packed up safely before the evacuation convoys arrive," he reminded her. The convoy wouldn't even leave Exeter for another week, but it would be in Chimera in eighteen days. Thirteen Garudan days.

"We have time, and it is better done right than damaged," Razhkah said. "You will get your blood price of information, Ambassador."

He shook his head.

"At this point, Razhkah, the exchange of information is guaranteed. I am more concerned about *protecting* the history and knowledge of your people than accessing it. The Lachai and your records may be at the top of the evacuation list, but so are many of your historians and scientists.

"We want to preserve what makes Chimera *Chimera*," he insisted. "Yes, the more we can learn from your archives, the better positioned we are to fight this war, but we do want more than that out of this."

The armored face of a reezh was still difficult for him to read, but he thought he saw some level of relaxing tension in Razhkah.

"I know," she conceded. "But I have spent longer than most members of our races live concealing and protecting this knowledge. I recognized my duty to reveal it to deal with Nemesis's approach to the Kazh, but it is difficult to let it entirely go into the hands of others."

"We would strongly prefer that it never wholly go into the *hands of others*, Lachai Razhkah," Connor told her. "That is part of what I wanted to speak to you about today."

He'd been trying to set up this meeting for days and had been surprised to be invited to join her in the archive. She probably had been avoiding him, but she recognized that, and the invite was probably some kind of peace offering.

"We are transporting all of this to other worlds," she said, gesturing around her. "I will travel with it, but I recognize that I will no longer have full control."

"My Queen has asked me to make you an offer," Connor replied. "We would like to bring *all* of the Lachai—the knowledge, the people, their families, everything—to Mars. We intend to build a new institute: a research facility to start, but expanding to educational and intercultural as time goes on.

"While this institute would act as a centerpoint for our studies of the old reezh magic, it would also act as the face of reezh–human relationships into the future." He met her lower eyes as evenly as he could.

"On the slopes of Olympus Mons, long ago, reezh agents set into motion the rediscovery of human magic for the darkest of reasons," he reminded her. "Tens of thousands of our people died in the labs the Eugenicists built with reezh help.

"Right now, that remains the biggest piece of what humanity thinks of your people. The authors of that atrocity were human, but it was the reezh that made it possible.

"But you are not those reezh. So, on the slopes of Olympus Mons once more, we want to lay the foundation for a new future. Where human and reezh work together, to reach new heights of science, magic and civilization.

"A plan for the future beyond this war, Lachai Razhkah. And the Mage-Queen of Mars has tasked me to offer you the leadership of this new institute, for as long as you are willing and able."

Razhkah was silent as he laid out the pitch, and then for some seconds afterward. Long enough that he started to worry.

"And this would be where all of these archives of the Lachai would go?" she finally asked.

"Yes. Under your control more than anyone's," he confirmed. They both knew there would be other factors, of course—but there would have been other factors if the archive stayed on Garuda, too. So long as it wasn't secret, knowledge of this importance couldn't escape politics.

"I will need to consider this offer, Ambassador," she finally said.

"Of course. A ship is being prepared to meet you at Mackenzie," he promised. "It is... within your power, Razhkah, to ask that we do not move the archives to Mars. We would prefer not to leave them at Mackenzie, but I can see how bringing it all to the heart of our power could be concerning."

He hoped that by leaving that option out there, he could avoid her concerns. His Queen's determination to do fairly by the reezh of Chimera was honest. Connor's phrasing and presentation of it were, well, somewhat manipulative—but the offer was complete and honest.

It was Mage-Queen Kiera Alexander's job to provide the compass and soul of the Protectorate's morality. It was Connor O'Hannagain's job to make sure that the Protectorate's goals were achieved.

In his opinion, both tasks were equally important.

The Garudan wind around Twin Sphinx was as brutal as ever as Connor stepped outside the Joint Museum and nodded his farewell to Tollo. The young reezh was both more and less somber after visiting the shrine than she had been when she brought him in, but she seemed to appreciate the chance to check on her brother, so to speak.

He tucked himself out of the wind, his pair of Protectorate Secret Service bodyguards materializing as if by magic to flank him.

"Car is on the way," Sarvesh Ansel, his senior PSS agent, told him. "Did we get what we need?"

"I think so," Connor confirmed. "She's thinking about it, but she's a tough old lady. If she was going to tell me to pound sand, she'd have done it immediately."

A notification on his wrist-comp told him that Chambers had tried to reach him while he was in the underground archive. He waited long enough for the car to arrive—it was more secure than outside a public institution!—and then returned her call immediately.

The Mage-Captain hadn't flagged her contact as urgent or priority, but his naval attaché was his link into the military affairs that dominated thoughts in the Chimera System.

"Roslyn, you needed something?" he asked.

"I do," she confirmed. "I need you to be my date to a dinner this evening."

Of all the things Mage-Captain Roslyn Chambers could have said, that was probably the one that he *hadn't* expected. Attractive as the naval officer was, she was also fifteen years younger than him and, despite a certain je ne sais quoi, not in line with his usual preferences.

"I beg your pardon?" he asked, his tone sharper than he meant because he wasn't used to actually being flummoxed.

In response, she laughed at him.

"Sorry, I couldn't resist," she confessed. "I have a dinner invitation to meet Admiral Wang tonight. He's bringing a few others, including Minister Hsieh Ai Ling, and I'm going to need covering fire.

"I'm asking him about the Prometheans he's hiding from us."

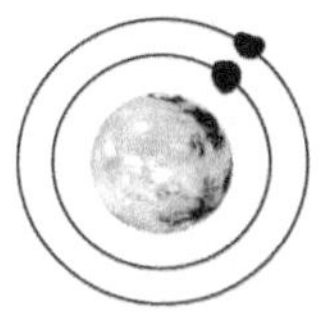

CHAPTER 11

had been expecting when she'd been asked to meet the commanding admiral of the local navy and one of the local heads of state. It was a sprawling concrete block on the outskirts of the setting, the name painted on the outside in black letters easily three meters tall.

Their host led her and O'Hannagain through the main dining area, where massive buffet-style tables of vegetables and sauces appeared to naturally guide diners toward a set of grills where chefs in tall white hats—one of them reezh, which made the hat look extremely incongruous—were grilling up the diner's selections for them.

It turned out that the interior had been cleverly designed to make roughly the back quarter of the building nearly invisible from the inside. There was an entire second restaurant hidden inside the Grill, Roslyn realized as they were guided through a drapery-covered set of double doors.

That second restaurant was a series of private dining rooms with subtle but clear security systems—not least a pair of looming matched human-and-reezh guards just inside the double doors to discourage anyone who stepped through by mistake.

Their room was at the end of the top floor, past a set of less-looming bodyguards who could have been pressed from the same mold as O'Hannagain's PSS detail.

"Your security can check the room," a woman, solely marked as the leader of Hsieh's security by a gold pin on her tie, told them. "Then they'll join us back out here."

She grinned. "The Grill will feed us all; don't you worry."

"Ansel," O'Hannagain said calmly. He glanced back at the Marine watching Roslyn's back. "Corporal Sydykova?"

Argyris Sydykova was one of Roslyn's minders. She might not be a starship Captain anymore, but she'd discovered swiftly that Kovalyow had no intentions of letting her wander around unescorted. The fire team was definitely from *Thorn*'s Marine contingent, so she supposed they were probably even still technically assigned to her.

For now, the stocky Marine accompanied Ansel into the dining room. The two of them spent at least two minutes in there while Roslyn tried to appear patient, then emerged.

"It's clear. Unsurprisingly," Ansel declared with a nod to his Chimeran counterpart. "I hope your principal isn't too bothered by our scans."

"She's used to it. The Admiral's Marines did the same thing, even if they left overt security to us after that," the Presidential Detail commander replied. "I think they figured providing the heavy fire support covered their part."

Roslyn Chambers had once been Flag Lieutenant to Mage-Admiral Crown Princess Jane Alexander. If the Marines treated this like hers would have for Alexander, there were at least a sniper, a ground team, an antiaircraft team, and spotters for all of the above in place around the building.

"Shall we, my dear Mage-Captain?" O'Hannagain asked.

"Let's."

The dining room was private and highly secured, but it was still built to the same almost-hyperbolic level of utilitarianism as the rest of the Khan's Grill. The table was a solid slab of wood on concrete supports, all of it seemingly solid, though the chairs were comfortable enough as Roslyn took her seat.

"This place is a bit of a surprise," she admitted to her hosts.

Admiral Wang sat across from her, his grin somewhat forced but anchored on real humor. Hsieh Ai Ling was to his left, with his Flag Captain, Natalia Falkenrath, to his right.

Falkenrath was as broad and tall as Wang himself, but Germanic and blonde to his Mongolian and dark. Hsieh Ai Ling was a study in contrasts to either of them, taller than both but whip-thin and with hair so dark as to be blue.

Like every time Roslyn had seen Hsieh, everything from her makeup—a dusting of pale violet today that brought out those tones in her eyes and hair—to her hair and clothing was impeccable. Roslyn knew she was attractive, even gorgeous to many people's eyes, but Hsieh Ai Ling managed to make her feel plain and dumpy.

It was just the five of them, and Wang's smile was accompanied by a questioning expression.

"Will Captain Morales be joining us?" he asked. The senior RMN Mage-Captain had been on the invitation list, but Roslyn shook her head.

"We were hopeful until an hour or so ago," she said. "But some of the questions around making sure we can support *Righteous Guardian of Liberty* when she arrives turned into, ah, 'spirited discussions' that required the senior Navy officer to have an opinion."

Most likely, even the two civilians in the room could translate that into *People started arguing and Captain Morales had to go be the responsible adult.*

"As always occurs, I'm afraid," Falkenrath agreed. "We appreciate the chance to make sure we're all on the same page in a less-formal setting. All of us are in enough meetings, including with each other!"

Though there weren't many meetings, Roslyn knew, that had both the military and civilian components of both nations involved.

"Should we have involved Minister Ojak, then?" O'Hannagain asked.

"While the Khan's Grill can feed reezh, Ojak ate here once and then refused to do so ever again," Hsieh observed. "I am reliably informed that the reezh version of this cuisine is very much an acquired taste."

"The human version can be too," Wang agreed. "I first came here shortly after I'd arrived, when Minister Hsieh's predecessor had gone so far as to look up both that I was theoretically ethnically Mongolian and that this style of restaurant was sometimes called a Mongolian grill."

Roslyn could guess just how related the food style was to anything actually served in Mongolia on Earth—and that was with her closest approach to the region having been while in orbit.

"Fortunately for Minister Davids, I am rather fond of mixed stir-fry," Wang continued. "So, despite his interesting assumptions, it was fine. It helps that the Khan's Grill is very good."

Roslyn noted there was a small stack of menus and grabbed one.

"Do you have a recommendation for what to get, then?"

All three of the locals had several recommendations. It also turned out that while they couldn't go out and do the Grill's "make your own bowl" standard while in the secured private dining rooms, the waiter was perfectly happy to do so for them.

"Are... you *sure*, ma'am?" the waiter asked as Roslyn finished listing the spices and ingredients she wanted.

She glanced down the list of options again.

"Yeah, that sounds about right," she confirmed. "Is there a problem?"

"No, I've just... well, frankly, I don't think I've ever seen someone put that much pepper in something and expect to be able to taste the number of other spices you're asking for," the young man admitted.

"How many Tau Cetans have you met?" Wang asked. "Because I suspect the good Captain is going to be just fine with that... mix."

"Please, it's just a slightly modified Tau Ceti *f* south continent vindaloo," Roslyn told them. "It'll be fine. So long as the proportions are right."

"We do have some Tau Ceti masala packages for... coffee, I believe?"

"Do you have regular masala chai? Spiced tea?" she asked. "For once, I think it might be too late in the day for coffee for me."

"We do," he confirmed. With her order done, he turned to the others, and Roslyn chuckled as she collected the menus to make his life easier.

"Are you trying to confuse the staff?" O'Hannagain asked as the door swung closed behind the waiter.

"No. This is just the first place I've seen in months that looked like they might actually be *able* to do a prawns and escargot south *f* vindaloo," she told him. "Worst case, it should still be the first actually spicy thing I've had in a few weeks."

"Tau Cetans," Wang said, echoing his earlier comment. "I spent time in the Mage-Captain's system when I was much younger, an exchange program between the LSDF and the TCSDF."

The Legatus and Tau Cetan System Defense Forces had been the two largest Core World militia forces for a long time. The LSDF had become the core of the Republic Interstellar Navy after the Secession, with most of the RIN's senior officer corps being drawn from its ranks.

Technically, the LSDF wasn't the RIN, but the mention of it still made Roslyn suppress a shiver.

"Perhaps I will one day visit your home system, Captain Chambers," Hsieh suggested. "The expanse and complexities of the modern Protectorate are news to us. We knew the rest of humanity existed, of course, but we had no contact with them until Admiral Wang arrived.

"Now we have contact with the Protectorate, and that would be enough of a shock."

"Except you have to uproot everything and move your entire people to our worlds now," O'Hannagain said, his voice gentle. "It is not a pleasant place to be, Minister. We will do all within our power to make it smooth, but to evacuate like this is a nightmare no one would desire."

"Indeed. Of course, that is a journey I am unlikely to take until this is all over," Hsieh replied. "I will not flee the danger until my people are safe. Key members of Parliament and the Dyad governments have been selected to join the fixed list for the first convoy, but Ojak and I will remain until the end."

Roslyn could respect that. She could argue either way, but the fact that the locals were sending a government-in-exile with the first convoy countered many of the points she would make. Someone would be at Mackenzie to speak for the exiled Chimerans.

"Her Majesty wants to make certain your people are taken care of," O'Hannagain promised. "A Hand will meet your selected representatives on Mackenzie, to act as Her Voice and Her Power. Your citizens will be welcomed, Minister; we swear this on the honor of the Mountain and the Mage-Queen."

It was very rare for an RMN officer to swear upon the honor of the Mage-Queen herself. It had been drilled into Roslyn at the Academy—both as a student and then again as an instructor—that for *any* representative of the Protectorate to swear on the Queen's honor bound the Queen as strongly as if Alexander had said the words herself.

Roslyn had pledged the honor of the Mage-Queen to the Chimerans before. O'Hannagain had too, she knew, if potentially only by implication and treaty. But the words still had weight, even in repetition.

Especially since even Roslyn hadn't known a Hand was on their way to Mackenzie. That was new—Kiera didn't have as many of the roving troubleshooters-slash-judges-slash-diplomats-slash-enforcers as her father had kept. Many of her father's were dead, and she'd only picked a handful during her own reign. The Link made them less necessary, overall, but to have a Hand present made the Queen's interest very clear.

"Both I and Ojak thank you, Ambassador. In Mars we have found a stronger and more willing ally than we would have dared hope. Even if it is only through Mars that we face this threat at all," she concluded.

The tone was wry, but the words were pointed.

And true.

"We do not choose the hours before us," Roslyn said quietly. "We only face the times we are given. I doubt Nemesis chose to die above the world of our ancient enemy, but that was the only destination their choices left us all.

"Now we face the enemy we awakened, and we fight to preserve who and what we are."

It had been Roslyn's ship that had destroyed the stolen *Rose*. She'd jumped her sister ship at close range and basically executed the cruiser and its crew with antimatter fire. There'd been no chance to summon the Nemesis ship to surrender. The Kazh's ships had already been boarding her. To preserve as many of humanity's secrets as she could, Kay and his minions had needed to die.

But it was Roslyn Chambers who had killed them.

"We have plans," Wang declared. "You have spent more time with our Evacuation Commission than I have been able to spare. Do you have any concerns, Captain?"

"None," Roslyn replied, almost surprised at her certainty. "Your people are expanding the Commission's personnel as quickly as they can, and the plans they've put together are extraordinary.

"We're still two weeks from the first convoy arriving, and I have confidence that they will be ready for them. Any lessons we learn from that, we'll have ten days to incorporate before the second convoy arrives and picks up even more people."

"It's hard to believe the numbers you're giving us for those convoys," Wang admitted. "Eight million evacuees in the first convoy. Eighteen in the second. Another, what, ten million seats you expect to add before the second flights?"

"Yes, sir," Roslyn confirmed. "A mix of civilian and military shipping. We *may* have the colony ships, who are most of those ten million extra seats, in the second convoy.

"But." She tried not to swallow audibly as she steeled herself for the next part. This was why she'd needed to have this meeting. She lifted her gaze and made sure to meet Wang's eyes directly.

"The second wave is anchored on fifteen Republic planetary invasion ships," she stated calmly. "And before Admiral Wang points it out, I will be clear, Minister: those ships can *only* function with Prometheans aboard.

"We asked the survivors of the RIN under our care to volunteer, and sixty-two of them agreed to put themselves back in starships to help save your people."

It was Falkenrath who responded most clearly, a shocked exhalation of breath as the ex-Republic Commodore leaned back in her chair.

"Holy shit," she said. "I... don't know if I could, in their place."

Wang sighed.

"We all know this party has an invisible guest," he pointed out. "Except perhaps the Ambassador?"

O'Hannagain glanced at Roslyn questioningly.

"The senior Promethean aboard *Chimera* runs systems overwatch wherever the Admiral goes," she told him. "So, Cam is present, even if she wouldn't normally say anything. I suspect from the Admiral's comment that she *does* have something to say?"

Wang tapped a few commands on his wrist-comp and a new voice emerged.

Cam—born Cameron Boyce, a young boy on the UnArcana World of Mercedes, then murdered and turned into a brain-in-a-jar to power a Republic warship after being Tested as a Mage at age eleven—used a computer-generated voice of a young woman of roughly her chronological age of twenty.

"Thank you, everyone," she said. "I will be somewhat less crude than the Commodore, but I am equally stunned. I, unlike the rest of you, *know* what is in my cousins' minds. I chose to *remain* aboard a warship. I am not certain I would choose to return to a Prometheus Interface, once removed from it."

"The Mage-Queen asked personally. She was prepared to accept *no* for an answer, but with the lives of innocents at stake, they have stepped up," Roslyn said. "As you say, Cam, it is difficult for any of us to truly comprehend the sacrifice they have agreed to.

"The Protectorate intends to reward their actions as fully as we can. But the numbers leave us a small problem."

"I don't understand," Hsieh admitted.

"I do," Cam told the politician. "The evacuation convoys are designed and scheduled around having three Mages capable of three jumps per standard day. Nine light-years per day pseudospeed. The timing for Prometheans is different, but four Prometheans can match that number of jumps.

"With sixty-*two* Prometheans, there is an extra ship that is falling behind the others. Am I correct, Mage-Captain?"

"You are, Cam," Roslyn confirmed. "All sixteen ships have left Sol. The first fifteen will arrive in Exeter in under two weeks and leave around the same time the first evac convoy reaches here."

And with the other ships gathered, would be transporting the best part of twenty million people, even if the colony ships didn't make it. She hadn't seen any solid information on when those would enter the theater beyond *The company is working on it.*

"But that last ship is going to be slow, and we have already asked as much as we can from our Prometheans. Your Navy Prometheans are needed where they are, which gives me a second reason to face a question we have all studiously avoided to date."

Wang shrugged slightly and squared his shoulders, facing her impassively. "Which is, Mage-Captain?"

"Did you give your Prometheans a third choice between death and volunteering?" she asked. "From what I know of you, it would seem out of character if you didn't, but no one has mentioned civilian Prometheans on Garuda to me."

The big Admiral was silent for several seconds. His next words were addressed to the empty air, not to any of the people in the room with him.

"Cam? It's not my call. I swore an oath."

"It's not my call, either," the Promethean replied. "I'm asking the others."

Wang met Roslyn's eyes and shrugged slightly. Hsieh, for her part, looked completely confused.

"Four to one. Without Lisa and Trevor, it'll have to do," Cam finally said.

Lisa and Trevor were the Prometheans aboard *Barracuda*, still absent on their mission to the Primes.

"Why do you want to know, Captain?" Cam continued.

"Regardless of where they are now, every Promethean that we know of was created by the Republic of Faith and Reason," Roslyn murmured. "Created by killing Mages that were often identified by the Royal Testers of the Protectorate. Mages *we* failed to protect. Mages we unknowingly handed over to monsters.

"Guilt be *damned*," she growled. "We owe every Promethean every scrap of help, aid, protection… anything and everything we can do. If there are civilian Prometheans on Garuda, they should be on the first evacuation ships, right next to the families of the CSN's personnel.

"Yes, we need to ask if any of them will volunteer to operate the ships of the evacuation fleet," she admitted. "Two more volunteers could see another million people evacuated every trip after the first."

There was no way they could get any volunteer Prometheans from Chimera to a rendezvous with the *Saladin*s in time for the first evac run. But they could still add another of the big ships to the second wave.

If they got it, but that wasn't part of the calculus that mattered for this discussion.

"Tell her, Admiral," Cam said.

Wang nodded, then glanced at Hsieh.

"We lied," he said bluntly. "To everyone. We told the Chimerans nine Prometheans chose life and to serve on our ships. My senior officers and engineers know the truth, of course, but even in the human component of the CSN, we have generally omitted any mention of the third option we gave our Prometheans.

"The one Mage-Captain Chambers correctly assessed that we did offer."

"I don't understand," Hsieh told him. "We would have gladly protected and helped those children."

"I know that now, Ai Ling," the Admiral admitted. "But as I already said, I swore an oath. That I would guard the children my service had damned with my life, my soul, my sacred honor. Even my oaths to Chimera and the Dual Republics are lesser than the oaths I swore to *them*.

"Do you understand that?"

Roslyn stepped on O'Hannagain's foot as she saw him start to say something. There would be time for them to ask questions and argue with Wang, but *this* moment, *this* exchange, was between two dear friends— one of whom was just discovering that the other had concealed fundamental secrets for the entire time they'd known each other.

Everyone was silent for at least ten seconds, then Hsieh Ai Ling reached over and squeezed Wang's hand. Despite her own height, her hand was slim and delicate against the Admiral's massive fist.

"I do, Emerson. I just wish you and your people had accepted they could trust us to help," she whispered.

"By the time we were certain of you, we'd already set our plans in stone," Wang admitted. He looked over at Roslyn. "Nine ships held fifty-four 'Prometheus Drive Units,'" he continued, the bitterness in the technical phrasing harsh.

"Nine volunteered to continue in service. Thirty-two chose mercy, euthanasia via an overdose of painkillers and disconnection of the life-support apparatus. Thirteen wanted life but could not endure to remain in the Prometheus Interfaces of a warship.

"We set up a covert facility in orbit around the ninth moon of Leviathan." That was the outer gas giant of the Chimera System, a planet that few even visited given the easier course toward Ifrit and the far-greater ease of extracting hydrogen in a place where solar power was easily generated in vast quantities.

"It's assembled from cargo containers and a few prefab pieces the Chimerans provided that are still listed as spare parts on the CSN's inventories," he concluded. "A few long-duration atomic batteries, a few data relays for a lightspeed network update from Garuda to get entertainment files, life support for a caretaker crew to keep the systems running and to, well, talk to them."

"Counselors, I'm assuming," Roslyn guessed.

"Recruiting them was more difficult than it could have been, but yes," he confirmed. "We have an eleven-person psychiatric treatment team we recruited from Garuda on site. They do what they can, but the situation is... difficult."

"Would your Prometheans and psychiatric staff be comfortable transferring to the Phobos facility?" Roslyn asked. "While we wouldn't be able to get them there quickly, everything is in place there to provide all of that."

"That is a question for them," Wang said firmly. "But... you are correct that we can't leave them in Chimera. We can move them to Garudan orbit once the evacuation convoy arrives."

Which would leave them concealed and reasonably safe if something went wrong before then. Roslyn could respect that.

"Would you be prepared to ask them to volunteer to back up our Prometheans aboard the *Saladin* transport *Shirkuh*?"

"Ahem." Cam didn't have a throat to clear, which meant that the sound she made wasn't quite right. Her intent was clear, though, and Roslyn wished that the Promethean had some kind of icon to look at to acknowledge her.

"What did you do?" Wang, clearly more used to his adoptive cyborg children's foibles, asked.

"We have not set up a Link relay to the Sanctuary," Cam pointed out. "But I did summarize all of Mage-Captain Chambers' points and arguments and send them over... about thirty seconds ago.

"As you say, Admiral, this is their choice."

"So it is," Roslyn agreed. "I hope you were clear, Cam, that we are asking for volunteers. They will all be evacuated on the first transports either way."

"Of course," Cam confirmed. "I would not have suggested that Admiral Wang reveal the Sanctuary's existence if I did not trust you, Mage-Captain. I do not know if my cousins will volunteer, but we trust you enough to ask."

Given how badly the Prometheans had been betrayed and failed by basically *everyone* in their lives before Emerson Wang, that single phrase meant more to Roslyn than she could ever explain.

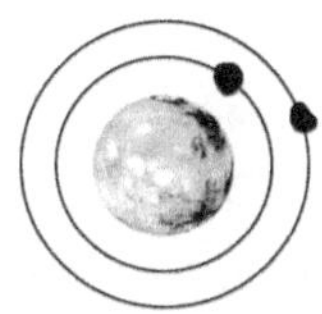

CHAPTER 12

"WHILE I WON'T PRETEND I WOULDN'T LIKE a few more and bigger ships, it's damn good to see you, Admiral Adamant," Mage-Captain Morales said in the Link conference.

Righteous Guardian of Liberty, *Lord of Righteousness* and *Lady of Freedom* had been in Chimera for roughly an hour, and the three Martian warships were still far enough out to require the FTL communicator for the senior officers to meet.

Mage–Vice Admiral Janet Adamant smiled calmly and nodded to the woman she was relieving.

"There may or may not be time for any formal kind of ceremony, Mage-Captain," she noted. "I assume command of Chimera Station. You are relieved."

"I stand relieved," Morales confirmed. "Trying to hold this system with two cruisers is something I'm very glad not to need to try."

Roslyn and Mage-Captain Blom shared the chuckle. With Mage-Commander Matthias Beck—formerly Roslyn's executive officer on *Thorn* and now the man running the RMN shore establishment on and above Garuda—they made up the half of the conference call already at the Chimeran planet.

"Our resources still aren't what we would like," Janet Adamant warned grimly. "Your *Salamander*s are, ton-for-ton, heavier sluggers than my *Honorifics*. The ships have been refitted, but my companions are all pre-War.

"Add in that the Chimeran Space Navy has been hammered, and we're well short of what the CSN and Mage-Commodore Banderas had to hold this system with. We'll do what we have to do, but... you'll understand, Mage-Captain Chambers why I'm a touch concerned about your request to dispatch one of our destroyers as a courier."

"We don't *have* any couriers," Roslyn replied, a bit thrown by Adamant's smooth change of subject. She hadn't even realized that the request for a ship to transport the Chimeran Promethean volunteers had made it that far up the chain yet. "But we do have six local civilian Prometheans who have volunteered to help fly evacuation ships if we evac the other seven with the rest of the civilians."

"I don't think anyone is going to blink at evacuating the Prometheans on the first flight," Adamant agreed. "And that would get two more of the big transports in the evac convoys eventually, yes. But we have exactly eleven warships of our own here."

"And we need the *Cataphract*s for missile defense," Roslyn said. She wasn't arguing her own point, she knew, but the relative priorities had to be very clear.

"Everything we are doing here, Admiral, is to cover for and protect the evacuation of the civilians," she continued. "For one of the *Saladin*s, we'll need to take four of our volunteers all the way back to Sol. But *Shirkuh* is already on her way, just falling farther and farther behind her sisters every day.

"The faster we can get volunteers to her, the faster she can be here and the more lives will be saved. It is..." Roslyn considered her words, then shrugged. "It's not my task to make the decision of whether those lives are worth forty-eight half-megawatt RFLAM turrets, sir. But my math says that if we get the new volunteers moving inside the next few days, *Shirkuh* will be able to join Evac Convoy One when they return to Chimera for their second pickup in about forty days.

"If we wait until *Shirkuh* gets here or have her meet the Prometheans at Mackenzie, she'll end up joining Evac Convoy Two for their second arrival—in fifty days. An extra ten days of cycling a million people every thirty days..."

"That math does start sounding very clear, doesn't it?" Adamant's Chief of Staff, Commodore Kai Nedbálek, noted. Nedbálek was a short man with pale skin and mousy brown hair. His gaze was piercing as he studied Roslyn, though she met his eyes calmly.

"Those ten days equate to a third of a million people evacuated that might not be safe otherwise," he continued. "Like the Mage-Captain, it's not my place to make that call, but it *is* my job to make recommendations, sir. If we had a courier ship, we'd send them. As it is, well."

"We replaced the courier ships with the Links because we need their Jump Mages for warships if we're going to fight this damn war," Adamant concluded. "Who's the most badly damaged of the *Cataphracts*, Mage-Captain Morales?"

"*Nikephoros*," the senior Captain replied instantly. "Mage-Commander Balik got lucky in some ways. Her ship took an ugly hit early in the fight, but she managed to get through the rest of the battle almost untouched.

"Unfortunately, our resources have been almost entirely dedicated to getting *Firebelly* back online," Morales continued, nodding to Blom. "*Nikephoros*'s worst holes have been patched and she has most of her defensive suite, but her offensive weapons are in rough shape."

Which probably explained why Mage-Commander Alexandrea Balik's ship *hadn't* taken more fire as the Battle of Chimera continued.

"But the Mage-Commander has a full Mage contingent and no holes in the hull, correct?" Adamant asked.

"Two of her Mages died in the battle, sir," Morales admitted.

"All of *Thorn*'s survived, but my ship didn't," Roslyn said quietly. "And... frankly, Mage-Ensigns Jain, Magro and Sigourney are very junior. Sigourney was jumped out of her last year in the Academy to fill out *Thorn*'s Mage complement.

"I would be *delighted* if those three young officers—and, if possible, some of the other very young Ensigns we filled out *Thorn*'s crew with—were sent somewhere else."

"Then that will work very well, won't it?" Adamant said firmly. "Commander Beck, I imagine those officers are in the shore establishment you've set up?"

"Yes, sir," Beck confirmed.

"Let's get the pieces moving," Adamant ordered. "Evac Convoy One left Exeter four days ago. They'll be here in seven days. Everything I have seen suggests that the Chimerans will be ready to load those ships when they get here.

"I know we can't fit many people on a destroyer, especially not if we're putting six Prometheans on her, but if there are any people the locals want to be *very* sure get out, let's ask," she continued. "No ship leaves Chimera, my friends, without evacuees on board.

"God alone knows if we'll be able to save everyone—but until He answers, we will save every single person we can."

Roslyn's office in the Embassy was nicer than any space she'd ever had assigned to her before. Most of her better spaces had been on warships, after all, with limited space and amenities.

In the small office building the locals had given to the Protectorate, she got one of the three corner offices on the top floor—the fourth corner was a meeting room, and the third office was set up to be used as one if needed.

That gave her a space only slightly smaller than the one O'Hannagain was using for his own workspace, with windowed walls looking out at the mound of the Last Ship and the Legislature Building.

Sunlight was streaming into the space the morning after the meeting with Adamant, making it difficult for her to use the screen on her console, and she was debating between relocating to the seating area with more shade versus closing the blinds when someone knocked crisply on her door.

"Baars?" she asked. Her steward wouldn't usually knock, though no one was likely to show up at her door without making it through both Baars and Kovalyow. She wasn't expecting to be interrupted.

"Just me, Skipper," a familiar voice said through the door and her tension relaxed. Matthias Beck was one of the few people her minders *would* let up to her office without checking in—and they would know that she and her former XO hadn't managed to see each other in person since she'd taken the attaché job.

"Come in, Beck," she told him.

The graying officer opened the door with crisp precision, stepping inside and bracing to attention.

"Good morning, sir!" he greeted her like a cadet she'd called on the carpet at the Academy, and she shook her head at him.

"Get in and sit down," she ordered, gesturing toward the set of chairs. "I'm guessing Baars is a minute behind you with drinks?"

"She said something of the sort," Beck agreed. He looked around the spacious office as he followed her instructions, and whistled softly. "I see that I need to angle for more diplomatic jobs. Nice office."

"If we had a true full embassy, I'd be relegated somewhere downstairs," she warned. "But since even with the dozen crew I roped in to back up my attaché role and the security, we've got less than forty people in a building with enough space for five times that."

"Some benefits for organizing the end of the world, I suppose," he said quietly.

That dark thought was interrupted by Tajana Baars, arriving with coffees as expected. Roslyn's was spiced, Beck's was black. The steward had known the XO's drink choice by heart long before they'd had to give up their ship.

"You're good, sirs?" Baars asked as they took the drinks. "I can round up snacks if you need."

"Matthias?" Roslyn asked. "I've eaten and need to get through enough datawork that eating more is unwise, but we can grab something for you."

"I'm fine, thank you, Tajana," he said.

"What did you need?" Roslyn asked as the steward slipped out. "As I imagine one or both of my minders told you, I have a datawork slot this morning that can be interrupted."

"Checking in, mostly," he admitted. "Our little shore establishment is finally mostly on top of our affairs. While you're definitely not part of what you and Morales dumped on me, you are planetside and I'm supposed to back you up."

Having someone of equal rank to the destroyer COs to corral the logistics ships and work with the locals—as well as manage the hundreds of *Thorn's* crew that were on Garuda and in desperate need of something productive to do—had been a godsend, from what Roslyn could tell.

"My biggest job is the Evacuation Commission, and the locals are in prep mode there," she told him. "Six days until we have Evac Convoy One here, and the Commission has the full list of ships and seats. You got the list of supplies EC-One needs to make the last few changes for passengers?"

"We did. The CSN and my people are working on it," he confirmed. "I expect everything to be in orbit by the time they get here. Did you get the list of who is leaving on *Nikephoros* from the locals?"

The destroyer had a surviving crew of three hundred and eight, and her engineer insisted they could carry another three hundred. Space, from what Roslyn remembered of her own time aboard destroyers, would run out before the life support did.

One hundred of those extra seats were RMN personnel. The other two hundred had been offered to the locals.

"I'm supposed to have it within the hour," Roslyn said. "Because the main convoys have so much space, they never really prioritized among the Alpha List. They decided to use the lottery system they've set up for everybody *else*."

She chuckled.

"After Razhkah point-blank refused to leave before her archives did, anyway. I could have told them how that was going to go."

"So could anyone who has spent five minutes around her," Beck agreed. "I did want to thank you, though."

"Thank *me*, Matthias?"

"We got Jain, Sigourney and Magro on their way out of the system," he reminded her. "With the argument that Jump Mages on *Nikephoros* were more useful than Jump Mages on Garuda—and, sadly, the fact that Captain Balik's tactical officer was killed in the fighting—I even got Mage-Lieutenant Thomas aboard.

"Despite some discussions, every RMN officer or crew joining *Nikephoros* is from *Thorn*," he concluded. "I tried to avoid that, but the truth is that there were few survivors from the ships we lost."

She nodded grimly. Space battles tended to leave few wounded or dead behind. Antimatter explosions and multigigawatt energy beams vaporized what they touched, including humans.

There was a silence between the two of them, the shared thoughts of two people who'd worked together in a difficult job and watched those around them pay the price.

Roslyn broke the silence with a sigh and raised her coffee cup in a toast.

"To *Thorn*," she said. "She kept us safe until it was time to pass us into the care of others. What ship can do more?"

Not every member of *Thorn*'s crew had survived—but most had. For a ship that was permanently crippled, that was all she could ask. Her last command, the destroyer *Voice of the Forgotten*, had taken a similar number of casualties when she'd been crippled at Exeter—but *Voice*'s smaller crew meant that those deaths had been a larger portion of the people under Roslyn's command.

"To *Thorn*," Beck agreed. "She's not dead yet, you know."

Roslyn took a mouthful of coffee, swallowing and repressing a gasp as she realized it was too hot. Exhaling sharply, she gave her former XO a level look.

"We both know those scuttling charges are getting blown," she stated. "Or we wouldn't have just signed the papers to send four of *Thorn*'s six Jump Mages back to the Protectorate."

"Fair enough," he conceded. "Hell of a thing, Skipper."

"I'm not your Captain anymore, Matthias," she said. The RMN culture was fascinating in some ways, she realized. As the Captain of the ship, her using his first name was considered an equal level of informality to him calling her *Skipper*.

"Until we have new ships and new Captains, you're the Skipper for everyone from *Thorn*, Roslyn," Beck told her, his tone very serious. "You *earned* that. We walked into and out of hell at your side. We won't forget that."

She was saved from having to reply to that heavy statement by a message alert on her wrist-comp. Only a few things would actually notify her audibly while she had a quiet work session scheduled, and she checked it to avoid addressing Beck's words.

"We have the list from the Evacuation Commission for *Nikephoros*," she told him. "Two hundred names. The Commission is testing their call-up infrastructure on them and are requesting that *Nikephoros*—or the shore establishment, I suppose," she noted with a small smile, "set up four shuttle flights for specific locations this evening local time. Twenty-seven hundred Twin Sphinxes time, so..."

She started trying to do the conversion in her head, but Beck beat her to it.

"Nineteen twenty OMT," he told her, giving the time in the clock of faraway Olympus Mons.

As part of the terraforming of the new capital planet, the planetary rotation had been accelerated to match Earth's. Somewhat terrifyingly, most people counted that as one of the *smaller* pieces of what the first Mage-King had done to the planet he'd claimed as his personal dominion.

"Twelve hours to get two hundred people sorted out with all of their lifelong belongings and ready to board shuttles," Roslyn concluded. "I'm glad that part of it isn't my job."

"I'll talk to Mage-Commander Balik, get the shuttles sorted out," Beck promised. "We'll—"

Whatever he'd been about to say further was interrupted by a red alert blazing up on both of their wrist-comps. If they'd had a ship to report to, it would have been a recall.

As it was, it was simply a notification that the long-range sensors had detected multiple unscheduled contacts.

The Kazh had returned.

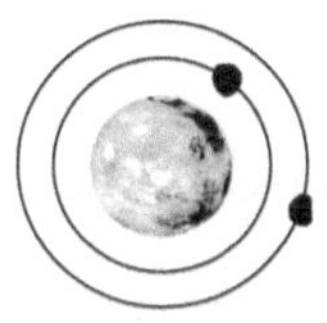

CHAPTER 13

CONNOR WAS UNDER NO ILLUSIONS of how much he could influence the course of a space battle. He was *also* painfully aware that the next round of fighting in the Chimera System would establish not only how long he had to evacuate people from this planet but also his own personal safety.

He'd asked to be added to the same warning list as all of the senior naval officers. The flashing crimson alert on his wrist-comp interrupted a call with two members of the Western Republic's Economics Department leadership—a call that was giving him fascinating information on the reezh perspective on money and finance.

"I apologize, Directors," he told the two reezh. "It appears the Kazh have returned. I suspect all of us have more important things to do in that situation than discuss arrangements for crop scheduling over the next few months."

The main concern of the reezh bureaucrats had been how to balance food production against the rapid drawing-down of the working population scheduled for the immediate future. No one had even considered changing the evacuation itself at all, but there were a lot of different moving pieces to the food-supply chain of an advanced world.

Connor was talking to the reezh side of the equation to head off any problems before they became problems. It was his old job of acting as a neutral arbiter, with extra weight from the entire situation.

"We are grateful for your understanding," the senior Director, a reezh woman named Izhal, told him with a bow of her armored frill. "Fare well."

The channel cut out and Connor pursed his lips as he tried to make sense of the alert. All he could really make out was the military equivalent of *Danger, Connor O'Hannagain, Danger,* but he was reasonably sure there was more information in the original message, let alone in the networks he had access to.

As if in answer to his confusion, his door slid open and Roslyn Chambers walked in. Somehow, the presence of an active threat changed the entire manner of his new attaché. The danger was clear in her eyes, but her spine was straighter, her eyes were sharper, and there was something in the air around her.

Part of that something was defensive shields, he realized as she walked over to his desk. The Mage had conjured a bubble of force and solidified air that moved with her, probably able to stop bullets or minor things like anti-armor rockets.

"Mage-Captain," he greeted her. "I'm glad to see you. Does this fall into the category of making sure the Ambassador understands the military situation?"

"I can't see anything else that would do so more," she told him. "Plus, I don't *have* a battle station right now. And you have slightly better holographic projectors here than in my office, per the system diagrams."

"Please, make free with them," Connor said with a wave at the desk with its built-in console.

Chambers could have done a lot with her wrist-comp, but this appeared to be a step beyond what the portable system's input tools could manage. The only command from her wrist-comp brought up the console's own controls, a holographic keyboard and haptic pointer-control field projected onto her side of the desk.

A few seconds later, the holoprojector in the room whirred to life and a scale model of the entire Chimera System filled the room. Hazily, as the bright light streaming through the windows washed out the three-dimensional images quite badly.

The blinds closed and the model zoomed in on the regions of concern. New icons populated the air in the middle of Connor's office, and he waited calmly as Chambers set up her initial point.

"What do we have, Mage-Captain?" he finally asked as the image seemed to settle onto a scale that showed Garuda, with a series of green icons in orbit, and a chunk of space with the planet on the side closest to them—and a collection of red icons on the far side.

"My worst-case scenario on timing and... possibly my best-case scenario on numbers," she replied. "Can you read the icons?"

"I can read that there's about fifteen of the enemy," he admitted, studying the array of cylindrical images. He thought they were to scale with each other, marking three different sizes of Kazh ships, but they definitely weren't to scale with the overall size of the display or Garuda itself.

"Sixteen," she corrected. An icon flashed, making it clear it had been hiding behind one of the others from his angle. "One big bastard in the middle, the fifty-million-tonner we flagged as Type Twos. Three Type Threes. Five Type Fours and seven Type Fives."

"Battleships, cruisers, frigates, destroyers? Or am I misremembering?"

"Roughly their equivalents in our order of battle, yeah," she confirmed. "Though the five-megatonners in the Protectorate are all militia ships, and their Type Threes are bigger than our cruisers."

"They have a battleship to our battleship but fewer cruisers. Is this... handleable, Mage-Captain?" Connor asked. He hated asking that question. He felt like he sounded scared. He *was* scared, true, but not as much as he felt the question made him sound.

"The odds were a lot worse against us last time," she murmured. "They're badly outmassed, but they still have more missile launchers than we do."

Numbers totaled up in a section of the display, a piece she'd obviously added for his understanding. They had estimates of how many launchers the given sizes of Kazh warships possessed, and the numbers flowed out in black-and-white math.

Two thousand two hundred launchers for the enemy. With missiles that were longer-ranged than anything in the Martian or Chimeran arsenal.

Fifteen hundred and thirty for the defenders. Plus another fifteen hundred for a few salvos if *Chimera* got her gunships into space. The first salvos would be heavily in the defenders' favor.

"With the gunships, the odds are different, though, right?" he asked.

"Maybe. It depends on what Adamant and Wang are thinking... There they go."

Connor followed her gesture and studied the movement of the green icons in orbit. He couldn't read the new vector data added to each of the ship icons, but he could tell they were moving to meet the enemy.

"What are they doing?" he asked.

"The orbital defenses are basically useless without investment no one is planning to put in," she told him. "So, Wang is taking the fleet out to meet the Kazh again. We've got a lot of unrepaired damage, but as you say, the gunships double our initial punch.

"The problem is that the Kazh will get their punch in *first*." She shook her head. "And we're still limited by the CSN's lack of gravity runes. The Kazh are coming in at two-point-eight-five gees; we're heading out at three.

"The RMN ships could out-accelerate them, but right now, we need Wang's people."

"Or we'd leave *Chimera* behind, at least," Connor guessed. "I thought carriers weren't supposed to get into the thick of things."

"They aren't. But they're the biggest ships the RIN built, so they have a lot of missile launchers. We can't afford to leave her behind."

Connor didn't know Chambers well yet, but he could tell that it was almost physically painful for her to be down there on the surface, explaining things to him and utterly unable to influence the clash taking place above them.

"How long?" he asked.

"They emerged close. One-point-five light-minutes. Closer than I would have risked without recent data, so I suspect they *have* data from the last fleet," she noted. "Combined with the timing, we have to assume they have an FTL communication ability. These guys left within days of the last Battle of Chimera."

The last Battle of Chimera. That sent a chill down Connor's spine. They were going to be numbering battles in this star system now. Assuming anyone lived long enough.

"How long?" he repeated.

"Seventeen hours for the Kazh to reach Garudan orbit. A bit under six before they reach their missile range of our defenders, assuming no one changes acceleration between now and then. Missile ranges then stack up pretty quickly—Morales's *Salamanders* have Samurai birds that can match the enemy in range."

"Will they close the whole way? What happens if they open fire on the planet?" he asked. Everything Chambers was telling him sounded like the defenders had the edge and would stop them, but even a single ship could cause catastrophic damage if they opened fire on Garuda itself.

"That's the real question, isn't it," she said, and her tone sent another shiver down her spine. "They won't be in active range of the planet until well after the fleets intersect, but planets don't dodge very well. If they decide to repeat the Burning here, well."

Her silence said everything Connor needed to know.

They sat in Connor's office in silence, watching the icons crawl across the air in the room. After about ten minutes, his wrist-comp pinged softly with an incoming call from the Dyad.

Gesturing for Chambers to stay out of the way, he accepted the call. Holographic images of Ojak and Hsieh appeared on top of his desk, the reezh and human looking equally tired.

"Ministers," he greeted them. "I am aware of the situation. As I understand, our combined fleet is advancing to engage the intruders. The odds, unlike last time, are in our favor."

"They appear to be," Ojak agreed, the reezh's gravel-filled tones even lower-pitched than usual. "But I will not put deception beyond our enemy."

"Thought deception does usually require some form of communication," Hsieh pointed out. "Which is what we wanted to talk to you about, Ambassador."

"I am here to assist if there is any way Mars can," Connor said. "Of course, our fleet is already arrayed to defend your world, so..."

"We attempted to communicate with the strangers, much as before," Ojak said flatly. "Only silence has answered us. You may have a different response."

"Or the same," Hsieh said with a sigh. "But it seems worth the try for a representative of the Protectorate to challenge the Kazh. It may raise some concerns they don't have right now."

Connor reflected on that. It was possible. There were ways he could phrase such a challenge to make it even more clear that the Kazh were crossing dangerous lines. Even so...

"I don't even speak their language, Ministers. How much do we want to rely on automatic translation?" he asked. He wouldn't want to use a live interpreter. It needed to be clearly his message.

"It is unlikely to make things worse," Hsieh pointed out. "I will forward you the most up-to-date program we have, Ambassador. I am not certain if they will listen to you more than us, but the chance remains, does it not?"

"It does," he agreed. "Send me the program, Ministers. I will decide on my approach and send my message."

Connor was surprised to see Roslyn shifting her seat around in front of her desk and linking her wrist-comp into his console systems as the call ended.

"Mage-Captain?" he asked.

"Compose your message," she instructed. "I just pulled the translation program and am setting it up. We could grab someone else, but I'm already here, aren't I?"

He chuckled and gestured for her to go ahead. He would have some questions about how she'd sliced the attachments out of his email without access to his messages later, but for now, it was useful.

She was running systems security for his building, he supposed. Shaking that thought aside with a twitch of his head he hoped even Chambers wouldn't notice, he focused on the situation in front of him.

It was quite clear that the Kazh had decided they knew who the Chimerans were and intended to bring their old colony back under control. While the expanded RMN fleet there might give them pause, they wouldn't *know* the human ships weren't native to Chimera.

They might, thanks to *Rose* and Nemesis, know more than he liked. But he suspected they didn't know they were pissing off a nation with more *everything* than them.

He smiled grimly and looked up at Chambers.

"Ready to translate, Roslyn?"

"Got it all set up. Do we want to send video or just audio?"

"Video." He looked behind him and grimaced. Nothing about the space screamed *the Protectorate of Mars* to him. "Wait, do we have... Um."

He could recode the screen behind him to show something, but it wouldn't really serve. For a moment, he completely blanked on what he needed.

"Flags?" the Mage-Captain suggested. "I think so; let me ping Kovalyow. I'm guessing we want this to look as imperiously Martian as we can manage?"

"Exactly, Roslyn," he agreed. He grimaced. He didn't blank like that very often, but he was, he supposed, stretching well beyond his experience in arbitrating interstellar business deals.

"We've got the Protectorate, the Navy, and the Kingdom flags on their way," his naval attaché said after a moment of prodding at her wrist-comp. "That's a wallscreen behind you, right?"

"Yes. I'm going to set it to plain gray, I think," he said, opening up the software on his own wrist-comp. The wall shifted to a single flat color. The blinds tinted slightly, changing the amount of light coming through as he concealed the tactical hologram, and he activated just enough artificial lights to focus on him.

Roslyn waited until he was done and then made a few adjustments of her own, leaving them flagged separately so he could reverse them. They were small changes, but he nodded as he saw her point—the lights he'd set up had highlighted him, but they'd also washed out his coloring.

A knock on the door announced the arrival of the three flags. Kovalyow led in two strapping young Marines carrying flagpoles with the banners and set herself to arranging them behind the desk.

The three flags were all clearly interrelated, evolutions of each other. The Kingdom of Mars flag was the mountain of Olympus Mons with the royal crown superimposed on it on a green field. The *Protectorate* flag was the same mountain with the crown moved above it and the whole symbol then laid onto a red planet, on a black background. The Royal Martian Navy then took the Protectorate flag and put a stylized rocket ship in the center.

Kovalyow and the Marines set the banners up in a clear progression, starting at the Kingdom on the left and putting the Protectorate flag directly behind Connor himself as Chambers set up the cameras.

"I think we're good. Thank you," he told the NCO and her minions. "Chambers?"

"You're live when you're ready."

CHAPTER 14

ROSLYN WAS FEELING UTTERLY OUT OF PLACE. At the
very moment that she was having her people fuss with flags, thousands
of RMN spacers were charging into battle above her head. The weight of
metal was in the defenders' favor, but the technological edge was toward
the enemy—and they'd only carried the day the last time by pure luck.

Whatever happened in space, there was nothing she could do to impact
it. Her job was to make sure that the Martian Ambassador knew what was
going on and had the tools to do his job. It just... wasn't what she was used to.

Fortunately, she seemed to be doing decently at that new job, and she
had the translator program up and running as she checked all the recording gear and gave the nod to O'Hannagain.

There was no stage fright or hesitation on the big redhead's part. He
returned her nod, leveled his gaze on the main camera pickup like a rotating turret, and spoke in a level tone that she'd heard others use before.

In fact, she suspected *she'd* used it before. He was using the diplomatic equivalent of a Captain's command voice. She wondered if it would
work as well on hostile aliens as it did on ill-behaved cadets.

"Ships and forces of the Reezh Kazh," O'Hannagain began. "You are
making a great mistake. I am Ambassador Connor O'Hannagain of the
Protectorate of the Kingdom of Mars, and it is my solemn duty to inform
you that this star system is under our protection.

"If you continue your approach without communication, the brave
spacers of our Royal Navy will be forced to drive you from this system with

fire and steel. You will be committing a knowing act of war against the Protectorate, and my Mage-Queen's stance is simple:

"If you attack this star system, the Protectorate will destroy you. Withdraw. We offer a second chance only because we believe your last attack was a mistake.

"Mars does not offer third chances."

A small gesture, invisible from the camera, told Roslyn to cut the recording.

"Do you want to review it?" she asked.

"Gods, no," he said with a surprising chuckle. "I have very little self-consciousness, Roslyn, but even *I* will start second-guessing myself if I rewatch my ultimatum! Translate it, send and be damned."

"You don't think it will make a difference?" Roslyn figured the odds were low, but she agreed with the Dyad Ministers that it was worth trying.

"These aren't people who came to talk," O'Hannagain said heavily. "Nothing I have seen in the histories the reezh have shown us make me think the Kazh has one ounce of give in them. I'd be delighted to be wrong, but..."

He trailed off and tapped a command to restore the holographic display. The two fleets had grown closer, but the change was barely perceptible on this scale.

"It's worth trying," Roslyn told him. "You're the only one who can send that message, after all."

"Adamant could," he countered. "But for us, at least, a civilian speaker carries slightly different weight." He looked at the array of red icons.

"Not least, with humans, people *expect* threats from the military officer," he noted. "When the civilians deliver harsh ultimatums, a lot of people begin to realize you are actually serious."

There was a long minute of silence.

"Almost six hours until anything happens," he murmured. "What do you naval people *do*?"

"Depending on the situation, eat, maybe even sleep," Roslyn said. "Most Captains will be on the bridge for a lot of the closing time, just in case. We make sure everyone is fed and prepped for vacuum, but it's often a long wait, even after everyone has committed to their vectors."

"Have they? Committed, that is?" O'Hannagain asked.

She studied the icons.

"I don't know Wang and Adamant's plans in detail," she noted. "I do know they're going to stay between the Kazh and the planet, so they'll start decelerating shortly before entering missile range. So, technically, they *haven't* fully committed to their final vector—but that's an expected change.

"I think the Kazh are committed. If they are heading for orbit, their turnover won't be until just before everyone enters beam range," she explained. "Whether they head straight in or for a zero-zero, the missile clash will start before it matters."

The two fleets were going to be in missile range for a very long time. It would take over two hours after they could fire missiles for them to reach the range of the lasers and particle beams involved.

"What if they just... leave?" O'Hannagain asked.

"It's possible," she admitted after a moment's thought. "This does appear to be a scouting force. Even with the edge we know they've got on a ship-by-ship basis, they're outgunned."

"And from what I saw last time, they are badly outmatched."

A flush of pride filled Roslyn at that statement. It was true, she knew, but it still meant a lot to hear it from the diplomat, a career group historically known for dismissing the military.

"I don't pretend to understand how that works," he continued wryly. "But every piece of hard analysis I was given said we were going to get wiped out, but you won. This time, the hard analysis is in your favor. So, we're safe, right?"

It was funny. The Ambassador was very smart and very good at his job—and part of his job was making the people around him believe he was infallible.

So much so that it had taken the explicit question for Roslyn to realize he was looking for reassurance.

"Basically, Connor, from the way they fought last time, the Kazh haven't seen a real war in a long, long, *long* time," she told him. "Where every senior officer and noncom out there"—she gestured at the holographic display—"is a veteran of the Rebellion. A solid majority of the spacers too, both ours and the Chimerans'.

"Their hardware is better. Their software is better. But their doctrine is shit and they don't have the experience to see it. They'll *get* that experience, but they haven't had enough time to incorporate whatever lessons the survivors of the last fleet picked up."

He glanced back at the red icons, then returned his gaze to her.

"Meaning?"

"This time, the question isn't *are* they going to jump out," she told him. "It's *when*. This is a scouting force. The real burden on the Admirals is making sure we don't lose too many people or give away too many secrets convincing them to leave."

They had food brought up as the hours ticked away. As everyone had expected, there was no response to O'Hannagain's message. It would have consequences, Roslyn suspected, but that wasn't an issue to raise until the system was clear again.

The numbers she spent those hours running again and again were similar. They told a sequence of events she didn't like, but reality didn't have much sympathy for her feelings.

"How long now?" O'Hannagain finally asked. The big man was sitting on his desk, staring at the holographic display with a waxed paper cup full of something fizzy and nonalcoholic.

Roslyn had taken one sniff of the sickly sweet beverage and passed her own cup over to him when he seemed willing to drink the soda. Baars had also brought coffee along with the meal, and she was content with that.

"Reezh are still over twenty-one million kilometers away," she reminded him. "Everything on the display is over seventy seconds out of date."

"Meaning?"

"The combined fleet entered missile range of the Kazh warships thirty seconds ago, and we won't see what happened for another forty," she told the civilian. "Their missiles have ten thousand gravities of acceleration and more flight time than anything in our arsenal.

"They get the first round all to themselves."

"For how long?"

Roslyn was reasonably sure O'Hannagain knew more of this than he was pretending to. Though he might also have forgotten it or simply asked questions of someone else during the last battle. The math was straightforward enough.

For her, at least. But she lived and breathed three-dimensional acceleration calculations, and what was "basic" to her probably wasn't to the Ambassador.

"It's complicated," she admitted. "The *Salamanders* can fire before the reezh missiles hit, but they only have forty of the long-range missile launchers. I'm... not Vice Admiral Adamant, but I might even hold fire until the Chimerans are in range."

She met the civilian's gaze and answered before he asked.

"About twenty-five minutes," she told him. "We saw the Kazh firing once a minute last time, for a total of forty-six salvos. They won't fire at that rate at extreme range."

O'Hannagain seemed prepared to accept that as an expert opinion, though she'd been prepared to explain the difficult realities of command-and-control loops at fifty light-seconds. The Kazh's missiles were smarter than the RMN's but not enough to make up for the lack of feedback from their control ships.

"They should be in range now on the display, right?" the Ambassador asked.

Roslyn checked the time.

"Twenty seconds ago, give or take," she agreed. "They haven't fired."

"Any idea what they're playing at?"

"They're alien crews flying alien warships operating to alien doctrine and unknown objectives," she reminded him. "That said, I think they *do* have data from the last battle. They know they have a major range advantage on us and are choosing accuracy over risk-free fire."

"So, the ships that got away checked in."

"They had to. Probably within hours of leaving Chimera," Roslyn said grimly. "These people have probably had decent scan data of the entire Battle of Chimera for their entire journey here."

That was the first time she'd said aloud what her math had concluded: that the Kazh fleet had clearly had an FTL communicator and had phoned home immediately. There was no other way for this fleet to have arrived this quickly.

Which meant, unfortunately, that the *next* fleet was going to arrive in about the same amount of time. With far-better intelligence.

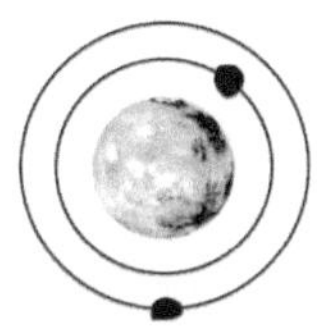

CHAPTER 15

IT WAS ALMOST A RELIEF WHEN the Kazh warships *did* fire, a swarm of red icons that were uncountable to the naked eye on the display. Roslyn immediately added the number beneath the crowd of icons—twenty-two hundred missiles, matching her expectations exactly.

"Well, that tells us one thing I expected," she murmured.

"Which is?"

She'd almost forgotten that she was neither on the command deck of a warship nor alone. O'Hannagain's office systems weren't a bad substitute for the tactical displays of her old bridge, giving her a solid handle of what was going on.

Though, on her bridge, of course, she could have *done* something about what she saw.

"Masses and armaments are a perfect match for the ships that were here last time," she told him. "Standardized classes. These ships almost certainly also came from the Nine itself, not one of the controlled Primes."

They knew there was a fleet of warships at one other Prime that still paid allegiance to the Kazh. A second Prime was under Kazh control, but the only warships there were obviously an occupation force.

The third Prime she'd managed to visit was independent, a discovery that had sent the Chimeran ship *Barracuda* on its long-range diplomatic mission. They might make friends there... but she suspected it wasn't going to be soon enough to matter.

They'd thought they had more time.

"Is that good or bad?" he asked.

"Neither," she admitted. "It's information. We know that the two sets of ships we think the Kazh can deploy are different sizes, so these ships came from the Nine itself. I don't know what that means.

"The distance they fired at, though, confirms what I thought. They know quite a bit about the last fight here—they fired just before they came into range of our Samurai missiles."

Not that the Samurai missiles would have reached them for a few minutes yet. They could be stepped down in acceleration for an extreme-range mode, but there wasn't much point in sending forty missiles against a battleship on its own, let alone one with fifteen escorts.

"That's... a lot of missiles."

"And our people can handle them," Roslyn said firmly. She had her doubts, but she wasn't going to air them to Connor O'Hannagain.

For now, she joined him in watching in silence as the tempest descended on the allied fleet. A single salvo of missiles blazed out from the defenders, barely half the number of weapons the reezh had launched.

Even without the gunships, Roslyn knew the fleet had more launchers than that, which told her what was going on. She was unsurprised when those weapons exploded as they interpenetrated with the enemy salvo, antimatter warheads ripping apart the incoming missiles and turning the space around them into a mess of radiation.

"Still twenty minutes until you expect them to shoot back?" O'Hannagain asked, his tone almost sick.

"That's the best way to stack everything we've got into a single salvo. The enemy's defenses are good. Long-range fire is a waste of time without overwhelming numbers, so waiting until we have the CSN's launchers is necessary."

Even as she calmly tried to explain the mess to O'Hannagain, every part of her body screamed to be out there, taking a cruiser or destroyer into the teeth of the enemy. Adamant and Wang weren't doing anything different from what she would—the situation didn't lend itself well to clever stunts, though she suspected there were games in motion.

Instead, she stood calmly in the Ambassador's office, a coffee in her hand while she watched numbers update as the enemy missiles entered the defensive envelope of the fleet.

The display she was getting wasn't detailed enough for her to judge the enemy jammers and sensor heads, though the way the salvo disintegrated into static told her a lot. A shiver of memory ran down her spine, and she *knew* that the laser turrets defending the fleet were losing lock.

But there were a *lot* of the standardized Rapid-Fire Laser Anti-Missile turrets out there, ranging from five hundred megawatts to a full gigawatt per beam. She couldn't track the fate of individual missiles, but the cloud of jamming died before it reached the fleet.

The second salvo of missiles was right behind it. This one had been programmed to expect the intercept salvo and kept most of its numbers. From bitter experience, Roslyn knew that the radiation cloud of the prior salvo's destruction would cause chaos with their seekers anyway.

The second salvo got closer but still didn't reach the fleet. The third was closer still, and it took an effort of will not to hold her breath as the fourth salvo reached out for her comrades.

New icons were added to the display when the fire was over, and Roslyn looked at them with grim eyes.

"Captain?" O'Hannagain asked, something in his tone and use of her title warning her that she was showing more than she should.

She took a moment to compose her features before turning back to him.

"Damage codes, Connor," she told him. "*Righteous Guardian* and *Scharnhorst* are both hit. We're not getting enough information for me to say if the damage is bad, only that they are damaged."

Roslyn could probably access that level of information, but she didn't need it. She wasn't trying to command or organize the battle. Just follow it and make sure the key civilians did.

"They're launching," she realized aloud as a blaze of green icons lit up the display. Not just the thousand-odd missiles of the interceptor salvos that had bought them time but the full fifteen hundred–plus of the massed launchers of the combined fleet—plus the fifteen hundred from the two hundred and fifty gunships.

"That certainly *looks* impressive," O'Hannagain said. "May it be enough."

It didn't need to be. The Kazh scout fleet had been spacing its missiles out by about three minutes. In the three-minute gap between salvos four and five, the defenders sent nine thousand missiles hurtling toward the enemy—and then made turnover to make sure they stayed between the planet and the oncoming warships.

The next eight and a half minutes were hell. Three more Kazh salvos hammered down on the defense fleet. Damage icons now marked every ship larger than a destroyer, though they'd been spared any true losses.

With even the massive Samurai missiles stepped down to match the Chimeran Excalibur Vs in acceleration, the salvo seemed to inch across the screen before it finally dived down on the enemy warships.

The reezh ships had their own defenses, and missiles died or lost course by their hundreds. The Martian and Chimeran missiles were no match for the sheer power of the enemy's electronic-warfare systems—but the spacers operating them had known that for over three weeks.

Unlike their enemy, the defenders *had* seen real war and they had a damn good idea of how to fool, avoid or ignore the vastly overpowered jammers and decoys the Reezh Kazh had equipped their fleets with.

Hundreds of missiles survived to connect, and over half of the red icons vanished from the display. The largest ships remained, but Roslyn doubted they were untouched. The attackers had drawn first blood, but they'd also taken the first losses.

Thirty seconds before the second salvo reached the enemy ships, they vanished from the scope with the abrupt suddenness of a jump.

She heard O'Hannagain exhale a long sigh.

"So, that's it, then," he murmured.

"Maybe," she cautioned. "They could have gone anywhere."

But he was probably right. Most likely, they'd gone to find friends.

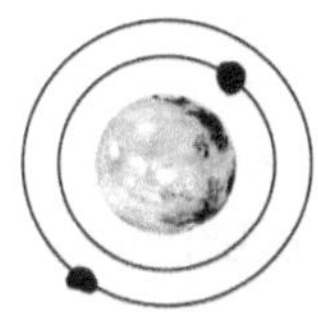

CHAPTER 16

JANE ALEXANDER SIPPED HER COFFEE and watched as the last of Second Fleet's staff took their seats. A holographic simulacrum of the Second Battle of Chimera was running at a hundred times actual speed above the table as stewards moved around, filling coffee cups and water glasses.

They weren't her wartime staff. Those officers had been scattered, promoted, moved into billets suited to their skills. None had risen quite so dramatically as now Mage-Captain Chambers, her Flag Lieutenant seven years earlier, but all of them were serving the Navy well.

At that moment, she wished she could reclaim them all.

Commodore Peta Soból took her seat at the opposite end of the table, the Chief of Staff the perfect example of the half dozen senior officers around the room. Soból was competent, phlegmatic and reliable, but there was a spark missing that Jane couldn't quite explain.

Her Communications, Intelligence, Logistics and Personnel Officers were of a similar ilk. Senior Captains all, the two men and two women were among the best the Royal Martian Navy had to offer.

They just hadn't been forged in the crucible of war like the staff she'd defeated the Republic with.

"Everyone has had a chance to review the reports and sensor footage from Chimera," she said. "Admirals Wang and Adamant did a solid job of driving off a force that was no match for their own, but the situation we are left with is something of a mess.

"Your assessments."

That was mostly addressed at Soból and Captain Coskun Xiao, her Intelligence Officer.

Xiao was the first to say anything, though the dark-skinned Chinese man in an Arabic-style white turban took a sip of his coffee to give the others a chance to say anything.

"This was a scouting mission," he stated. "That much is obvious. They made no attempt to truly close with the defending fleet. They retreated as soon as they took casualties.

"The more-interesting piece, I find, is that the order of battle we saw yesterday could not have been assembled out of the known Kazh survivors of the First Battle of Chimera. There may have been some ships from the original attack force present, but there also needed to be new ships."

"Suggesting?" Jane prompted.

Xiao replied with a one-shouldered shrug.

"These ships were drawn from elsewhere," he said. "The most likely source is one hundred and eighty light-years away, suggesting that our enemy's command-and-deployment loop is approximately twenty-four days—the elapsed time between the departure of the first fleet and the arrival of the second."

"That would require a sustained speed of fifteen light-years a day, minimum," Captain Nikos Giannino said. The Logistics Officer wasn't disagreeing with Xiao, though the swarthy Greek officer and the Turkish-Chinese Xiao rarely *agreed*, either.

"Any ship in our fleet is supposed to manage sixteen," Xiao pointed out. "We could certainly have sent couriers back from Chimera to the Nine, mustered a fleet and deployed to Chimera."

"Except that if we could actually do something comparable, we would have a lot more ships at Exeter," Giannino countered. "Like us, most of their ships are almost certainly tied up in existing duties. I imagine their large vessels have similar logistical limitations to ours as well.

"The Republic Interstellar Navy, as the only force we know that used a similar atrocity to the Kazh for jumps, was standardized at ten light-years per day," he noted. "That was with five Prometheans aboard, jumping twice per day each."

"We can't assume that the Kazh Engines of Sacred Sacrifice have the same principles or limitations as the Prometheus Drive," Xiao warned.

"That's correct," Jane said, cutting off the discussion before it grew more heated. "But it does give us a point of comparison, doesn't it? If they were using a similar speed to the RIN fleets, these ships would have left the Nine eighteen days before they reached Chimera.

"That would have given our enemy roughly six days to receive the information on the First Battle of Chimera, make a decision and a plan, assign units and then work up those ships and the logistics for a minimum thirty-six day journey."

She saw her staff chew on that. A week was about what Jane would have expected from the Protectorate, a standard that her nation and navy were currently failing to meet. The RMN hadn't drawn down after the war, but they had definitely found new uses for all of the ships they had!

"But that's impossible," Soból finally said. "That would require them to have some form of faster-than-light communicator. None of the records of the Reezh Ida suggest they had anything of the sort."

"The last records of the Ida we have access to date to shortly before the Protectorate was founded," Jane reminded her officers. "We cannot assume that nothing has changed in the intervening centuries. *We* have certainly advanced technologically."

There was a line of discussion, one that she gave quite a bit of credence to but wouldn't raise in public, suggesting that the widespread use of magic in the Protectorate had caused a significant level of stagnation. The basic engines and weapons suites of the modern Protectorate warship, after all, were recognizable evolutions of the ones deployed by the first Protectorate warships in the twenty-third century. The only major step change in two hundred years had been the mass deployment of antimatter—and *that* had been due to magic.

"Which scenario we are facing will be relevant in the medium and long term," she warned. "Right now, the key point is that twenty-four days appears to be the likely timeline before the next attack. That is how long we have to get Second Fleet into position in Chimera."

That raised the furor she was expecting, and Jane waited it out, drinking her coffee as her staff worked through the fundamental issues.

"Giannino," she finally snapped, silencing the argument. "How long until we have enough of the logistics train in place for us to move forward?"

"Another week, sir," he said. "A few days before the forces detached from Nia Kriti are scheduled to arrive."

That would bring Second Fleet to the greatest strength Jane was likely to have for some time. Without those ships, she might come up short against whatever the enemy did—but those ships could follow in their own time.

"We will prepare to relocate Second Fleet to Chimera as soon as our logistics train is complete," Jane decided. It still didn't feel right, with a shiver down the back of her neck that reminded her they were leaving Chimera vulnerable.

But without the logistics to keep her fleet operating, they'd rapidly turn into decorative asteroids. Dreadnoughts were *not* designed to be self-sufficient for more than a week or two.

If she had enough warning... but that twenty-four-day cycle said she was okay to wait.

Probably.

They only had one data point, after all.

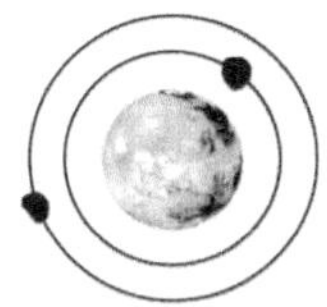

CHAPTER 17

"I APOLOGIZE FOR THE DELAY, SECRETARY KARIM," Roslyn told the head of the Evacuation Commission. "There was some question over how much refit work the ships would be able to do in Garudan orbit."

"I hope the supplies we've promised will help with that," Karim told her.

"They will. That's why we have the final numbers," she said.

Baars put a coffee cup at her elbow and slipped back out of the room.

"We are impressed," Shozha told her, the reezh's face unreadable. "Would you care to explicate them for the team?"

The Commission's leadership team had grown, Roslyn noted. She'd mostly been meeting with Karim and a working group of mid-level bureaucrats. Hopefully, her information had been making it up the chain.

"The core of Evac Convoy One is eighty *Bushido*-class troop transports," she told them. "Sixty of those transports have been refitted for civilian passage, and we have solid numbers on their capacity. The other twenty are currently running light but carrying a division apiece of either the Royal Martian Marines or the Protectorate Guard. A total of four hundred thousand soldiers, plus additional equipment that we intend to make available to the Republics of Chimera Army.

"Thanks to the supplies you've agreed to provide, we know we will be able to refit them within forty-eight hours to meet the same standard as the other sixty."

Roslyn tapped a few commands on her wrist-comp to pull up the last numbers.

"There are also fifty-two civilian ships of various sizes. The final total we can confirm is eight million, seven hundred and eighty thousand, six hundred and fifty seats."

It was a *lot* of people, but Roslyn knew that everyone in the room was comparing it against the task ahead.

"We have confirmed with the planetary government of Mackenzie that they are setting up receiving facilities to handle the evacuees."

"We... would like more information on that," Karim said grimly. "There are too many horror stories of refugee camps and similar fates in our past. I have faith in the Protectorate's promises, and anything will likely be better than occupation by the Kazh, but..."

"I understand," Roslyn told him. She dug through her wrist-comp for what she was looking for, then flipped the image over to the holoprojector.

The conference room was as well equipped as any she'd ever been in, though her wrist-comp did need conversion protocols to talk to the software. The windows automatically dimmed as the image appeared above the table: a city of immense towers arranged in concentric circles of decreasing height toward the outer ring.

Even at the small scale of the hologram, the streets and smaller buildings around the stepped towers were clear. They were mostly empty, but there was just enough traffic to strongly suggest that it was the real image it was.

"This is where one set of bastards helps save us from another," she told the Evacuation Commission. "This was built as Ridwan City, named for the commander of the First Legion who conquered Mackenzie and a number of other planets with a leftover force of Republic ships and ground troops.

"It has been tentatively renamed Chimera Landing. Despite being built for a population of twenty million, less than ten thousand people currently live there—caretakers for a city no one wanted or needed except for a self-aggrandizing dictator."

The Commission's members studied the towers, the scale taking a few minutes to sink in. None of the towers quite reached arcology status, but Admiral Ridwan Muhammed's ego hadn't settled for anything small for his planned capital.

"Thanks to the First Legion's insistence on building themselves a brand-new capital city, Mackenzie has found themselves in possession of a massive amount of construction equipment and trained workers they weren't entirely sure what to do with.

"The Protectorate has employed them for the last few years doing reconstruction work around the region," Roslyn noted. That had served the dual purpose of accomplishing said reconstruction and of pumping a large amount of outside cash into the local economies.

The worlds conquered by the First Legion had been rogue colonies, settlements created by people who wanted to escape the Protectorate for their own reasons. Once liberated from the Legion, they'd all voted to join the Protectorate so long as their own unique government structures were respected.

Only the caste-based theocracy out of the strange mess had actually created a problem—and that structure had been sufficiently unstable after the Legion conquest that it had collapsed like wet paper when the Mountain, in the person of Queen Kiera's Hand Shea Riley, made noises about declining their request.

"The ships we were using to haul them around make up about half of the civilian transports of Evac Convoy One," she concluded. "That has provided Mackenzie with an absolutely massive amount of personnel and equipment to take on city-building projects—and for all of its heritage problems, Chimera's Landing makes for a surprisingly good template."

"The Mackenzies are... building entire cities for us?" Shozha's voice was slow, with boulders in her throat instead of gravel. "I am... we are..."

"The Protectorate promised you safety," Roslyn reminded them. "My Mage-Queen will not break her promises. A crude collection of tents on a windy plain would not keep your people safe—and while Mackenzie's southern continent, Arran, is not the most pleasant place in the galaxy, it is as habitable as Garuda's temperate regions and currently home to only a few people."

Arran was, from the reports Roslyn had read, actually *nicer* than most parts of Garuda. The Chimerans' planet was windy and cold, survivable but unpleasant for both species. Arran would be decent for the humans—and probably significantly more comfortable for the reezh!

"I do not know if the debt we are incurring can be repaid," Karim said levelly. "Only that we must be grateful beyond any words or reason."

"My Queen's oath makes her Protector of all humanity," Roslyn told the Chimeran politician. "*All* of it. And neither her spirit nor her Navy's honor would see us evacuate the humans and leave the reezh behind.

"We are counting, I have to admit, on your people setting to work once they arrive," she warned. "We will provide a great deal of equipment, but there is farmland to be cultivated, empty factories to be turned into industry and, well, cities to be built for the next waves."

Even with all of the equipment in place on Mackenzie, the first clone of Ridwan City/Chimera's Landing was going to take almost two months to complete—and Roslyn wasn't convinced she believed that estimate.

Even with magic and modern technology, that seemed impossible.

"We will make certain our evacuees are warned," Shozha said with a chuckle like a breaking rock. "They may well be pleased to know there is work and opportunity awaiting them. We would all rather stay in our homes, but..."

"Nemesis took that from you," Roslyn finished as the Director trailed off. "We failed to stop them, which leaves this the best we can do until we can expand our fleets. We were not ready for this war."

"Would you ever have been?"

She turned to look at the man who'd spoken. He hadn't been introduced, but he wore the dark green uniform of the Republics of Chimera Army, with a double-eagle insignia matching the one the Republic Space Assault Force used for Lieutenant Generals.

A quick glance confirmed that it said *O'NEILL* on his uniform and she nodded to him.

"General O'Neill, correct?" she asked.

"Lieutenant General Jacques O'Neill," he confirmed. "I don't know your Protectorate well, Mage-Captain. I was born here in Chimera and, frankly, I expected the worst thing in my army career to be disaster relief.

"With your war with the UnArcana Republic over, would you have expected anything else?"

Roslyn paused to consider the question.

"Thanks to the organization that Nemesis grew out of, the Keepers, we had some idea of what was out there," she admitted. Arguably, they'd known thanks to Nemesis itself, but Roslyn would swallow broken glass before she gave *them* any credit.

"We kept the knowledge limited, but enough people knew that we were expanding and upgrading our fleet. Given another year or two, we would have had a significantly stronger fleet.

"That was why the ships like *Rose* and *Thorn* existed," she explained. "Our task was to locate the people behind the Olympus Project and see what, if any, danger existed. Instead... well, we all know what happened instead."

"We do," General O'Neill allowed. "You expect to be able to fight the Kazh, given time?"

"That is the plan. New ships are being ordered, construction plans accelerated. Training regimes expanded." Roslyn spread her hands. None of these things would be fast, but the Parliament of the Protectorate had responded to the attacks on Chimera with as much certainty and speed as anyone could have hoped.

"But not soon enough to save us."

"No," Roslyn agreed without hesitation. "Hence this Commission. Hence the vast construction projects on Mackenzie. We will save as much of what makes Chimera *Chimera* as we can. The people, the history, the culture.

"Cities, monuments, ships... these can be replaced. The hands that built them and the memories they honor cannot be. We will save everything we can."

"And when you are ready for this war, Mage-Captain?" Secretary Karim asked, the politician taking over for the General. "What happens then?"

"Then we will liberate Chimera," Roslyn told them. "We will defend your system with you as long as we can. If we are forced to retreat, we will return. My Queen has pledged nothing less, Secretary Karim."

"Of course," he conceded, then turned his attention to the rest of the room. "We now know how many people we can fit on the first evacuation convoy. That gives us a great deal of work to do—and our processes are new.

"Let's go through it all, my friends. The clearer we are to start, the smoother the process will be and the safer our people will be."

CHAPTER 18

"IF I HAVE MY MATH RIGHT, the Promethean transports should be joining you shortly," Kiera Alexander told her aunt with a mischievous smile. "I hope you'll find some pleasant surprises in the mix with them."

Jane gave her niece the most reproving look she could deliver to her sovereign. Mage-Queen of Mars or not, Jane Alexander had over six decades on her brother's younger child. She put every one of those years into her eyes as she glared down her kin.

"There aren't supposed to be *surprises* in the evac convoys, Kiera," she growled. "Pleasant or not, we need to make certain that the Chimerans know what they're getting when we arrive. The more information they have, the better off they are organizing the on-load."

"I am the Queen," the young woman replied, utterly unperturbed by her aunt's glare. The years of familiarity worked both ways, Jane reflected. "While I wish my surprises added to the number of seats for the evacuation, they won't change that. You will find them up your alley, though, I hope."

"You do realize it is beneath the Mage-Queen of Mars to conceal information for a prank?"

"It's not a prank," Kiera replied, her tone suddenly flatly serious. "The declaration of war only passed seven days ago. We were operating under a special dispensation from Parliament prior to that, which means the RMN wasn't supposed to send ships out to Exeter beyond the agreed funding.

"Shifting ships around from the frontier fleet bases was one thing—the reality is that no one is going to blink at anything we do—but detaching ships from *Sol* was going to draw attention nobody wanted.

"So, some ships moved without formal orders, you get a pleasant surprise, and now that the declaration *has* passed, no one is going to poke at the exact timing."

Jane shook her head.

"And this, Kiera, is why you make a better Queen than I do," she admitted. "Desmond got the twisty brain in my generation. I'm a good Admiral, but I'd make a terrible politician."

"We do what we must to serve the Mountain and, through the Mountain, the people of the Protectorate," the young Queen said. "I had good teachers and have good advisors.

"But I'm not ready for this war."

Jane hadn't been expecting that admission and she sighed.

"None of us are, Kiera," she reminded her Queen. "War isn't a thing we want, ever. We prepare for it, we build ships and train people for it, but we don't want it. And so, we're never truly ready for it.

"But when the alternative is to allow a state that we know has burned hundreds of worlds to ashes to conquer one more? To watch a people that we would happily be friends with in better times conquered and enslaved?

"We did not choose this war, Kiera, my Queen. We only choose the values we are prepared to fight for and the lines we will not let others cross. Those choices, and the actions of Nemesis and of the Kazh, leave us here."

"I know. I just wish they'd talk to us."

Jane nodded grimly.

"That part bothers me," she admitted. "Both we and the Chimerans have tried to talk to them and received only weapon fire in response. That, too, leaves us little choice."

Before Kiera could say anything, a chime sounded on Jane's desk and a nervous-sounding voice interrupted.

"Sir, Admiral... multiple contacts jumping in. CIC databases are calling them *Republic*!"

"And that's my cue, Kiera. Because despite the fact that everyone *knows* who's coming, the arrival of a dozen Republican warships isn't going to go without a panic attack," Jane said wryly.

By the time Jane Alexander strode onto her flag deck, barely a minute and a half later, most of the initial panic had been smoothed by the arrival of the identify-friend-or-foe beacons from the incoming ships.

"Our guests, I presume, are the core of Evac Convoy Two?" she asked Commodore Soból lightly.

She was neither bothered nor concerned by the semi-panicky message she'd received from the Bridge Officer of the Watch. She'd drop a quiet word in Captain Do Pei's ear later, as much to make sure that the Lieutenant Commander in question—who was *just* old enough to have seen Republican warships in action during the war—didn't get his fingers slapped as anything else.

"Yes, sir," Soból confirmed. "Fifteen *Saladin*-class planetary invasion ships under Commodore Chinedu Okorie aboard *Saladin* herself. Escorts... four cruisers, six destroyers, under Mage-Captain Máiréad Agramunt in... *Victory at Midway*? I'm not familiar with that ship."

"I'm familiar with Agramunt and *Victory at Midway*," Jane said slowly. "I'm guessing one of the other cruisers is *Last Stand at the Alamo*?"

Soból checked.

"Yes, sir. *Victory at Midway* and *Last Stand at the Alamo*, plus the *Salamanders Olm* and *Fire Salamander*."

"Mage-Captain Agramunt was responsible for the initial workups and test flights of the *Victory*-class battlecruisers," Jane told her Chief of Staff—who had access to that information and should probably have been up to date on just what the RMN's Bureau of Shipbuilding—or Bu-Ships—had been up to.

"*Midway* and *Alamo* are the only two completed *Victory*-class ships I'm aware of, though the ordered class was thirty," she continued. "We'll want to discuss their readiness carefully with Mage-Captain Agramunt, though I doubt she or Admiral Medici would have brought them if they *weren't* ready."

"The destroyers are all *Virtue*-class ships, sir," Soból added, clearly recognizing what *those* were. The smallest of the new-generation ships, the *Virtues* had been deployed in enough numbers that people knew what they were.

That was why they'd gone through three classes of destroyers during and since the Rebellion but only one class of cruisers or larger ships. The *Salamanders*, *Peaces* and *Mjolnirs* had all been built under the same scheme as the *Cataphract* class, but a whole new class of destroyers had come and gone while the larger ships only saw a new iteration of the existing classes built.

"All right." Jane stood by her chair and studied the big holotank at the center of the room. The new big green icons would join the existing cluster of green icons—including three that dwarfed everything in the system except the two dreadnoughts.

"Set up a Link conversation with Commodore Okorie, Mage-Captain Agramunt and General Badem," she told Captain Jundt, her Communications Officer. "I'll take it in my office as soon as they're ready."

Okorie was the first person to pop up the holographic screens around Jane, a broad smile playing across his dark lips.

"Your Highness," he greeted her. "I understand several people will be joining us, but with your permission, I'd like to add two more. I presume this will be something of a coordination-and-planning meeting for Evac Convoy Two, yes?"

Jane studied him silently for a moment, then realized who he had to mean.

"Promethean representatives?" he asked.

"Yes. Miz Spencer and Mr. Connors continue to speak for their compatriots in most affairs, and I believe they would make a useful contribution to this meeting," Okorie said firmly.

"Plus, they're almost certainly listening in on your coms?" Jane asked, remembering what Kiera had told her about the Phobos Special Rehabilitation Facility.

"Oh, I've given that pair access; they are *definitely* listening," the Commodore confirmed immediately.

For a man who had spent his entire career in the Logistics arms of the Royal Martian Navy and had never held anything resembling a major command before, Commodore Okorie seemed to know exactly how much forgiveness to ask.

"Include them," she instructed, a moment before Mage-Captain Agramunt appeared in a second screen.

Máiréad Agramunt was a Taran woman with brilliant green eyes, shockingly red hair, and a slimly tall frame to rival that of the Royal family. A Mage by Right, discovered by the Royal Testers at age eleven, she'd risen to her current rank and role from about as much poverty as anyone could find in the Core Worlds.

"Commodore, Admiral," she greeted the officers waiting for her. "I take it our Promethean friends will be joining us?"

Summoned by Jane's command as opposed to Agramunt's comment, two virtual avatars created a third window around her desk. The window's occupants were seated behind a clone of Commodore Okorie's desk vaguely stretched to allow two seats.

Mikayla Spencer had either been intentionally testing the Mage-Queen when she'd met Jane's niece or had decided to tone down her expression now she was in auxiliary military service. Her avatar was still an anthropomorphized fox, but the breasts and hips had been reduced to more-ordinary proportions and she wore a gray civilian shipsuit with a Mage medallion at her neck as the only insignia.

William Connors had shifted from his RIN uniform to a matching gray shipsuit with medallion—and it took Jane a solid ten seconds to realize that his ears were now long and pointed like a fantasy elf's.

Given that he still had the gaze and bearing of the not-quite-officer he'd been for the First Legion, Jane had to wonder if that had been the price he'd paid for his companion being less over-the-top.

"Mage Spencer, Mage Connors," she greeted the two. "Welcome to Exeter and Base Deveraux."

"Deveraux." Connors rolled the name around his virtual mouth like he was tasting it. "It was Exeter Fleet Base before. You renamed it for Sharon?"

"We did," Jane confirmed. "Sharon Deveraux died liberating this system from the First Legion, with the sole and *only* purpose of her defection being to save the thousands of innocents trapped in the work camps here.

"Naming the base for her was a tiny marker of the immense debt that the Royal Martian Navy, the Protectorate and the Mountain ourselves owed her. We cannot repay that debt. We can only honor her sacrifice."

"Thank you," the ex–First Legion Promethean said. "I knew I made the right decision volunteering for this, Admiral Alexander. I did not think I had any doubts—but I am even more certain now.

"Sharon Deveraux deserved better than the First Legion."

"So did you all," Jane told him. "It is for the memory of those we have lost that we strive to protect the innocent, Mage Connors. Even if Base Deveraux wasn't the most convenient place to stage our operations toward Chimera... it is most definitely the most *appropriate*."

That it was convenient helped, though there were arguments for assembling the evacuation convoys at Mackenzie. With the Protectorate's investment and construction, however, Base Deveraux's logistics capabilities now exceeded the old First Legion capital system, and ships like dreadnoughts and colony vessels required those facilities.

The last member of the meeting, General Fedora Badem, appeared on the meeting a few moments later. The Marine Corps General couldn't have looked less like the stereotype of a Martian Marine if she'd tried, being a petite woman with shoulder-length raven hair and pale skin.

Only her hard, flinty eyes and the fine white lines of scarring across her face suggested the truth.

"Thank you all for joining me," Jane told them all. "General Badem, this is Commodore Okorie, Mage-Captain Agramunt, and the Ship's Mages Spencer and Connors."

Badem nodded once crisply.

"The Prometheans," she said.

"Yes. Commodore Okorie will be taking command of the ships of Evac Convoy Two, under your overall authority," Jane informed the Marine. "Can you give him a quick rundown of what Convoy Two currently has?"

"Yes." Badem moved slightly, focusing her eyes on Okorie.

"We have twenty *Bushido*-class transports, currently loaded with second-wave forces for the Chimera stay-behind plan," she noted. "That is three divisions of the Protectorate Guard and one of Marines, eighty thousand soldiers. The ships themselves are expected to provide final evacuation transport of one hundred thousand personnel apiece, a total of two million.

"Additionally, we have two hundred and twelve civilian vessels, rated for passenger capacity in aggregate of another one-point-seven million. That is excluding the colony transports, of course."

"We have only received three of the ships the Derry Colony Expedition Corporation promised so far," Jane noted. "We are aware of where the other three *are*, and the DCEC is keeping their promise. They've been redirected to Mackenzie at this point, to rendezvous with Evac Convoy One when they get there in twenty-six days."

"That said, Derry's ships are some of the largest currently in operation," Badem noted. "The three they have provided us have been refitted while en route by ship's engineers, like everything else in Evac Convoy Two.

"They're guaranteeing six million people across the three ships."

"Which has nothing to do with the fact that Derry is getting paid on a per-evacuee basis," Jane said drily. "Cynical as I am, though, I do trust their engineers, and the increase makes sense."

"We've run the same refits while on our way," Okorie said. "Each of the *Saladin*s is clear for a million people once we offload the leftover RSAF hardware."

"Can Chimera even use as much hardware as we're delivering?" Connors asked, the Promethean's tone curious. "I know some equipment was delivered by Evac Convoy One, but we have a significant percentage of the *entire* equipment list for the Republic Space Assault Force stored on these ships."

"We didn't have time to send out a call for ex-Republic personnel willing to help protect Chimera," Jane pointed out. "So, the only people who actually know how to use those systems are already on Chimera and have, hopefully, been training the locals in using them."

She wasn't entirely convinced on the logic of a heavily armed stay-behind force, given that the Kazh would have orbital superiority, but she supposed it was better to put the guns in the Dual Republics' hands and let them make the call.

"How quickly will Evac Convoy Two be ready to move out?" she asked.

"The Commodore and I will need to touch base directly on a bunch of details," Badem noted. "The ships already here still need a few finishing touches, and I imagine the *Saladin*s require fuel at the minimum.

"Unless Commodore Okorie's ships are in a very different state than I expect, tomorrow will be the earliest we can move," the General concluded.

"Tomorrow would be my expectation," Okorie agreed. "What about escorts?"

"I can certainly continue on with the four ships temporarily under my command," Agramunt noted, "but I imagine you would like to retain *Victory at Midway* and *Last Stand at the Alamo* with the main fleet body."

"You are correct, Mage-Captain," Jane confirmed. "The two most modern cruisers in the Navy are ships I want at my side, not escorting the convoys. But Evac Convoy Two will require an escort."

She paused in thought, then shook her head.

"Tomorrow gives us time to make decisions," she told the others. "Badem, Okorie, get the replenishment and preparation of Evac Convoy Two underway. If at all possible, I want the convoy ready to leave by twelve hundred hours OMT tomorrow."

"I believe we can do that," Okorie promised. "Presuming there is fuel available."

CHAPTER 19

THE ITCH BETWEEN JANE ALEXANDER'S SHOULDER blades wasn't going away. There in Exeter, her fleet was safe—but fleets didn't exist to be safe. They existed to keep other people safe.

Chimera wasn't safe right now. Not with a single RMN battleship and a handful of cruisers backing up the Chimerans' own ships. Adamant was a solid officer, but she didn't have the firepower to stand off another attack.

Even the first force from four weeks earlier would overrun what remained in Chimera. She needed more ships there, but the logistical math was straightforward.

The RMN logistics ships in Chimera were capable of handling BTG Romana's original strength: a battleship and six cruisers plus destroyer escort. Chimera's own infrastructure could manage hydrogen fuel, but she had only the crudest estimates of how much antimatter the accelerator ring could produce once it was online—and by the time it was online, she'd have the refinery ships and Transmuter Mages currently on their way.

Without those ships and Mages, operating her capital ships was critically dependent on Base Deveraux's refineries and antimatter stores. Even Deveraux didn't have enough Transmuter Mages on hand to keep up with Second Fleet's consumption for any kind of operational tempo—if they did, Jane would have loaded them all onto her ships and transferred to Chimera weeks before.

At the maximum pace her fleet could sustain—a bit less than double the nine light-years per day the Evac Convoys were targeting, with three Mages or four Prometheans per ship—she could reach Chimera in a week.

At which point she'd be able to stay in the allied system for about two days before she had to turn right back around and bring all of those ships back to Exeter. *Maybe* three—and if Second Fleet fought a major battle there, they wouldn't have the fuel to make it back to their logistics chain.

Her dreadnoughts and battleships could operate for eighteen days without refueling. The cruisers could go longer, the destroyers mostly less—but the destroyers could refuel from the battleships and dreadnoughts, trading a day of endurance on the heavy ships for a week extra on the escorts.

Seventeen days. That was a hard limit, and it meant she couldn't bring her fleet forward to Chimera.

Except...

She had *some* logistics ships already. They wouldn't be enough to sustain her entire fleet, but combined with Chimera's own hydrogen extraction...

Jane barely even realized she'd opened up her console until she was halfway through running the numbers.

Her last logistics ships—unfortunately, the most key ones for maintaining a dreadnought battle group—weren't due to arrive for eight more days. Like the Evac Convoys, they would take eleven days to reach Chimera from Exeter, arriving *after* the original expected date of the Reezh Kazh attack.

Now they didn't know when the next Kazh attack would be, but Jane's guess was twenty days. That would see the logistics ships reaching Chimera, well... at roughly the same time as the next wave of the Kazh. Twenty days.

Her existing logistics ships and the Chimerans' own logistics infrastructure could buy her somewhere between five and ten days. Even on the low end, it was more than she needed.

She tapped her coms.

"Soból, Giannino, I need you in my office now."

The two officers listened as she laid out the scenario. Neither said anything, which was ahead of what Jane had expected, if she was being honest. She'd been prepared for argument, objections, even outright denial.

Instead, her Logistics Officer and her Chief of Staff heard her out. Giannino was running numbers on his wrist-comp, but Soból was studying Jane's own math.

"If something goes wrong, sir, we will run out of fuel in Chimera," she noted. "Depending on when we arrive and when the Kazh arrives, we could easily end up in a situation where we have *ships* in Chimera to fight but no fuel to fight with."

"The worst-case scenario I see, Commodore, is that we have limited delta-v to maneuver with," Jane countered. "We will have to limit our maneuvering, even in the face of the enemy, to sustain enough power for the battle lasers.

"But we are in far better shape with sixteen capital ships in the Chimera System when the Kazh arrive than *three*, even if we are limited in our maneuverability."

She snorted.

"For that matter, Adamant's lack of numbers means she needs to stick closely to Wang's two capital ships and limits her to low levels of acceleration anyway. We're not giving up a maneuverability advantage we haven't been able to *use* yet."

The battle plan rattling around the back of her head didn't call for them to use it against the first attack, either. The dreadnoughts alone would be a shakeup for the Kazh. If Jane could keep the Kazh thinking that her ships lacked magical gravity that could counteract thrust for a while longer, she would.

So far, her enemy had stuck to the same handful of gravities of acceleration as the Republic warships had. That had removed maneuvers outside of jumping as a major component in the battle to date.

But it also meant that Second Fleet, capable of *fifteen* gravities of acceleration thanks to their magical protections, could potentially outmaneuver their enemies.

"This is extraordinarily... risky, sir," Soból finally said, the pause in the middle of her words suggesting that she'd stopped to self-censor something she couldn't really say about her superior officer.

"No, it isn't."

Both Jane and Soból looked at Giannino, who'd just finished running the math on his wrist-comp.

"Your numbers are too conservative, Admiral," he told her. "Give me twenty-four hours to reshuffle our tanker capacity in favor of antimatter over regular hydrogen, and I can all but guarantee that we will have enough fuel left to fight a battle when the logistics convoy arrives."

"Antimatter is only half of our fuel situation," Soból countered. "And the Chimerans' fuel-scooping and refining capacity isn't up to handling our needs for extended periods."

"No, but their military capacity was built around three capital ships and another two cruisers," Giannino pointed out. "Ships that haven't been drawing fuel for four weeks—and, in general, they have built up significant reserves as a strategic security.

"They wouldn't be able to provide fuel to keep our ships going indefinitely, but they can provide enough fuel to keep Second Fleet online for a week—probably two—while still maintaining a solid reserve for their own ships."

Giannino shook his head.

"I apologize, sir; I should have seen the opportunity myself. We were focused on the fact that we couldn't get the entire fleet and logistics line in place before the expected first attack and missed that we could utilize what we had to get the fleet in place before the *next* one."

"Especially since our expectations around the attacks have shifted," Jane murmured. "Soból, Giannino. Can we move out in time to accompany Evac Convoy Two tomorrow?"

Her Chief of Staff could clearly tell she'd been overridden and, wisely, kept her mouth shut.

"Not quite," Giannino said slowly. "But we could detach half a dozen cruisers and send them ahead with Evac Convoy Two and then have the rest of the fleet catch up after a day or so.

"We have more Mages than any of the transports. We can be in position to escort them for most of the journey."

"And if the Kazh show up sooner than we expect, we will be in place to give them a damn ugly surprise," Jane said. Her satisfaction was probably audible—though she was more relieved than she was prepared to admit that Giannino's numbers had agreed with hers.

That Chimera had already been attacked once while Second Fleet was a week's journey away grated on her. She had no intention of letting it happen again!

Even if she figured the risk was probably closer to Soból's assessment than Giannino's.

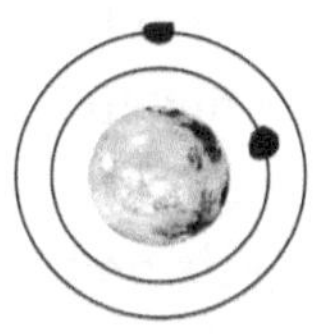

CHAPTER 20

ROSLYN STOOD IN HER OFFICE, WATCHING new icons flare into existence on a holographic display exactly on schedule. The hundred-plus starships of Evac Convoy One were on time and in formation, emerging two light-minutes from Garuda.

Four cruisers flanked the transports, their sensors sweeping the region of Chimera surrounding them without trust. The CSN cruiser *Antoinette* had moved up to secure the arrival point ahead of them, but the ex-Republican ship had been careful to keep the range long enough that she didn't pose an immediate threat.

Even scheduled and expected, no one wanted to risk friendly fire—and the value of the transports was so high at that moment that the escort could take almost no risks.

Acceleration numbers popped up on her display as the flotilla began to move. Many of the ships were civilian, limiting the cruisers and the troop transports to a mere gravity and a half—though even the *Bushidos* weren't capable of the fifteen gravities of RMN warships.

Twenty-seven and a half hours for them to reach Garudan orbit. Roughly the same for them to get from Garuda out to where they could safely jump. Civilian ships had basic jump matrices, runic constructs that could only amplify the standardized jump spell, and the troop transports' matrices weren't much better.

Without the unrestricted spell amplifier of a Martian warship, preferably backed by either a Promethean or a highly trained and experienced Navy Jump Mage, no one wanted to jump close to a planetary gravity well.

"Mage-Captain?" Baars' voice interrupted. "Secretary Karim is requesting a quick video meeting, if you have the time to spare?"

Baars knew, as well as Roslyn did, that she'd cleared the hours around Evac Convoy One's expected arrival. Even if everything went smoothly and according to plan, the next thirty-six hours or so were going to be full of demands on Roslyn's attention and time.

"Connect him, Chief," Roslyn said.

The map of the star system shrank into the background. A screen unfolded up from Roslyn's desk as she took her seat and Karim's weathered face appeared in front of her.

"Mage-Captain Chambers," he greeted her. "You know, I only just realized part of me didn't truly believe that the Evac Convoys were coming. Just a niggling doubt—one your people have laid to rest in style."

"We do what we can, Secretary Karim," Roslyn replied with a chuckle. "The first step is going to be getting our boots on the ground. That doesn't fall under the Commission's role, but I imagine the Eastern Minister's First Secretary has some idea how the planning for that is going?"

"The truth is that your landing force outnumbers the entire Republics of Chimera Army. Fortunately, we always planned for the potential of needing to dramatically upsize the army in a true emergency, so we have housing for roughly a million soldiers at bases across the planet."

He smiled.

"I understand that our officers are talking to your General McConnell to arrange appropriate quarters to start. I imagine that there will be entertaining plans for where those troops end up, given the nature of their role."

"Any underground bunkers or command centers you have will come in handy, I suspect," Roslyn agreed. "Though I believe McConnell has brought enough gear to build some of his own."

"We have started expanding some of our own concealed facilities as well," Karim agreed. "But speaking of command centers, I've imposed on Admiral Wang to allow several key Evacuation Commission members to be present in the Planetary Defense Command Center when Evac Convoy One arrives in orbit.

"I want to give my compatriots a sense of the size of the Protectorate's commitment to Chimera—and I would appreciate it if both you and Ambassador O'Hannagain were able to join us."

"I will have to check with Ambassador O'Hannagain for his schedule," she admitted, "but I am at your disposal for the next few days, Secretary. We need the loading to go as smoothly as possible."

"We are ready, Mage-Captain," Karim promised. "It will go smoothly."

She believed him. It was, after all, his people's lives on the line if it didn't.

Roslyn found Connor O'Hannagain standing at his window, staring out at the dome of the Last Ship. She figured he knew she was standing in the door, but she rapped on the frame regardless.

"Come in, Roslyn," he told her.

"Wanted to be sure. You looked lost in thought."

She crossed over to stand next to him, detouring for a moment to check her suspicion. The coffee on his desk was cold and forgotten, barely touched.

"Something's on your mind."

"Someones, mostly," he corrected. "About two billion of them. The people I don't see a way to save."

"I wasn't under the impression that miracles fell in the diplomatic toolkit," she reminded him. "More Mage-Admiral Alexander's, if anyone."

He snorted.

"I've heard rumors of what a member of the Royal Family can get up to. I believe they are powerful Magi, but *miracle* doesn't work for me."

Roslyn shivered at an old memory. Even with the Rune of Power inlaid into her forearm, there were distinct limits to her powers. One of the ones that was beaten into Navy Mages, especially, was that they couldn't reliably stop lasers. Missiles, bullets, even mass-driver slugs if they were desperate—anything physical could be stopped with solidified air or fields of energy.

Controlling or blocking energized photons was a lot harder. It was supposed to be impossible—but she'd watched Jane Alexander do just that when they'd escaped from Republican imprisonment together.

O'Hannagain caught her reaction and glanced over at her.

"You know something I don't, don't you?" he asked.

"I know a lot of things you don't, Ambassador," Roslyn told him archly. "Some things, though, even Mage-Captain Chambers doesn't know, if you catch my meaning."

He raised his eyebrows at her, then sighed.

"But Kiera Alexander's friend might?"

"She might know some things," Roslyn conceded. "But those aren't hers to share."

"I understand." He looked back at the radiation dome at the center of the city. "You know, part of me still finds it ridiculous that they built their entire city around a dome they *knew* contained an ongoing meltdown."

"The dome is solid enough to justify it," she told him. "Though I don't even begin to conceive of how they built a fission pile that is managing to *still* melt down after several centuries."

"One of your Navy engineers explained it to me. Or tried to," O'Hannagain admitted. "My eyes glazed over somewhere in the middle of *sequential fission chains*. Those being the only three words I remember from the lecture."

Roslyn had... some idea of what that might mean, but no idea of how it could be achieved. On the other hand, everything she'd seen suggested that the Reezh Ida had been astonishingly advanced in both technology and magic.

Fortunately, it didn't seem like the Kazh had advanced much on the Ida's technology in the years since the Burning.

"So, your mulling over *someones* is including staring at a nuclear reactor that hasn't quite managed to die in the lifetime of the Protectorate," she noted. "Anything productive coming out of the circle?"

"Mostly, I'm glad the question of making balanced deals is dead," he said grimly. "The only thing we want from Chimera is going on a ship tomorrow because *they* need it evacuated as much as we do.

"Not that Razhkah has decided if she's going to Mars or not yet. I think the old woman is intentionally fucking with me at this point."

"I saw Kiera's offer. She'll have the best researchers from two species to go through those archives, and if she's half the historian I think she is, the fact that they've never been able to properly analyze the Lachai's archives has to bother her."

"I hope so," he agreed. "These are damn fine people, Roslyn. If I could get my hands on Kent Riley..."

"You'd have to get in line," Roslyn said flatly. "And don't take this the wrong way, Connor, but you've never killed anyone. Most of the people who'd want to tear Kay—or Riley, or whatever we want to call him—to pieces *have*."

"Don't... take that into your soul if you can avoid it."

She blinked. She hadn't expected that particular tidbit to fall out of her mouth. Roslyn didn't really regard *killing people* as her job. It was just often an unfortunate necessity in her actual job, which was protecting people and civilization.

She didn't like that part of her career—but she had to admit that it didn't bother her as much as she sometimes thought it should, either.

"Somehow, a conversation that started with me lamenting that we weren't going to be able to save everyone got even more morbid," O'Hannagain said wryly. "What did you need, Roslyn?"

"The Evacuation Commission wants to make a big deal out of seeing Evac Convoy One arrive," she told him. "Karim, Shozha and presumably a couple of other members are going to be at the main Planetary Defense Command Center to watch the troop landings and the first shuttle flights back up. They asked you and me to be there."

"Huh." O'Hannagain turned away from the mound to study the city. "Media."

"Connor?"

"There will be media," he echoed, expanding on his single word. "I suspect the *couple of other members* will be either well known or simply photogenic. The Commission wants the entire star system to see what they're doing to save everyone—and that we are with them, working together as one."

"Which we are," Roslyn pointed out. His tone wasn't condemnatory, though he had caught an aspect of the situation she hadn't. "Is there any reason for us to decline the invitation?"

"No, quite the opposite," O'Hannagain said swiftly. "We have as much reason to make certain everyone knows we're working together as the Commission. I am... mostly making sure you realize what we're walking into.

"How familiar are you with media and news, Roslyn?"

"Connor... I was the commanding officer of a Royal Martian Navy warship through some of our ugliest incidents since the end of the Rebellion," she reminded him. "I was, for what I recognize as political reasons, made something of a darling child and mascot of the Navy *during* the Rebellion, as I managed to pick up my collection of Medals of Valor.

"I've dealt with enough media to be surprised they haven't managed to dig up things I don't want to talk about—a problem I'm reasonably sure I'm safe from here!"

No one in Chimera, after all, could access the detention records in Tau Ceti. Juvenile-detention records, like Roslyn's, were supposed to be sealed and inaccessible after a certain point, but that was always... more fluid than anyone would prefer.

"Forgive me, Roslyn, I tend to think of you as a military officer and forget some of the context," the Ambassador told her. "We should be fine."

Something in his tone suggested that he knew exactly what she'd been thinking—which was concerning in itself. Even the RMN seemed willing to forget that particular part of her pre-service history these days.

"I just wish I didn't *know* that everything we're doing isn't going to be enough," Roslyn admitted.

"Me too. At least the Crown Princess is on her way. That's going to be an ugly surprise for the Kazh when they come back."

"Three weeks, maximum," she said grimly. "Less, most likely. I'm expecting seventeen days. But I *think* that we'll have Second Fleet in place and Evac Convoy Two on their way by the time it happens."

"That's all we can hope for at this point, Roslyn," O'Hannagain reminded her. "Well, that and that the third wave is based on the reports from the first two. If they send a force that they know will overwhelm a pair of battleships, my understanding is that two *dreadnoughts* will be a very rude wake-up!"

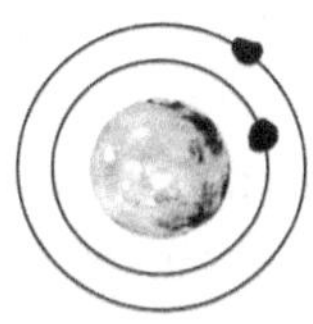

CHAPTER 21

DIPLOMACY LED TO SOME INTERESTING discussions and decisions over what to wear. Mage-Captain Chambers didn't need to worry about it as much as Connor did, he knew. Everyone on the planet knew her by face and reputation—they'd be more surprised on the occasions she showed up in civilian dress than her showing up in uniform.

Connor had brought a carefully designed selection of clothing in his limited luggage. By mixing and matching pieces, he could assemble a stylish outfit for any of the Protectorate's Core Worlds—and most of the other systems, too.

In his opinion, Garuda's current high fashion was based on telling the planet's ever-present wind to go to hell. He wasn't entirely sure how the locals wore the ankle-length toga-like wraps without either being carried away or losing the garments.

He'd still acquired several versions of it as well as a suit cut in the local style—a far broader opening at the shoulders than the current quite-tight Martian style—and had dressed in local fashion for several events.

Matching the people around him was a sign of respect that meant something, even if that meaning was sometimes registered more subconsciously than anything else.

For the show-and-tell around the arrival of the Evac Convoy, though, he needed to be very clearly Martian. His favorite suit came out: a tight-collared blazer in a red so dark it looked black in most lights. A dark-blue tie joined it, with a pin of the crowned-mountain Seal of the Protectorate to hold it in place.

He looked up as the door to his bedroom opened, surprised and about to snap at whoever dared intrude. He held his tongue when he saw it was his aide, Zahid Kootenay—who also wore the hat of a counterintelligence operative with the Martian Interstellar Security Service.

Kootenay was a spy, but he was a spy tasked with helping Connor, so he was an asset. At that moment, the chubby blond secretary was carrying what looked like a shopping bag.

"Ah, the mahogany suit. A good choice, sir," the other man told him. "You want to be as Martian as possible for this, of course. I have some items that could help with that."

"Of course you did," Connor said with a concealed sigh. "What did you have in mind?"

The first things out of Kootenay's bag were a pair of epaulets of a style that was bone-deep familiar to Connor. He hadn't worn them in years, but the angled fabric patches were part of the not-quite-uniform of a Member of the Dáil Taran, his home system of Tara's highest legislature.

Then, his epaulets had been marked with the tartan and crest of his district. This set were black, with green and gold leaves around a helm and a white banner with... two shamrocks, a rabbit and a red moon.

"What... no... that can't be..."

"The Sept O'hAnnagain family crest from Ireland, on old Earth," Kootenay told him, nailing the slightly more guttural tone of the original Irish versus Connor's smoother pronunciation of his family name. "I got the crest and the standards from a lovely lady in Ireland; though these copies were made up here in Twin Sphinxes. Hand-crafted by a reezh artist."

The secretary smiled as he attached the patches carefully to Connor's jacket. The pads on the underside were identical to the ones Connor had used as an MDT, able to latch themselves on to almost any fabric without damaging it.

"The local crafting seemed like it might help."

"That it might," Connor conceded. "As does the call back to home for me. Thank you."

"Not the only thing I spent your money on, sir," Kootenay told him. "Take off the jacket? I had the measurements, but I need to be sure on this."

Confused, Connor obeyed. He watched as Kootenay took a few strange-looking strips of fabric and wrapped them around his waist and up over his shoulders.

It wasn't until the secretary produced the holster and placed it at the small of his back that he realized what the man was putting on him.

"I'm not going to go armed to this stunt, Kootenay," he warned. "The biggest threat I'm expecting is awkward questions, not assassins."

"And you'll have Sarvesh with you, I know, but as this situation grows more critical, you need to get into the habit," his secretary insisted. The holster clipped on to the harness, and Kootenay stepped back.

"Can you reach that?" he asked.

Connor knew most people underestimated the speed and flexibility of large, muscular men. That was part of why he worked quite hard to maintain both. He tested and, yes, he was quite certain he could draw a firearm from the holster Kootenay had attached to him.

"I can reach it. And I will consider wearing a gun in the future, sure, but not for this. Not today."

"We don't know if the Kazh has agents on Garuda," Kootenay pointed out. "So far as we know, the original reezh church died out here before the human colonists ever arrived, but religions have a habit of surviving in quiet corners where no one expects them.

"The odds are low, yes, but it is possible that we could have a fifth column."

"And when we see evidence of that, I'll worry about it," Connor replied—though the scenario did give him some pause. "What is the holster sized for? Macy-Six?"

The Martian Armaments Caseless Six-Millimeter or MAC-6 was the standard sidearm of basically every Protectorate service he knew of. It was a weapon he was familiar with and knew to be reliable as anything.

"I have a Macy-Six holster, but that's not the one you're wearing," Kootenay told him. "That one is for that monster hand-cannon you had custom-smithed."

Connor blinked in surprise, then walked over to his luggage. The bottom of one of his cases had a locked section that required both a thumbprint and a code before it opened, revealing several individual sections.

Most of the ammunition for the two guns was kept in different suit-cases, though there was one filled magazine for the MAC-6 and one over-sized speedloader for the *monster hand-cannon*.

He left the speedloader in place as he put a second keycode in to un-lock the larger gun case. Connor was more concerned about the weapons being stolen than having to use them—as Roslyn had pointed out the previous evening, he'd never fired a weapon in earnest in his life—though there *was* a code that he could input on the top lock that would unlock the inner locks at the same time.

The monster in question was nestled into a custom-cut foam holder. On the surface, it was a revolver built to scale with Connor's own massive hands—though he knew perfectly well that a conventional revolver built to that size would break anyone's wrists.

There were subtle features built into the weapon to manage recoil, but part of what made it useable at all was that the rounds it was designed to fire were quite light. The cartridge was fifteen millimeters across, but the actual projectile was a third of that.

Custom-built to his hand, the revolver was one of the few—if not the only—sidearms chambered to fire the discarding-sabot tungsten pene-trators the Royal Martian Marines used to counter combat exosuits. The Protectorate Secret Service used a mind-bogglingly expensive but still mass-produced carbine to fire the same round, but that was the only pen-etrator-dart weapon that didn't count as a heavy weapon.

And then Connor had paid a truly ridiculous amount of money to a woman familiar with the PSS weapon to engineer all of its features into a revolver. It wasn't a weapon that could be concealed—its main covert nature was in misleading people as to its use, not in invisibility.

Except that Kootenay took the unloaded weapon from him and slid it into the holster he'd put on Connor. The weight shifted, Kootenay tight-ened a strap, and then it felt like it vanished.

"This wouldn't work if you were ten centimeters shorter or narrower across the shoulders," the spy noted. "But because you are almost as over-sized for a man as that thing is for a gun, yeah, we can make it vanish.

"Put the jacket back on."

Connor did, then inspected himself in the mirror. Even turning to the side, there was no hint in his profile that he was carrying a massive handgun.

"Huh. That's good to know and might be useful," he conceded. "For today, though, I'm not going to try to bring a firearm into the Chimera PCC. Anything else in that bag of yours?"

CHAPTER 22

THE TWO PROTECTORATE REPRESENTATIVES were led into the main space of the Planetary Defense Command Center by a pair of Wang's troopers. Technically just one regiment of the Republics of Chimera Army these days, they still wore a modified version of the uniform of the Republic Space Assault Force.

Connor had no real concerns with them, though he noted that Chambers watched them like she'd found out a friend's pet was a venomous spider. They were polite and courteous enough, even allowing Agent Ansel to keep his sidearm, but he understood that the uniform had memories attached to it for his companion.

He hadn't been a Republic prisoner of war. Chambers had.

"Not a bad setup," Chambers said as they stepped out into the tiered auditorium. "We're, what, a hundred and fifty meters below ground?"

"One hundred eighty," the familiar voice of Admiral Wang said behind them.

Connor turned and offered his hand to the Chimeran commander. Wang was one of the few people whose fingers didn't completely vanish in the Ambassador's grip.

"Most of the PDCC predates even my arrival," Wang continued as he traded salutes with Chambers. "We updated the software and replaced the sensors feeding this place, but a lot of the computer hardware was good enough that there was no point updating it."

A holographic globe of Garuda hung above the central pit at the bottom of the room. Seven circular terraces rose up from it, each five meters wide and hosting two circles of consoles and screens. Dozens of CSN and RCA officers and specialists were working away in the room, managing the dozens of day-to-day tasks required even without a threat of hostile invasion.

It was quite clear where they were supposed to be going. There was a broad set of stairs leading down to the hologlobe and a slightly more decorative section of carpet on the bottom of the terrace.

Karim and Shozha were already there, with Lieutenant General O'Neill and another Commission member whose name Connor didn't know—and four perfectly turned-out medias, two human and two reezh, with both shoulder-mounted and flying camera-drones buzzing around them.

"Well. Ambassador, Mage-Captain. The first transports have entered orbit and we're about to begin landing your Marines," Wang told them. "Shall we go talk to the world?"

"I am delighted you both could make it," Secretary Karim greeted Connor and Chambers as the two Martian representatives joined him next to the hologlobe. "Allow me to introduce Miss Ombeline Sydne Aukema and Mr. Nymphas Sadiqov. Miss Aukema is a host for the Meridian East Daily Update, our largest video news service, and Mr. Sadiqov is the lead reporter for the Republic Nexus, a news association providing source information for many smaller services."

Miss Aukema was a blonde woman who came up to about Connor's shoulder, carrying enough weight to draw the eye away from what Connor saw to be *very* sharp blue eyes that seemed to weigh and assess him and his companion very carefully.

Sadiqov, on the other hand, only came up to Connor's chest. The man was easily thirty centimeters shorter than the Ambassador—but almost as broad across the shoulders as the Taran man. There was muscle there, but the man was as broad front-to-back as he was side-to-side, with a brilliant grin and an aura of cheer that was hard to miss as he offered Chambers his hand.

"Mage-Captain, an absolute delight. Ambassador, an honor." He nodded to Connor as Aukema monopolized the Ambassador's hand.

The word *monopolized* had come without thinking as her handshake lasted slightly longer than was expected or appropriate. There was a twinkle in Aukema's eye as she saw him register her lingering, and a twitch of the eyebrow that might have been a wink.

"Please, Secretary, do not exclude our companions," she told Karim, her voice having the slightest touch of what Connor would have sworn was a French accent. "Ujan and Akuzh hold similar roles in Western Republic media as Mr. Sadiqov and I hold in the east.

"I'm afraid I can't pronounce the names of their services, but they have similarly expansive audiences."

Akuzh stepped forward, a reezh woman with an unusual reddish tone to her pebbled skin. She bowed slightly, looking at Connor over her armored frill with her upper eyes.

"Ijazheedan Kochak is not beyond Ombeline's voice at all," Akuzh said brightly. The reezh news host had less of the gravelly undertone Connor had grown to expect of reezh than he'd heard from any of them before. "The name translates as *News from the Sphinxes*, and I host our evening videos most days."

"Kochak Kochak is our equivalent to the Nexus," Ujan added. The male reezh media was short for his people, with pale gray skin of a smooth luster that seemed rare among the people. "And yes, the name means *News News*, if you were wondering."

"Media, Ambassador, officers," a uniformed member of the CSN called for their attention. "*Horatio*'s launches have begun. If you take a look at the globe"—the man gestured as he was sure he had everyone's attention, including the cameras—"you will see the icons marking the tracks of the shuttlecraft."

"So, Ambassador O'Hannagain, do you know what troops were aboard *Horatio*?" Aukema asked with a smile. "The Protectorate has sent a great deal of help our way, but those details haven't yet been shared."

"I'm afraid I haven't been keeping up with that level of detail," Connor replied with a matching smile. "Mage-Captain Chambers is my naval attaché and is far more up to date on such information. Mage-Captain?"

"*Horatio* is a combat transport of the Royal Martian Marine Corps," Chambers said instantly. "Her passengers for this voyage were the Eleventh Heavy Armor. I am not authorized to share where they are deploying, I have to admit, but they will be in place to help protect Chimera shortly."

Connor nodded his thanks to her. He presumed that the hologlobe footage was being blurred out in the final videos or something similar, as even he could work out that the group of transports was heading toward Twin Sphinxes.

"Only twenty-five of the transports are carrying troops," Connor told Aukema, fully aware of both the cameras now pointing at him and her twinkling eyes. "I believe, and Mage-Captain Chambers will correct me if I am wrong, that ten of the transports are carrying divisions of Royal Marines and the other fifteen are carrying units of the Protectorate Guard."

Which was about ten percent of the Guard and almost a quarter of the Marines. Even after the war, the Protectorate did not maintain massive forces of ground troops.

"Another ten ships are carrying gear that we are handing over to the Republics of Chimera Army," he continued. "The remaining thirty ships will also be launching shuttles within the next few minutes, but they are launching empty. All of the shuttles will be refueled on the surface and take on their first loads of evacuees—but that last group has no need to offload anything and is heading directly to the loading sites."

More tracks marking shuttle flights were appearing on the globe, and he realized that Aukema had managed to move herself to put the hologram behind him and Chambers. Ujan's drones were similarly aligned, though the other medias seemed to be content to let Aukema take the lead on the questions.

"How long do you expect all of this to take?" she asked. "Or is that a Mage-Captain Chambers question?"

"I would say it was a question for the Mage-Captain—or for Admiral Wang—except that I've asked the same thing more times than I can count," Connor told the reporters. "The timelines here are a focus of everyone's attention, Miss Aukema. Most of the ships in orbit are able to load immediately, a process that's going to take about sixteen hours. The transports that were carrying the Marines and Guard need to spend about twenty hours refitting their internal spaces.

"The sorts of voids and open holds necessary to transport aircraft and armored vehicles aren't very useful for carrying passengers. Materials are already being moved in as the troops land to refit those spaces to provide beds and facilities for the evacuation.

"All told, Evac Convoy One is expected to be on their way in about thirty-two hours, leaving the Chimera System twenty-two hours after that. They will have been in-system for about three and a half days and loaded almost nine million people."

"And how many of those people are human?" Akuzh asked. The red-tinged reezh reporter's tone was just as smooth and bright as it had been greeting them, even though her question was quite accusatory.

"That would be my question to answer, Akuzh," Karim interjected. "The loading plan for Evac Convoy One contains approximately four million four hundred thousand humans and four million three hundred thousand reezh.

"The lottery-allocated seats are evenly split, but the decision was made early on that priority would be given to the family members of the Chimera Space Navy and Republics of Chimera Armies personnel who will be evacuated last. Despite Admiral Wang's enthusiastic and determined recruitment efforts, the truth is that the CSN remains seventy percent human.

"The difference in Evac Convoy One's population distribution is entirely due to the preference for military families."

"A preference, of course, that we all see the logic behind," Sadiqov said quickly, the cheerfully tubby reporter heading off any argument. "Further seats will be selected purely on the lottery basis, yes?"

"Exactly, Mr. Sadiqov," Karim agreed. "And, as I understand it, further convoys will be larger?"

"That is correct," Connor said. "Evac Convoy Two has a large number of civilian transports whose crews have volunteered for this mission, accompanying heavy transports operated by Promethean volunteers from the former Republic.

"Several colony ships, designed to carry upwards of a million people under normal operation, will be joining Evac Convoy One before they return here. More ships will join each convoy as they become available."

He smiled for the cameras, knowing that he had the attention of millions across the planet.

"And I must reiterate the *volunteer* basis of many of those ships," he told the Chimerans. "Major colony corporations have agreed to delay their expeditions—their entire reason for *existing*—to place their ships at the disposal of the evacuation. Hundreds of starship owner-operators have volunteered to put their time and the ships that are their very livelihood at your service.

"The Mountain has mustered the official resources of the Protectorate for this evacuation, yes. My Queen, my government, our Navy—we have committed vast resources to both protect your world and to bring your people to safety.

"But hundreds of ships that will carry millions of people to safety are not coming because the Mage-Queen of Mars ordered them into motion," Connor said quietly. "They are coming because you are in danger. Because *people* are in danger—and so, they, people just like you, will take on personal and financial risk to help."

Those crews and owners and the companies behind them would be well compensated for their efforts, but Connor didn't need to mention that. Certainly, the people around him at that moment knew that—and they also knew, just as he did, that the money was irrelevant to the tens of thousands of spacers who had heard the call, finished their current jobs and set their course for a star system they'd never heard of.

"It is the Mountain and the Mage-Queen that have sworn to help you," he concluded. "But is the *people* of the Protectorate who are rallying to your side."

CHAPTER 23

"CAPTAIN CHAMBERS, A MOMENT OF YOUR TIME?"
The party, such as it was, had been slowly dissipating as the medias realized that there was only so much excitement to watching dots and tracks move across the holographic planet. There were, Roslyn knew, other reporters and camera people and hosts at many of the landing sites.

Especially at the loading sites for the evacuation, where Karim's people were organizing what she hoped were orderly lines of literally tens of thousands of people.

"Of course, Mr. Sadiqov," she told the reporter. She stepped aside from the structured chaos of the command center and gestured for him to follow her. "How can I help you?"

"The nature of my reporting versus Miss Aukema's is such that I like to provide more details on the people involved than her videos really have time for," Sadiqov told her. "I also have a few questions about the details of the evacuation, information to put alongside the pictures my colleagues are taking as we speak."

"Ask as you wish, Mr. Sadiqov," Roslyn instructed. "Even more so than Ambassador O'Hannagain, there are questions I can't answer due to military security concerns and, well, to make certain the evacuation ships and shuttles are as safe as possible."

"Of course, Captain. Or is it *Mage-Captain*, correctly? I'll admit the difference is confusing to those of us Chimerans who have long forgotten what little we learned of the Protectorate outside boring classes on what was basically ancient history," he said cheerfully.

"Either is correct," she assured him with a smile. She tapped the gold medallion at the hollow of her throat. "It's arguable, in fact, whether *Mage-Captain* is even a rank. Anyone wearing one of these medallions is a recognized Mage and deserves that title on a day-to-day basis. My military rank is Captain, but as I am supposed to also be addressed as Mage, the RMN simply merges the two titles in basically all contexts.

"Certainly, I am not offended by it being forgotten." She thought for a moment, then sighed. "I should note that there are almost certainly some Mage officers of Her Majesty's Navy or Marines who would be offended, but that is inevitable."

"There are always people who cling to every jot of supposed respect they can claim, I know," the reporter agreed. "You are obviously not one of them. I heard something about you also being a Marine?"

Roslyn chuckled.

"I hold the rank of Colonel in the Royal Martian Marine Corps," she conceded. "I tend to forget. It's an honorary rank whose main purpose is to grant me the second salary in recognition of acts of service."

"As opposed to the Medals of Valor, which are purely honorary, as I understand?" he asked, his eyes flickering to the sapphire pin on Roslyn's uniform jacket.

It was the only military decoration she ever wore, and it rendered any other ribbon or badge redundant. That tiny pin marked her as one of two living people in the Protectorate who had been awarded the Medal of Valor three times.

"It is... a bit painful to hear them described that way," she said slowly. There was a lot of blood and memory tied up in that tiny pin. "But fundamentally, yes. There is no cash award to go with a Medal of Valor. There is a significant pension adjustment for the first one, though."

"Not something high on your own list of priorities, I imagine, as the youngest full Mage-Captain in the RMN?"

"You know quite a bit about me, Mr. Sadiqov," she said calmly. "Are we still in background detail?"

"Mostly. I bounced across a few rumors, as I asked questions about the woman some say saved our planet and some say damned it," he told her, his voice level and nonjudgmental as he spoke. "The one I'm actually concerned about right now, though, is with regards to Mage-Admiral Alexander, the commander of the relief fleet.

"Is it true you served with her before?"

"I was Her Highness Crown Princess Mage-Admiral Jane Alexander's Flag Lieutenant for much of the UnArcana Rebellion, yes," Roslyn confirmed. "A glorified secretary, if you were wondering."

"Or, one might suggest, an understudy for her various staff officers and a very junior apprentice to the Admiral herself?" Sadiqov said lightly. He made a small tossing gesture. "Be that as it may, is it true that the Admiral has deployed her fleet and is on her way?"

Roslyn smiled.

"I can't answer that question, Mr. Sadiqov. The exact position of Second Fleet at this moment is classified as we move to make certain that Chimera is safe from the Kazh."

It *was* true, but the decision had been to keep that under wraps until Evac Convoy Two arrived with its "reinforced escort" in nine days.

"Of course. Thank you." Sadiqov glanced back toward the hologlobe for a few moments, then turned his attention back to Roslyn. "Can I ask about the *Bushido* transports and their shuttles, Captain?"

"Why, are you stalling for time, Mr. Sadiqov?" Roslyn asked, a moment of suspicion hitting her.

He grinned childishly.

"Not for any dark motives, but a little bit," he admitted. "I am, to borrow an ancient phrase, wingmanning for my counterpart."

Roslyn looked back toward the hologlobe and spotted that Ombeline Aukema had managed to inveigle O'Hannagain into helping her pack away her drones. The news host was, she judged, close to the Ambassador in age and seemed quite determined to keep his attention.

"I fear she may be too old for him," she told Sadiqov in mock concern.

"Wait," he said quickly, "is the Ambassador one of *those*? A... connoisseur of younger women?"

Roslyn laughed aloud at the reporter's face, but also moved quickly to correct any misconceptions her joke had created.

"No, I don't think," she told him. "I honestly have no idea of Connor O'Hannagain's personal relationships or interests in that area. I barely know what the man's hobbies are. We're colleagues—technically, he's my boss."

Sadiqov chuckled and his shoulders relaxed.

"That is fair. Forgive me; Aukema may be a solidly capable woman but she was basically a mascot to the Nexus newsroom when she first started out, and part of me still sees her as the team little sister!"

"I understand how that goes," Roslyn conceded. "And since my boss still seems occupied, what was your question about the transports?"

It took O'Hannagain almost fifteen full minutes to help the reporter pack up her drones and finally join Roslyn at the exit from the command center. Fifteen minutes in which she'd explained more about the *Bushido*-class transports and their associated assault shuttles and specialized dropships—designed to deliver a full battalion of tanks or infantry in a single drop—than she'd realized she'd known.

"I apologize for occupying so much of your time," Sadiqov told Roslyn as the Ambassador approached. "I will leave you to your no-doubt-busy day."

"Thank you, Mr. Sadiqov. I hope my answers have been of some use to you," she replied to a grin and a wink from the reporter. He might have been keeping her occupied while his friend made a pass at O'Hannagain, but he'd also made good use of his time.

She suspected the articles coming from the Republic Nexus were going to be more accurate than many she'd seen over the years, both because she had a sense of the man's integrity *and* the depth of the answers she'd provided.

"I see I am at least not holding us up," O'Hannagain murmured as the reporter moved away. There was no hint of irony in his tone, but Roslyn picked it up anyway.

"I take it you have a private interview with Miss Aukema later?" she asked, her tone equally lacking in implications.

He didn't quite blush as they stepped out into the corridors of the underground base, but his cheeks definitely gained a touch of color his fair Taran coloring made very clear.

"A dinner scheduled, at least," he conceded. "We shall see what the media thinks she can get out of me in a more-private setting, of course. A woman like Aukema is... unlikely to do anything without multiple motives."

"A diplomat would know," Roslyn agreed. Their security detail formed around them as they followed the signs toward the elevator. She was surprised to see that the Chimerans weren't insisting on escorting them, a sign of trust she wasn't sure *she'd* have extended in their place.

"I doubt her interest is entirely professional *or* personal, just as mine is neither one nor the other," O'Hannagain noted. "She is attractive enough, but it is also strongly to our benefit to forge warm relationships with the Chimeran media. I've been working on it, but this is an opening I can't pass up."

Roslyn almost missed a step at the sheer level of double entendre in his last sentence—and now he *actually* blushed as he realized what had come out of his mouth.

"Damn. Professional diplomat and negotiator, with years of training to make certain I say the right thing, and phrases like that *still* come out of my mouth."

"We all have our lapses in our professional skills," she told him with a chuckle. "There's a reason that no Mage jumps without someone else checking their math. Well. If we have a choice."

Roslyn had definitely made jumps without having someone double-check her math. She'd made jumps without doing math *at all*, but those had been under... extreme duress.

The elevator doors closed behind their party, and O'Hannagain shook his head at her.

"I'd assign you a punishment duty for that, Captain Attaché, but I just made you talk to the media. How was your impromptu interview with Mr. Sadiqov?"

"Warm, if not as warm as your chat with Aukema," she replied. "I think we made the right impression here today."

"A hundred-plus starships arriving to evacuate from the enemy they know is coming won't hurt there." He sighed. "I just wish we could conjure a hundred-plus *warships* to make sure they didn't have to run."

CHAPTER 24

DEEP SPACE BOTHERED A LOT OF PEOPLE, Jane Alexander knew. She wasn't one of them, but she could at least see the reasoning. Second Fleet and Evac Convoy Two hung in the void, counting out the two hours and forty minutes between scheduled jumps.

She had the wallscreens of her office turned to show the space surrounding *Mjolnir*—similarly to the simulacrum chamber that allowed the big ship to jump, though unlike the simulacrum chamber, these weren't fiberoptic links to the outer hull.

Even Jane couldn't do magic from these screens. Somehow, her magic knew that *this* was a reproduction and that the fiberoptics in the simulacrum were the "real" light from outside the dreadnought.

That was a reality Mages were long used to, though no student of magic had ever worked out *why* it mattered.

But the screens let her track the fleet around her. Fifty-eight other warships held formation around *Mjolnir* and the convoy, the stars of their running lights forming a constellation of ordered lights.

If Second Fleet was a constellation, Evac Convoy Two was a *galaxy*. Two hundred and fifty ships gleamed in the night, orbiting the three colony ships—the only vessels large enough to have a clear shape to her eyes at this distance.

The Royal Martian Navy owed the big colonizers a debt Jane suspected few realized. The Protectorate had settled on its immense battleships long before, tens of millions of tons of metal and magic, but the size increase of those mighty warships had been incremental, a million or two tons in a generation of ships.

It had been the colony corporations, looking to maximize the amount of cargo and people they could move with a limited number of Mages, who had pushed the scale of ships past that. The three Derry Corporation colonizers lacked *Mjolnir*'s density and total mass, but their dimensions dwarfed her.

The dreadnought was a full kilometer long, a pyramid four hundred meters across at its base that rose eight hundred to its square peak, still a hundred meters wide. That peak was surmounted by a hammerhead holding her heaviest weapons, itself half a kilometer wide and two hundred meters across.

The colony ships were cylindrical hulls fifteen hundred meters long and five hundred wide. At a *mere* eighty million tons, they were theoretically light enough to float if they landed on a planet.

Of course, a colony ship would only land once, on its final voyage. The Derry ships were probably two or more decades away from their turn as the central fixture of a new world. Older ships would serve that role for Derry itself, with the big new vessels being sold back to the company that managed them.

On this journey, none of the hundreds of ships in Jane's viewscreens would land. Shuttles would—in untold thousands, the vast numbers necessary to bring millions of innocents from the surface to their chance of safety.

"Sir."

The single word announced that she wasn't alone in her office anymore, and the Admiral turned to see Commodore Soból standing in the open door.

"Commodore. What do you need?" she asked.

"Commodore Okorie has confirmed. Evac Convoy Two is clear to jump in fifteen minutes. I've taken the liberty of advising Second Fleet to jump on the same timeline."

"A good call; thank you," Jane said. At least Soból was learning. The woman wasn't quite where Jane wanted her to be yet, but that would take time.

"Take a seat, Peta," she continued, gesturing the other woman to a chair.

Her Chief of Staff obeyed, perching on the edge of the seat and waiting in silence.

"You didn't just wander in here to tell me about the jump," Jane pointed out. "We're still a full day from Chimera, and while we're being cautious, I don't expect a Kazh intercept."

"I was wrong, sir," Soból said quietly. "To argue against coming in early. I've gone over the timeline with the Operations team, and the dates are looking... ugly. The logistics ships are no faster than Evac Convoy Two. If we'd waited for them, there was a sixty percent chance the next Kazh attack would arrive before we got there."

"I judged it fifty-fifty myself," Jane admitted. "And you were *not* wrong to argue. Even if, with more information, it is clear that your position was less defensible than you thought, it is your job to argue with me. To be the point of view I missed."

"Yes, sir."

That was as much as she was going to get out of Peta Soból on that point, and Jane swallowed her retort.

"The Ops team," she said instead. "How are they working up?"

"I'm not able to devote as much attention to them as I expected," Soból admitted. "They seem solid, but none of them seem quite... willing to act as an informal leader, I suppose.

"When we didn't receive an Operations Officer in time, I believed I would be able to step in and fill the gap. I've tried, but I can tell that the team is suffering for not having a clear leader. The personalities are just a touch too strong for them to find alignment on their own."

She shook her head.

"We need an Ops Officer, sir," she concluded. "The only suggestion I have would be to promote one of the Commanders heading up the shifts, but..."

Jane waited for Soból to finish her thought after trailing off, then considered what the Commodore had already said, and sighed.

"Those personalities you mentioned. Out of three Commanders in the Ops team, I'm guessing none of them would really accept one of the other two being put in charge over them?"

"They're professionals and I think they'd sort it out," Soból hedged. "But it would take time and might cost even more efficiency. And this fleet is almost certainly going into battle in the next ten days."

"So, you have a problem but no solution," Jane noted. "And, like any good officer, you hate coming to your boss without a solution."

"I should have been able to spend more time managing that team, sir. I feel I've failed both you and them by not having an answer. The team is functional but not as efficient as I know those officers and analysts can be."

That was Jane's fault. Not because she'd trusted Soból to manage the team—the situation she'd created had left that the only possible solution, weak as it had been—but because Operations was one of the most critical roles on her team and she'd held her ground to get an officer of her choice in the role.

Instead, she'd ended up with nobody.

"That responsibility is not yours, Peta," she told her Chief of Staff gently. Soból knew as well as Jane why they didn't have an Ops Officer. "And while the end result is going to be close to what I wanted, I recognize that both you and the Operations team have suffered for my stubbornness."

"What you wanted, sir?" Soból asked.

"Get the orders drafted before we hit Chimera. We'll be stealing Mage-Captain Chambers from her diplomatic role." Jane shook her head. "I wanted Mage-Commodore Kulkarni, but apparently, she's Mage–*Vice Admiral* as of a month ago and will be watching our back against the entire coreward frontier."

Indrajit Kulkarni had been her Operations Officer through the war. Like many of her other officers, that had boosted Kulkarni's career to new heights. But while Kulkarni been Jane's Ops Officer, Roslyn Chambers had been Flag Lieutenant and Kulkarni's apprentice.

"Chambers knows how I think, and her career since working under me shows she has the spine and the steel to do the job," Jane noted. "I was planning to leave her in her attaché role for a bit—it will look good when she faces her Commodore board in a few years—but the needs of the service demand."

Soból looked thoughtful.

"She is young," the Commodore pointed out. "That may give her trouble with her new subordinates. I think she's *younger* than two of them, though I'd have to check."

"If Roslyn Chambers hadn't learned to deal with that particular variety of foolishness by now, I suspect a lot more people who served under her would be dead," Jane replied. "She'll do. And anyone who gives her flak will discover just *why* that young woman has three Medals of Valor."

One earned saving Jane Alexander's life.

CHAPTER 25

ROSLYN WAS UP LATE, digging through the last datawork round with the Evacuation Commission before Evac Convoy Two arrived, when O'Hannagain drifted into the not-quite-mansion that was serving as the Embassy Residence.

Among her hats was security for the Embassy, so she had the camera feeds running on one screen in her office—not least because the Ambassador had been out late for his "private interview" with the redoubtable Miss Aukema.

There was a certain degree of flush to the big man's coloring in the camera that suggested he'd had a very good night—as if the fact that he was returning to the Residence six hours after his dinner had ended wasn't proof of that.

She was surprised, though, to see him detour when he spotted the light in her suite. She had enough warning that she could have shut down the security feed if she hadn't wanted him to know she'd been watching.

He knocked.

"It's unlocked," she told him. "I saw you through the cameras."

If O'Hannagain didn't think she was watching the security cameras on both the Embassy buildings, he didn't know her as well as she thought he did.

"Good evening, Captain," he greeted her. There was a slight lilt to his voice, a native Taran accent he didn't normally show.

"I take it your private interview went well?" she asked.

"A gentleman does not kiss and tell, though I can make no promises about medias," he said with a chuckle. He pulled a chair over to him and took a seat.

The suites in the house were split into three spaces: a bedroom, a front sitting-area-slash-office, and a luxurious en-suite bathroom. All three were floored in stone tile with solid plaster walls painted a matching pale tone.

The furniture was wooden, and the chair O'Hannagain had grabbed was probably older than the two of them combined. There were trees on Garuda, she knew, but they were few and far between around Twin Sphinxes. The only wood she'd seen in the capital was used for furniture, and someone had applied a phenomenal amount of care and skill to the chairs, especially, in the Embassy Residence.

"You're not here to brag, so what are you after, boss?"

He blinked at the address, then shrugged.

"You know, you and Sarvesh are the closest thing I have to friends on this planet," he murmured. "Tonight was a pleasant arrangement, but part of the entertainment of time with someone like Miss Ombeline Aukema is, well, the game itself.

"We both want something more than just the obvious. There ends up being more than one negotiation going on at the same time."

"And did you get what you wanted out of the evening?" Roslyn asked archly.

He laughed.

"Maybe. As much as anything, I hope that I managed to defuse Ombeline's main ask without burning goodwill we're going to need with the media going forward."

"From the sounds of it, there was still some *goodwill* left afterward," she reminded him.

His face and tone were serious now, and she realized he was both more serious and less drunk than she'd realized.

"She wanted me to move her little sister and said sister's family to the top of the queue to get off-world," he said quietly. "I told her that I have no control over that—that we and the Commission have explicitly set it up so *no one* has any direct control over it.

"I'm not sure she believed me. I think she's hoping I may still find a way, but..." He shook his head. "I understand where she's coming from, but that was a decision for the Chimerans to make. I suppose I could put the family on the military ship that's supposed to be taking *Thorn*'s crew home in a few days, but that would be abusing a lot of things."

Roslyn had left taking care of that in Commander Beck's capable hands. Some of *Thorn*'s people were remaining behind to keep doing the shore establishment roles they'd taken on, but it had been made clear that Second Fleet was bringing their own logistics people to take that over.

The RMN needed experienced cruiser crew, well, crewing cruisers. *Thorn* wasn't going to be fighting anytime soon, so there was both a moral and a practical reason to want to bring her crew back to the Protectorate, where they could be assessed by counselors and sent to new cruisers as they came online.

"The last I checked, the plan was to load the remaining wounded and shipless onto another of the *Cataphract*-class destroyers and send them home once Second Fleet arrived," Roslyn said carefully. "If all of the shipless were going home, there wouldn't be enough space for *us*, let alone passengers. That said, enough of us volunteered to remain that there might *be* a half dozen bunks to spare."

The big man leaned on the arm of his chair and looked down at his knuckles.

"I'm not sure if says good or bad things about me that I'm barely tempted," he told her. "I'm reasonably sure Ombeline knew it was a long shot, but I do worry that pissing her off could lead to problems down the line.

"A media of her presence is an asset—to us, but also to the people who might try to impede us."

"I haven't seen much of that," she noted. "Though I imagine the Evacuation Commission is getting some flak."

"Ask Karim if you want to know; I'm *aware* of it but not really a target of that," O'Hannagain said firmly. "There is definitely a faction—both grassroots and members of the Dual Legislatures—that blames us for the situation. We're doing a lot, which helps, but they think we should be doing more."

"We're doing what we can. We probably *should* be doing more, but we don't have the ships," Roslyn said. "What do they *want*?"

"For us to save them from the problem we created without actually inconveniencing them in any way," he explained. "There will always be people who will see any inconvenience or interruption in their lives as a conspiracy against them, and, frankly, the kind of evacuation we're arranging isn't a small interruption.

"But, as you say, we're doing everything we can. We got the Lachai and her people and the archives out. We got the CSN's and RCA's families out. What else can we do?"

"If I knew an answer to that question, Connor, we'd be doing it," Roslyn said.

"Same." He sighed. "Need anything from me, Roslyn? You look like your computer is going to eat you."

"Nothing you can help with," she replied. "Just finalizing the numbers on Evac Convoy Two. A few of the civilian crews have rearranged things and think they can cram in another few hundred souls."

"That's good. What does that get us to?"

"Twenty-four million, six ninety-seven thousand, five hundred thirty," she told him. "Minimal refit work on the ships coming in this time, but loading will take longer than it did for Convoy One. Twenty-five million people versus nine."

"The numbers barely make sense. Until you compare them to how many people we need to get out and you realize they're nothing," he said heavily.

"And that, Connor, is the other reason I can't sleep."

CHAPTER 26

"**WELCOME BACK** to the Command Center, Ambassador, Mage-Captain."

"Colonel Razhko." Connor let Chambers return the Republics of Chimera officer's salute—odd as it looked on a reezh, where they saluted to the top of their frill rather than the hat no reezh wore—and responded with a simple nod.

"There is no media today," the reezh officer noted. "I have you on my schedule, but the landing isn't for another day and a half, correct?"

"That's correct," Connor agreed, letting Razhko guide them back down toward the central floor. There was no official gathering at the Planetary Defense Command Center for this, because no one had admitted to the media or the public that anything outside of the original plan was happening.

Everyone knew that Evac Convoy Two was due in the next hour or so. But only the most-trusted people in the military and government knew that Second Fleet was expected to arrive ahead of them.

"Ambassador, Mage-Captain," Wang greeted them. The lack of *official* gathering meant that the CSN's commander was wearing his day-to-day uniform. Connor didn't know for certain, but he suspected that Admiral Wang spent much of his time on Garuda inside this room.

The Chimeran fleet could be commanded from any of its capital ships, but the places on the surface that could provide command and control across a star system were fewer.

But while Wang was almost certainly a regular attendee in the Planetary Defense Command Center, Connor was quite certain that the Dyad Ministers weren't. Ojak and Hsieh stood next to the Admiral, both studying the holographic display. They had an unusual paucity of aides with them, but it was clear that they, like Connor, were there to see Mars's promise kept.

"I do have some news for you, Admiral," Connor told Wang as he stepped up to join the Chimeran officer. "We confirmed the arrival of *Nikephoros* in the Solar System a few hours ago. The volunteers are cross-shipping to the invasion transport *Az-Zahir*, and the civilian Prometheans are due to arrive at Phobos by midnight Twin Sphinxes time.

"You can communicate with any of them whenever you want," he concluded. "I hope that is a promise you will consider fulfilled."

"You and your Mage-Queen have made many promises, Ambassador O'Hannagain," Hsieh Ai Ling said, stepping up next to Wang. She was ever so slightly closer to the Admiral than was appropriate, but that was normal for them.

Connor had to wonder if the situation between the two Chimerans was as obvious to them as it had to be to everyone around them. He supposed there were reasons the military leader of the Republics and one of its two civilian executives couldn't act on the feelings between them, but *damn*, was it painful to watch.

"We have made all of them in the fullest of faith and intention, Minister Hsieh," he told her. "The evacuation of innocents has begun. The Prometheans are now on Phobos with their cousins. *Shirkuh* will reach Mackenzie roughly a day after Evac Convoy One, and will be with them when they return here. *Az-Zahir* will take more time. She should arrive in Mackenzie shortly after Evac Convoy Two leaves to return to Chimera— the plan is for her to wait there to join Evac Convoy One for their third voyage."

"All of which expects we shall have the time for these evacuations," Ojak said, their stony tone clear as to their fears.

"Contacts!" one of the analysts barked. "Multiple contacts at one light-minute!"

New icons blazed into existence on the hologram, ship after ship emerging from their last teleport far closer than the civilian fleet behind them would mirror.

"And there is the promise we made that will buy that time, Minister Ojak," O'Hannagain replied as new data filled out on the globe.

"What even *are* those?" Ojak asked, staring at two icons that blazed like miniature green suns above them.

"I've seen them once before, but they weren't friendlies then," Emerson Wang said. "Those two are dreadnoughts, Minister Ojak. The mightiest vessels humanity has ever built.

"Vessels even the Kazh should fear."

The Planetary Defense Command Center was home to one of the handful of Link FTL communicators the Protectorate had provided the Chimerans, allowing the unofficial but quite real gathering of the Dual Republics' leaders to take over a conference room and connect with *Mjolnir* and *Righteous Guardian*.

As the holographic conferencing system came online, Connor noted as fact something that he'd suspected since watching the hologlobe in the main space for the first time: Chimeran holographic technology was probably better than Protectorate.

It wasn't an immense difference, a matter of sharper resolutions and a better level of intentional translucency, but it resulted in the images of Jane Alexander and Janet Adamant being both more true to life and more obviously transmissions.

The choice on the translucency was interesting, but Connor also knew that Protectorate holoprojectors *couldn't* manage light pass-through with sufficient accuracy to pull off the holograms he was greeting.

The tech should have been on the list of possible trade goods when he'd been sorting out just what Chimera had to offer the Protectorate, before the question had become moot. It wouldn't have been enough on its own, but it was a reminder that not everything the system had to offer was obvious.

"Vice Admiral Adamant, Admiral Wang, Minister Hsieh, Minister Ojak, Ambassador O'Hannagain," Alexander reeled off her greetings with the smooth practice of a lifelong politician and commander. "Captain Chambers. Good to see you all."

Connor inclined his head to the Mage-Admiral. Martian protocol didn't call for great signs of deference or delegation to the Mage-Queen, let alone the primary heir, but respect was owed.

"We are delighted to welcome you to the Chimera System," Hsieh told Alexander. "We appreciated the urgency of your arrival."

"My staff have been discussing your supply needs with your people since you left," Wang noted. "As I'm sure they briefed you, we can't sustain Second Fleet indefinitely. However." He glanced over at his two politicians.

Connor spotted the infinitesimal nod Hsieh gave him. Whatever sign Ojak gave was beyond his ability to read reezh body language, but Wang clearly got the go-ahead he was looking for.

"However," he repeated. "We're not fools and we're well aware that you have detected the accelerator ring at Ifrit. So long as it was offline, we didn't see any real reason to mention it. My impression is that the technical schematics in my possession are equal or superior to any the Protectorate would possess for the accelerator in Legatus. There was little assistance we needed or that Mars could provide."

"You might have been surprised," Alexander told him with a chuckle. "But deploying such assistance would have been difficult. Since you are mentioning it now, though..."

"Preliminary pulse runs were executed last night," Wang informed them. "We knew we would have the ring online soon, which was why we had missile-production lines ready to go—the lines your people have been providing antimatter for us to operate.

"While we won't reach anything resembling full production on the Ifrit Accelerator for weeks, I am informed that we are expected to produce one hundred kilograms of antimatter today. One thousand tomorrow. Scaling will slow from there, but our missile-production lines have been running at four hundred missiles per day.

"Thanks to Vice Admiral Adamant's Mages, we have sufficient munitions for a full combat load for the entire Chimera Space Navy. Until the logistics line for Second Fleet arrives, I am prepared to place the full output of the Ifrit Accelerator at your disposal," he concluded.

Connor was only vaguely aware of how much antimatter was needed to operate a warship, only that *outside* of the context of warships, a full ton of antimatter was considered an absolutely mind-boggling amount.

"That will help," Alexander confirmed. "What limited logistics we do have are capable of making the in-system jump to load up at Ifrit without requiring intrasystem travel.

"Is there a plan for if Chimera falls?"

If. That was being diplomatic, and the diplomat in the room knew it. Everyone there was planning around the assumption that Chimera *would* fall. Even with Second Fleet in the system, all the Kazh had to do was move one of the *several* massive fleet groups Roslyn's scouting run had spotted in the Nine to crush them under sheer weight of metal and numbers.

"Charges have been placed throughout the structure," Ojak said grimly. "There was discussion about attempting to use its destruction as a weapon, but I believe the conclusion was that it was too risky for whoever remained behind."

"More than risky," Wang explained. "A crew would have to remain on the ring until the last moment to make certain the antimatter beam was on target. It would be a one-shot weapon—one that would require several dozen people at least. None of whom would survive."

"We shall use it as long as we can for its designed purpose," Alexander assured them. "I will not ask anyone to take on a suicide mission."

Not given a choice, anyway. Connor knew that much. Chambers's own recent activities spoke to that. The RMN cruisers had jumped into close range of the Kazh fleet to use their amplifiers to save the surviving heavy units of the main fleet.

That any of the cruisers had survived had been a miracle, from what he'd seen. That had been a suicide action, one the Captains had taken on without consulting their crews.

The Navy wouldn't send people on suicide missions *lightly.*

"In any case, that the Ifrit Accelerator is online should ease our logistics concerns until my logistics flotilla arrives," Alexander agreed. "Admiral Wang, you and I will need to sit down in person once *Mjolnir* reaches orbit. Would you prefer aboard *Chimera* or on the surface?"

"*Chimera* will work perfectly, Mage-Admiral," Wang told her.

Connor was starting to feel redundant. Alexander was quite capable of handling the diplomatic part of her job, at least, without his help.

"Ambassador." She turned her attention to him even as he was considering his presence in the meeting unnecessary. "You and I will also need to meet. Would it be possible for you to come aboard *Mjolnir*?"

"Of course, Mage-Admiral," Connor agreed. "I should be able to maintain communications from the shuttle. Few of my appointments need to be in person, though it is important that I remain on the surface overall.

"Mage-Captain Chambers"—he nodded to the young woman—"has been serving as my attaché and will be able to handle anything on the surface that requires a face-to-face meeting."

"Mage-Captain Chambers will need to come up to *Mjolnir* with you," Alexander said. "Do you have a civilian second? I am realizing I'm not aware of any augmentation to your staff since your arrival."

"I have handled multisystem, multitrillion deals with the staff I have here on Chimera, Mage-Admiral," Connor pointed out. "I believe I can handle matters here, though Mage-Captain Chambers' military knowledge has been of immense value."

He knew that the young woman would likely be surprised by just how profusive his praise was. Given the chance, she'd claim she was just doing her job—and she might have been, but no one had *done* that job for a long time.

"Mage-Captain Chambers' actions in this system have been in the highest traditions of the Royal Martian Navy," Alexander said, presumably in acknowledgement of his words.

"In any case, it is still some hours before *Mjolnir* makes orbit. Four of my cruisers remained with Evac Convoy Two, and I am deploying four more to sweep their expected route.

"It is not necessary, Admiral Wang," she noted, before the local commander said a word, "but since we now *have* the ships to spare for extreme paranoia, I am inclined to indulge said paranoia with regard to the evacuation flotillas."

"I have grown quite used to the constricted resources of the Chimera Space Navy, Mage-Admiral," Wang said after a moment. "The RMN additions to date have been helpful but not the kind of fundamental shift that the presence of Second Fleet entails. It will take some getting used to."

"We will sort out how to deploy those resources together, Admiral," she promised. "I have two final details to take care of.

"Firstly, Vice Admiral Adamant?"

"Sir." Jane Adamant's holographic image straightened to formal attention. She knew what was coming, even if Connor could only guess.

"You've done a fine job, more than we expected to need and beyond what we dared hope. More formal markers will follow, I'm sure, but know that you have the thanks of the Mountain.

"I relieve you as Commander, Chimera Station."

"I stand relieved, Mage-Admiral. I have only done my job," Adamant noted.

"You, Janet Adamant, have not spent *nearly* enough time around Damien Montgomery for that kind of self-effacing bullshit," the Mage-Admiral said drily. "We both know no one expected the Kazh to return until around *now*, not over two weeks ago."

Connor hadn't met Damien Montgomery, the Prince-Chancellor of Mars, the head of the Protectorate's day-to-day government, in person. Formerly Kiera's Prince-Regent and, before *that*, First Hand to Mage-King Desmond Alexander the Third, the man had a well-known reputation for not quite being convinced he was actually *important*.

Even after being formally adopted into the Royal Family. Connor wasn't certain exactly how said adoption worked in terms of who his "adoptive parent" was, but there was no question that Damien Montgomery was second in line for the throne in the Mountain.

After Jane Alexander herself.

"And my last point is going to give my poor Ambassador a headache," the Admiral continued. "Mage-Captain Chambers."

"Sir."

"You and I will need to select your replacement as naval attaché to the Chimeran Embassy carefully, but you are being transferred to my staff," Alexander said firmly. "The myriad confusions of the Navy have left me without an Operations Officer. Given your experience on my staff in the Rebellion, you'll be an excellent fit."

Connor couldn't say he was surprised. Disappointed—Chambers had been just as useful as he'd told the Mage-Admiral—but not really surprised. He'd known his attaché had served Alexander directly before, and he'd more than half-expected her to get scooped up.

"On one condition, sir," Chambers said, to the Ambassador's surprise. And, from the impression he got of the room, everyone else's, too.

"Officers generally don't place conditions on arguable promotions, Captain," Alexander said—but her strict words were undermined by the amusement in her tone. "But I know you, so you may as well spit it out."

"I need to remain the Protectorate's representative on the Chimeran Evacuation Commission," Chambers said levelly. "That is... not a job I feel I can leave half-done."

Given the expressions on the two locals whose faces Connor could read, Chambers had once again arranged a healthy deposit into the account of mutual respect that made Connor's job possible.

CHAPTER 27

THE GARUDAN WIND WHIPPED across the landing pad, making even the usually dangerous heat of a just-landing shuttle a welcome break—from a safe distance, at least.

"I could get used to this place," Matthias Beck said with a chuckle, the Commander half-shouting to be heard over the wind. "Any idea why I'm being pulled upstairs?"

"Nope," Roslyn lied. As Beck's most recent commanding officer, she'd been asked to sign off on the datawork for his promotion as a courtesy. A Mage-Admiral didn't *need* a mere Captain's signature to promote anyone, but Roslyn's mark on the files meant that there was no question as to why Beck had been promoted.

Courage under fire and *stepping outside of standard duties in the service of Mars* were at the top of the list of reasons. It was an off-cycle promotion on merit, one that required a board of senior officers to confirm.

A Mage-Admiral, two Vice Admirals, and Beck's most recent commanding officer counted. He'd get his new insignia on *Mjolnir*, and Roslyn wasn't spoiling the surprise.

"The light is green. That means it's safe to board, right?" O'Hannagain asked.

There was no way the Ambassador was that oblivious to shuttlecraft safety standards. He'd been bouncing between worlds for years. Which meant that he was covering what he knew was a lie on Roslyn's part.

Roslyn knew both that O'Hannagain could read people well and that she couldn't lie for shit most of the time. She could mask her emotions behind a shield of command, but that was a different story entirely.

"It does. Let's go," she told her two companions.

The Admiral had sent a fully armored assault shuttle for them. Exo-suited Marines had stepped out onto the pad while it was still superheated—the ability to do so was the original main purpose of the big suits of powered armor—and now moved out to flank them, coordinating with the Secret Service and Marines seeing the Ambassador and two officers to the shuttle.

A small cluster of NCOs followed a few steps behind, led by Baars and Kovalyow. A trio of enlisted spacers were handling the luggage for the three people expecting to stay on *Mjolnir*, and Roslyn found herself concealing a mix of amusement and bemusement at the fact that she now went everywhere with an entourage.

"Our flight path is clear all the way to the flagship," the copilot announced as the shuttle's Chief helped them get everything seated and locked away. "We have the screens on. I know Mage-Captain Chambers has seen dreadnoughts up close, but I figured the rest of you would want the view."

"Like you wouldn't believe," Beck agreed brightly. "There's pyramids and there's *pyramids*, right?"

The young Lieutenant chuckled and gave them a thumbs-up.

"Only thing even close to it is the colony ships," he agreed. "And those are still a good day out."

Roslyn wasn't as familiar with *Mjolnir* as some of her sisters. *Durendal* had been Alexander's flagship during the Rebellions, but that ship was currently in the Tau Ceti Naval Yards, being refitted.

Mjolnir, according to the notes she'd reviewed since being advised of her new job, had already undergone the refit to the 66 Standard. A lot of the work on the dreadnoughts had been superficial—none of the ships were more than ten years old, after all—but just cleaning out the ships' atmosphere and restarting everything was needed every few years.

The weapons fit was still the same across the class. Mass, engines, all of that was identical to what she remembered. The notes suggested the interior would be different—*Mjolnir* had been the first, the nameship of the class, while *Durendal* was the sixth of the original order—but most of the 66 Standard changes were computer hardware and software.

Not enough to bridge the gap between Protectorate and Kazh systems, she judged, but any narrowing of that gap was useful.

"And there she is," Beck said behind her.

Roslyn followed her former XO's pointing finger and saw the ship. Beck had waited until *Mjolnir* was distinctly visible as opposed to just one of the many dots of light now filling Garudan orbit.

"That's... Huh." O'Hannagain leaned back in his chair to study it. "I've seen the reports and even seen *Masamune* at a distance before, but it's different to see it from this close and realize that no, it doesn't look much like what we expect our warships to look like."

"It's still a pyramid, we just put a great honking weapon platform on top of it," Roslyn told him with a chuckle. "It's where all the big Samurai launchers live."

On *Mjolnir*, anyway. The new ships had given up the Samurais for an entirely new standard of missiles. Unfortunately, Second Fleet didn't have any ships equipped with the new Wyvern attack missiles.

The ship grew on the screens as their shuttle approached, and she heard O'Hannagain inhale as the scale of the ship truly began to sink in. There were dreadnoughts in Mars's orbit, and pictures were available on the system-nets across the Protectorate, but very few people actually got to approach the leviathans of war that now underpinned Martian might.

"I thought *Pax Romana* was big," O'Hannagain said quietly. "But *Mjolnir* makes it look like a toy."

"Not quite that bad," Beck corrected, though Roslyn could hear some of the hushed awe in the Commander's voice. "*Pax Romana* was half the length of *Mjolnir* and actually bigger at the base. Sixty percent of her mass."

"It's incredible that we can build things like that. Magic and science combined. Makes one feel invulnerable."

The Ambassador's words echoed in the shuttle, and Roslyn shivered.

"The problem is that anyone who might come after us has things that can make our dreadnoughts very, very vulnerable," she told her friend. "*Mjolnir* is bigger than the biggest Kazh ships we think are FTL-capable... but they have bigger ships in their home systems. And we have no evidence that they're limited to the same kind of volumes and masses for jumps that we are.

"Assuming they're stuck with the same limits we are is dangerous."

Roslyn wasn't going to point out that she was one of the people who'd made the assessment that the bigger ships couldn't jump—primarily on the basis of the fact that the Kazh had clear divisions between their forces in the Nine.

Several major fleet formations had been positioned across the system, and the truly monstrous ships hadn't been part of those formations. They'd been positioned like the in-system defense ships she figured they were: in high orbits of the inhabited planets or hovering protectively over key industrial nodes.

"We'll learn what their real limits are, I suppose," Beck said.

The shuttle was silent as they approached their destination, Roslyn's new home.

"I am no soldier," O'Hannagain said softly, "but my impression is that kind of lesson comes at far too high a price."

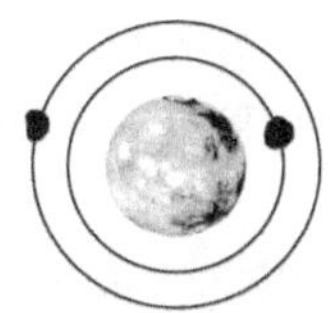

CHAPTER 28

"ATTEN-HUT!"

A hundred boots slammed into the deck as the honor guard came to attention. The Marines formed a clear file between the shuttle ramp that had just touched the deck and where Jane Alexander, Commodore Soból and Mage-Captain Do waited for their guests.

From the way the trio paused, none of them had been expecting a full honor guard. O'Hannagain and Chambers were first to move, Beck taking only a second longer to fall in behind his old CO.

Jane led her companions in saluting Chambers a full second before the young woman could. The Sapphire Medal of Valor earned the Mage-Captain that privilege, though Jane knew it occasionally bothered Chambers.

Hopefully more occasionally now than when she'd been a Lieutenant. She'd had at least one Medal of Valor for basically her entire career, after all.

"Welcome aboard *Mjolnir*, Ambassador O'Hannagain, Mage-Captain Chambers, Commander Beck," she greeted them. "I'm delighted to have you all with us."

"And we are pleased to be here," Chambers said instantly. "I presume you have a pile of work for me that's taller than I am, but you also have a meeting with the Ambassador."

"That's true, but I also need just a few minutes with Commander Matthias Beck here. With you, of course, Mage-Captain Chambers."

Chambers returned her grin and stepped to one side, a small gesture bringing O'Hannagain with her. Jane was pleased to see how well she and the civilian worked together—that was promising for Chambers' future career.

"Commander Matthias Beck," she said crisply. "Attention to orders."

Beck's spine snapped straight. He took one step forward and saluted again, just in case.

"It appears the traditional notices and documentation have gone astray due to the exigencies of the service," Jane told him. "However, an informal promotion board sat on your case over the last week. The officers involved have reviewed your record and your situation, including the unfortunate incident in the Tau Ceti System.

"Do you have any further commentary on that matter beyond what is in the files?"

Beck managed to hold the attention pose without so much as a shiver, though Jane knew the memory of that mess couldn't be pleasant. Like the rest of the original non-Mage crew of *Thorn*, the Commander had been hit with Nemesis's Orpheus-Ultima magitech nanoweapon. His will had been taken over and he'd been forced to run the ship for several of Kay's Nemesis minions.

He had even shot at Roslyn Chambers. He had missed. Chambers, thankfully armed with a nonlethal SmartDart stungun, hadn't.

"The situation was not one any of us anticipated," Beck said quietly. "The consequences of it will be what they will be, sir. I recognize the necessity that certain acts cannot be forgotten or forgiven, regardless of the reason behind them."

"That is an argument that was considered by the board, Commander Beck," Jane told him. "So were others, including that it is in the best interests of the Navy to reward loyalty, duty and competence. To stand behind our officers who rise above the worst injuries to continue doing their duty.

"Your promotion board was unanimous, Matthias Beck, and it is my privilege to inform you that you are promoted to the rank of Captain of Her Majesty's Royal Martian Navy as of twelve hundred hours Olympus Mons Time today.

"You may do the honors, Mage-Captain Chambers."

If Chambers had been promoted further herself, tradition said she'd give her XO a set of her own Captain's bars. Since Chambers still had need of that insignia herself, a human chain of noncommissioned officers had seen the velvet case shifted subtly across the hangar into her hands.

Now she stepped forward and opened the case, revealing the shining gold of a brand-new set of Captain's bars: four thick bands instead of the three thick and one thin bar Beck currently wore.

The man seemed in shock for a moment, until Roslyn reached up and gently removed the insignia from the collar of his shipsuit. He shifted enough to make it easy for her to pin the new icon in the same place, and then took his old insignia from her in awe.

"You knew, Skipper," he said accusingly.

"I was drafted to the board," Chambers told him. "And as Admiral Alexander said, the decision was unanimous."

Jane set her two officers off on the courses required of their duties. Beck would return to the surface and continue commanding the RMN's shore establishment, even as that establishment began to rapidly expand.

He'd be going back with another thirty staffers, and his main purpose aboard *Mjolnir* was to meet them, but Jane enjoyed springing pleasant surprises on her people.

Chambers was sent to get her quarters sorted out with her two personal NCOs. Jane would introduce her to the Operations Team herself, but that could wait until after her other meetings.

"Coffee, Ambassador?" she asked. "I know I can't keep you up here for very long."

"As I said when you proffered the invitation, much of my work is messages and video calls," O'Hannagain replied. "I can do that in motion, no matter where I am. Once we reached a certain point, Chimera became a far-easier posting."

"I understand some of the initial discussions were… difficult," Jane allowed. She didn't wholly agree with the stance that the Protectorate needed to get something out of Chimera for defending them to be worth it, but she could see where it came from.

"You don't agree with the negotiating position I took," O'Hannagain observed. "You are hardly alone in that. Most of the Parliament would have backed just about any deal I made, but the deal I was *aiming* for would have brought over many of the holdouts."

"As an RMN officer, it goes against the grain to demand *payment* for our services," she pointed out. "We exist to honor the Mage-Queen's Protectorate, not to bring coin and trade back to the worlds Parliament represents."

"The description of the position I took as *requiring payment* is a misnomer," the Ambassador said sharply. "It is one I have heard before and I understand where it comes from, but it entails a fundamental misunderstanding of both what I sought from Chimera and *why*."

"What we received from Chimera, in terms of the Lachai Archives and access to them, does rather strongly resemble a payment," Jane said. "And that was what you were after, wasn't it?"

O'Hannagain sighed and looked down at his hands.

"Can I get that coffee before I try to explain myself?" he asked wryly. "I am quite certain you will understand once I've explained, but I could use the caffeine."

Jane eyed him levelly, then crooked her finger. A tiny spark of power opened a panel on the wall, revealing it to be a two-sided cupboard containing two tall latte mugs. A second bit of magic floated the two mugs over to the desk.

"Thank you, Charlene," she sounded loudly and clearly, knowing that so long as her side of the cupboard was open, her steward could hear her.

She smiled at O'Hannagain as the panel slid closed and the mugs settled onto the desk.

"You asked for coffee?" she asked.

He looked down at the foamy drink, then shrugged and took a sip.

"This is… quite good," he observed. "How did you know it was ready?"

"Charlene is an extraordinary steward," Jane said mildly. "She also sent me a message when the drinks were done."

She took a sip of her own drink, letting the delicate balance of flavors—coffee, vanilla and coconut weren't delicate *flavors*, but the perfect balance between them took skill—run over her tongue.

"You were telling me that you weren't *actually* trying to extort a price from Chimera for our assistance," she reminded him.

"Unsurprisingly, I had this exact conversation with the Dyad Ministers," he observed. "It boils down to this, Admiral: the Protectorate will fight for Chimera on the Mage-Queen's word alone. No one questions that.

"But how *long* will we fight for them? How many resources will be poured into a conflict that Parliament sees as the Mage-Queen's war? How strong will the public resolve to fight for someone else hundreds of light-years away be?"

He took another sip of the latte, actually closing his eyes to savor the flavor. Jane wasn't sure if he was doing that because he was truly appreciating it or just to buy time—or, potentially, to make a positive impression on her.

"History warns us that wars fought for someone else far away tend to lose steam," O'Hannagain finally said. "No matter how high and pure the cause, there has to be something *more* for the commitment to stand. There have to be ties that bind, economic, societal, familial... more than just the cause. More than just the Mage-Queen's word.

"It was never my place or my job to deny Chimera assistance," he concluded. "We were *going* to fight for them. It was my task to find reasons to fight, to create ties that would bind the Protectorate and the Dual Republics together, so that our alliance would endure."

"Huh." Jane studied the immense man sitting across her desk. He leaned back in his chair, returning her regard levelly as he held his latte mug up so he could smell it.

"You're not wrong about the historical record of this kind of fight, I suppose," she conceded. "Most of my own historical studies only reach back as far as the Eugenics Wars, but there is a clear argument that the United Nations could have ended those wars early on if they'd truly committed to them."

Instead, the UN had sent six Expeditionary Forces to Mars over a hundred years, each ending in defeat after varying periods of time. There was *also* an argument, she knew, that if the Eugenicists had been willing to let things lie after the Third Martian Expeditionary Force, the war might have petered out after that.

The Eugenicists hadn't believed that and had launched counterstrikes, leading to the second half of the war. Jane had little sympathy for either side of that war, though she had to admit that being the grandchild of the final product of the Eugenicists' bloody-handing research experiments left one side as the definite *villains* of the piece to her.

"The references I dug out for comparison were older," O'Hannagain said. "Proxy wars and colonial fights from the second half of the second millennium.

"Of course, now all of that is irrelevant. We are evacuating as many of the Chimerans as we can, and the question of what happens to them is... wide open," he said grimly. "No one has been quite so blunt as to point out that the sanctuary cities on Mackenzie will be under Protectorate jurisdiction, but the Chimerans know.

"If Chimera falls and we don't retake her quickly... the Dual Republics die. The people and culture we can save become part of the Protectorate. Even the best of intentions won't prevent that."

"Shit deal we've offered them," Jane concluded.

"And yet they're taking it, because their historians tell them that a return to the Reezh Ida in the form of the modern Kazh is worse." O'Hannagain looked grim. "I'm guessing you don't have a miracle in your pocket that you expect to hold this system with, Admiral."

"I suspect the next attack will be dramatically more powerful than the first one," Jane warned. "But I do expect to hold it off. They have reason to believe that the defenses will be as strong as they were originally. Unless they scout in advance again, they will have no idea what is waiting for them.

"The attack after that?" She grimaced. They'd pulled basically every ship that wasn't needed where it was out of the Protectorate. Some of the system militias had stepped up, allowing more ships than she'd expected to be deployed.

Most of the militias simply didn't have the plans and structures in place to do so without more time. Give them three more months—maybe two, but she was figuring three—and the various cruisers, frigates, destroyers and suchlike of the Core and MidWorld system fleets would take over from the Navy.

That would free up ships for her—but the earliest she was expecting real reinforcements was at least three or four months away.

"It depends on how quickly they ramp up and how fast they come back," she finally told O'Hannagain. "We'll hold Chimera through the next round. I can't guarantee anything after that."

"That's more than we've promised them, honestly," the Ambassador admitted. "I've told them we'll hold as long as we can, but they have a good idea of the odds. They might not know how many ships we have in total, but they recognize that we've brought as many as we can."

Once the Nia Kriti ships caught up with her, Jane Alexander would command a full fifth of the warships of the Royal Martian Navy. More, if she counted the eight cruisers she had assigned to the two Evac Convoys.

"I need you to keep inside the Dyad Ministers' heads, Ambassador," Jane told O'Hannagain. "Them placing the Ifrit Accelerator at our disposal is a godsend, but we shouldn't have been surprised.

"I want to know what they need as soon as they do, if not before. If they're starting to doubt our commitment to this alliance, I need to know. We're going to fight for them, and I want to make sure they know it."

"I don't think they knew until this morning that they were going to be *able* to commit the Accelerator to supplying you," O'Hannagain said, "but I see your point. I've been keeping my finger on the pulse of most of their society. Right now, they're scared, and they see us as the big sibling they never had before.

"We're in a good place. I worry about what happens if we keep winning, though."

Jane paused before responding to that, rolling the thought around her head.

"What do you mean?"

"You think we'll beat the next attack handily," he pointed out. "That'll put us and the CSN at three for three against Kazh attacks. People are going to start wondering if they really need to evacuate at that point, aren't they?"

She took a swallow of her coffee, as if the caffeine would soothe the headache that popped up at *that* thought.

"We need to keep them moving," she told him. "We'll win one more fight. We might manage two, if the Kazh screw up. They won't screw up twice."

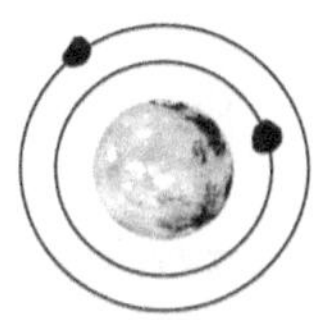

CHAPTER 29

NONCOMMISSIONED OFFICERS HAD WAYS and connections no mere Mage-Captain could match. Patience Kovalyow had been on *Mjolnir* for exactly as long as Roslyn had, but when she'd finished going over the order of her quarters with Baars, the Master Chief already knew where her office was and was ready to guide her there.

Walking around the desk, Roslyn dropped into her chair and looked up at the graying NCO.

"Feels like home," she quipped.

"Does it, sir? I've never been on a dreadnought before."

"I was on *Durendal*, but you knew that," Roslyn noted. "Flag Lieutenants rank a closet somewhere near the Admiral's office, of course, but I spent a good chunk of my time in Captain Kulkarni's office."

She waved around her at the utilitarian space. The desk had all the electronic systems and computer connections she could want, backed up by two wallscreens. There were spots for bookshelves, but the space came with the desk, three chairs and the flag of the Royal Martian Navy hanging from a pole in one corner.

"Kulkarni had definitely made it more her space than this is mine yet, but it's basically the same. The layout of the dreadnoughts isn't as different as I was afraid of—which means the main Ops Center is to the left down the corridor and the Flag Bridge to the right."

"And the Admiral's office is about halfway between here and said Flag Bridge," Jane Alexander said, the Crown Princess of Mars stepping through the still-open door.

"I can be elsewhere," Kovalyow said instantly. She hadn't even taken a seat yet.

"No, please sit, Chief," Alexander told her. "At least some of this, I'll want you both for."

Kovalyow waited for Alexander to take one of the two chairs across the desk from Roslyn, then carefully sat in the other. Roslyn's Chief didn't seem overly comfortable having the Admiral on the "wrong" side of the desk—but then, neither was Roslyn.

"I don't think this office has been touched in six months, maybe more," Alexander said, looking around. "I'll talk to Charlene. I'm quite certain we can get you more-comfortable chairs, if nothing else."

"It works for me, sir," Roslyn promised. "We have a few things in a case from my office on *Thorn*. They'll make their way here soon enough."

She'd lost most of a decade's accumulation of clutter when *Voice of the Forgotten* had been destroyed at Exeter. The only things she'd replaced had been the light sculptures made by an artist who'd been in Tau Ceti Juvenile Penitentiary with her.

"There is a nonzero chance I'll be sitting in the chairs in your office, Commodore," Alexander said drily. "You're getting more-comfortable chairs."

Roslyn shivered at the title. There could be no question of who *Captain* was referring to aboard a warship. While only Commodore Soból—who Roslyn hadn't met yet—was a full Commodore out of Alexander's staff, the various Captains would all be addressed as Commodore.

The only real cue was that, by tradition, the *Mage* part would be dropped for that particular courtesy promotion. The commanding officer of a ship was the only Mage-Captain aboard, even if said officer was only a Mage-Commander—as Roslyn had been for a while.

"As you command, Admiral," she finally said. "The *Commodore* is going to take some getting used to."

"Just don't let it go to your head," Alexander warned. "That's a whole other conversation. One to have in private, potentially with a beer."

That was mildly ominous, but Roslyn just nodded.

"You wanted Patience here, so I assume this isn't catch-up time," she noted.

"No. This is prep for what comes next. You literally just sat down, so you haven't had a chance to review your direct reports' files yet. Pull them up on the wall."

Roslyn took a moment to make certain that the door was closed. Anyone's full personnel file was a confidential matter, and the seniority of the three O-5s whose files she was opening didn't make that any *less* critical.

But all three of the women in the room had the authority to see the files in question, so she obeyed Alexander's command. The wall to her left lit up, three of the standard how-ugly-can-we-make-you-look headshots of the Royal Martian Navy topping text just large enough for Roslyn to read if she had a chance.

Two women and one man. Commanders Shahnaz Rostami, Moran Miyajima and Pranav Sharm. Only Miyajima was a Mage, her image the inevitably ethnic mongrel of a descendant of Project Olympus and her name a similar multiethnic mess.

"All three of your Commanders are solid, competent officers," Alexander told her juniors. "You will swiftly find that our flag staff has an immense abundance of such people. They are reliable, dependable, sensible and a lot of other words that end in *-ible.*

"What they lack, in my opinion, is a combination of a full understanding of how I operate and a certain spark of aggression and imagination," the Admiral warned. "There is nothing wrong with any of the officers heading Second Fleet. I would be delighted to have any single one of them on my staff.

"Overall, however, I find the stable solidity of the team a touch concerning," Alexander concluded. "I am hoping that time will improve their understanding of my methods and free up the imaginations I'm sure they have from fear of the Crown Princess of Mars.

"Until then, I am going to need to rely on you to provide that spark of aggression, Chambers. I know you can do that. Your record since leaving my staff has proven that relying on you has never been a mistake."

"My record is and always has been a litany of falling into nightmares and managing to not die," Roslyn pointed out. "If Chief Kovalyow doesn't regret hitching her star to me yet, she probably will."

"I volunteered, sir," the Chief said calmly. "If we have problems with the Commanders, I'll make sure to buy their Chiefs some beers and get a feel for the situation."

"The biggest problem is that while you have seniority over all three of them, you are younger than all of them except Miyajima," Alexander warned. "And Miyajima was one of your classmates at the Academy. She was lucky enough to be on the right side of the Protectorate when the war started and avoided such joys as *battlefield promotions* and *Medals of Valor*."

Roslyn had to check the file to confirm that. Even with the black-and-white text confirming that she and Moran Miyajima had been at the Tau Ceti Naval Academy at the same time, she still couldn't remember the face in the picture.

Meeting her in person might jar something loose, she had to admit. RMN file photos were universally terrible.

"I have been younger than many of my subordinates for most of my career, sir," Roslyn said. "It shouldn't be a problem. Matthias Beck, for example, is significantly older than I am and was explicitly placed under my command to compensate for my inexperience. We had a solid partnership by the end.

"I am grateful that everyone agreed with me that he deserved his next step—and I wanted to thank you, sir, for letting me be part of it."

"If we can manage things like that, where officers people know are there to stick the bars on them, we do it," Alexander replied. "Keep that in mind as time goes on, Chambers. You won't be making those calls on your own for a while yet, but there are conversations you're going to be in."

"Beyond the age concern, is there anything I should be aware about with these three?" Roslyn asked, gesturing to the pictures.

"They've been theoretically answering to my Chief of Staff since Second Fleet formed, but Commodore Soból wasn't able to dedicate as much time to them as anyone would like. All three are exactly the kind of intelligent, strong-willed people we *want* heading up Tactical and Operations teams," the Admiral said.

"Without proper leadership, they have degraded to being somewhat at loggerheads. Each shift and team are effectively operating independently of each other. That has been fine so far, but... I expect this fleet to be in action inside a week.

"I need my Fleet Operations Department able to work as a team when we put all three shifts on deck, Chambers. Making that happen will be down to you."

Roslyn nodded slowly, looking back at the three faces on her wall.

"Then I should get moving on that," she declared. "Patience, can you check where the Commanders are and get them all to report to the Ops Center?"

"Do you need an introduction to them?" Alexander asked.

"No, sir," Roslyn demurred after a few seconds' thought. "I think this will work better if I'm not seen as hiding behind anyone else's rank."

CHAPTER 30

DESPITE ALL OF THE SIMILARITIES between *Durendal* and *Mjolnir*, stepping into the Operations Center drove home to Roslyn that she was standing on a very different ship. The role of the space was the same: an adjunct to the Flag Bridge that allowed the Operations Department to provide the support the fleet commander needed without taking up the entire Flag Bridge.

As Operations Officer, Roslyn's post was on the Flag Bridge itself, but this was the space that she was responsible for where most of her people would work.

The Center on *Durendal* had resembled nothing so much as an administrative office. It had been arranged as a glorified cubicle farm, with clusters of four workstations tucked together in sections divided by narrow but passable walkways.

That had been an experiment, Roslyn had been told, and from the state of *Mjolnir*'s Operations Center, the experiment had been regarded as a failure. It was obvious that the 66 Standard refit had seen a lot of work done in there, to the point where the space still smelled ever so slightly of fresh paint.

The workstations were still grouped in sets of four, and that was the only constant. The Center had been clearly divided into three sections, each holding the thirty-two stations required for one of the three shifts. All ninety-six workstations were oriented toward a central point, where a brand-new set of holoprojectors duplicated the main tactical display from the Flag Bridge.

If Roslyn had been setting it up, it would have been an exact duplicate of the Flag Bridge display, mirroring in real time so that the Operations staff knew what the Admiral was seeing on the big projection.

"Commodore on deck!"

Roslyn concealed a smirk as Kovalyow's voice cracked out, parade-ground perfect—but having waited a good twenty seconds to let her boss get a feel for the new space.

"At ease, everyone," Roslyn ordered as analysts began to rise. As she'd anticipated from the layout, only one of the three segments was currently occupied. Bravo Shift—Commander Rostami's people—was on duty, with almost two hours left before it passed over to Charlie.

"Commanders, report to me," she continued as she took in the people in the space. *Her* people now, though she only knew the shift leaders by name so far.

Those three, two of them summoned by her quiet request to Kovalyow, converged on her with the expected alacrity. The trio was a matching set of darker skin tones, with Miyajima's Martian-vague brown the palest of the three.

Rostami was the current shift officer and the first to salute. A tall woman from the Svarog System with dark hair and eyes to match her Arabic coloring, her features were a touch too broad and her nose too sharp and prominent for her to be conventionally attractive.

"Commodore Chambers, welcome to the Operations Center," Rostami said loudly. "May I introduce my fellow shift leaders?"

Roslyn saw the spark of irritation in Commander Sharm's eyes but gestured for Rostami to continue before the other Commander said a word.

Sharm was the most senior of her three commanders, a forty-five-year-old Earth-born officer from the Indian subcontinent. Shorter and even darker than Rostami, he had a neatly trimmed beard and sharp amber eyes that showed his emotions far too easily.

"Commander Pranav Sharm has the privilege of commanding our Alpha Shift," Rostami told Roslyn, gesturing to the man. "Mage-Commander Moran Miyajima heads up Charlie Shift, and I, Commander Shahnaz Rostami, command Bravo Shift—currently on duty."

Roslyn nodded to each of them in turn, spending a moment studying Moran Miyajima to try to place the other woman. There hadn't been that many ethnic Martians at the Tau Ceti Naval Academy, and most of them had been from the Mage-by-Blood First Families like hers.

Miyajima wasn't one of those families, so the other student should have stood out. She was an average-looking officer in many ways, shorter than Roslyn but taller than Sharm, with the blue eyes and faded-parchment-brown skin nearly unique to the mongrelized ethnicity that now dominated Mars.

It was only as Miyajima bowed her head slightly in acknowledgement of Rostami's introduction that she finally clicked in Roslyn's head. Tucked away in the back row of almost every class, her head down in her notes, so determined to succeed that she'd pushed away friendly overtures from Mages and mundanes alike.

That had been Moran Miyajima. Mage by Blood, descended from Mages, but somehow convinced that her place at the Academy hung by a thread—more so than Roslyn, whose place definitely *had* prior to her battlefield commission.

"Thank you, Commander Rostami," she told the Bravo Shift Commander. "Now. Commander Miyajima, brief me on the status of the Operations Department."

"Sir, this is my—"

"I asked Commander Miyajima, Commander Rostami," Roslyn cut the other woman off smoothly. "Any of the three of you should be able to provide me with a general briefing, even if the events of the current shift are out of scope. Is that not right?"

"Yes, sir," Miyajima said, her voice clicking the final pieces into place. That soft soprano could be sharp, dismissive, even rude, but something in the way the Mage never raised her voice meant no one had pushed her.

Much of that dismissiveness was gone now, to Roslyn's ear at least, with sharpness replaced by firmness. Her voice was still soft, but there was no mistaking that Mage-Commander Miyajima had grown up quite a bit from Mage-Cadet Miyajima.

"The Operations Department is currently seven hands under strength," the Mage-Commander noted. "That is excluding the Operations Officer and attached personal staff, which would bring the shortfall to twelve.

"In the main operating shifts, those shortfalls are mostly in the more-junior ratings, and our Chiefs and Petty Officers have, so far, successfully substituted experience for numbers. How well that will hold up in a real crisis is, of course, uncertain.

"Coordination with Communications and Logistics has been functional, but we have suffered from the lack of staff-level representation on occasion. Fleet-wide exercises have been taking place on a staggered basis, with Captains-only exercises alternating with command-staff exercises on a roughly three-day cycle coordinated by Commodore Soból."

Miyajima's gaze flicked over the other two Commanders.

"I can't speak to morale or discipline issues in the other two shifts, but my people's mood is good. We are here to do a good thing, and my people want to make sure it gets done. We haven't had much chance to meet the locals, but our impression of Chimera is highly positive to date."

"Thank you, Commander." Roslyn nodded to the woman and stepped forward, moving up to the main display, with the three officers and Kovalyow following in her wake. She studied it for a moment, then pointed to the obvious cluster of pale green icons.

"That is why we are here, people," she reminded them. "Evac Convoy Two. Two hundred and fifty ships carrying almost twenty-five million people. As of my last update, nine million people had been moved into orbit and the entire convoy is expected to be moving by oh six hundred OMT.

"Once they reach Mackenzie, we will have evacuated almost thirty-three and a half million people from Chimera to the Protectorate. Impressive, isn't it?"

"Yes, sir," Sharm said behind her, his voice firm and showing no sign of the several-second pause before anyone had spoken.

She turned back to face them.

"It only leaves two billion, one hundred and sixty-eight million people in this star system," she said flatly. "That's not counting us, and I shouldn't need to remind you that Second Fleet alone makes up almost half a million people.

"Each evacuation flight we can get out is millions of people moved to safety, but we are looking at six months or more to evacuate the entire system. You three, more than anyone outside the flag staff, know the information we have on the military capabilities of the Kazh."

They were silent. From their expressions, Rostami and Miyajima got it. Sharm... understood but didn't agree.

"We are the Royal Martian Navy, sir," he said flatly. "We have faced these aliens at a disadvantage in numbers and, on paper at least, technology *twice* now. Their lack of proper combat doctrine is quite clear."

"Do you know how combat doctrine improves, Commander Sharm?" Roslyn asked him gently—softly enough that only the four officers and Kovalyow could hear her. "*By fighting.* The timelines we have seen for the arrival of new Kazh forces suggest they are in possession of FTL communications. We don't know the exact form, so we have to conclude that they have something equal or superior to the Link.

"That means, Commanders, that they have full sensor and tactical data from the First and Second Battles of Chimera. The Shining Shield of the Nine, the Kazh's navy, is not stupid. They will take all of that data and compare it against their existing doctrine.

"They will iterate. They will refine. And, may I remind you, between the two systems we know the Kazh controls, they command no less than *eighty* warships we estimate are capable of going toe-to-toe with our dreadnoughts.

"Our doctrine is better. Our crews better and more experienced. But quantity has a quality all its own, Commander Sharm. None of us like it, but eventually, we are going to have to concede this system.

"Our job, in Operations, is to make certain that Admiral Alexander has every possible option to push that off."

She smiled.

"So. Let's adjourn to my office and go through what options we've put together for the big boss, shall we?"

The meeting that followed was both better and worse than Roslyn had expected. The individual Operations teams had put together decent analysis and some solid tactical options. A bit of polishing here and there, and she'd have a package of options she'd be willing to put before the Admiral.

There was only one glaring problem.

She leaned back in her chair, holding her coffee mug in her hand and taking a moment to inhale the scent of cinnamon and nutmeg from her café masala.

The three Commanders were all seated across from her in the same standard, uncomfortable seats that Alexander had decided to replace sixty seconds after sitting down in them. That replacement would take more than a couple of hours. She had to note that, without even thinking, Miyajima had ended up between the senior shift leaders.

"Thank you, Commanders," she said slowly. "Those were three excellent presentations, put together on quite-short notice, and the teams seem to be performing decently.

"Now. Would one of you care to guess at the glaring problem that the last sixty minutes has made obvious to me?"

The silence was a clear answer. Roslyn let it stretch, glancing around the room to see if her subordinates would meet her gaze.

She was surprised when Miyajima met her gaze and giggled like a naughty schoolgirl.

"You mean the fact that there is zero cross-training, zero cross-analysis, zero cross-work, almost zero *anything* between the three different Operations shifts?" her former classmate asked brightly.

Miyajima smiled at the other two.

"I gave my shift's update last," she reminded them. "That made it, as Commodore Chambers noted, *blatantly* obvious how much repeat work my team had done. We have been working at cross-purposes and failing to coordinate."

There was, Roslyn noted, no attempt to discount her own involvement on Miyajima's part.

"Commander Miyajima has it," she confirmed. "All three of your records make it clear that you are good at your jobs. The work you've done confirms that. You're smart, capable people.

"What the *fuck* went wrong?" she growled.

There was a chilly silence, then Sharm breathed a long sigh and looked down at his coffee.

"I believe the fault is mine, sir," he said flatly. "With the lack of a direct superior, it seemed obvious to me that, as senior officer, I should act as the effective Operations Officer. At least in terms of setting priorities and so forth for the department.

"Since I was quite certain in that position, I created problems that should not have existed, giving orders I had only arguable authority to give, and Commander Rostami stepped in to cut me short.

"In hindsight, her action was intended to protect her personnel and manage their workloads," he observed. "At the time, some... hasty words were exchanged, and the Commander and I have been on the most formal of terms since."

"You were a damn bull on a power trip in a pottery shop," Rostami growled. "I told you to go through me to assign tasks to my staff, and instead, you just stopped *talking* to me or my people at all!"

Miyajima coughed delicately.

"That may, Commander, be because the phrase *If you bother my people again, I'll slice off your balls* passed your lips prior to that calmer email," she pointed out.

Roslyn turned her gaze on the youngest officer.

"Your shift is no better, Mage-Commander. I see your senior officers having a miscommunication escalating to a personal conflict. Your shift, however...?"

"I joined the staff from the cruiser *Righteous Dignitary of London*," Miyajima said. "I was Mage-Captain Fischer's Tactical Officer. This was my first flag staff appointment, and, for at least the first few days, I didn't realize that the shifts *weren't* supposed to be running completely siloed from each other.

"After that..." She shrugged helplessly. "I made some inroads with the senior Chiefs to make certain I had access to some high-level information on the other shifts, but it was clear to me that resolution was going to require mediating between my seniors. As the most-junior shift leader, that... was going to take some time."

All three of Roslyn's senior subordinates had the grace to look embarrassed. Roslyn hadn't really regarded Miyajima as having failed somehow in the divide continuing—but she had wanted the other woman's point of view on the mess.

"I am *not* the most-junior person in this room," Roslyn said, echoing Miyajima's concern. "You both have admitted some level of fault in this mess."

Rostami *hadn't*, really, but she'd had the sense not to dispute Miyajima's quote of her own words. She would either go along or be dealt with. Roslyn would make it work either way.

"What happened and why are now water under the bridge," she told them all, firmly. "Going forward, we will act and work as *one* department, not three. Despite our issues, we have been able to provide the support needed so far, and I have confidence that we will provide what the Admiral *expects* going forward.

"To start with, we will now be having handover meetings at the beginning of each shift," she informed them. "I will be sitting in on these initially, to make sure that I am up to speed on everything."

And to both make sure the meetings happened and that no one started a fight in them.

"Beyond that…"

CHAPTER 31

"YOUR MAJESTY. We are always delighted to speak with you."

Kiera smiled and returned the formal nod of acknowledgement of Crispin Kerekes, Governor of the Mackenzie System. Kerekes was the first person elected to that position, replacing an appointed military governor only nine months after the Protectorate had taken control of the system from the First Legion.

No one was quite sure yet whether the Governor would take on the pre-Legion title of Chéad Cainteoir—First Speaker. That was being debated between the new Protectorate-style legislature and the old tribal councils, currently more informal than they had been before.

Most of the tribal councilors and elders who'd run the collection of clans and tribes that divided Mackenzie's population into non-geographical voting blocs when Admiral Ridwan Muhammad and his fleet had arrived were dead.

Muhammad had brooked no alternative governing structures to his strictly imposed military hierarchy. Mackenzie's semi-ethnic divisors were informal enough to leave the First Legion unsure of their use.

So, they'd just killed anyone who'd claimed to be on the tribal councils.

"And We are delighted to see that Mackenzie flourishes once more," she told Kerekes. "We understand that the evacuation convoy arrived yesterday?"

"They did, Your Majesty," he confirmed. "They entered orbit this morning and the offloading has begun. Chimera Landing is a city of the confused and afraid right now, but we have plans and are speaking with the leaders of the evacuees.

"It will take time for them to get settled," he noted, tapping a command on his desk—a plainly utilitarian chunk of local wood, an intentional contrast to the Legatan-made monstrosity Muhammad had used—and bringing up an aerial feed of the constructed city.

"I never expected to be *glad* for the First Legion's desire to build a new capital," Kerekes said. "They did a lot of damage to the social structures of this region. We gained from our liberation, not from our conquest."

"You might have made contact with your neighbors without them or us," Kiera allowed. "But We are glad to have you all. And We are relieved that you are present and willing to take on the Chimerans."

"My people were under the boot of a tyrant all too recently, Your Majesty. If we can save anyone from the same fate, we will." He smiled sardonically. "And, frankly, Mackenzie has resources and potential our current population cannot take advantage of. Every new body on our world is another chance to move our entire people forward.

"We welcome our newcomers, and we will do all in our power to make them at home. Making sure that there was food for the reezh has been almost as large a struggle as getting the second city built!"

Hopefall was the name of the second metropolis that the construction teams were assembling.

"If there is anything the Mackenzie government needs to make this process smoother or more complete, you have only to ask," Kiera told him. "Parliament has assigned significant resources to this project—and if Parliament's resources somehow come up short, the Mountain *will* find what is needed."

The Royal Family of Mars might not be as mind-bogglingly wealthy compared to their citizens as some monarchs of the past, but Kiera had personal resources that would put many planetary governments to shame.

"We are determined to see this done, Your Majesty," Kerekes assured her. "The Chimerans will find only hope here, you have my word."

"Thank you, Governor. Do you know if the Lachai Razhkah has made planetfall yet?" Kiera asked. "We need to speak with her."

Because the old reezh had yet to actually give Kiera or anyone else an answer, and it was going to be embarrassing if Kiera had sent a specialized high-security fast-packet freighter to Mackenzie to pick up Razhkah and the Lachai Archive only for the woman to say no.

"So. You're the Mage-Queen."

Something about Razhkah reminded Kiera of her aunt. Old, yes, but carved from steel and granite. Razhkah looked more like she was carved from marble, her skin a smooth white that made her look distinguished no matter what she wore.

The dark gray robe she wore offset it perfectly. The Lachai looked like the aged scholar she was, though her surroundings were more modern. Razhkah was seated in what appeared to be a bureaucrat's office.

"I have that honor and that responsibility, yes," Kiera agreed. From what Kerekes had said, Razhkah *had* taken over one of the offices being used to process the arrivals and assign them housing.

"You want to know if I'm going to accept your offer."

"That doesn't take any great leaps of insight." The Queen chuckled. "The ship that's on the way to pick you and your people up is expensive to operate, but I can live with some embarrassment if I've guessed wrong."

"And if I were to refuse to even move the archive? Yes, you want to bring many of my people and researchers and such to Mars with me, but they are already here. This seems to be quite the impressive city of nothing you found for us."

"A monument to ego that will now serve to support those who need it," Kiera said. "I can think of no better fate for Ridwan's egopolis. I think he'll be incoherent for *hours* once he finally hears."

Razhkah was silent for a few seconds.

"I did not realize that the conqueror of Mackenzie and others still lived," she observed.

"He was aboard his flagship during the battle." Much as she might like to dismiss the former Admiral of the First Legion, Kiera Alexander couldn't deny Ridwan Muhammad's personal courage. "While he did not surrender his ship or his fleet himself, he did survive the fight.

"He is now serving a sentence for his crimes against these worlds in a secure facility. I dislike signing death warrants, Lachai Razhkah. I may not see a way for Ridwan Muhammad to pay his debt to society, but I will not take the chance away forever."

Not when he was no longer a threat. Kiera could afford to be ideological when there was zero chance that a broken old man could find the resources to threaten her realm.

"You didn't answer my question, though," Razhkah pointed out.

The Mage-Queen of Mars smiled, knowing that the reezh Mage was testing her—and probably assessing the surroundings of the office Kiera spoke from. Everything in the Mountain was built to very specific concepts of luxury and expense. The furniture was simply... solid. It was functional, if only rarely refitted with the latest in comfort technologies, and designed to last forever.

Kiera's chair was probably worth more than some shuttles—and that was ignoring the fact that it had been the office chair for three Mage-Kings, a Prince-Regent, and now a Mage-Queen.

And those were just the five people she was *certain* of.

If Razhkah took away from the surroundings that the Mage-Queen lived a utilitarian life, she would not be entirely wrong—but Kiera suspected she was the type of person to recognize the truth of that office.

"I did answer your question, Lachai Razhkah," she pointed out. "If Chimera Landing is to become the site of the Lachai Archive, then I will need to send many of the resources intended for our Institute to Chimera Landing.

"If hosting the Institute of Interspecies Thaumaturgy in Chimera Landing is the price for you to lead it, then Mackenzie will be home to my Institute. If it is simply that Chimera Landing is where you will keep the Lachai Archive, the Institute still must study those documents and archives—and so, whoever leads it, it would need to be in Chimera Landing."

There was a sound like rocks falling on each other, and it took Kiera a moment to be sure Razhkah was laughing.

"You are quite determined, I see."

"I am the descendant of a man raised to be breeding stock who overthrew his enslavers and freed all Mages," Kiera warned. "I will not force you to do anything you do not accept, Lachai Razhkah. But the Lachai Archive may be the key to the future of our combined people's magic.

"There are things learned on Mars that will not leave this world. You will have opportunities if the Institute is on Mars that you will not have in Mackenzie, but I will not force you to bring the Archive here, nor will I force you to—"

"Enough, Mage-Queen of Mars," Razhkah interrupted her. "You argue against your own cause because you know it will work. The path you ask me to walk is the clear route for both of our people.

"I am old and I am stubborn… and I am lost in these days of crisis. I fulfilled my duty to reveal the truth of our past and somehow thought that would be the end of things. Now I realize that the work only now begins.

"I will come to Mars, Your Majesty. I will lead your Institute. I will learn your secrets and dig up the ones of my own people that I have forgotten, and we will build something new from the pieces of both."

"Thank you. I can't promise you won't regret it," Kiera admitted. "But we will dig through these mysteries together." She sighed. "As much as I have time to, anyway."

"I look forward to it. For the salvation of my people, it is far too small a price to pay."

"I hope, in time, that you will accept that it was never a price," she told her new Director of Interspecies Thaumaturgy. "We were always going to do all we could for Chimera.

"What this might allow us to do, together, is liberate Chimera in the future… and, perhaps, free the rest of the reezh from the chains that bind them down."

CHAPTER 32

BY NOW, CONNOR WAS SPENDING at least some time every day in either Hsieh's office or Ojak's, keeping up with the current concerns, fears and needs of Mars's new ally.

When he entered Hsieh's office this time, he saw that Admiral Wang was joining them. He concealed a moment of amusement when he saw that the two locals were almost exaggeratedly seated apart, with the desk between them and Wang pushed an easy thirty centimeters back from the furniture.

"Admiral, Minister," he greeted them. "I have a full update on the progress of offloading Evac Convoy One, though you should have the reports in your inboxes."

"Of course. Take a seat, Ambassador. Coffee?" Hsieh asked.

There was already a third cup of black coffee on the table. The question was almost ritual by this point, but he smiled and nodded as he took his seat and cup.

For all that Garuda's climate was terrible by the standards of *both* its settler species, it had its microclimate areas, and some of them had proven to handle coffee beans with astonishing facility. If they hadn't been planning on evacuating the planet, he'd have made suggestions about setting up trade routes.

It was funny. The longer he was on the world, the more small things he found that would have provided value to a long-term trading relationship. None would really have justified the expenses of the defense, but once that treaty was signed, those trades would have helped solidify the bonds needed to keep the Protectorate in play.

Instead, well, the main service the Protectorate was providing was sanctuary.

"Evac Convoy One has almost completed offloading," he told them after a sip of the rich brew. "They expect to be on their way back here by the end of the day, Garuda time."

Which meant early morning by the standard clock and calendar of the Protectorate—Olympus Mons days but Earth's months and years, as opposed to Garuda's thirty-three-hour days and almost four-standard-year orbital period.

"We expect them to reach Chimera again in fourteen standard days. They've picked up three colony ships, one of the ex-Republic transports and several hundred more civilian transports. Mage-Captain Chambers will provide exact numbers to the Evacuation Commission, as before."

"Her new job will not cause issues there?" Wang asked.

"It was her condition of taking the position on Admiral Alexander's staff," Connor explained. He knew that Chambers had a long-standing relationship with the Royal Family in general and had served under Jane Alexander, but he still hadn't expected her to set conditions and make them stick.

Even knowing that the Mage-Queen had attempted to make Chambers her representative in Chimera, he might have underestimated just how connected his former attaché was.

"We appreciate it," Hsieh told him. "Despite the vast resources we've committed to it, the Evacuation Commission is running on a thin wire. The disruption of changing the RMN linkage could be expensive."

"And so that change will not happen," Connor agreed. "Evac Convoy Two, to continue my report, will arrive in Mackenzie in one week. We expect them to return to Chimera roughly ten days after Evac Convoy One, with a similar but smaller expansion of their carrying capacity."

Mostly new civilian shipping, from what he'd been told. There was only one Promethean-crewed *Saladin* left, and she wouldn't reach Mackenzie until several days after Evac Convoy Two left.

Even for a ship that could carry a million souls, there was no value in delaying the entire convoy for her. The question, which was thankfully not Connor's to worry about, was whether it was worth bringing her on her own.

"Thank you. Some good news is a relief," Hsieh told him. "There are days it seems the clock only brings doom."

The general sense of impending catastrophe loomed over all of Garuda, but Connor sensed she was referencing something else.

"Is there something Mars can assist with, Minister?" he asked slowly.

"Not quickly or easily," she admitted. "You know that we sent an embassy to the Ordin System, aboard the cruiser *Barracuda*."

"That was before I arrived in Chimera, but I was briefed, yes," he confirmed. "Have you heard from them?"

"No. As of today, they are overdue," Wang said. "Potentially, that's good news. We only allowed a week for them to carry out negotiations in that timeline, but the relatively low speed of our ships versus yours—or the Kazh's—means that *Barracuda*'s crew were given specific orders to leave the embassy behind and proceed home if possible."

"But you sent sensible officers who would recognize the importance of building the relationship over blind adherence to orders, I presume," Connor replied.

"Indeed." Wang shook his head and took a sip of his own coffee. "Captain Joto was an officer in the Chimeran space forces before my fleet arrived, one of the few to make the transition over to my fleet with minimal delays.

"They are not only my best reezh officer; they are one of my best *Captains*, period. I trust their judgment. But we are now into the time where every day suggests another delay."

"And each day builds the chance that *Barracuda* is not returning," Hsieh concluded. "Or, perhaps worse in some ways, that they may return too late, after we have been forced to abandon our world in the face of the Kazh's assault."

"We will shortly have vessels capable of scouting the Primes," Connor told them. "They have been slower to arrive than anyone would like, and their journeys out to the old reezh worlds will be long even with full Mage complements.

"I will speak to Admiral Alexander and make sure one of those ships is directed to Ordin," he promised. "We will learn *Barracuda*'s fate if we can, Minister, Admiral. If the news is good, the Protectorate will want to open our own channels there."

And if the news was bad, the stealth ships that belonged to the Martian Interstellar Security Service were the closest thing to invisible the Protectorate had ever built. Even the explorer cruisers like *Thorn* had been a pale shadow next to the *Rhapsodies'* ability to vanish.

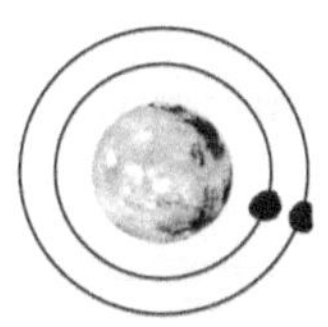

CHAPTER 33

"WELCOME TO CHIMERA, Vice Admiral Ryland," Roslyn greeted the woman on the video screen. "How can Fleet Ops help you out?"

Vice Admiral Vladislava Ryland was the Nia Kriti–native officer who'd been second-in-command of the fleet base there. When Mage-Admiral Hammond had sent two battleships and six cruisers to join Second Fleet, over half of his heavy ships in total, he'd put her in command.

"The Admiral and Commodore have given me a rundown of where everything is going to go administratively," Ryland said cheerfully. "I was hoping Ops would be able to give me the orbits for my ships—the last orders I'll be giving most of them!"

Pax Excellence's Flag Bridge was slightly blurred but visible behind the blonde Admiral. Her battleship flagship was a welcome sight, with the *Peace*-class ships still the second-heaviest warships in Second Fleet's order of battle.

Ryland's own arrival had allowed Alexander to split her battleships into two forces of six ships apiece, with Ryland in command of the newly redesignated Twenty-Second Battle Squadron.

Roslyn tapped out commands on her console without even looking around the Operations Center. She knew what her people had been doing and the last set of coordinates—for the *Honorific*-class cruiser *Marquis de Honestie*—filled in as she pulled them off.

"I'm firing them over right now," she told Ryland. "I mark your ETA as about ninety minutes. And while I am not our Logistics Officer, our constraints have been starting to tighten around my planning. I am relieved to see your charges, Admiral."

"There are few convoys in this universe I would wonder if two battleships was too light an escort for," Ryland noted. "But I have to admit this was one of them. I'll make sure those orbits get passed on."

She paused, then shrugged.

"On a personal note, Commodore Chambers, I wanted to give you some very belated thanks," she continued. "Twice over, in fact. My nephew was aboard *Stand in Righteousness* at the start of the war, and he credits you pretty highly with getting them out alive."

Roslyn shivered at the name. *Stand in Righteousness* had been the destroyer she'd served her cadet cruise aboard. But where most RMN officers had three cadet cruises over the four years of their training, Roslyn had only served one. Hers had ended with the beginning of the war, a battlefield commission and a Medal of Valor.

"We all did our part, sir," she told Ryland. "Those were some terrifying days."

"I can only imagine. My *second* thanks, however, is because *I* was taken prisoner when the RIN took Nia Kriti, and every analysis I've seen says the warning you and *Stand* got out is the only reason I was freed as quickly as I was."

"That, sir, was most definitely our duty," Roslyn said. "But you are most welcome for the personal benefits you received from—"

"Contact!"

Roslyn's head jerked over to where Chief Lam Carsten, the second-most senior NCO of Alpha Shift, had just barked the one-word report.

"What have you got, Chief?" she asked, then realized she was still live on the channel to Ryland.

"Apologies sir; I have to go."

Ryland simply nodded and cut the channel.

Commander Sharm was standing at Chief Lam's shoulder by the time Roslyn joined him, but the same information was now showing up on every screen in the Operations Center. On the big display—now mirrored to the Flag Bridge display, as per Roslyn's instincts—there was only a large red splotch marking an unknown emergence.

"Computers are running analytics," Lam reported. "Multiple jump flares at three light-minutes. The same distance as the first Kazh fleet."

Roslyn nodded grimly.

"Numbers? Are the Shining Shield sending another scout or…?"

"We're reading at least forty contacts," another analyst, not one of the handful whose names Roslyn knew so far. "Likely more."

"We don't have engine signatures yet, so we can't resolve masses. We're still working on the jump flares themselves," Sharm noted. He was mostly letting his people answer Roslyn's questions.

"What can we give the Admiral?"

She was looking at three different screens, absorbing the information on them all at a glance. Not every officer could do that, she knew. It was part of what made her as good at her job as she was.

"Forty-four to fifty-two contacts," the analyst updated his estimate. "Chief Lam?"

"Minimum half a billion tons total mass," the Chief noted. "We won't have much more than that until they light off their drives."

"Understood. Punch it to the main display."

Roslyn could have done that from her own station, but she needed to be in amidst her people. Lam knew what she needed, though, and the red splotch on the main hologram solidified into a red diamond marking a probably hostile contact.

The numbers they'd just discussed appeared alongside it, marking a range of almost ten ships and a minimum mass that didn't come any-where *near* the total mass of Second Fleet.

For the first time, the Royal Martian Navy had the edge over their enemy.

"Sir, your place is on the Flag Bridge," Sharm murmured into Roslyn's ear. "Mirroring our screens and getting our updates, but you need to be backing the Admiral up, not getting your hands in the data yourself."

Roslyn was silent, watching the information flicker across the screens, then slowly nodded.

"I'll have Kovalyow get Bravo Shift up here to back you up," she promised. "It's not battle stations, not yet... but we're the flag staff, and that means we need more hands right now."

She couldn't call up everyone. The earliest they were going to hit battle stations was still hours away. The Shining Shield force was still a full day from Garudan orbit.

She gave Sharm a firm nod, then turned on her heel to report to the Admiral.

CHAPTER 34

JANE ALEXANDER HATED the combination of time and distance that defined the modern battlespace. Three light-minutes was a vast distance by any objective standard, but it was close enough that she could see her enemy.

And far enough that the Shining Shield would take a day to cross it if they matched the acceleration of the last force to visit Chimera. There were other options—Jane was already running mental numbers on jumping a portion or all of her fleet out to ambush the enemy—but so far, the Kazh fleets had settled for a standard sublight advance both times.

"Enemy engines are live."

Jane turned from the main display and saw Roslyn Chambers slip into the Operations Officer station. There were three analysts up there—with space for six, but nothing to the numbers actually needed to run a fleet of over a billion tons of warships—and Chambers had clearly read the report off one of their screens.

"We are resolving numbers now. Estimate is now fifty on the dot. All ships brought their engines online at two-point-eight-five gravities three minutes ago."

"How many capital ships?" Jane asked.

"Four Type Ones," Chambers told her. "Looks like six Type Twos. Enemy appears to be following the two-to-three ratio we've seen before. Eight Type Threes, twelve Type Fours, twenty Type Fives."

As the Ops Officer spoke, the main holodisplay updated. The red diamond separated into individual symbols, most of them clusters of small icons Jane couldn't make out the details of, centered on the four blood-red shapes marking the Shining Shields' equivalent to her dreadnoughts.

"Any immediate markers that these are different classes from before?"

"Seventy megatons, fifty, fifteen, five and one," Chambers reeled off. "Masses appear identical across the board. What emissions we can resolve cleanly at this range appear to match as well.

"Some of these may be the survivors of the previous two attacks, but the evenness of the two-to-three ratio suggests an entirely new force, sir," the young woman concluded. "If they received the sensor data based from the last mission and calibrated their force to utterly overwhelm Adamant's task group, well."

She waved at the display.

"This is what I would have sent, Admiral."

"I agree," Commodore Soból noted. "Even assuming another reinforcement on the scale of Admiral Adamant's task group or a full doubling of the ships present when they scouted Chimera, this would be an utterly overwhelming force."

"Shame that they underestimated what we could deploy," Jane said with a smile. "Xiao, what's your assessment on their course of action?"

It was her Intelligence Officer's job to guess what the enemy would do, after all.

"They've gone the same two rounds with us that we have with them," the Turkish-Chinese man noted. "It's reasonable to assume they've drawn much the same conclusions: their hardware is significantly better, their software is moderately better, and our doctrine blows theirs out of the water.

"Vice Admiral Adamant's people didn't see any adjustments to jamming or electronic-warfare protocols last time, but those were lighter ships in a clear scouting formation. *This* is a serious attempt to drive us out of Chimera and take control of the system, so I would presume we will see revised electronic-warfare systems and protocols.

"Most relevantly to the guessing game, though, they have to realize that whatever edge they have isn't going to make up for a two-to-one tonnage disadvantage."

"So." Jane leveled her best *Stop fucking around and get to the point* stare on Captain Coskun Xiao. "The guessing game, then, Commodore?"

"In their place, we'd pull back," Xiao noted. "But we saw the scouting force push, hard, to test what they saw. Once the situation was clearly against them, they bailed. I would expect something similar on a grander scale."

A direct push for Garuda, to see whether the billion-plus tons of alien warships the Shining Shield saw were real. Jane didn't know of any way to fake a force on the scale of Second Fleet, but she was sure someone could come up with a way.

"Didn't we just establish that they know their doctrine sucks?" Chambers asked, the Operations Officer putting in her two cents.

From several of the expressions around her, not all of Jane's key staff officers realized that was what she *wanted*.

Soból, to her credit, took it in stride and seemed to realize what was going on.

"We don't have a lot of information to go with other than what we know of their base capability," she said. "What would *we* do with that?"

"We know that Prometheans can jump more accurately than any Mage, thanks to the computer integration," Xiao pointed out. "We have yet to resolve any identifying features as to which of their ships are using Mages versus their equivalent."

"On that note... Shinkawa, get me a live link to Wong," Jane ordered as a thought occurred to her.

Captain Masami Shinkawa gave her an acknowledging salute before setting the flag Communications team to work. Ten seconds later, an image of the Chimeran Admiral appeared on Jane's display.

"Admiral, a question for your Prometheans," she told him. "Two questions, actually. Can *they* tell which ships have Prometheus-style drives aboard?"

Wong looked oddly perturbed but spoke into thin air.

"Cam, you heard the question," he said.

"I have not noticed anything distinctive," the Promethean said, her computer-generated voice carrying an edge of concern. "Even knowing which ships among the CSN and RMN possess Prometheans, I cannot discern any difference via *Chimera's* scanners or my own magical capabilities."

Which was fair, Jane reflected. That meant there was exactly one person in the star system who *might* be able to tell the difference: her. The only Rune Wright, able to sense the flow of magic for hundreds of light-years.

Well, so far as humanity knew, anyway. Who knew what the reezh had?

"To answer what I guess to be the second question," Cam continued, "a *Prometheus Drive Unit* is not more accurate than a Mage. Only a fully Awakened, active Promethean with significant direct control of the ship's sensors and computers can achieve the kind of precision you are speaking of.

"While I cannot guarantee that the Engine of Sacred Sacrifice shares the limitations of its sister atrocity, that appeared to be an unavoidable result of the coma-like state of the Mage in question. Unless the reezh are using Awakened minds on par with myself, I do not believe they can duplicate the maneuvers the CSN is capable of."

"So, our Mages can dance around them, but if they have their own Mages, the math changes," Jane concluded. "Thank you, Admiral, Cam. Please, stay linked through. We're considering our options and what we expect the enemy to do."

"They are doing exactly what I would expect based off the last two incursions," Wong noted. "Which means I have to assume that they have a trick up their sleeve."

"That is where my staff and I appear to have ended up. We're wondering what *kind* of trick," Jane said with a chuckle.

"Sir, I think I see it."

Giannino spoke hesitantly, the Logistics Officer seemingly concerned that his input wasn't wanted as a battle loomed. Like Xiao, he didn't have any staff present on the Flag Bridge. Of course, unlike Xiao, Giannino actually headed up the single largest chunk of the hundreds of human beings that made up Jane's flag staff.

"What do you see, Nikos?" Jane asked. Even if she hadn't figured the man who lived and breathed logistics might see something the rest of them didn't, she had a strict unofficial policy: in the questions-and-planning phase, *anyone* could speak.

"Their vector is for Garuda right now, but if they adjusted their vector by sixty-five degrees about halfway to their current turnover and kept accelerating, they'd miss the planet by over twenty million kilometers—and be on a direct course to arrive at the largest processing node in the Chimera Belt, Belt Processing Six, in fifty-one hours."

"Chambers, can you— Thank you."

The Ops Officer had put the course Giannino was suggesting on the display as a dotted red line.

"They'd make final turnover around when we would expect them to hit Garudan orbit by our current projection," Chambers told them. "They'd never be in range of the planet, but if we sortied at three gees in the next hour or so—and were *limited* to that—we'd probably be able to force a passing engagement."

The CSN *was* limited to three gravities, and even that was putting a lot of strain on their crews. Second Fleet, with magical gravity present on every deck of every ship in Jane's fleet, was far less limited.

"After which whatever was left—and they could probably manage to get the Type Ones through intact—would obliterate a key resource supply for Chimera's defenses and incidentally kill three million people," Wong said grimly.

"It's one option they have," Jane agreed. "While they don't have the precision of true Prometheans, they are still likely to be able to microjump in the system."

She considered the display.

"Chambers, Soból, Shinkawa: make sure a note gets to the ship Captains," she ordered. "If we can disable and disarm any enemy vessels, leave them. We need something to pick through after this."

The previous battles had been brutal clashes, with the very survival of the planet on the line. Profligate use of antimatter warheads and massive battle lasers had left very little behind of the enemy.

There hadn't even been a chance to pick through what *was* left, for that matter. The focuses of the RMN and the locals had been very, very clear. Now, though, they would have a chance to get prisoners and debris to examine.

Jane hoped.

"The enemy has a few options. What are ours?" she asked.

"We can accelerate at fifteen gees to their three, sir," Chambers said instantly. "We can go out to meet them, as Commodore Banderas did, and play in to the doctrine they're expecting of us until they pull whatever trick they're planning out of their hat.

"If they divert for the Belt, we can go to full acceleration and intercept them. If they jump past us, we can jump right after them. We can make them commit and then hammer them."

Jane nodded slowly, looking around at her officers and Admiral Wang.

"Regardless, I think we need to see to the safety of Garuda," she noted. "Admiral Wang, with your permission, I'd like to handle this battle with Second Fleet alone. I'll leave Cruiser Squadron Twenty-Three, under Commodore Mared Peng, to back up your ships, but I will need you to catch anything that sneaks past us."

"We can do that, Admiral," Wang confirmed. "We've been updating and expanding the defenses. With eight of your cruisers and the CSN, we can play backfield. Just... don't miss anything *too* big."

"I'm not planning on it, Admiral Wang," Jane promised. CruRon 23 was her *Honorific*-class ships, older and more lightly armed than the *Salamander*s and her two *Victories* but fully refitted vessels that had given the Republican Interstellar Navy a headache throughout the Rebellion.

"First option is we hold our acceleration and controlled jumps in reserve," she reminded everyone. "Move the way the enemy expects us to, let them commit, then cut them off. Any other thoughts?"

"We can simply hold position until they commit one way or another, sir," Soból said. "With Second Fleet in high orbit, we can prevent even a genocidal attack on the planet. Once they've made a choice, we can follow through, the same as if we maneuver out now."

"Not completely true," Giannino pointed out. "I'm not a Jump Mage, but my understanding is that teleporting from this close to a planet is something we should reserve for emergencies? We have greater flexibility than a civilian jump matrix, but it is still risky."

"My preference will always be for a minimum of twenty light-seconds, outside of a direct threat," Chambers confirmed. "Which is part of why I suggested we get moving for almost any scenario."

"And what course would you suggest, Commodore Chambers?" Jane asked.

"We used in-system microjumping against the Shining Shield in their first attack," the Ops Officer observed. Chambers was the only person in the conversation except Wang who had been present for that attack. "Holding back that capability doesn't serve us. They *don't* know that we can out-accelerate them as thoroughly as we can.

"Given the force imbalance, I would suggest holding back on that capability for as long as we can. I would suggest that we short-circuit whatever plan they have." Chambers shrugged. "We advance to six million kilometers clear of Garuda and then jump right on top of them. I'd recommend around seven to eight million kilometers away—avoiding the range bracket where they can reach us with missiles but we can't return the favor, but not going all the way into laser range.

"That fleet does have more missile launchers than us, but our anti-missile doctrine proved effective both times we've fought them. We're better off playing in our missile range than having to close through theirs."

"And if they immediately jump again?" Soból asked.

"That's part of why we have to leave Admiral Wang behind," Chambers replied, clearly having picked up on that part of Jane's thoughts. "Every ship in this fleet has at least four Jump Mages aboard. We can jump out to meet them and then jump to follow them."

She shrugged.

"If we have to do it a *third* time, we're leaving behind Admiral Ryland and the two battleships she brought from Nia Kriti, but I'm prepared to take the bet that the Kazh don't have the Mages, living or murdered, to make multiple tactical jumps with an entire fleet."

Jane didn't even need her people to do the math, though she knew it was being done. Five and a half hours to get twenty light-seconds from

Garuda. The Shining Shield would advance nineteen light-seconds toward the planet in the same time—assuming they didn't change acceleration, which was possible.

There would still be over two light-minutes between the two fleets. No one would be in weapons range. Even if the Kazh were feeling paranoid, they might not be at full defensive readiness at that distance.

"For now, we maneuver out to meet them," she ordered. "Three gees, direct-intercept course. If they play games, we adjust. We prepare to make a combat jump once we're at six million kilometers from Garuda.

"Leaving the *Honorifics* and the CSN behind, how many launchers do we have?" She was still looking at the holographic display, but she knew who would have the answer.

"Six thousand eight-ninety-two Phoenix Nine launchers, three-forty Samurai Deuces," Chambers replied after barely a second. "Based off the prior encounters, Bandit One will have over nine thousand of their launchers."

"And that, people, is why we don't want to let them use their range advantage," Jane said flatly. "I am prepared to trust our antimissile doctrine, but I am not going to sit here and take missiles without being able to respond.

"Get the fleet moving."

"Sir. There is one more thing," Captain Jundt said, her voice calmly firm.

"What is it, Isadora?" Jane turned from the main display to meet her Communications Officer's gaze. Jundt was as solid as the rest of the staff, but her role didn't lead to her speaking up much. Communications was a department that was invisible when it worked well, and Isadora Jundt's team was working perfectly.

"We have the unquestionable advantage in numbers and tonnage this time," Jundt pointed out. "Admiral Adamant had that last time, but the last force was a reconnaissance. This is a real fleet that is badly outmatched.

"Shouldn't we make at least one more attempt to talk to them?"

Jane swallowed a sigh. Fortunately, it was Chambers who spoke first.

"The locals tried to talk the first time," the young Mage-Captain reminded everyone. "They didn't answer. Both the locals and Ambassador O'Hannagain tried to hail them last time. They didn't answer.

"We don't actually know for certain that this *is* the Shining Shield of the Reezh Kazh," she continued. "We're going off intercepts and scraps of history. They haven't said a word to us here in Chimera.

"I would feel perfectly fine blowing them to debris and memories without saying a word. That said... Commodore Jundt is right. We don't know anything, and the situation is different enough that they might talk.

"I just wouldn't hold my breath."

Jane waited. Chambers had summarized her own objections and then turned them around on her to agree with the Coms Officer. That was a surprise, if she was honest, but a healthy one. The young woman had saved her life once but had been very junior even then.

She approved of the officer Chambers had grown up to be.

"I feel we have something of a moral obligation to at least attempt communication with an alien force, sir," Soból finally said, the Commodore sounding like she expected Jane to argue with her. "That is and always has been the doctrine of the RMN, though it has come up very rarely."

"I was going to fall down on Chambers' *blowing them to debris and memories*," Jane admitted. "But I can recognize when I'm wrong. Admiral Wang." She turned to the screen with the Chimeran officer. "Would you be able to provide an interpreter? I feel this should not depend on a software translation."

"The CSN would be delighted, Mage-Admiral. I can have an officer transfer to your flagship within a few minutes?"

CHAPTER 35

CONNOR O'HANNAGAIN'S MAIN JOB at that moment was to keep the locals calm. Thanks to Kootenay and Ansel, he'd managed to confirm that the Dyad Ministers had retreated to the Planetary Defense Command Center.

With Captain Beck in tow, he'd descended into the fortified bunker to join them. No one seemed surprised to find him there, a reezh officer guiding him to the central command deck without blinking a single one of her four eyes.

"There isn't going to be much going on for a while yet," the newly pro-moted Beck told him. "This part is slow and boring as well as terrifying."

"I thought war was ninety-nine percent boredom, one percent utter terror?" Connor asked.

"Yep. What they forget to mention is that a good chunk of the bore-dom is *also* terrifying, Ambassador."

Connor snorted in amusement as he led the way down the steps to the clear space next to the main holotank. As he'd expected, Ojak and Hsieh were both there. A single aide accompanied each of them, along with a CSN Commodore and an RCA General.

He didn't know the two military officers and they weren't what he was there for.

"Ministers," he greeted the planetary executive. "I see the situation proceeds... apace."

"So it does," Ojak said roughly. "Your Admiral Alexander has left our entire fleet in orbit and moves out with her own ships only."

"We both know why, Ojak," Hsieh countered. "We have five ships left. Admiral Alexander has *seventy*. With the eight cruisers she's left under Wang's command, Garuda is protected even if the Admiral's plan doesn't work perfectly."

"Do you know her plan, Ambassador?" the reezh Minister demanded, turning his lower and upper eyes on O'Hannagain.

"I could likely request that she or one of her officers brief you, Ministers, but no. I am not privy to the Admiral's intentions," Connor told them. "I attempt to be aware of the limits of my skillset and not jog the elbows of the experts outside of them."

"Within those skills, you are quite talkative, though," Ojak observed. "Your mediation on the Agricultural Supply Board was quite effective, I have to concede. You have our thanks."

Hsieh was silent for a moment.

"I was not aware of any incident with the ASB that required mediation," she finally said. "Should I be?"

"The vagaries of random selection, Minister Hsieh," Connor told her. "An unexpectedly high number of reezh agricultural workers were evacuated on the second flight. Some adjustments of the supply chains were required, and certain corporate partners were insistent on contract terms that would prevent that adjustment.

"Compromise was possible, and I helped people find it. That was all."

A major Eastern Republic grocery chain had been unwilling to lower the contracted amounts a major agricorp was expected to provide them. Those amounts were higher than the stores needed, but keeping the contract would have prevented backfilling the Western Republic's supply chains for their reezh counterpart.

The *compromise* had been O'Hannagain pointing out that they could either cooperate or the Republics would legislate. If the Parliaments had to get involved, the company wasn't going to like the deal they got.

It was surprising how quickly people got in line when reminded that the alternative was going to leave them worse off.

"Well, we appreciate your presence and wisdom, Ambassador," Hsieh told him. "I only wish it had more impact on the Kazh."

"So do I," Connor said fervently. "I have faith in Admiral Alexander, Ministers. She has a powerful fleet and led our Navy to victory against the Republic that once commanded Admiral Wang."

The one that had created the Prometheans. He didn't need to make that point.

"Ministers, we are being copied on a transmission from *Mjolnir*," a reezh tech announced. "Admiral Alexander has sent a message to the incoming ships. Captain Neejoh of the CSN is acting as her interpreter."

"Play it for us, Chief," the CSN Commodore ordered.

The holographic display of the system shifted slightly, allowing a two-dimensional screen to take shape in front of the Ministers and their companions. Admiral Alexander was seated in a raised chair on her Flag Bridge, though most of the details of the space had been blurred out. A reezh officer with unusually dark, almost obsidian skin stood at her right hand.

"Approaching vessels," Alexander declared, waiting a moment for Captain Neejoh to repeat her words in reezh.

"I am Mage-Admiral Jane Alexander, Crown Princess of the Protectorate of the Kingdom of Mars," she continued. Another pause for translation. "I command the Second Fleet of the Royal Martian Navy and I am tasked, by order of my Mage-Queen and the Parliament of the Protectorate, to guard our ally, Chimera, against any and all threats.

"Twice now, ships have attacked this system without communication or demands. Twice now, the Chimerans, aided by ships of the Royal Martian Navy, have driven those attackers off."

Even with the translation, there was a silent moment after that.

"I have no choice but to assume you represent more of these unknown and undeclared enemies. Without any communication, there can be little confusion or deception, but I will be clear.

"You do not have the numbers or the power to challenge my fleet. You have faced Chimera, aided by Mars, before.

"Now you face the power of Mars. I will not permit this system to be taken by force. We are prepared to open diplomatic communications and assess whatever concerns lie between you and the Dual Republics of Chimera, but we have sworn our guardianship of this star.

"If you advance, you will be destroyed. Withdraw and speak. Advance and die. These are your choices."

The message ended and Connor smirked inwardly. Ambassadors could give ultimatums, but sometimes it took a soldier to give a very clear, blunt threat.

Except it wasn't even a threat. Alexander was simply telling the Kazh what was going to happen.

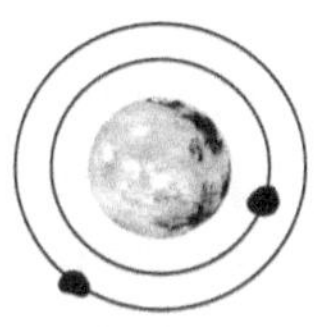

CHAPTER 36

ROSLYN HAD ALMOST FORGOTTEN the strange dichotomy of being on the fleet staff as battle approached. On the one hand, the staff were often busier than individual ship commanders, collating information and assembling alternatives for the Admiral. At this stage, there was very little for the ship Captains to do beyond keep their ships following their assigned courses and their crews steady.

On the other hand, the hours during which fleets approached each other dragged on just as infinitely for the staff as for the line officers. For five full hours, the two forces simply pointed their ships at each other and accelerated.

"Range is forty-two-point-four million kilometers," she quietly told Alexander. "Three minutes to Point Alpha."

"Thank you."

Roslyn stepped back from the Admiral and reviewed everything at her station. Every Ship's Mage and Mage-Captain in the fleet had been reviewing their calculations for the jump from Point Alpha to the enemy position for hours. Enough of them had asked Fleet Navigation to validate their numbers that Captain Usman Abbas had asked Operations to help.

Roslyn was the only member of the Operations Team who could actually jump a ship, but the calculations were something that anyone with training could double-check—and the margin of error on a jump of barely two light-minutes was ridiculously tight.

Just not as bad as it would have been had they jumped from Garudan orbit.

Her staff had checked over the jump calcs and flagged what corrections were needed. Now, between her people and Abbas's, the fleet was ready. *If* the Admiral decided to execute on that plan.

It was Roslyn's job to make sure there were other options available, but she couldn't see any new ones. Even if the enemy diverted toward the asteroid refineries, Second Fleet could increase their acceleration by enough to intercept them. This wasn't a fight the attackers could win or even avoid.

The tactical jump might be *too* aggressive, but it also avoided the risk of losing ships and people before they could even fire on the enemy.

"Alpha Point in one hundred seconds, sir," the senior Ops NCO on the bridge, Chief Tora Hakim, reminded her. Hakim hadn't moved from her station in six hours, only pausing to drink from a cup of coffee the stewards made certain stayed full.

"The fleet firing plan is ready?" Roslyn asked Hakim. She knew the answer. The two of them—and all three of her shift leaders—had been bouncing said plan back and forth for most of the long flight.

"Nailed down. Bracket distribution."

"Thanks." That meant they were sending half of their missiles against the biggest targets, the four seventy-megaton Type One warships, and half against the smallest targets, the twenty one-megaton Type Fours.

The dreadnought-equivalents would probably survive, though the hope was to nail at least one of them. The escorts, equivalent to the RMN's destroyers, would hopefully be completely wiped out. That would reduce the enemy missile defense by a significant chunk.

Alexander had already seen it, but Roslyn sent over the final version with a summary.

"Fifty-fifty bracket distribution," she told her boss. "All Samurais on the high end. Two salvos, then narrow the bracket and repeat. Reassess at salvo five."

By the time they were launching their fifth salvo, they'd see the results of their first. The missiles had some ability to independently retarget normally, but they knew that this enemy had enough jamming and electronic warfare to render that unreliable at best.

"Execute immediately after jump," Alexander responded.

The Admiral rose.

"All-ships channel," she ordered. That took precious seconds, but she got her channel.

"Second Fleet, we stand where the RMN always has: between the innocent and those who would do them harm. That is our task and our oath: to maintain the Protectorate of the Mage-Queen of Mars.

"I know none of us will fail that oath today. Execute jump on my mark."

A heartbeat passed and Roslyn saw the time click green on her screens.

"Mark."

The universe flickered. Not everyone could register the sensation of a jump. Some Mages could. Some non-Mages could. Many of both Mages and mundanes couldn't tell any difference unless they were looking at a display showing them the world outside the ship.

Across a jump of two light-minutes, even that might not make enough of a difference. Unless, of course, that jump took a fleet of fifty hostile warships from over forty million kilometers away to six.

Dozens of confirmation reports blazed across Roslyn's displays. The weapons of sixty-two massive warships were synchronized to her computers, but the Captains and Tactical Officers of those ships had their own part to play. To get seventy-two hundred missiles into space in a synchronized salvo took dozens of officers and tacticians alone—across the entire fleet, the salvo involved thousands upon thousands of people, all working to the plan Roslyn had created.

It was a rush, only expanded by the surge of green icons on the main holotank as those missiles blazed into space.

"All missiles launched as per the plan," she reported. "Jump plus three-point-five seconds."

"Well done, Commodore Chambers," Alexander told her. "Soból, Xiao. Enemy disposition?"

"As expected," the Chief of Staff replied. "No significant vector alteration in the two minutes since our lightspeed data. No sign they were anticipating our jump. Electronic-warfare systems at standby."

The question in Roslyn's mind was how long it took the enemy's electronic countermeasures to come online. The Shining Shield's ECM was better, using both more powerful emitters and more sophisticated sequences than the RMN had access to.

There were signs that it was less randomized than she would prefer if it was *her* defense systems, but exploiting that was less easy than it might sound.

"Commanders," she addressed her subordinates in the Operations Center. "This is where we earn our paychecks. I want to know the moment there is any sign of ECM coming online over there, and I want to know the moment the first missile hits the void."

"We're on it, sir," Miyajima said before the senior pair could speak. "Twenty seconds until we can see their reaction."

Lightspeed limited things both ways. It would take twenty seconds for the invaders to see Second Fleet's new location—and they would see *two* Second Fleets for well over a minute—but it would also take twenty seconds for the Fleet to see what the Shining Shield did in response.

For those first few seconds, their missiles hurtled into space unchallenged. Then light completed its loop and they could see the enemy reaction.

Or... complete lack thereof.

"Enemy is continuing on course. No sign of weapons fire or active defenses," Roslyn reported as the seconds ticked by. "That doesn't make sense."

"It makes a pattern, perhaps, but one we're still putting together," Xiao noted, the Intelligence Officer sounding like this was an intriguing behavior of some insect he was studying. "How long, I wonder, before they wake up someone who can authorize them firing back."

Roslyn bit back the accusation that the other Captain had to be joking. No, Xiao was deadly serious. The man had a list of degrees ending in "ology" the length of her arm to go with his military credentials.

He was thinking out loud, not joking—and the lack of response on the part of their enemy suggested some level of tactical rigidity. Or a trap.

"They weren't this rigid at the First Battle of Chimera," she warned. "They could be decoys of some kind. A trick."

Even as she said it, though, she was running through the sensor data. The vastly reduced distance gave them a far-clearer image of their enemy, and there was no sign of a trick. Those were massive warships over there, in a formation that seemed organized by weight rather than any tactical purpose.

"Profile change," Rostami's voice snapped in her ear. "Sensors just went live across the Kazh fleet. Missiles launching, but it's not synchronized."

Roslyn passed that on automatically as she watched the reezh fleet finally act. A single Type Two had fired first—almost immediately followed by three of the Type Threes. Then two of the Type Ones, followed by half of the Type Twos and the remaining Type Threes.

The enemy launch had been spread over a period of fifteen seconds. Nine thousand hostile missiles were coming their way, but the solid punch that would make them truly devastating had been diluted.

"I see." Xiao's tone of almost-academic fascination was still present, grating on Roslyn's nerves. "The next salvo, I suspect, will be more synchronized. What we're seeing here is the officers who are senior enough or feel they have enough other connections to open fire without orders, followed by others using them as a shield—and then, finally, the 'appropriate' orders being issued."

"A quite-hierarchical structure, at a level where we're used to seeing a minimum level of tactical independence."

"We saw that before, though," Roslyn objected. Her planned second salvo blazed out of Second Fleet's launchers, hurling themselves toward the enemy in pursuit of their earlier cousins.

"Once battle was joined," Xiao pointed out. "I suspect that they have more flexibility while in active conflict—or, potentially, that this rigidity is the result of the personality of a specific commander."

"Even in that case, though, it speaks to a flawed system that would permit it," Alexander said. "Regardless, it has bought us a small measure of advantage I didn't expect. Let's finish this, people."

At its most basic, space combat was a numbers game. But, in Roslyn's opinion, you could simplify *anything* down to that, from politics to dating. You didn't have to convince all of the voters or potential lovers, just *enough*.

She didn't need to get every one of the seven thousand–plus missiles she'd thrown across the void through. Just enough. The problem was that unlike politics or dating, *enough* wasn't a quantity she could know.

"Day late and a dollar short," she said aloud as new icons flared onto the displays. "Enemy electronic-warfare systems are coming online. From the first missile launch, two hundred twenty seconds."

"Marking that down," Xiao confirmed. "One data point does not a conclusion make, but it's a start."

"And today, it's not enough," Roslyn said fiercely. She lost control of her missiles as the reezh jammers came fully online, but it didn't matter. She'd retained direct links long enough that the individual Tactical Officers had dialed in their targets.

There was more than electronic warfare attacking her missiles, though. The Kazh fleet was well supplied with their own antimissile lasers. With the full data from an entire fleet's sensors, Roslyn could assess those defenses more accurately now—and she was both unimpressed and glad that the enemy didn't seem to know what to *do* with their weapons systems.

"Enemy defenses appear anchored on a fifteen-hundred-megawatt pulse laser," she told Alexander. Xiao was getting her data analysis as she was pulling it together, but Alexander just needed the summary.

"Pulse recycle, throughput and rotation speeds are all superior to the systems in our RFLAMs," she continued. "But they appear to be single-chamber units. Overall beam density is only about seventy percent of ours and, well..."

"Half a gigawatt kills a missile as well as three times that," Alexander finished for her.

The RFLAMs on old RMN battleships were gigawatt-range systems, intended to function as much as close-range antiship weapons as antimissile systems. Everything newer than the *Peace*-class battleships, though, used half-gigawatt systems. They cycled faster—and so long as a beam could kill an antimatter missile, more beams was straight up better than fewer.

While every individual beam on the Shining Shield ships was better, their overall defense was weaker. In the previous battles, that had been covered by their ECM—and even with sixty-two starships and hundreds of drones, Roslyn's sensor clarity around the enemy was degrading as she watched.

Part of that was the explosion of hundreds of antimatter warheads, a radiation cloud that was always a factor in space combat. Most of it was the enemy jamming.

None of that, however, muted the cataclysmic eruption as however many missiles were left of Second Fleet's first salvo struck home.

"Spread the drones wider," Roslyn ordered her team. "I want to get numbers on how many we've hit."

Between the delay in the enemy opening fire and the higher acceleration of the RMN's missiles, she would get three full salvos in before the first one reached Second Fleet. The dramatically longer endurance of the reezh missiles didn't help them when the humans jumped this close.

"Clean sweep on the Type Fives," Sharm reported. "Not sure on the Ones. We've still got a lot of big energy signatures out there."

"Correlating analysis from the Tactical teams," Rostami added. "I mark it as one probable in the big boys. No definites."

"Not bad at all," Roslyn told them. "Retarget the lower bracket of salvo two if we can."

"Miyajima's working on it," Sharm said. "If anyone can pull it off, it's her."

That was a confidence in the junior Commander that Roslyn wouldn't have expected from her juniors. The pressure of an actual fight seemed to have blown away whatever cruft remained from their earlier friction.

"Sir." Roslyn raised her voice and turned to Alexander. "Clean sweep on the Type Fives, one probable on the Type Ones. Second salvo is targeted on Ones and Fives; we're attempting to retarget on the Fours, but it may come down to the onboard targeting."

She grimaced.

"With their jamming, it may come to that anyway, sir," she admitted.

"Coordinate outer-zone missile defense, Commodore Chambers," Alexander ordered. "Leave the offensive to your juniors and inner zone to the ship's Tactical teams. The first line of defense is yours."

"Yes, sir."

Roslyn passed that on to her people and pulled up an entire new range of screens around her. It made sense, after all. There was only so much direct control they could exert over their missiles now. With the later salvos, they could basically pick a quadrant of the enemy formation and pour fire into it.

They could still control their own defenses, and there were tens of thousands of missiles heading their way.

Even if her first salvo had wiped the enemy from the universe, the Kazh would still have launched four of their own. The first salvo was a chaotic mess, but they still couldn't ignore it.

Roslyn's team had already been working on the solutions, and she flagged to all of them that she'd entered the system. There was only so much one human being could handle, even with Protectorate computers, so she quickly checked and refined the allocation of responsibility between her people.

Between the Flag Bridge and her Operations Center, ten people were working with the various ship Tactical Departments to run the defense. Each of them had taken over a zone of the outer defense, and there wasn't much to change there.

She moved on to the incoming fire itself. Her hands flickered across screens and controls as she grouped, assessed and allocated missiles in batches of five hundred to a thousand. The zone division might have been enough on its own, but by the time Roslyn was done, her people—and the ships they were communicating with—knew which missiles were hitting which zone.

Her attention moved to the second salvo—as her own second salvo impacted. Even with her focus on the defenses, she knew that she couldn't be completely oblivious to the overall pace of the fight.

Reports flickered across her screen, and she spared a few seconds to look toward Alexander.

"At least six lesser ships destroyed along with one *definite* Type One kill," she told the Admiral. "Not sure if the losses are Threes or Four. The jamming is throwing us off."

She knew, without even watching, that the first salvo of reezh missiles was already doomed. Her work on the second salvo was more difficult, but the concept was the same. Some of those missiles would make it through the outer-defense zone.

Second Fleet's third salvo claimed another squadron's worth of lesser vessels. The enemy was down over half their total numbers, but most of their mass was in the Ones and Twos—and only one of the big ships was definitely gone.

And then her screens were clear, and they were *all* gone.

"They jumped," Roslyn reported the obvious before anyone else said a word.

"Fuckers. Did they leave the system or jump for a target?" Alexander demanded.

That wasn't a question Roslyn's sensors could answer. Her focus was still on the incoming missiles—their danger level went down without their motherships, but it certainly didn't go *away*.

Seconds ticked by and missiles exploded around the fleet. With no enemy to fire at, Second Fleet's offensive missiles could be turned to a defensive role, obliterating their counterparts in job lots.

A handful of missiles made it through, but they were exclusively targeted on the dreadnoughts and battleships—ships that were built to take just those hits.

"We have them, sir," Jundt snapped. "They jumped deep into the stellar gravity well and are on a rapid approach to the refinery complex Giannino flagged as a concern before."

Roslyn didn't see that on the sensors—and wouldn't have, she realized, since the Chimera Belt processing complex was almost four light-minutes away.

"When did the complex get a Link?" she asked, then saw Giannino flush and cough.

"General Badem requested half a dozen units to provide to defense units she was distributing throughout the system," the Logistics Officer said. "She had the authority to requisition them."

"Yes, she did," Alexander agreed. "And that may have just saved a lot of lives. Are they giving us telemetry or just an update?"

"Give me a moment," Jundt replied. A moment later, a new voice crackled on the bridge.

"This is Major Orfeas Coenen," a drily calm voice reported. "My tech team is looking at interfacing what sensors we have with this black box of ours, but it may take a few. We weren't expecting to get in trouble quite this quickly, Your Highness."

"That's war for you, Major. Do you have a distance and a vector on the enemy?"

"Too damn close and too damn fast," Coenen told the Admiral. "Estimate maybe six million klicks. They haven't opened fire yet, but they aren't slowing down, either."

"Chambers?" Alexander asked.

"They'll start accelerating if they haven't already," Roslyn guessed. "This is a drive-by, sir. They'll hit the complex with a couple of thousand missiles as they pass by, but they're going to push to get out of the system.

"This pass will do real damage, but it looks like a stunt for the sake of clearly doing something rather than a real plan," she concluded.

"Which fits the odd hierarchical attitudes we're seeing," Xiao said. "What do we do?"

"Major, I need proper coordinates," Alexander growled.

In that moment, a new feed popped up on Roslyn's displays.

"We have telemetry, sir," she told the Admiral.

"Sixty-three degrees by one-twenty-five from a stellar line," Coenen said in the same moment. "Distance approximately six million kilometers. Apologies, Admiral. I don't have my good sensors up yet.

"Our shuttle got here about an hour before these guys showed up in the system."

"What do you have, Major?" Alexander asked.

"A hundred satellites with four Phoenix IXs apiece… except we've only got thirty of them out of crates and only ten of them are in space," the Marine admitted. "Otherwise, three assault shuttles and two Viper SSM units with mag-treads."

"They can't do anything, sir," Roslyn murmured. She had to pull up the details on the Viper. A mobile armored vehicle loaded with specialty surface-to-space missiles, it would give a starship in orbit a real bad day, but two of them weren't going to do much against a fleet.

"Understood, Major," Alexander informed Coenen. "Do everything you can to protect the complex's civilian population. I assume they have rad-storm shelters. Get them into those shelters and make sure we keep getting sensor data."

"Yes, sir."

Alexander turned to survey her staff.

"All ships will calculate to jump to one million kilometers of the enemy in one minute," she ordered calmly. "Stand by to engage with lasers and amplifiers."

And hope, Roslyn supposed, that they really had killed two of the Type Ones.

CHAPTER 37

JANE ALEXANDER WAS ONE OF THE MOST powerful Mages alive, but even she could only do so much without an amplifier. *Mjolnir*'s simulacrum was a hundred meters and seven decks away, at the exact center of the enchanted starship. Only the Mage touching that simulacrum, currently Mage-Captain Do Pei, could unleash power through the dreadnoughts' amplifier runic matrix.

Without access to that simulacrum, the jump order was the last chance she had to influence the battle. *Mjolnir* and the rest of Second Fleet stepped through space at her order, leaving fully two minutes before the light of the Shining Shield's emergence would have reached them.

The Kazh, it seemed, had made the same erroneous assumption about the Protectorate that Jane had initially made about the Shining Shield: that they lacked FTL communicators. Or, she supposed, that there wouldn't be any sensors in position to cut the over-ten-light-minute time lag between the Chimera Belt and where they'd left Second Fleet.

Whatever their plan had been, they thought they had time to execute it—and their entire focus was toward Belt Processing Six. Emerging a million kilometers behind them, Jane's people had three full seconds of surprise, no matter what happened. The Kazh fleet's focus and conviction that they had at least two more minutes gave her another ten, at least.

Second Fleet's lasers arrived alongside the light of their arrival, and Jane realized she hadn't given target-priority orders. Soból and Chambers *had*, however, and every remaining Type Three and Type Four of the Kazh fleet died in that first torrent of coherent radiation.

The Mage-Captains of Second Fleet were delayed momentarily by the need to swap out with the Ship's Mage who'd jumped their ships. Even a short jump like this wiped out a Mage, and the juniors who'd teleported the warships had to stumble aside for their commanders to take over.

The magical power of the Protectorate followed its lasers by a handful of seconds, seconds the Kazh's distraction had bought them. A second salvo of beams hammered into the Type Ones and Type Twos, but even the forty-gigawatt beams of the dreadnoughts weren't the ultimate offensive weapon of the Royal Martian Navy.

Lightning and fire filled the void. The lasers were an afterthought, hundreds of them blazing through space with near-incalculable energy transfers.

"Clean sweep, sir," Chambers reported. "A few of them launched; we have missiles inbound on the processing node. Engaging with main beams."

Jane held her tongue. Even the "mere" three-gigawatt beams on the old *Cataphract*-class destroyers were overkill against a missile—and the forty-gigawatt weapons on the *Mjolnir*s couldn't slew fast enough to really *target* a missile.

But the RFLAMs would quickly lose the range against missiles flying away from them, and the big beams wouldn't. Plus, as the displays rapidly proved out, whatever evasion patterns the enemy missiles carried weren't programmed for fire from behind them—and their dead motherships couldn't *re*program them.

The Shining Shield had launched over five hundred missiles while they were dying. None of them made it within five million kilometers of Belt Processing Six.

Jane allowed herself an audible sigh of relief, then took a large swallow of coffee from the sealed cup on her armrest. Her steward had made sure she had her latte, though any pretense of foam hadn't survived the battle.

"Damage reports and casualty lists," she ordered. "As quickly as we can get them compiled."

"Already done, sir," Commodore Soból told her, the other woman's voice carrying a touch of awe. "We took four hits across *Mjolnir* and *Excalibur*, another eleven across the battleships. One breach on *Pax Pacifica*. No combat impairment reported on any vessels. Seven ships with armor damage that will require replacement."

Jane blinked in surprise, understanding Soból's tone. The Kazh's Shining Shield had brought over half a *billion* tons of warships into the Chimera System. Second Fleet had wiped them out in exchange for minor damage?

"Casualties?" she repeated.

"Sixty-three total," Jundt told her, the Coms Officer listening to someone else speaking on her headset at the same time. "Four fatal, all on *Pax Pacifica*. Prognoses are still coming in; some of the wounded are in rough shape. We may lose some more; no one is sure yet."

Every spacer and soldier lost was a price Jane hated to pay. It was part of her job to send people to their deaths, but if she ever found an officer under her command who wasn't bothered by that, she'd cashier them on the spot.

Still. Even sixty dead would have been an astonishingly light butcher's bill for a battle of this magnitude.

"Set a sublight course back toward Garuda," she finally ordered. "Admiral Ryland's Ships' Mages need to rest before they can jump her ships. We'll keep the fleet together—and our eyes open.

"Just because we *think* this is everything they had to throw at us today doesn't mean it was!"

Her people turned their attention back to their stations, but she could *feel* the mood in the room. The previous battles against the reezh empire had been a near-run thing and a scouting mission that hadn't tried to seriously achieve anything.

This was the first time the Shining Shield of the Kazh and the Royal Martian Navy had gone head-to-head with full fleets, and the RMN had basically *obliterated* their enemies.

Every officer in the room was feeling quite full of themselves. Every officer except two, that was, Jane realized.

Jane herself could see the consequences of this. They *knew* the Kazh had massive fleets to deploy, with the only question being how many murdered and living Mages they had to move those fleets with. With a crushing victory behind her, arguing for her reinforcements to be sent faster at any cost was going to be difficult.

More immediately, though, she could see that the *Chimerans* might take it as a sign that they didn't need to evacuate after all. If enough people started refusing to leave, the evacuation might start to get... difficult.

But that kind of looking for the dark cloud in the silver lining was the Admiral's job. Jane couldn't let herself let go to the euphoria of victory. The other officer who seemed darker in mood had less excuse, and Jane rose to walk over to the Operations station.

"Chambers," she murmured. "It's my job to borrow trouble for the future. What are you seeing *today*?"

The Mage-Captain looked up at her and shook her head slightly before pointing at her screen.

"Thirteen seconds, sir," she said quietly. "That's how long passed between us arriving and the last contacts fading, but there was a *lot* going on. So. Watch."

The sensor footage replayed on the smaller screen, zoomed in on the two Type Ones leading the enemy fleet. Lasers flared around them, then the star icons marking magical effects—and then the two massive ships vanished.

"We didn't kill the big ones," Jane concluded grimly.

"They jumped. We can pull Tracker-Commander Uesugi up from Chimera, but I've worked with Trackers enough to know we made way too much of a mess of the local area for them to find a trace."

Trackers were a strange mirror of the Gift of a Jump Mage. None of them—so far, at least—were Mages, but they could backtrace and analyze the aftermath of a jump in a way that required both training and a natural talent of some kind that *couldn't* be trained.

Only Trackers could allow a jump ship to be followed without knowing its course. The RMN had less than a dozen of them and ran a training program generally described as *demoralizing* for both trainers and trainees—because less than one in a hundred students actually had whatever spark allowed a Tracker to do what they did.

Jane hadn't spent much time working with the breed, but she knew that Chambers *had*.

"We'll send one of the destroyers for him anyway," she decided. "I'm quite certain you're correct, Roslyn, but we have to be *sure*. I doubt they jumped in-system again, not after losing the rest of their fleet, but if we can find their local base…"

Her subordinate nodded her understanding. None of the attacks so far had included landing ships or even fuel tankers. Just as Second Fleet had left their logistics ships in Garudan orbit, the Kazh were leaving their logistics ships somewhere else.

Quite possibly in deep space, making them impossible to find unless Tracker-Commander Uesugi got lucky.

CHAPTER 38

"I SEE THAT ADMIRAL ALEXANDER'S REPUTATION is hardly underestimated," Dyad Minister Ojak noted as they gestured Connor to a seat.

Connor had expected some kind of debrief after the battle, but he'd been surprised to be invited to Ojak's own home. The Western Dyad Minister lived in an underground burrow on the edge of Twin Sphinxes, a low geodesical-dome roof providing solar power while resisting erosion from the unending wind.

Underground or not, the house was a sprawling complex of tunnels and rooms with plenty of space for humans and reezh alike to walk around without banging their heads. Unlike most of the places Connor had been, though, the Minister's home had no concessions to human thought.

The halls and doors were built as flattened hexagons rather than the rectangles or circles a human would use. The angles were ever so slightly off, without a single true right angle in the place, and the slight difference was enough to make Connor's brain itch.

Whatever was being cooked through the door behind him smelled incredible, though, and he gave Ojak his best smile.

"Jane Alexander is often regarded as instrumental in the defeat of the Republic of Faith and Reason," he told the reezh. "She would be the first to point out that she was hardly the only person in Second Fleet—and that Second Fleet was only our *main* force, not our only one.

"But she is *very* good at what she does."

"An overwhelming victory over my distant cousins," Ojak noted. He looked up as Hsieh stepped into the room. "Thank you for making it, Ai Ling."

"I wasn't going to do anything else," the Eastern Minister said with a chuckle. "Thank *you* for being prepared to speak English in your home. I know that is an intrusion in this space."

"I... could attempt to muddle through with a translator earbud," Connor offered. It wasn't a good idea, but he felt the need to make the offer. He presumed that Hsieh could manage the reezh language, painfully guttural as it sounded to most humans, as well as Ojak could handle English.

"That is not necessary, Ambassador," Ojak told him. "You are a guest in my home; I will make certain you can understand what is discussed. Please, Ai Ling, sit. It is just the four of us this evening."

Connor realized that there were only three of them in the dining room—which was set for four, though it could easily fit ten without crowding—moments before another reezh entered the room with a vibe he could only describe as *bustling*.

"Apologies, apologies," the new reezh said in English only slightly thicker than Ojak's. "I was busy checking the ingredients on the dessert and missed your arrivals."

"Ambassador, this is my partner, Koja Lijak," Ojak introduced the other reezh. If Connor had learned the tells correctly, the Minister's partner presented as non-gendered like Ojak themselves.

Lijak was tall for a reezh, with the smoother skin Connor now knew to be a sign of aging and an agate-green coloring he'd rarely seen before. Their armored frill had been decorated with tiny silver chains, an affectation as rare as the reezh's coloring.

"I doubt that Nujika is likely to accidentally poison me *now*, Izhaj, Koja," Hsieh said with a chuckle. "She has only fed me a hundred times."

"It's not that simple, Ai Ling," Lijak replied, their voice calmly certain. "Thanks to Emerson's people, we know that humans born on Chimera have an adaptation to certain trace minerals that the main lineages are lacking. There are things that we can feed you that would make the Ambassador quite ill."

"I trust that your cook—Nujika, was it?—has it in hand?" Connor asked. "It would seem unfortunate to celebrate victory with a round of illness."

There was a warm humor to the trio in private that he found comforting. Little of his time with the two Dyad Ministers had been at all private, and even that had usually included at least one aide or another.

He realized that Koja Lijak might be the first reezh that Ojak had *ever* introduced him to. There was something cultural there he needed to pin down sooner rather than later.

"A victory indeed," Ojak confirmed. The reezh produced a bottle—hexagonal instead of round, of course—and poured four glasses half-full of a pale gray liquid. "Our cultures share the tradition you call a *toast*, I believe?"

"Variations of it that are understandable, I'm sure," Connor agreed. He took the glass, careful not to show any hesitation. Whatever the drink was, Hsieh seemed unconcerned about it, so it was safe for humans.

He was only now realizing that he had yet to encounter any kind of reezh food or drink.

"Most of our food and drink is cross-compatible, if you're wondering, Ambassador," Lijak told him with a soft click of her tongue. "As is our reaction to various chemicals. Enough isn't that an entire class of recreational drinks used by the reezh is dangerous for humans, but rich's active ingredients are chemically ethanol and caffeine."

"*Rich?*" Connor echoed, swirling the liquid in his glass as if it was a fine wine. There were some definite color undertones to the pale gray. It made for a fascinating distraction.

"There is no English translation," Hsieh told him. "It may not be much to your taste, but it is quite safe."

The Eastern Minister raised her glass.

"To the heroine of the hour, Admiral Alexander."

"To Alexander," Connor echoed, tapping his glass to Hsieh's and taking a brave sip of the rich.

It wasn't *unpleasant*, per se, but it tasted nothing like wine. The closest comparison he could think of would be Earl Grey tea blended with bourbon. The caffeine was probably stronger than the alcohol, he realized a moment after swallowing.

"Food will be a few minutes," Lijak said as they put the glasses down from the toast. "I will check on it before it is served, just to be safe."

"Lijak holds both a PhD in biochemistry from the University of Ochre City and the equivalent from the Atchakal och Maki," Hsieh told Connor, her handling of the guttural rocks-falling sound of the reezh words impressive.

"That is the University of Sanctuary City, to translate into English," Ojak explained. "During the period between the loss of contact with the Reezh Ida and the arrival of the Founding Expedition, you know that we lost much of our technology, yes?"

"I'm aware, yes," Connor said.

"During that time, we maintained what technology we did by a ruthless restriction of power usage and higher-end systems," Ojak noted. "A single citadel was maintained, while the rest of our people fell to steam engines and animal power. Maki—Sanctuary.

"Much of Maki's importance was degraded with the construction of Twin Sphinxes as a joint capital and the implementation of Terran-style technology, but it remains a major center of learning for the Western Republic."

"I do not normally apply my skills to making sure our guests can eat safely," Lijak added. "I work in a research facility studying crop-to-fuel conversions."

They shrugged.

"Our work is currently suspended, as we can no longer afford to spare the crops."

"I was under the impression that most research and academic workers were offered seats on the first two convoys," Connor asked.

"I was offered. I declined," the reezh said with the same calm certainty. "I will remain with Ojak. We will face the fate of our people together."

The two glanced at each other and their eyes flickered.

"That fate is not as much improved by today's events as we might want," Connor warned. "The numbers available to the Kazh are far too large. The fleet we saw was intended to defeat the defenses of this system if they had been doubled or tripled. They did not anticipate the level of reinforcement we were able to provide."

"And now they will anticipate a similar increase on your existing forces and assemble their next force around that," Ojak said, clearly following Connor's thoughts. "The next attack will be utterly overwhelming."

"They may take longer to assemble that attack," Connor said. "But that is the only bright side I can see, Ministers. Based off the previous timeline, I would expect us to be attacked in twenty-four to twenty-five days."

"Second Fleet will not be able to guard us against that attack," Hsieh concluded. "You must make certain, Ambassador, that Admiral Alexander is prepared to withdraw without risking her fleet if she cannot expect to achieve anything."

"Would you expect Admiral Wang to do the same?" he asked—and the slight flush to her face told him that he'd judged things between her and Wang correctly.

"We will give the order," Ojak said flatly, letting Hsieh find her equilibrium again. "I would hope that Emerson obeys, but we will have little means to enforce our authority at that point. Our Admiral will... find himself torn, I know, but he will understand his duty."

Torn was a small word. Connor was impressed by how much depth Ojak had sunk in to a single word in an unfamiliar language.

Wang would be torn between the people on the ships he could save and the people on the ships he *couldn't*—because not all of the CSN warships had Prometheans. He would be torn between the Prometheans he regarded as his children and the spacers he held as his responsibility—but also between the limited chance for the CSN and the fact that leaving would condemn the woman he clearly loved to occupation at best.

"We will need to keep the evacuation moving," Connor warned. "I fear too many people will see this victory as a sign they don't need to run."

"Some will," Hsieh said grimly. "Enough won't. We don't have enough seats on the evacuation flights for it to matter, Ambassador. Another thirty-three million against the billions who will remain? There are not so many fools on our world."

"And you two?" Connor asked.

"We will remain," Hsieh told him. "That is our duty. Our military prepares plans by the day for the proper use of the weapons you have provided us. The Kazh may take Chimera, but if they act as we fear... they will not find our world easy to hold."

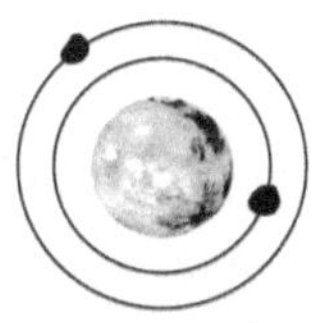

CHAPTER 39

"**YOUR MAJESTY, YOU HAVE AN...** interesting caller."

Kiera Alexander clipped the last piece onto the model spaceship in front of her and leaned back, considering her secretary's words. Cormac Mooshian was a solid presence, a former Martian Investigation Service undercover operative who'd entered her service as much as an extra bodyguard as her aide and secretary.

Those years of undercover placements meant he was very, *very* good at moving mountains to keep the Mountain in line and the Mage-Queen's schedule under control.

Part of that was buying her the time for her hobbies. The model in front of her was custom, assembled from specially printed pieces Kiera had drawn up herself. The *Thorn*-class explorer cruisers were still quite classified, for all that two of them had been at the heart of the mess with Chimera—one stolen and the other chasing it.

Four more were being built, but their intended mission was already over. They'd been supposed to find the Reejit—what they now knew to be the Reezh Ida.

Still, one of Kiera's few friends had commanded *Thorn* in that desperate pursuit of the stolen *Rose,* so she was making a model of the ship to give to Chambers. For Mooshian to interrupt that meant it was important—but because she was supposed to be locked away for forty-five minutes, she could take her time to answer him.

"Your next question, Your Majesty, is *Define interesting?*" Mooshian prompted her—earning himself a giggle high-pitched enough to surprise Kiera herself.

"All right, fine," she told him. The model was done and just needed painting, anyway. "My boyfriend is currently locked in a conference room with more PhDs than I can count as they finalize his course plan, so I'm out of proper distractions.

"Is *interesting* at least *good?*"

"I think so," Mooshian told her. "Complicated, though. Governor Kerekes wants to basically put you on the phone with a Colonel Salih Jusić."

Kiera checked the placement of the piece and then stood from her workbench.

"I'm not familiar with Colonel Jusić," she observed. "I'm not going to claim I know every officer in my militaries, but I make an attempt to know most of my senior officers."

"That's because *Mister* Jusić is no longer a member of any active military," her secretary said. "And his last service was with the First Legion."

She gave Mooshian a long, level look.

"I assume Jusić was not one of the Colonels and on up we imprisoned, then," she noted.

"No. I did a quick check after getting the request from Kerekes. He seems to be about as clean as anyone in the Legion, but we *know* some of them did far too good a job of destroying evidence."

The First Legion—originally the Republic Second Independent Cruiser Squadron, plus whatever other forces Admiral Muhammad had swept up when the Republic had surrendered—had conquered over half a dozen worlds, imposed its military hierarchy on those planets, and proceeded to treat the worlds and their people as a resource to be exploited.

Everything from out-of-hand executions to forced labor drafts had taken place under their rule, and they'd had evidence to justify *shooting* something like ten percent of the officers of "Colonel" Jusić's rank and higher.

"I presume the Governor had some assessment of *why* this Jusić wants to talk to me?"

"Oh, Jusić only wanted to talk to Governor Kerekes," Mooshian said with a grin. "Kerekes decided that this was something he'd toss up the chain.

"You see, it appears that Salih Jusić wants to volunteer to help Chimera."

Salih Jusić was a swarthy man with the shoulders and skin of someone who spent a great deal of time doing heavy labor outside in the sun. His eyes were a brilliant blue, as sharp and cold as ice as Kiera studied his image in the video screen.

He returned her regard levelly, letting her choose her time.

"So." She let the syllable hang. "I have very little enthusiasm for anyone who served the First Legion, Mr. Jusić. But the situation in Chimera is dangerous, and I'm told you think you can help."

"I believe so, Your Majesty," Jusić said, inclining his head in a small bow. "It depends, I suppose, on what you did with the *Saladins* when you captured them."

Evac Convoy Two would have arrived in Mackenzie that morning, Kiera realized. Anchored, as Jusić clearly realized, on fifteen of the Republic Space Assault Forces' planetary invasion ships.

And carrying twenty-five million people rescued from impending doom. The week since the Third Battle of Chimera had seen celebrations aplenty, but Kiera and even the majority of her Parliament, to her surprise, were clear that even that crushing victory didn't change much.

"There are two billion people who are the only reason I'm listening to you, Mr. Jusić," Kiera warned him. "I suggest you don't waste my time."

"I appreciate your patience, Your Majesty," he replied. "I was in the Republic Space Assault Force before I ended up out here. You will give me little sympathy, I know, for feeling that I was trapped in Ridwan Muhammad's nightmare. I saw no option but to obey and relay orders.

"And I know perfectly well that I am effectively on probation now. I would like to prove myself... and find some measure of redemption, perhaps, in my own mind."

Kiera let him speak. She had a mental timer running, but it wasn't as harsh as she'd implied.

"The transports at the core of Evac Convoy Two were seized by the Protectorate at the end of the war," he said. "And I *know* that they were loaded to the gills with military hardware.

"I know that because the one *Saladin* at the depot the Two-ICS was guarding gave us more equipment than our handful of divisions could actually use. Those transports arrived here full of civilians, so that hardware ended up *somewhere.*

"Would I be off base, Your Majesty, in guessing that it ended up on Chimera?" he asked.

"What does it matter, Mr. Jusić?" Kiera asked.

"Because while I know Emerson Wang by reputation, I doubt that he arrived in Chimera with a great many RSAF personnel," Jusić pointed out. "Which means that you have enough weaponry, tanks, mobile artillery, anti-air and anti-space systems, et cetera on Chimera to equip an army of a few million troops... and, what, three hundred people qualified to train on that hardware?"

Kiera didn't know the exact numbers, but he was in the right orders of magnitude.

"And you could help with this?" she asked, letting some of the sarcasm slip into her tone.

"Among other things, Your Majesty, to reach Colonel in the RSAF, I ran a training school for six months for the Legatus Self-Defense Force," Jusić told her quietly. "I am fully qualified to train on every key weapon system the RSAF used. Moreover, I know who out of the ex-Legion personnel on Mackenzie are qualified to train for those systems.

"I can put together a training detachment that can go to Chimera with the Evac Convoy when it returns. We'll augment and support training efforts for the use and maintenance of that equipment. Make certain that the locals get the best use they can out of a windfall that, currently, is mostly a pile of useless metal."

"And what would you get out of this, Mr. Jusić?" she asked.

"Well, I wouldn't mind a steady paycheck using my actual skills," he replied with a brilliant grin. "Not many people on Mackenzie will hire ex-Legion officers, Your Majesty, so I'm hauling crates to keep a roof over my head.

"It's honest work and I don't begrudge these people their anger," he continued before Kiera could say anything. "We damn well earned our fate. I will take a second chance if I can get it, though, and it sounds like Chimera could use me and anyone else I can scrounge up."

He shrugged.

"I was not a war criminal," he stated, firmly. "I have a good idea of who *was*, even if I couldn't prove it. I all but can guarantee that the people I would recruit *are* people you would want to give a second chance to, Your Majesty.

"But *not a war criminal* is a low bar to clear. I served the First Legion. Trained conscripts, fought in Muhammad's invasions, a dozen things I wish I hadn't. I didn't think I had a choice, but hindsight makes us our own harshest critic.

"I want to make things a bit right, a bit better, if I can," he concluded. "Plus, right now, I have mandatory counseling and check-in sessions and, like I said, am effectively treated as an ex-prisoner on probation.

"I want a chance at an honest life, using the skills I've learned—in the service of a state and a cause that are more worthy of them." Jusić sighed. "I'm pretty sure I can round up four or five hundred other ex-Legion people who feel the same way. If Chimera will take us, we'll probably stay there when the sitch is handled, but what I want is clear records and a recognition that we have at least attempted to pay our debts."

"You do realize, Mr. Jusić, that you will almost certainly be left behind in the evacuations?" Kiera asked softly. "You aren't volunteering to train a conventional army. You're volunteering to train a resistance force, even if it's one with vast access to the military hardware in question.

"You'll be trapped on Chimera with everyone else, conquered and occupied."

"Yes," Jusić said shortly. He shrugged again. "I'll make sure the people I recruit know that too. But we will stay behind. We will train the Chimerans to use the old Republic gear. When the time comes, we'll probably fight alongside the people we train."

"That's a high ask." Kiera was impressed despite herself. She didn't *want* to offer a chance at redemption to ex-Legion personnel, but Jusić made a good argument.

"*We* conquered and occupied, Your Majesty. Helping someone else stand against the same crimes is the only thing I can think of that might let me forgive myself."

Kiera nodded slowly.

"We can't delay the evacuation convoy's return to Chimera," she warned. "The timelines are tight. Evac Convoy Two is expected to get in and out before the next attack, but it's... tight."

"Give me the nod and a deadline, Your Majesty, and I will get as many people together as I can."

"Don't make me regret this, Jusić," she said, her tone hopefully carrying the full weight of her power and responsibility.

"I don't plan on it."

"Cormac," Kiera said in a raised voice, summoning her aide. "Start the paperwork: Salih Jusić is *temporarily* granted the rank of Captain in the Protectorate Guard, in charge of a training group he is to recruit on Mackenzie inside the next thirty-six hours.

"Make sure that the Convoy knows they'll be providing transport," she continued. She turned her gaze back to the video screen.

"Make it worth it, *Captain* Jusić."

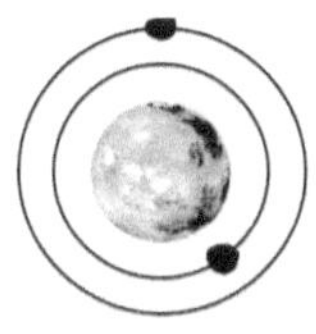

CHAPTER 40

"MAGE-CAPTAIN CHAMBERS. Thank you for joining us."

Roslyn nodded to Karim as her office screens lit up with the faces of the Evacuation Commission. She had a small screen-in-screen effect showing her own image, which showed that her holographic avatar in the Commission's conference room was flickering oddly.

She'd learned just how good the Chimeran holoprojectors were, which meant that the problem was on her end.

"Apologies for the delay, Secretary, Director," she told the lead members of the Commission. "We're having some technical difficulties with my office setup."

Roslyn's training and experience were focused on tactics and navigation, along with magic. Still, she had some passing familiarity with holo-systems and took a quick glance around her desk at the pickups mapping her for the transmission.

She reached over and flicked one of them. It shivered on its mobile mount and then slipped back into the spot it *should* have been in.

"That appears to have helped," Lieutenant General O'Neill offered, the Army officer the only one who seemed prepared to acknowledge what she'd done.

"Thank you." She nodded to the man, though she did check the screen-in-screen to be sure that the hologram looked good to her.

"This should be a relatively quick update, I believe, unless there is something major," Director Shozha said crisply. "With the full run of two evacuation convoys, the Commission's systems are in place, and so far, while we have had plenty of problems, nothing has prevented us from loading on time."

"I do have a couple of updates," Roslyn warned. "One won't impact us soon but will impact Evac Convoy Two's loading in two weeks."

That timeline was assuming that Evac Convoy Two left Mackenzie on time. Given that the ships had just begun boosting from the planet's orbit to leave the system, that seemed likely to Roslyn.

"The other has been delayed, and I don't imagine anyone expects me to make apologies for that," Roslyn continued. "With the chaos here when Evac Convoy One left Mackenzie, we lost track of information we'd already received and had to get updated copies from both the Convoy and Mackenzie.

"Then, to throw a wrench into things, the Promethean volunteers from Chimera decided that they weren't going to be late, thank you very much," she concluded with a small smile.

"I am not entirely certain how Cleo and her friends managed to get *Az-Zahir* this far this fast, but the evidence suggests they are uninjured from the experience."

Reading between the lines, the four Prometheans who had gone all the way to Sol to meet their ship had decided to push themselves to jump every ten hours instead of ten hours and forty minutes.

Possibly even *nine* hours. A perfectly reasonable, almost leisurely rate for a Jump Mage, but faster than any Promethean had done for extended periods. No unconscious Mage-brain trapped in an interface had ever managed that pace, and the general assumption had been that the Awakened Prometheans had similar limits in their new state.

It seemed that might be wrong—but that was a conversation for the Prometheans to have with each other, not living Mages.

"With *Az-Zahir* making rendezvous with Evac Convoy One, we now have a final definitive number on EC-One's capacity," she told the Commission. "With the civilian shipping that was waiting for them at Mackenzie, they are now up to well over four hundred starships and total seats of seventeen million, seven hundred and sixty thousand, four hundred and fifty."

It was fewer people than Evac Convoy Two had got out fourteen days earlier, but it was still the best part of eighteen million souls who would get to safety.

"That is excellent news, Mage-Captain," Karim told her. "I have never had the pleasure of meeting Cleo or the other Prometheans aboard *Az-Zahir*. I... am glad that they feel that they are citizens of our system, despite their isolation while they lived here."

"As I understand it, they did have access to our datanets and media libraries," O'Neill pointed out. "If there's ever a way to get absorbed into a culture, I imagine watching their movies for half a decade would do it!"

He wasn't wrong, Roslyn reflected. She'd figured something similar herself—but she also suspected that the single largest reason the six Chimeran Prometheans who had volunteered had done so was Admiral Emerson Wang. He was as much an adoptive parent to the civilian Prometheans he'd protected at Leviathan as the ones who'd stayed to serve on his ships.

"We'll get the wheels moving on announcing that and passing out tickets," Shozha declared. "Are there expected to be any delays in their arrival, Mage-Captain?"

"No," Roslyn said. "They are currently on schedule to arrive in the morning, OMT, on November twenty-ninth."

She had to pause and consider what that translated to in the local calendar and time, but Karim beat her to it.

"The thirteenth of Theta," the Arabic man told his reezh counterpart. "Late afternoon, Twin Sphinxes time."

Garuda had a long year by the standards of most human-inhabited planets, at almost four standard years. Combined with a thirty-three-hour day, that meant the locals tracked time by a year of twenty-four months—fourteen of them with forty-four days and ten with forty-three—named for the Greek alphabet.

In English, at least. She wasn't sure what the names in reezh were.

"Every soul we can move is a soul we know is safe," Shozha said firmly. "Make sure our people communicate that as they reach out."

"We are going to have more pushback than before," one of the Commission members noted. The speaker was a dark-haired man in his late thirties. He wore the same toga-esque garment as Karim and was a government official of some kind.

"Admiral Alexander's victory is a huge morale lift, but I have already heard questions over whether the evacuation is still needed," he continued as Roslyn wracked her brain for who he was.

Dennis Raymond, she finally remembered. The Eastern Republic Treasury's representative on the Commission. His job was, in theory, to make sure that they stayed on budget—but given that the budget was *yes*, he'd mostly just been taking the invoices back to his superiors.

"My understanding from the Dyad Ministers and Admiral Wang is that we have bought time, nothing more," Shozha said flatly. "Is this something the Treasury debates?"

Raymond snorted loudly.

"There are always going to be people in the Treasury who argue against spending the people's money, Director Shozha," he pointed out. "In this case, most of my compatriots do recognize that the Protectorate has shouldered the immense majority of the financial burden of this project.

"As a member of the Evacuation Commission, I have heard the question both in the Treasury and elsewhere. I have done my best to remind people of the reality, but hope is a powerful force."

"Hope is a positive force," Roslyn reminded them. "But reality is a cruel answer to any question. It is not the place of the Protectorate or the Royal Martian Navy to order your people onto transports."

For that matter, she wasn't entirely comfortable with the idea of letting the *Chimerans* order their people onto transports. She could see value to it, in extremis at least, but she was glad that wasn't going to be her call.

"We have always said that anyone can decline an evacuation seat," Karim reminded the Commission. "That does not change this week or next. Our people will remind our candidates of the harsh realities, but the choice remains theirs.

"We will always be able to fill any seats left empty," he concluded grimly.

There was a long pause.

"There was something else you mentioned, Mage-Captain?" Shozha asked.

"There was, yes," Roslyn confirmed. "When Evac Convoy Two arrives, we'll be offloading a number of new personnel. Former members of the Republic Space Assault Force, they have volunteered to serve as trainers and cadre to help the RCA master and deploy the large amount of ex-Republic equipment."

"You mean former members of the First Legion," O'Neill said after a moment, his tone a touch frosty.

"They also served in that organization, yes," she conceded. "They see this as some form of redemption, I believe. They have all volunteered to remain as part of the stay-behind force. Whoever they have served, they are prepared to place their lives alongside yours in the defense of this system's people."

"We will not turn aside help," Karim said. "The use of said personnel is a matter for the military to sort out."

"Of course. As they are arriving on our transports, though, we will need to consider where they will land in the context of our lift plan."

"How many volunteers?" Shozha asked.

"Just over two thousand, as I understand," she told the Director. "A dozen shuttles that will land full before they pick up our evacuees."

Roslyn was by no means used to the way that the Mage-Admiral in charge of the entirety of Second Fleet would sometimes just pop into her office to see what was going on. Alexander had the courtesy to not barge in during actual meetings, but no NCO in the Navy would stop her without a good reason.

"Roslyn. Coffee?"

It took her a moment to realize that the Admiral was *offering* coffee, not requesting one. Alexander put a tall thermos down on Roslyn's desk, then gestured to Roslyn's empty coffee cup.

"I know you like yours with spice, but there's already a few other bits in here, so you may want to go light," she noted.

"I'll take some, sure," Roslyn conceded. She took a look at her cup, with some cinnamon-scented black sludge at the bottom, then chuckled and slid it aside.

One of the many things Baars took care of was making sure that there were clean coffee cups in a small niche on Roslyn's desk. A new cup—bearing the commissioning seal of the now-lost *Voice of the Forgotten*—settled onto the desk.

The Admiral poured. The rich scent of the coconut milk and vanilla wafted across the desk, and Roslyn sniffed it consideringly.

"There are a few things I could do with spices with this," she told her boss. "But I wouldn't use the same masala for this as I would for black coffee."

"Fair enough. The Commission failed to eat you alive again, I see?"

Roslyn took a sip of the latte and nodded.

"They're held up on us getting them final numbers for the evac convoys," she noted. "We expected to have them within a day or two of Evac Convoy One departing Mackenzie, but, well."

"We all know what we were doing *that* particular day," Alexander agreed. "Any status updates I should know about?"

There would be a formal staff meeting in the morning, but Roslyn was, at least, used to the Admiral's need for updates at random times.

"The last of *Pax Pacifica*'s replacement plates was fused into place an hour ago," she told her boss. Between the ablative layers, the energy-dispersal webs and the complex lattice of composites and alloys that made up the more-inert pieces of modern armor, replacing damaged pieces of armor was a major undertaking.

"The fleet's munitions have been restocked and everyone is at expected fuel levels," Roslyn continued. "With our refineries and transmutation team on hand, we've been able to redirect the Ifrit antimatter supply back to the CSN, who are currently stuffing missiles full of it."

"Any chance they'll be fueling gunship antimatter drives soon?"

"They don't have any gunships left with them," Roslyn admitted. The Republic Interstellar Navy had built their ubiquitous gunships for three modes of drive operation: pure antimatter, antimatter-assisted fusion or standard laser-ignition fusion.

But maintaining the systems for the two antimatter modes was a pain, and the Chimeran Space Navy hadn't expected to have enough antimatter for it to be worth it for a long time yet. Even though the ex-RIN officers should have realized just how much supply the Ifrit Accelerator was going to put in their hands, they'd still been focused on missiles as their sole use.

"They took the antimatter-handling systems out of the ones *Chimera* arrived with, and the ones they built here never had them. Saved them five percent of the mass, with accompanying fuel savings and simplification of maintenance and construction."

"And without gravity runes, all it really does is extend their operating range," Alexander conceded. "I'm not going to object to any more options people put on the table."

"No. Are we getting any of those?"

The Admiral snorted.

"I just spent longer on the Link with James Medici than you did with the Evacuation Commission," she admitted. "Parliament told the system militias to work with us weeks ago, but *intention* and *capability* are unfortunately two separate beasts.

"With the best of intentions, only half of the Core World militia fleets and a tenth of the MidWorld militia fleets have enough training, hardware and information to be able to slot into our patrol and security patterns without a lot of work."

"And only half of the MidWorlds even *have* militia fleets," Roslyn murmured. Any Fringe World with starships likely only had one—and they most likely had sublight ships if they had any. MidWorlds would have sublight defense ships, but not all of them had Jump Mages and starships in their militias.

"Exactly," Alexander confirmed. "So, the systems that *can* step up have done so, but the need to train and orient in the other cases is keeping our ships tied down. Plus, we stripped a bunch of places bare to assemble what we have."

She sighed.

"So, we're not getting anything," Roslyn summarized.

"We're getting a lot. Eventually. A fifty percent reinforcement in battleships and escorts. In six to ten weeks, with zero chance of acceleration."

Roslyn nodded slowly. That would bring them up to sixteen battleships and over thirty cruisers. It would also bring Second Fleet up to almost half of *all* battleships in the Royal Martian Navy.

"We're already a fifth of the fleet, I suppose," she said.

"Exactly. This is a strategic nightmare," Alexander told her. "A good chance for you to watch and learn, I suppose."

Roslyn blinked and then took a long careful sip of her coffee to cover her confusion.

"Learn, sir?" she finally asked.

"Roslyn, you saved my damn life while I was drugged into a comatose lump; you can at least drop *some* of the *sirs* in private," Alexander said acidly. "And yes, learn. Surely you didn't miss that a term on a flag staff was just about the last box left to check on the *ready for flag rank* list?"

At the rate Roslyn was covering her reactions with her coffee cup, she was going to be pretending to drink from an empty cup soon.

"The thought had not crossed my mind," she admitted honestly. "I am one of the most junior Mage-Captains in the Navy *and* the youngest by several years. Mage-Commodore Banderas made it quite clear that while he respected my achievements, he was concerned about my lack of experience and seasoning.

"While I may not assign the late Mage-Commodore's words the weight he would like, he was not wrong, either."

Alexander had a mouthful of coffee as Roslyn started the last sentence and nearly choked. She took a gasping breath, waving away Roslyn's concern, then coughed and breathed in more steadily.

"Banderas was a good officer but always a touch convinced that *his* opinions were correct and carried the weight of said correctness," the Admiral finally said. "He died a hero—and I will not besmirch that one iota, but... you seem to weight his assessment correctly."

"I *am* the youngest Mage-Captain in the fleet, and I *am* short of experience," Roslyn said. "I feel my record speaks for itself in the weight that should be assigned to *my* opinions, but among those opinions is the one that I am by no means ready for the next step in my career. Your Highness."

Alexander held her hand over her heart, coffee cup and all.

"*Your Highness?*" she echoed back. "I don't think I quite deserved *that*, Roslyn. Not when you're being so damned sensible."

Roslyn gave her boss her best *reprove the subordinate* look. It washed off the much-older Admiral like light off a mirror.

"I will admit this staff left me appreciating having people who aren't *quite* so sensible and dependable around me," Alexander said. "But there is great value to having a steady foundation on which to build the clever plans.

"That foundation, Roslyn, is what you have to build. By watching and learning as Fleet Operations Officer. But also by making decisions and taking command. You'll be on the command deck of one of the new *Victories* soon enough.

"But you won't be a Commodore soon."

"Am I supposed to be offended by that?" Roslyn asked. She was honestly closer to relieved. She didn't think she'd engaged in the kind of desperate heroics that had acquired her several of her earlier promotions recently, and while she was realizing she *preferred* command to staff work, she wanted a new ship.

Not... she didn't know what. A squadron?

"It would offend some people to be told that," Alexander noted. "But I'm not surprised that *you* aren't offended." She shook her head. "It will begin to grate," she warned. "Because you *will* be ready before the Navy is. Barring things going very wrong in your immediate vicinity again, you won't face a promotion board again at *least* until you are no longer the youngest Captain in the RMN."

Roslyn had to pause and think that through. At twenty-eight years old, she was seven years younger than the median age an officer made Mage-Captain. That was the median, not the minimum... but if Alexander's assessment was close to the mark, that was a reasonable metric.

Seven years. That would be the longest she'd been any single rank—but on the other hand, if she was going to be at any rank for that long, Mage-Captain was a good one. She'd command her own ships for that time. Get the experience everyone agreed she needed.

"I can live with that," she told Alexander. "I'm senior enough to command my own ship but junior enough to mostly control what politics I get involved in. I'm doing good work and helping good people.

"I don't need money, I don't fame and I don't need shiny bits of metal. When the Protectorate needs me to do more, I'll step up. Until then, give me a cruiser and I'll waltz Her Majesty's enemies to their final dances."

"Be a bit for that, I think," Alexander replied. "I'm quite fond of our current setup. Just... felt that was a bit of heads-up you should have. The weight of your early rise is going to hold you back."

"I never expected anything else," Roslyn said. "I hope to avoid things going wrong enough in my vicinity that I end up needing to be a hero again. Most people with the sapphire pin died earning it."

There had been nineteen Sapphire Medals of Valor awarded in the two hundred and sixteen years of the Protectorate's history. Nineteen people who had managed to earn *three* Medals of Valor over their career.

Fourteen of them had died earning the third. There was only one other living holder of the Sapphire Medal—and Roslyn hoped that she would one day be able to meet the Marine Corps' General Josef Bako.

That would require her *not* dying, which seemed an all-too-likely consequence of the kind of act that would force Parliament and Mage-Queen to decide on a gemstone for someone with *four* Medals of Valor!

CHAPTER 41

"**WELL, AMBASSADOR O'HANNAGAIN,** we've been going back and forth for a good hour tonight, and I appreciate your patience in answering all of our viewers' questions," Ombeline Aukema said cheerfully.

Connor inclined his head gracefully to the woman sitting across the desk from him. The cameras were still rolling, with everything from an old-fashioned two-dimensional video pickup to hologram-mapping pickups mounted on the walls around the interview room.

There, in Meridian East Daily Update's own offices, there were no flying drones doing the recording. This studio was custom-built from the bones out for its current purpose.

"Part of my task here, Miss Aukema, is to make certain that Chimera's people—as well as her government—are aware of what the Protectorate is doing to help them and place a high value on our alliance," he told her. "We not only need to do the things we've promised to do, but we need to be certain that the people who can take advantage of them *know* those things are happening!"

"I could not have said it better myself," Aukema replied.

Connor now knew, thankfully, that the constant cheerful bubbliness was at least partially a show. Ombeline was certainly both cheerful and bubbly in private, but it was a much-less-performative variety that he figured would take longer to grate on him.

"While our questions have varied across a vast range of subjects this evening, from the unclassified basics of the military supplies the Protectorate is providing the Republics of Chimera Army to the cuisine of your homeworld, we have only had an hour to chat," Aukema declared. "Is there anything you want to make sure that our citizens know that we haven't covered?"

Connor had been on the Update twice a week since the arrival of Evac Convoy One and meeting with Aukema. He'd also given interviews to the Republic Nexus, as well as Ijazheedan Kochak and Kochak Kochak, the major reezh news services.

Adding in his time spent with the other, less-major news services, on Garuda, he was up to an average of two interviews a day. Not all of them were as friendly as his "chats" with Aukema.

"There is, though I'm afraid it's not as cheerful as any of us would like," Connor told her. He focused on the larger 2-D pickup directly in front of the desk.

"My understanding is that the first wave of notices from the Evacuation Commission went out today, for the third evac flight," he said levelly. "Talking with the Dyad Ministers and our own representative on the Commission, Mage-Captain Chambers, there is a real concern that some Chimerans are going to look at our victories over the Kazh in the three battles that have taken place here and believe that we are secure and safe."

He was probably laying this on a bit too thick, but he *had* to. This was a case where the most *effective* thing he could do was be completely, brutally honest.

"Unfortunately, our assessment of the forces available to the remnant of the Reezh Ida is that they far outstrip the forces the Protectorate can place at your defense without more time than we expect them to give us," he warned. "There is a chance that we will see another scouting force before we see a third true attempt at conquering Chimera, but only a chance.

"The grim reality is that our shared enemy is almost certainly able to bring a larger attack force than the Protectorate can stop. If you've received a notice, if you have a place on the evacuation flights, please, please, *please* take it.

"The government, the military and even the *people* of the Protectorate have moved mountains to put together these Evac Convoys. They are not as large as we might like, but they can carry more of you to safety than we dared imagine when we started planning them.

"Those of you who have lucked out in the lottery must take those tickets," he urged them. "I know this sounds dismissive of the rest of you. We all know that only a few tens of millions of reezh and humans can be evacuated. Hundreds of millions will remain."

He hated that. If he could have waved a magic wand and conjured fleets upon fleets of evac transports, he would have. But even the might of the Mage-Queen of Mars did not extend that far—and he supposed she'd have conjured warships to protect Chimera before she magicked up transports to evacuate it.

"We are not forgetting or abandoning you. As I discussed with Miss Aukema earlier, vast reserves of equipment have been provided to the RCA. Over *half a million* soldiers of the Royal Martian Marines and Protectorate Guard have landed on Garuda. None of those soldiers are leaving.

"*I* am not leaving," he reminded them. "Neither are your governments, the spacers of the Chimera Space Navy, nor the soldiers of the Republics of Chimera Army. There is a reason the families of your military personnel had first call on the evacuation transports.

"The Kazh may take Chimera. They may conquer your world and occupy your cities. Both Chimera and the Protectorate will do all within our power to prevent that, but the odds are against us all.

"If we withdraw, we will return," he promised. "We will not leave you under the boot of a church alien even to the Chimeran reezh. The Kazh may have more ships today, but they have a handful of star systems at most.

"The Protectorate has over a *hundred*. We are already building ships and recruiting Mages, but these things take time. Mars will come back for those we must leave behind. I swear this, upon the honor of Mars, our Mage-Queen, and the Mountain of Olympus Mons itself."

Later, after dinner and the evening's other entertainments, Connor took a few moments to indulge in just how comfortable Ombeline Aukema's bed was. The mattress used a mix of foam and adjustable-tensility springs to provide a perfectly calculated level of firmness for an individual's weight and current level of activity.

There were similar mattresses in the Protectorate, but it was a well-done example of the type. He couldn't even register the adjustments, but the fact that it was holding him up to the same level as Ombeline was impressive.

The interviewer was tall and curvy but that hardly matched the mass of his height and breadth.

"I got a notice," she told him, rolling over to sit on the edge of the bed, her naked back fully visible to him. "From the Evacuation Commission."

"That's good," Connor said. "You should take it."

"I can't. It's the cart on one side, the hauler on the other," she countered. "I'm a public-enough figure that taking it is setting a good example, but I have a job to do here, Connor. I have to stay; I have to keep the news rolling."

He considered his next words very, very carefully. Ombeline was a good interviewer and a solid presence on the air, but her administrative and editorial roles were as part of a committee.

The news would keep rolling without her.

"Yet... the impact of a major public figure taking the notice would be huge," he said quietly. "You may underestimate it. We're *worried*, Ombeline. It's unlikely that we'll run out of people to send, but if enough people decline the notices, we could actually delay the flights."

"You're staying," she pointed out.

"Because we have to show that we aren't abandoning the people we have to leave behind," he countered. "Yes, twenty-nine divisions is a bit more meaningful than one Ambassador, but I'm the one people see. You understand that."

"I do. Symbols are everything. That's why *I* have to stay." She paused. "And I can hope that stepping aside gives my sister a chance to get a notice."

Connor swallowed his first response again. The odds for Ombeline's sister getting an evacuation notice were the same, no matter what she did. Adding a single place back into the lottery wasn't going to help a woman with a husband and two children get a spot.

"She didn't get one, I take it," he murmured.

"I'd have heard. I haven't heard a peep from her all night," Ombeline admitted. "I need her to be safe, Connor. Do you have siblings? Wouldn't you take even a tiny chance to help keep them safe?"

"Only child, sorry," he said with a sad smile. "I do understand, though. I think you should go, but it's your choice. No one can make it for you."

"No. No one else can. I have to stay and speak for the people of Garuda, for as long as I can."

Connor couldn't argue that point, he supposed. It was part of why he was going to stay, after all.

CHAPTER 42

"DIRECTOR LAMONTE," JANE ALEXANDER SAID, putting a great deal of frost in her tone. "I understand that you have a... *special* relationship with the Prince-Chancellor. I am even personally grateful for your own involvement in the scouting operations against both the Republic and First Legion.

"Hell, I owe you my own life, personally. So, understand the level of frustration it takes for me to say this, Director," she told the woman on her com screen.

"Where. The FUCK. Are my scout ships?"

LaMonte was a small woman with currently bright-red hair—and the Director of Stealth Ship Operations for the Martian Interstellar Security Service. She also wore at least three other hats that Jane knew of, at least one of which was classified to high heaven and back.

"Would it help if I said I was dragging my feet to keep my wife and husband from taking command of one of the *Rhapsodies*?" LaMonte said, her own voice carrying a touch of acid sarcasm that Jane probably deserved.

"I needed those ships weeks ago, Director. I needed to have one of them in Ordin last week, so I could tell the locals what the hell happened to the cruiser they sent on an embassy."

"We promised *one* ship, three weeks ago," LaMonte confirmed. "And if MISS had its way, that ship would have been a week early. The unfortunate reality, Admiral, is that we don't have the level of control we would like over such *minor* things as high-velocity micrometeorites."

Jane blinked. Most modern warships had armor that could shrug off space debris. Even they could suffer an unlucky impact that damaged something critical. It was rare but happened—and while the *Rhapsody* stealth ships were armed, they were most emphatically *not* armored.

"Why wasn't I informed?"

"We told you *Rhapsody in Velvet* wasn't going to arrive on schedule," LaMonte said. "What more did you need to know? That *Velvet*'s Captain had some of the worst luck I've seen in sixteen years as a starship officer or engineer and ran into an entire *cloud* of high-speed space dust in deep space? That we were damn lucky she was only a day's jump from Sherwood and the Defender Yards there?"

The spy shook her head grimly.

"The timing on this was absolutely atrocious from our perspective," she noted. "Like the Navy, we were in the process of updating our ships to a new standard—arming them with Wyvern missiles, specifically. Because we only have ten of the things to begin with, we had three in for regular work before we pulled another four.

"So, counting *Velvet*'s bad day, I had eight of ten ships in shipyards three weeks ago," LaMonte concluded. "Critical as the Chimeran situation is, I do, in fact, have at least two other places I absolutely *must* have a spy ship right now!"

And Jane could name them off the top of her head. A ship had to be in Legatus—the former capital of the Republic was still a Core World and was the only system the Protectorate *hadn't* given a choice on rejoining.

If she was honest, Jane could think of at least four or five places that should have a stealth ship in them, though she wouldn't have prioritized all of them over her need for a scouting force.

"There are no explorer cruisers left in service, Director. I need your scout ships," Jane said quietly.

"I know. The good news is that you're getting stealth ships with four Wyvern launchers and the munitions for them," LaMonte said. "The bad news is that they're leaving Tau Ceti *today*. Three ships. *Rhapsody in Armor*, *Rhapsody in Blue* and *Rhapsody in Bohemia*.

"They should reach Chimera in fifteen days."

Jane nodded. That was far later than she'd like, but it would have to do. Though…

"I presume they have Links," she said grimly. "Because that is when we're expecting the Kazh to make their next real push. We will need to divert them if we're forced to fall back on Exeter."

She had a window for when the next push would arrive. Twelve to fifteen days. She was hoping for the end of that window—because the first day or so overlapped with when Evac Convoy Two would be in Chimera.

"They do. We'll pass contact information on to your staff so you can keep in touch," LaMonte confirmed. "I'd suggest sending them directly to the Primes, but they're following a straight course from Tau Ceti to Chimera. They'll need rest and resupply before they move on."

"We'll make it happen, either here or in Exeter," Jane promised. "I just…"

"You needed them three weeks ago," the other woman conceded into the silence. "I could use twice as many of them as I have, but they're expensive, complicated and fragile. Even more so than your explorer cruisers."

"And when I get those stealth cruisers, I will happily use *them* for scouting as well. Right now, Director LaMonte, your people are my only hope." She paused, considering what LaMonte had said before.

"Are your wife and husband on the ships coming our way?" she asked gently.

"Yes," LaMonte said flatly. "Mike Kelzin commands *Rhapsody in Bohemia*—fitting, since he's responsible for her name—with Xi Wu as Senior Mage. I'd be with them if I could be, but I am chained to a desk."

She did not, Jane noted, even say where that desk was. LaMonte might have been an engineer and a stealth-ship Captain instead of a more-traditional spy, but she'd still spent the last decade working in intelligence.

"I have every intention of keeping those ships safe, Kelly," Jane promised. "Even *without* knowing your spouses were aboard, I need them."

"I know. And they'll be there. Mike and Xi are the best I've got. If anyone can find your answers in that haystack of stars, it's them."

CHAPTER 43

THE PLANET WAS UNDER EXISTENTIAL THREAT. Massive fleets hung in orbit, with tens of thousands of spacers aboard. Further tens of thousands of troops, both Chimeran and Protectorate, drilled and trained across the planet in preparation for when they *knew* they would have to lead an armed resistance.

But life went on, even political life, and that meant there were parties. And because she both owned multiple dresses and knew how to play the game, Roslyn Chambers found herself occasionally sent to stand in for the Royal Martian Navy.

It was part of how Jane Alexander managed to avoid attending over ninety percent of the events she was invited to, after all.

That left Roslyn wearing a long blue high-collared dress in a Twin Sphinxes garden—absolutely *delighted* that the length of the garment allowed her to wear much of her shipsuit uniform under it to proof against the chill and the wind.

"Mage-Captain." The almost Valkyrie-esque shape of Commodore Falkenrath emerged from the crowd, a pair of local wineglasses—designed to maximum volume versus available surface for the wind to hit—in her hands. "A drink?"

"Thank you, Commodore," Roslyn said. "I take it that Admiral Wang is exactly as present as Admiral Alexander tonight?"

"Exactly as, yes," Falkenrath agreed with a cut-off chortle. "Our host tonight is critical to many of the CSN's logistics, so she gets a high-ranking guest, but she doesn't get Emerson. Not tonight, anyway."

Roslyn nodded, not even pretending that she'd learned more about their host than the woman's name—Felicity Darwell. Darwell was rich, ran an industrial combine of some import, and was important enough to at least *think* that the Mage-Admiral should attend her parties.

"This, too, is part of the job," Roslyn noted. "I see Mr. Sadiqov over there, planning a tactical assault on the buffet table. In the interest of interstellar public relations, I believe I should assist him."

"Better you than me," Falkenrath muttered. "The man takes a *no* like a gentleman, but he definitely likes women who can punt him into next week."

Sadiqov was short, but he wasn't a small man. It would take both height and a good deal of muscle, Roslyn supposed, to get airtime on the reporter—both of which Falkenrath *had*. If the woman had been interested in him in any sense, that was.

"Not a skillset I have on surface appearance," Roslyn conceded. She could toss the reporter across the room with a twitch of her thumb, but that wasn't the same thing. Plus, she was hopefully too young for the man.

"And you're better at dealing with impromptu interviews than I am," Falkenrath said. "I've learned the skill, but you have a talent. Go impress him some more, Mage-Captain. The better press the RMN has here, the easier both our jobs will be!"

Sadiqov's primary goal had definitely been the deviled eggs. After he'd convinced Roslyn to try them, she'd seen his point, and their not-quite-impromptu exchange had taken place around bites of the spiced egg dish.

"You are one of the few to have seen the Nine in person," he noted after a few minutes of more regular questions. "There is much discussion over the assumption that Chimera will fall, that Mars can't save us. You have seen the might of our enemy."

"I have," she agreed carefully.

"Can Chimera hold?" he asked flatly. "And if we fall, can the Protectorate retake our system?"

"The Nine is…" She searched for words. "A fortress-system," she finally said. "Every orbit is guarded by fortifications and fleets of warships. I do not know if the Royal Martian Navy could ever assault the Nine itself."

Not least because she knew the enemy had a planetary-scale amplifier, equal to the mighty arcane artefact that guarded Sol. Possibly superior, even, given that the Olympus Mons Amplifier had been built by a group of Reezh Ida operatives operating hundreds of light-years from their territory with whatever resources they had on them.

"If even a quarter of the ships we saw in the Nine carry jump matrices or their 'Engines of Sacred Sacrifice,' we cannot hold Chimera against them," she conceded. "But, as the Ambassador said in his interview a few days ago, we have a hundred star systems. They have a handful.

"We have not dedicated any great portion of our industry to the materiel of war, Mr. Sadiqov. We are changing that now. We will not have the fleets to protect Chimera tomorrow. We may not have the fleets to retake Chimera in six months.

"In a year? In two years? When the economic, scientific and magical might of the Protectorate has been turned to this task without diversion or distraction? We will."

"I hope you are correct," he murmured. "These are terrifying times for my readers. And for myself, I must admit."

"We will do all we can, Mr. Sadiqov. And a few things we probably shouldn't," she added with a small grin.

"And we of Chimera appreciate it." The reporter scarfed his last deviled egg and grinned at her. "I see higher powers than I are descending on you, Mage-Captain. I must abandon you to your hunters, I'm afraid!"

"Not *quite* that quickly, my friend," Aukema's cheerful tones declared.

Roslyn turned to see the other reporter approaching from behind her, her hand tucked through Connor O'Hannagain's elbow.

"You don't need to run away; I'm not working that much this evening," she continued. "I have a case of drones over by the front door for my closing interview with Mrs. Darwell."

"Of course you do," Sadiqov said with a grin. "But for now, you are showing off the latest in exotic off-world fashion accessories, I see."

"I prefer not to think of myself as a mere fashion accessory," O'Hannagain rumbled.

Roslyn doubted that Sadiqov knew the Ambassador well enough to judge whether he was being teased or actually yanked up short. *She* could tell when O'Hannagain was teasing, and from Aukema's smile, the Ambassador's new girlfriend could too.

"But you make such a fine one," Roslyn interjected before Sadiqov started to apologize. "Did anyone establish what we were doing here *other* than looking fashionable?"

"We are celebrating the departure of Evac Convoy One, of course," the Ambassador told her.

Evac Convoy One had jumped out of Chimera around midnight the previous day. That was a local day, which meant that it had been over a day earlier by the clocks of Second Fleet. Evac Convoy Two was less than a week away—and this time, Roslyn had given the Evacuation Commission the number of places on time.

Another twenty-eight million, fifty thousand, two hundred and sixty people would be whisked to safety in a week, before even Roslyn's worst-case estimates for the Kazh's arrival.

"Every ship that leaves this system is a victory," Roslyn allowed. "I believe Mrs. Darwell's people were integral in some of the refits for the Evac Convoy One ships, for that matter."

She'd been wracking her mind for where she'd heard of their hostess before all night. The woman was the CEO of the Dar-Kan-Ray Combine, who had provided a large portion of the beds and—critically important!—prefabricated toilet systems installed in the *Bushido*s.

"Hence the party," Sadiqov allowed.

"Ombeline, can you take Mr. Sadiqov over to the buffet and grab us drinks?" O'Hannagain asked softly, slipping his arm away from his escort.

"Of course," she agreed instantly. "I need to start checking over my gear for the final interview, too, once I've got the drinks."

The two reporters nodded warmly to the Martian representatives and vanished with surprising grace and speed.

"Useful to have medias who know when to give us space," the Ambassador noted. "It's good to see you again, Roslyn. Work in space has been keeping you busy."

"A hundred and twenty thousand spacers on seventy starships," she replied. "It's a lot to keep track of, but I'm keeping up on the Evacuation Commission, too. Plus, I think the Admiral thought this would be a break for me."

O'Hannagain chuckled.

"Even more than you or me, this was the environment Jane Alexander was born in, I suppose," he observed. "I can handle parties like this, even enjoy them, but it is work."

"Exactly." Roslyn surveyed the crowd. "I probably need to circulate again. You need something?"

"Yeah. Wanted a chance to talk to you without Ombeline. She's sweet, but she is still a media and has her own take on everything," he admitted. "The timeline I'm seeing on the next Kazh attack versus the next evac convoy... it's tight."

"It is," she confirmed. "Worst-case scenario my people have run, though, has the convoy basically waving to the Kazh from across the star system. And I doubt we're looking at the worst case."

"Why not?"

"Look at how long it took us to get seventy warships lined up here, and we *aren't* in a multistellar cold war," she reminded him. "They *have* the ships to overwhelm us, but I doubt they're all rigged up for multi-week journeys and interstellar invasions.

"Prepping all of that will take time. Assuming the recon fleet arrived as quickly as it could, it took them twenty-four days to assemble a scout squadron and get it here. I imagine they used some of that time to prep the actual attack force—and they probably didn't expect to need a second, *larger* assault force.

"We'll have some time. My worst case is they arrive on the same timeline as the second real attack, and I can't see them pulling that off."

"Not unless they are very paranoid," O'Hannagain murmured. "We don't know our enemy well enough, Roslyn. We need information and friends."

"I agree. You sound like you have something in mind," she noted, carefully.

"The Chimerans sent out *Barracuda* but haven't heard anything from her. She's seventeen days past her earliest return, and they're starting to make noises about *overdue, presumed lost*."

Roslyn shivered. That was never a good set of words for a warship.

"We need to make contact with the Primes. Scout them all, learn who is definitely Kazh and talk to those who aren't."

"We're getting scout ships. More than that will require, well, real warships," she warned. "We're not sending you or anyone else into the Primes without backup."

"I prefer that," he said. "Look, I'm still talking to the locals, but everything they know is centuries out of date. Between myself and a few friends back home, I'll have a plan put together in a few days."

"Can you make sure Alexander sees it?"

"That's more on Commodore Soból than me, but just it coming from *you* should get it that far," she reminded him.

"I would hope so," he agreed. "But I also know that both as Operations Officer and as the woman who saved her life, Jane Alexander values your input."

She sighed.

"Send me your draft plan in advance," she told him. "If it's half-decent, I'll make sure Alexander sees it."

CHAPTER 44

"ALL RIGHT. WHERE ARE WE AT, COMMANDERS?"

Roslyn surveyed the three people in her office. None of her shift leads were what she'd call *comfortable* with each other yet. Sitting in the chairs in front of her desk, they looked like she'd called them onto the carpet to face some kind of punishment.

As per usual, Miyajima seemed least bothered by everything. The Mage-Commander seemed pretty unbothered by anything, from what Roslyn had seen, a trait that was probably going to serve her well.

Rostami and Sharm were still seated on opposite sides of the youngest officer, but at least they weren't trying to glare at each other over her head anymore.

"We ran through the set of exercises you left last night," Sharm reported. "Miyajima's team ran the Op Force while Rostami worked with the BatRon commanders as their Fleet Ops Officer. Admiral Alexander stepped in to help me adjudicate."

Roslyn nodded her approval. The scenario had been to test how well Vice Admiral Ryland and Mage–Vice Admiral Adamant handled losing Alexander and sharing command of the fleet.

If Roslyn and Alexander were nicer people, they might have made the situation Ryland and Adamant faced something resembling fair. Because they were, instead, the people who needed to make sure Second Fleet got out of disasters alive, the Op Force Miyajima had been running had seen its weapons tuned up from the sensor records of Kazh ships… and four times Second Fleet's tonnage.

"It was a no-win scenario," she observed. "How'd they do?"

"Not bad," Rostami assessed levelly. "I mean, we lost sixty percent of the fleet, including both dreadnoughts, but that was more on Miyajima having Admiral Alexander on hand to ask questions of—combined with her own sneaky mind."

The young Mage-Commander smiled beatifically.

"Ryland and Adamant both assumed the target on the board was Chimera," she noted. "Whereas, to me, it was *Second Fleet.*"

"Alexander agrees," Roslyn said grimly. "It's going to make for some interesting days in the near future. How badly did you mangle the Admirals?"

"As Rostami said, they lost both dreadnoughts and two-thirds of the battleships—but got most of the destroyers and cruisers out. In terms of cohesion, they did better than expected, which meant that the Op Force got pounded pretty thoroughly in exchange."

"Might be the best we can hope for," Roslyn allowed. "Let's run up a few sets of scenarios for us to try out internally.

"Any departmental issues I should know of?"

It was a good sign that her officers looked to each other to answer that question rather than assuming they knew. They were improving—faster than she'd been afraid of.

The Third Battle of Chimera had helped, she knew. Standing shoulder to shoulder under fire made for strong bonds that minor personality conflicts didn't undermine.

"I'm going to be getting some draft plans from the Ambassador for supporting diplomatic initiatives in the Primes," she warned her Commanders. "I'm going to give them to each of you to critique separately. Improvements are better than destruction, to be clear, but if the plan isn't workable, I want to know that, too."

She'd take her own look at O'Hannagain's papers, too, but her respect for the Ambassador could easily lead to her assuming he'd thought of something he hadn't put in the files. Her people wouldn't have that bias.

"Whatever we come up with will go to the Admiral," she concluded. "Diplomatic missions into the core space of the enemy are definitely in our area of operations, but we want to make sure we can do those missions as safely and effectively as possible."

Two hours later, well past the end of her shift, Roslyn finished burning through the messages that had piled up from her spending eight hours on the surface. As the Operations Officer, she wasn't Alexander's second-in-command or backup, but she *was* the Admiral's right hand, the person tasked with turning the plans in Alexander's head into reality.

And sometimes the plans in other people's heads. She stared at the last message, willing for the counterarguments to take shape through her fatigue—but the argument was impressive.

Between the Martian and ex-Republican equipment delivered to the surface, the Dual Republics were currently in possession of over eight thousand mobile surface-to-orbit missile platforms.

The Marines had distributed Viper SSMs to a lot of places across the star system, but they'd still left fifteen hundred of them on Garuda. Each of them packed six missiles, using a dual-booster mode to lift the weapons high enough for an antimatter rocket to carry them the rest of the way.

Limited by size and how much antimatter anyone was willing to put in a weapon on a planetary surface, their range was only about a light-second. The Republic's Mobile Defense Unit, Type Nine, was comparable but with a fusion engine instead of the antimatter drive.

That required a larger missile, so the MDU-9 only had four weapons aboard. Except there were almost seven thousand of them in the stores offloaded from the *Saladins*, leading to the easy conclusion of *quantity has a quality all its own*.

The surface-based launchers could put over thirty thousand missiles into orbit. It would give someone an extremely bad day—and probably a worse one when they discovered that every one of those mobile launchers had a trailer with a full set of reloads.

Now several of the local commanders were suggesting that the ground forces prepare for an actual fight, using the SOM batteries to hold off the attacking fleets and forcing them to besiege the planet from a distance until the RMN could return.

Roslyn wasn't going to deny she saw the temptation. No one *wanted* to surrender Garuda to the enemy. They were almost certainly going to have to give up the star system, but if they could hold the Kazh away from the planet, that would keep the vast majority of the people there safe.

She wasn't sure they even had enough trained personnel to operate all of the thousands of SOM launchers. The arrival of the volunteers from Mackenzie would help, but she still figured they'd only get maybe half of them online.

There was a problem in the mess, she could feel it niggling at the back of her mind, but it wasn't coming to her at that moment.

She'd sleep on it and see what Alexander said.

CHAPTER 45

"WITH THE COUNT DOWN TO MERE DAYS before things get complicated in multiple ways, I see that everyone is coming up with entertaining ways to make our lives difficult," Jane said drily to her key officers.

There was a lot of coffee in the meeting room. While only Jane was drinking her particular mix, all of the coffee came from her Magna Madagasca properties. She wasn't Montgomery, obsessed with sampling coffees from all over the galaxy and cycling through the best of them. She had her flavor and she'd made absolutely certain she would *always* have it.

She watched Chambers take a few moments longer at the coffee station than the others and raised an eyebrow at her Operations Officer.

"Find something interesting, Roslyn?" she asked.

"Poking around historical records and found something that is a touch ridiculous, but I wanted to try it," Chambers replied. She held up her cup, which had a similar hue to Jane's own, though a touch... *oranger?*

"There was a fad for a while of *pumpkin spice lattes*, but I checked. There was no pumpkin in most of them, just a spice mix that looked like a sweetened masala to me. I had everything to try it, so I did."

"That, at least, isn't adding new plans to the mix," Jane allowed. "Peta, do you want to give everyone the rundown on the two potentially useful, potentially disastrous ideas that landed in our inboxes this morning?"

There were a few chuckles, but most of the faces around the table were tight and tired. Evac Convoy Two was due back in the system in less than twenty-four hours—and the window for the Kazh's return opened forty-eight hours after *that*.

"The first plan we have comes from Ambassador O'Hannagain," Soból told everyone. She nodded over to Chambers. "The Ambassador had the good sense to run the concept and structures by our Operations Department, who ran his wants against our actual capabilities and came out with a scheme that may actually work.

"Basically, the Ambassador wants to open diplomatic contact with the non-Kazh Primes of the reezh," the Commodore summarized. "That won't be straightforward, for two reasons: one, we don't *know* who is and isn't under Kazh control at this moment in time—and, two, the Chimerans already reached out to the only independent star system we know of.

"*Barracuda* is over three weeks past her earliest report-in date," Soból noted. "Officially, the CSN is basing their *overdue* timeline on her mission taking two weeks in Ordin, which means she is only nine days overdue.

"She will not be declared missing, presumed lost until December twelfth, OMDT."

Jane nodded grimly.

"I've spoken to Admiral Wang," she told her staff. "He gave specific orders for *Barracuda* to leave the diplomatic contingent behind and return within ten days if at all possible. Without any idea what is going on in Ordin, he has privately assessed them as lost.

"Ordin is no friend to the Kazh, according to the records and video that Mage-Captain Chambers retrieved while she was in that system, but they appear to also be hostile to us. The enemy of our enemy, sadly, is not always our friend.

"Sometimes, they're so terrified that xenophobic isolation is the only option they have left."

"Just because I understand what they might be thinking doesn't make me any happier if they killed *Barracuda*'s people, sir," Xiao said grimly, the Intelligence Officer looking almost as thoughtful as he did furious.

"Much as it will surprise some of us, I am in agreement with Coskun," Giannino noted, his aside glance at Xiao exaggerated for some level of comic effect.

"In terms of the Ambassador's plan, my main concern is logistics, of course," he continued. "I see that Ops has us deploying four cruisers to escort the embassies. Given that we will also need to support the MISS stealth ships no one has mentioned yet, I imagine we'll want to forward-deploy at least two such groups along with a logistics train."

"The first stage is definitely scouting out the Primes I wasn't able to visit before," Chambers told him. "If you look at section B of the plan, deploying a single supply ship cuts the operational loop for the stealth ships—who *are* in that part of the plan—by weeks.

"We won't want to leave that supply ship unguarded, but we won't need major forces until Phase Two. Even the Ambassador knows we need to scout the target systems before we try to talk to anybody."

Jane's own experience with Connor O'Hannagain was that he was surprisingly sensible for a politician. Even the dullest rock in the shed would probably know they needed to find out who would talk and who would shoot before walking in the door, though.

"I see no reason not to move forward with the Ambassador's plan, as updated by our own people," Jane said. "We'll be held up a few more days as we wait for our stealth ships to finally arrive, but once they're in place—and have had a day or so to rest; they've flown directly from Tau Ceti—we'll kick off that operation.

"That one actually makes *more* sense when we dig in to the details," she concluded with a small smile, then took a large swallow of her coffee. "The *other* big idea we have in front of us looks good on the surface, but the details make me twitchy. Peta?"

Soból nodded again and leaned forward slightly, making sure she had everyone's attention.

"General Badem has passed this on to us, as she feels that it falls into areas she can't judge," Soból explained to everyone. "Also, because Admiral Alexander is the commander in chief of Protectorate forces in this star system, including Marines and Guard."

A responsibility Jane was honestly fine with. She knew when to ask the ground-pounders their advice on the situations that involved them, but she wouldn't trust a Marine General to do the same in turn.

It might have been a disservice to Marines in general—and definitely was a disservice to General Fedora Badem—but Jane Alexander hadn't gone into what had then been her father's Navy and earned her rise to Mage-Admiral because she wanted to let someone *else* have control of her fate.

"We have a large number of mobile surface-to-orbit missile launchers on Garuda. Several others have been positioned throughout the system to protect specific installations, but enough remain on Garuda to put tens of thousands of missiles into orbit at a time.

"Reloading the launchers takes a lot longer than a shipboard or fixed installation would, but the RCA's General Staff is looking at the options and want us to help set up a firing plan. Captain Jusić has been consulted on the capabilities of the ex-Republic equipment, and he agrees that, in theory, the systems should be able to synchronize with our platforms."

"They will need telemetry feeds from orbital sensors—either dedicated satellites or links to existing stations," Chambers warned. "Their range drops from three hundred thousand kilometers to *one* hundred thousand if they're reduced to their onboard systems."

"Is that with or without networking the sensors from the various launchers?" Xiao asked.

"With," Chambers confirmed. "They need targeting data from above the atmosphere to be able to use their full range—and even that full range pales next to any antiship weapon a starship carries."

"Because, unlike a starship, SOMs need to think about leaving the atmosphere around their launch sites breathable," Jane pointed out. "Mobile or not, the launchers need to be stationary to both fire and reload. Once the Kazh realize they're present, their life expectancy is likely far too short to start the kind of siege that would give us time to return."

"There's another problem," Xiao said. "The Burning."

The single word sent a chill rippling through the room, and Jane cursed in her head as she realized what he meant.

The Reezh Ida had burned *their own colonies* to ash on an immense scale when they couldn't retake them by storm. Chimera was surrounded on three sides by dead star systems, where their former masters had destroyed much of their own civilization rather than lose control of it.

"The SOMs don't have any capability to protect Garuda from antiship munitions fired at the planet," Jane's Intel Officer continued. "We don't *know* that the Kazh are as willing to be genocidal as their ancestors were, but I can't sit here, amidst the ashes of a thousand dead worlds, and say we should gamble two billion lives on the chance that they *aren't*."

"That does rather put an ugly bow on the whole thing, doesn't it?" Jane said quietly. "We'll want to sit down with the Generals anyway, make sure we're all on the same page on their plan, but we're also going to throw a large bucket of ice water on that plan.

"Those surface-to-orbit missiles will make a hell of a difference when we come back," she reminded them all. "One of my biggest concerns is going to be enemy ships with ground-attack weapons in orbit of Garuda trying to hold the planet hostage. If the stay-behind forces are in position to shove thirty-odd thousand missiles up the tailpipe of anyone who tries that particular stunt, I will feel much better about this."

There was a considering silence at that, then Jane nodded sharply as she made her decisions.

"Roslyn—if General Badem isn't planning on sitting down with Jusić and the locals the moment the training cadre hits the ground, she isn't half the officer I think she is," she said flatly. "Get yourself in that meeting. I want a voice in the room where it happens—and I think that voice needs to be the officer who saw the Burning first and got the full horror of it firsthand."

From the way the redhead shivered and clenched her fingers on her coffee cup, Jane was sending the right person.

"Soból, get on the horn with Captain Beck and whoever is running O'Hannagain's schedule right now," she told her Chief of Staff. "We're still on the same page, but I think it's time for us to catch up in person. I know what I want to do with those embassies—but I also know that he has publicly stated he's staying on Garuda.

"I want to know who he's planning on sending to speak for Mars. Last time I checked, he didn't have that many diplomats with him, and if he wants to fall back on Her Majesty's Mage-Captains, I need to know that now so I can start picking the right brains to send."

CHAPTER 46

Connor recognized Ombeline's voice and turned to both raise an eyebrow in question and give her a warm smile. He hadn't expected to run into the reporter at the Legislature Building, though it was a pleasant surprise.

She didn't look like seeing him was pleasant, and his smile shifted into a mask as she stepped up to join him.

"In a rush?" she asked. "The big media scrum for the return of Convoy Two isn't until this evening."

"That's part of why I am in a rush," he admitted, starting forward again as she fell in beside him. Whatever she was unhappy about, it didn't appear to be *him*. At least, not at the top of the list, anyway. "I need to get up to *Mjolnir*, have a two-hour meeting with Admiral Alexander and her staff, and get *back* down to Twin Sphinxes in time for the cameras and parties."

He kept his tone light, but the time constraint was quite real. Only Garuda's thirty-three-hour day made having a "lunchtime" meeting at the Legislature with the leaders of key opposition parties, a meeting in space on Second Fleet's flagship, and a media scrum and the associated party in the evening possible.

"That's... a lot to cram into ten hours," she noted, sharing his own thoughts. "I—"

"Can walk with me to the car, if you want," he interrupted as gently as he could. "It's a ten-minute drive to the pad, for that matter, and you're cleared as not-a-risk by my security already, if you need to talk."

Connor knew he was many things, but he could read people, and he only used that against them when it was necessary. Whatever was bothering Ombeline Aukema *did* involve him, he judged, but she wasn't mad at him.

She was furious at somebody and upset and probably needed somewhere quiet to cry, either alone or with people she trusted, but she wasn't going to suddenly pull a knife on him.

"That... would work, I think," she said quietly. "I just found out context to news from a few days ago, and I..."

She trailed off again.

Now Connor actually began to worry. Ombeline was a video news reporter. Yes, she often ran from a script, but it was usually a script *she* wrote, and she hadn't blinked at going off it, in his experience. For her to have trouble finding words was new.

He thought he had his body language under control, but his bodyguards—Agent Ansel and one of his top women—closed the distance. They were normally so discreet as to be invisible, and Connor saw several people take a step back as the two Protectorate Secret Service Agents in their pristine black suits suddenly went from *background* to *perimeter*, clearing a moving bubble of space around the principal and his companion.

"We're almost at the car," he told Ombeline. "I think... you might want to sit down."

Kootenay had an impeccable sense of timing, and the armored black limousine the locals had lent them slid up to the curb at exactly that moment. It still took them a good minute to get into the vehicle and have everyone situated, but then Connor and Ombeline were alone in the secured back compartment.

"What's going on?" he asked.

"It's my sister. Christine got a spot on the convoy. She didn't want to give me the details, but I kept prodding, and her refusing to talk about it was strange," Ombeline told him in a rush of breath.

"So, you leaned on a source in the government," Connor concluded. She was a reporter; she *had* those sources. She was probably only slightly more inclined to use them for something personal than *he* would be—and Connor prided himself on his notorious refusal to be bribed or influenced.

"It's my baby sister. I had to know." Ombeline swallowed and shook her head. "She got three spots, Connor. Parent, two children. Under a military-family placement."

"Oh." The pieces fell together in Connor's head. "What does... did, I guess, her husband do?"

"Dave's an *agricultural scientist*," his girlfriend snarled. "He does *soil-chemistry analysis*. I was only passingly aware that the dumb fucking idiot flew drones in his spare time. He apparently aced the damn entry exams for the RCA's air and remote combat forces; he's going for fucking *pilot training*.

"Which gets Christine and the girls a ticket to Mackenzie and..."

Now she started crying.

"And puts Dave in the pilot seat of an atmospheric jet when the Kazh arrive," Connor finished for her, reaching over to wrap his arm around her.

She curled into his shoulder and sobbed heavily into his suit jacket for ten seconds. Fifteen.

Then she swallowed, took a deep breath and pulled back to look at him steadily.

"I thought she didn't want to talk about it because you'd done something," she said, and there was a hint of frost to her tone.

"I told you from the beginning, Ombeline, I can't influence the lottery for the evacuation," he reminded her gently. "Even if I somehow had access, *any* undermining of the validity of that system risked too much."

"I know." There was still a chill to her tone, which Connor could forgive. Her brother-in-law had just volunteered for a military service that was probably going to end up with him dying for their planet all too soon.

That *was*, though he wasn't so foolish as to say so to her at that moment, why signing up for the Chimeran military came with those guaranteed military-family spots on the evacuation convoys.

"I'm sorry; I shouldn't have bawled on you," she told him, every inch the professional again—if not quite up to her usual cheerfully bubbly persona. "That was more of an imposition than—"

"Ombeline, neither of us is under the impression that this is deep and enduring true love," Connor said, reaching out to cup the side of her face in his hand. Her cheek was still damp, despite her attempt to look composed. "We *are*, however, most definitely dating, and that comes with a list of responsibilities and duties I am traditionally obliged to handle with grace.

"*Human kleenex* is definitely on that list. I'm glad we bounced into each other. I enjoy your company and I'm glad I was able to be a shoulder for you."

She sniffed but didn't quite start crying again. She did, however, lean in against him again, allowing him to gently stroke her hair.

"Dave made his choice. Christine is probably even angrier at him than you are," he pointed out. "She didn't tell you because she knew it would upset you. Not the wisest course, but family and emotions make us do silly things."

"Thank you," she murmured into his shoulder. "For being here. I'm... not used to having anyone who would take this."

"My dear Ombeline, if that is the bar to be exceptional in your life, I feel you need better taste in partners!"

That got him a chuckle, and she sighed and settled her head on his shoulder. There wasn't much left of the car ride, but Connor let it pass in silence.

If his presence was enough comfort for her, then he would provide it as long as he could. Duty might call—but he could travel toward it and support her at the same time for now.

CHAPTER 47

"ATTEN-HUT!"

Four Martian Marines snapped to perfect stance on one side of the door. Matching them on the other side, four Republics of Chimera Army troopers did the exact same thing. Of the eight people securing the access to the Triangle's underground bunker, three were reezh.

It spoke to the intermingling of authority and responsibility, Roslyn reflected, that half of the people providing security there, inside the central command of Chimera's military, were Martians.

"At ease, people," she told the combined security team. "I hope I'm on the list."

If she wasn't on the access list for today, she'd either made a wrong turn somewhere inside the Triangle's utilitarian corridors and manicured courtyards, or she'd come down from orbit for a waste of time.

Since her shuttle had carried O'Hannagain up to *Mjolnir* and wasn't returning until his meeting was over, she hoped she was on the list.

"You are expected, Mage-Captain Chambers," the Marine Sergeant who'd called his fire team to attention told her calmly. No one had explicitly called the RCA fire team to duplicate the gesture of respect, she noted, the thought sending a warm fuzz down her spine as she gave the reezh Sergeant in charge of that side a warm nod.

"We will need to check your ID, of course," the RCA Sergeant insisted, his tone polite despite his choppy accent.

"Of course." Roslyn presented her wrist-comp to the local NCO. A double-jointed arm and hand skimmed a scanner across the device. The basic protocol for communication was the same as used by Wang's ex-Republic people, so the reezh hadn't even had to provide new scanners when the Martians arrived.

"You're clear, sir," the Sergeant said, stepping back. "Welcome to the Triangle, Mage-Captain. The Generals are already assembling in room delta-seven-nineteen."

"That's sub-floor delta, section seven, room nineteen," the Marine noncom explained. "There is a lift just through the big door. If you'll follow me, I'll get you on your way."

"Thank you both," Roslyn told them. "Do you need to check Chief Kovalyow's ID as well?"

Her aide smirked at her, as if reading her mind. Patience Kovalyow's job title changed depending on where Roslyn was posted, but the RMN was perfectly comfortable with the concept that any senior officer came with at least two permanent NCOs.

The locals probably hadn't *missed* Kovalyow's presence, but they'd definitely focused on Roslyn. Her face was the one that felt like it was plastered all over the planetary news half the time, after all.

The "lift" was closer to a three-dimensional tram. The controls took both Roslyn's and the Sergeant's ID codes to unlock, and were still complex enough that she figured they were a security measure in themselves.

She at least had a destination and was capable of reading both the Greek alphabet and Mongolian numbers. She could have found the buttons for floor delta and section seven on her own, but she was glad to have the help.

The Sergeant gave her a crisp final salute and stepped out of the elevator as the door closed.

"Mongolian numerals," Kovalyow said drily a moment later, having scanned the controls with her wrist-comp. "Someone was having fun."

"Either Admiral Wang or someone close to him," Roslyn agreed. "I studied Chinggis Khan as part of my correspondence catch-up on Academy work, so I still remember the basic numbers."

Her aide sighed and checked the screen more closely.

"At least the ETA is in English," she noted. "As well as reezh."

Roslyn checked the time and blinked in surprise. Either the Triangle bunker was smaller than she expected, or the elevator was moving faster than she thought. The first sub-floor was easily fifty meters farther underground from the basement where they'd been screened by security, which put delta at least another thirty or forty below that, but the tram was saying they'd arrive in twenty seconds.

"I guess our directions took us to the closest elevator," she murmured. "Efficient."

The next surprise came when the door opened, and Roslyn saw who was waiting to greet them. She knew General Fedora Badem from being in the same meetings together, but the General had inevitably been linking in from the surface, and they'd had limited direct interaction.

Badem gave her an Academy-perfect salute in her split second of surprise, which Roslyn returned with the grace of long practice. Even after all of these years, training and instinct told her to salute a superior officer first, Medal of Valor or not.

"General, I wasn't expecting quite so elevated a greeting party," she told the smaller woman. From the look of Badem, she could probably break Roslyn in half with one hand tied behind her back—and might manage to do so fast enough that magic wouldn't help the Naval officer.

She was still fifteen centimeters shorter than Roslyn.

"I wanted to get a chance to meet you in person on my own," Badem told her. "There aren't many Sapphire Medal holders, Mage-Captain, and fewer still who are single-handedly responsible for friendly relations with the only nonhuman state we've ever been friends with."

"There were many people involved in getting us to here, General," Roslyn insisted. "I can't argue the Medals, though. You know what they cost."

"I know Josef," the General replied. That was all the answer either of them needed. Josef Bako was the *other* living Sapphire Medal holder.

"This way," Badem continued, turning and striding down the hall with a determination and speed that belied her height. Roslyn had to hurry to catch up to the Marine.

"I'm mostly here as a subject-matter expert today, sir," Roslyn noted as she fell in beside Badem. "Is there anything you think I should be aware of?"

She heard as much as saw Badem make a sour face that she probably shouldn't have let a junior officer see.

"I am not in command here, Mage-Captain," Badem finally said. "That responsibility falls to General Edgar David of the Republics of Chimera Army. He's the Eastern Marshal, normally co-equal to General Kin Oronazh, the Western Marshal, but Oronazh voluntarily conceded high command."

It made sense that the Dual Republics military had the same Dyad command structure as they used everywhere else, but Roslyn could see problems arising in wartime from that. So, it seemed, had the locals.

"General David is good," the Martian officer insisted. "However, the RCA was a glorified disaster-relief force and gendarmerie until all of this started. An army whose main training was in backing up police and pulling people out of floods is a damn useful tool—but it lacks experience when the bullets start flying."

"Is he listening to you?" Roslyn asked.

"He is. But he is also in charge, and this is his planet. He will *listen*, but he will also make the decision himself. Do not talk down to him, Chambers. I've sent more than one Colonel of the Marine Corps to an asteroid or arctic base after they shoved their foot in their mouth here."

And, technically, Roslyn Chambers *was* a Colonel of the Marine Corps. She got the point.

"Thank you, General," she said. "I'd like to think I didn't need the caution, but we are all only human."

"Even the reezh, as you mean the phrase."

CHAPTER 48

THE MEETING WAS SMALLER than Roslyn expected, given the elevation of the officers she knew were involved. General Edgar David was the largest presence in the room by several measures, his gray-and-green RCA uniform clearly tailored to help conceal his midsection, but also loud-voiced and clearly the center of attention.

Next to him, General Oronazh faded into the background. She was an odd-colored reezh, with smoother skin than most Roslyn had seen and a marble-like pattern and sheen across her dark-blue features.

Two Lieutenant Generals sat with their superiors. Roslyn didn't know the reezh officer, but she did know Lieutenant General O'Neill, who gave her a nod across the room.

A Martian Marine Corps Major General was riding herd on the Protectorate contingent, which consisted of a Guard Lieutenant General—theoretically superior to the man keeping an eye on her, but taking it in good grace—along with Captain Jusić, part of the cause of this meeting, and a noncommissioned officer with insignia she'd never seen before

Instead of the angled stripes she was used to, the woman wore a version of the Seal of the Protectorate, the crowned mountain on red planet rimmed in gold and then flanked by a dragon on one side and a wolf on the other.

Roslyn had only seen the insignia of a Royal Martian Marine Corps Warrant Gunnery Sergeant in databases. A WGS was the highest non-commissioned rank in the Corps, someone who would almost never be assigned to a detachment of the size assigned to warships.

They were the senior NCOs for entire *army groups* of multiple divisions. The Protectorate didn't need very many of them, but with eleven divisions of Marines and eighteen of the Guard, it made sense that there would be a Gunny senior enough to run herd on the NCOs needed to run those massive organizations.

"I found Mage-Captain Chambers and her aide at the elevator," Badem announced, the stentorian parade-ground voice she produced surprising coming from her slim form.

"Good, good," David replied, his voice only a fraction less booming than Badem's. "Are we waiting on anyone else?"

He glanced around the room, then nodded sharply.

"This is everyone. Grab seats. This is going to be a long one."

There was no conference table, Roslyn realized. Just a collection of folding camp chairs in a rough circle. If there'd been any question about the purpose, David was the first to take one of them.

Oronazh followed suit, folding herself into the chair in a manner that was still disconcerting to Roslyn.

In a few moments, everyone was seated. Even in the surprisingly short chairs, Edgar David loomed over everyone else except the Warrant Gunnery Sergeant.

"We've a few newcomers today, though I think everyone knows who they are," David declared. "Mage-Captain Chambers has been critical in the establishment of the alliance between our governments. Her aide, Master Chief Kovalyow, has been better at avoiding the cameras, but I hope none of us are blind to the critical nature of the support provided by our noncommissioned officers!"

"Thank you, sir," Roslyn said.

"Our other addition is Captain Jusić, currently of the Protectorate Guard and in charge of our volunteer training cadre from Mackenzie," the General carried on, gesturing to the swarthy man sitting with the Martian officers.

"We have some specific items to go over before this is done, but I want to make sure we're all on the same starting page. General O'Neill, can you give us a rundown of our current positions?"

O'Neill straightened but didn't rise. His gaze flickered downward like he was reading a wrist-comp he wasn't wearing, then back up at the audience he'd clearly expected.

Roslyn didn't catch that he had an implant until a holoprojector filled the empty space amidst the chairs with a globe of Garuda.

"Thanks to the reinforcements we have received from our allies and our own recruitment efforts, we now have just under two million personnel in uniform," O'Neill declared. "Unfortunately, the value of Captain Jusić's cadre is born out of the fact that almost a third of the RCA personnel, roughly half a million troopers, are in some level of training."

Green icons scattered across the globe. Few of them were in places where Roslyn would traditionally expect to see military bases, but that was no surprise. Everyone in this room knew they were preparing for a guerilla war, not a stand-and-fight resistance.

"We have dispersed our personnel and equipment across the entire planet. Some of it has been moved off-world to various stations and asteroid facilities, though those will be more difficult to conceal operations from when the time comes," the Chimeran warned. "The largest portions of both equipment and personnel have been moved into bunkers underneath the Blue Rose Mountains and the Shelter Range."

"We have distributed caches across basically the entire inhabited region of the planet," the reezh officer sitting next to O'Neill added. "Most are simply food, ammunition and portable arms, but a few had secure-enough concealment that we have moved vehicles into them."

"Those caches will be critical for ongoing operations as part of the stay-behind plan, but the main Army groups will remain in concealment until the return of the Navy," O'Neill said grimly.

"The main protection of our forces will be an attempt to convince the invaders that they have neutralized our main strength before they even land," he continued. A half dozen icons, the ones positioned where Roslyn would expect to see military bases, flashed.

"These are our older bases, the ones that predate our contact with the Protectorate. While they would be extremely useful in our current training and organizing efforts, the decision was made to abandon them early on.

"Instead of containing soldiers and weapons, they currently contain large numbers of highly sophisticated decoys provided by the RMMC. Right now, any scanner in orbit would show them as being fully operational and home to almost three hundred thousand soldiers between them."

"Are we sure of this?" Roslyn asked.

"We have validated it with our CSN counterparts," David told her. "I certainly would not object to confirming it with Second Fleet as well."

"I'll make arrangements, General," she promised.

"Thank you, Mage-Captain. O'Neill?"

"Not much more to say, sir, unless we want to get truly down in the weeds," the junior General replied. "Thanks to our allies, we have vast numbers of aircraft, drones and armored vehicles, but our training regimes are lacking."

"I've had a chance to review the training programs you have in place, General," Captain Jusić said calmly. "The programs are good; you simply haven't had the time to train enough trainers to train your soldiers. That's what my people are here for."

"We are hoping you can help accelerate the process," David confirmed. "You should have received deployment orders already."

"We have," Jusić confirmed. "All my people except a small command team have divided into platoon-strength groups and are spreading out as requested to the various training facilities. We'll be at work by this time tomorrow, given how long your days are."

"That is excellent news. If the other plan we're discussing is going to work, we're going to need a lot of people trained up on the MDU-Nines."

The ex-Legion officer nodded slowly.

"The anti-orbital launchers," he said. "We certainly have people, including myself, qualified to lead training courses on them. They weren't high on the request list I received from you before, General, so I would have to double-check who among my volunteers is able to lead those courses."

"Thank you, Captain," David told him. He looked around the room. "Between the Protectorate's own equipment and the ex-Republic equipment we've been gifted, we have the capacity to launch almost thirty-two thousand surface-to-orbit missiles in a single salvo.

"To me, that suggests possibilities that should be built in to the planning for defending this system," he said. "Properly utilized, we could use Garuda and her defenses as an anvil for Second Fleet to hammer the enemy into. More directly, we could use the launchers to hold Garuda itself against the invaders for far longer than the Navies can protect us."

A new layer of icons speckled the planet. Each marked a suggested deployment zone for a brigade or more of SOM launchers—and Roslyn knew that if she zoomed in, they'd probably nailed down the locations for individual batteries if not individual mobile launchers.

At a glance, it showed complete coverage, making sure that any portion of the planetary orbit could be reached with thousands upon thousands of missiles, salvos large enough to pressure the defenses of even a dreadnought.

Except...

"It won't work, General," she told David, keeping her voice calm and level as she contradicted an allied flag officer astronomically senior to her. "And even if it *does*, the result won't be what you want."

"What do you mean, Mage-Captain?" the Chimeran asked. She was surprised by how unperturbed he was by his subject-matter expert telling him his plan was a nightmare in the making.

"The first problem, sir, is that you're conflating the threat profile of ship-to-ship missiles with that of a surface-to-orbit weapon," she explained. "We prefer not to have gigaton-range antimatter weapons on planetary surfaces, which means that both the Viper and the MDU-Nine are equipped with fifty-megaton fusion warheads, not the antimatter tips of a ship-to-ship missile.

"They have far less fuel, which limits their range dramatically but also limits their terminal velocity. A Phoenix Nine has a velocity at impact of almost twenty percent of lightspeed. A Viper SSM has a terminal velocity of *three* percent. They carry lighter warheads, requiring more hits to mission-kill a target, and are far easier to shoot down."

There was a reason that the moment there wasn't an atmosphere to worry about, everyone who could do so used ship-to-ship missiles from their ground bases. Viper SSMs and the Republic SOM-Bravo equivalent used a mix of scramjets and light fusion rockets to get up to about eight thousand kilometers, where they engaged their main drives.

"I haven't seen a full comparison, but I would estimate that it would take as many as forty or even fifty Vipers or SOM-Bravos to match the threat level of a *single* Phoenix IX to a modern RMN ship," she said grimly. "That's likely a conservative estimate, but it tells you what you're facing."

Those thirty-two thousand launchers were still the equivalent of a thousand antiship missiles in threat level—and certainly, there was a psychological impact to seeing thirty thousand missiles that Roslyn wouldn't dismiss! But that brought up the other problem.

"The other problem, sir, is the historical track record of the enemy," she continued, letting her tone go grim. "Most ships coming to Chimera from the Protectorate have simply bypassed the Burning. *Thorn* didn't, sir. I have stood on my command deck and looked at the worlds the Reezh Ida burned to ash because they couldn't hold them.

"If we successfully prevent the Kazh from landing on Garuda, they will simply pull back outside the range of our anti-orbit launchers and bombard the *planet* with ship-to-ship missiles. We cannot guarantee a one hundred percent clear rate against enemy salvos targeted on a *planet,* sir."

She didn't need to tell them that it wouldn't take very many hits to wipe out every living being on Garuda. The Kazh's Shining Shield used smaller weapons than the Protectorate, but it was a matter of a few percentage points.

Gigaton-range explosions would kill continents. There was a reason both the Protectorate and the Republic had drilled into their officers and then hardcoded into their weapons and targeting systems one simple, unbreakable commandment: *Thou shalt not fire antimatter weapons at an inhabited world.*

"Even with all of the launchers and systems at our command, General David, all a defense of Garuda can do is convince the Kazh to *destroy* Garuda, sir," she concluded. "If we are forced to leave, we will return."

The room was silent, the blinking icons on the holographic globe marking the perfect layout for a plan that would probably only get two billion people killed.

"Damn," David said quietly. "We have spent weeks building plans to dig into the ground and hide like scared rabbits, Mage-Captain Chambers. We saw a chance, especially with Captain Jusić's people, to actually fight for our world.

"But I grew up here. The Burning is distant in time but not space from Chimera, and we should have thought of that."

"In fairness, General, *I* didn't think of that," Roslyn admitted. "That fell to Second Fleet's Intelligence Officer, and trying to predict how our enemy can think is sort of his job."

"It's part of all of our jobs, Mage-Captain, and while I would prefer to fight for my world, I will not invite Armageddon for the sake of my pride."

General Oronazh snorted softly and leaned forward, but whatever the reezh Marshal had been about to say was cut off by a scream of alerts across the room as every wrist-comp in the space went off.

They were senior officers in a classified meeting in a secured bunker. There was only one alert, one event, that would reach any of their wrist-comps. Let alone all of them.

The enemy was early.

CHAPTER 49

"WELCOME BACK ABOARD MJOLNIR, Ambassador," the mustachioed Chief guiding him through the dreadnought told Connor. Chief Walerian Zawisza had been his guide and escort every time he'd been aboard, and he suspected the man reported directly to Admiral Alexander.

"Is there anything you're going to need while you're aboard?" Zawisza asked.

"I'm only here for the length of this meeting, Chief," Connor told the other man as they reached their destination. "If the Admiral's people haven't already made sure I have something to eat and drink for it, I'll be stunned."

"And I will probably have to ritually flog myself or something," the Chief replied, confirming Connor's assumption he'd have responsibility for that. "We can always miss something, though, or you could need something specific.

"I'm good, Chief."

"Then I leave you to the Admiral's tender mercies," Zawisza told him, opening the door with a gratuitously flamboyant bow.

Chuckling, Connor gave the man a nod in reply and entered the space. He was reasonably sure it was the same meeting room he'd spent most of his time talking to Admiral Alexander in, but given that it could also have been one of the meeting rooms on *Pax Romana*, he wasn't making bets.

The Navy liked standardizing things, and the room had the same ta-ble, chairs, projectors and flagpoles as every other Navy meeting room he'd ever been in.

"Ambassador," Alexander greeted him. She had three holographic screens projected around her—one from her wrist-comp and two from the room's systems. "Commodore Soból will be joining us momentarily, and we're ex-pecting to get a Link connection from *Rhapsody in Bohemia* shortly as well."

"The stealth ships are almost here, I understand," Connor replied.

"Within a few days. Captain Kelzin will fill you in once he links in." Alexander shook his head. "Fair warning: Kelzin is Director LaMonte's husband, and their wife is his Senior Mage. I'm not sure if Xi Wu will be joining us, but you irritate any member of that triad at your peril.

"You're a decently useful chap, but LaMonte *is* the short list for the next MISS Director, and all three of them claim Damien Montgomery as a close personal friend."

"I shall watch my step," Connor promised. "I am generally known to be... somewhat diplomatic."

"The question is more how well you teach that, Ambassador," Soból told him, the Xanthian officer stepping through the door and holding it open for a steward with a platter of coffees. "We are rather short on dip-lomats out here."

"We are short on diplomats *everywhere*," he replied, scooping a coffee from the steward's tray and dodging out of the man's path in a single movement. "We are going to have to improvise."

As if summoned by the word, the holoprojector shivered and two new figures joined the meeting. Having grown used to Chimeran holo-projector technology and standards, they were both lower-resolution and opaquer than Connor found himself expecting.

It was always interesting what you grew used to, he supposed.

"Improvisation is my middle name," Michael Kelzin, Captain of *Rhap-sody In Bohemia*, said brightly. "If the introductions got missed on your end, this is my wife Xi Wu."

The tall blond officer and spy gestured to the smaller, clearly ethni-cally Chinese woman next to him. She wore the golden medallion of a civilian Ship's Mage, and nothing in her posture suggested she was going to be deferring to her Captain or her husband in this meeting.

"You have spoken with both myself and Commodore Soból before, Captain, but this is Ambassador Connor O'Hannagain," Alexander introduced Connor. "Ambassador, this is, it seems, Captain Michael Improvisation LaMonte Wu Kelzin."

The gray-haired Admiral smiled winningly at the hologram of the stealth-ship Captain.

"Did I get *Improvisation* in the right place?" she asked.

"Close enough," he allowed. "Not many people remember to use the extra surnames."

"Like you, for example," Xi Wu said pointedly. "If we are being that formal, I believe I am Xi Trouble Kelzin LaMonte Wu."

Connor didn't know either of the pair nor their third spouse, but he suspected he was going to *get* to know all three over the next while—and that it was probably going to be an entertaining experience.

"I take it there are limited concerns about the scouting or embassy-delivery portions of the plan?" he asked.

"Not in the final version you handed us," Soból agreed. "How many did Chambers and her people file off?"

"A few," Connor admitted. "It was an educational experience."

"Operations plans are their jobs, Ambassador," Soból told him. "I'm glad the Mage-Captain and her people were helpful."

"Extraordinarily so, Commodore," he said. "Captain Kelzin, Mage Wu, I hope you have had a chance to review the scouting portion of the plan?"

"We have," Kelzin confirmed.

"Not much improvisation there," Wu said. "Beyond the normal for stealth scouting runs, anyway. Things can always go very sideways when you're trying to be invisible. We know, after all, that both *Rose* and *Thorn* were detected by the Primes—and while we are confident *Rose* was detected via amplifier, there are more questions around how Ordin picked up *Thorn*."

"We do know that," Alexander said grimly. She glanced at Connor, and he returned her gaze levelly. "I don't like the answer, and it draws on some of our more-classified secrets. I'm not clear on if you two are read in on it, but I *know* the Ambassador isn't."

"I was not briefed on any explanation for how *Thorn* was detected," Kelzin said grimly. "If we know the answer, I need to know, Mage-Admiral. I have three ships and a hundred people whose lives are going to depend on being able to avoid being seen."

Connor raised a hand.

"Mage-Admiral Alexander, it sounds like Captain Kelzin and Mage Wu have a need to know," he told her. "I would suggest you brief them. I am not so certain of *my* need to know and would be perfectly fine to step outside for a few minutes."

"We can also have this conversation later, if the Ambassador is fine with us clearly leaving him out," Wu noted.

"I think that may be best. Apologies, Connor, but there are things the Mountain must keep under wraps," Alexander told him.

"I'll survive," he assured her. He was intrigued and would try to find out some of what was being hidden from him regardless, but he was confident that the Alexanders wouldn't hide anything from him he needed to do his job.

"The scouting plan is straightforward enough," Alexander noted. "As is the plan for getting your embassies to the various systems. We'll move one logistics ship up into deep space near the Primes along with the spy ships.

"As soon as we have a better feel of what the Primes are doing, we'll send eight cruisers and two more logistics ships to join that one," she continued. "The plan is to—"

The scream of an alert tore through the room. Connor had a sudden flashback to his rooftop dinner with Roslyn Chambers, where she'd been hit with a recall alert in the middle of their conversation.

Both Soból and Alexander's wrist-comps were flashing red.

"Admiral, I think you should take that," he said quietly.

Alexander hit the button. She hadn't been waiting for his permission, he assumed.

"Alexander. Report," she barked.

"Sir! We have jump contacts at the ninety-light-second mark," a voice Connor didn't know reported. "Energy signatures suggest Reezh Kazh. Mass estimate… is unclear, sir. Well over a billion tons."

"Understood. Order the fleet to Condition Two," Alexander barked. "I'll be on the bridge momentarily."

She turned back to the meeting.

"I think this all just got pushed back in priority," she told them grimly. "Kelzin?"

"Admiral."

"Divert to Exeter," she ordered. "I may reverse that order in a few days, but… for now, get the hell out of here."

Connor didn't know the two MISS officers well, but he suspected neither liked that idea. They still nodded, almost in unison, and cut the channel.

"What about me, Admiral?" he asked softly.

"Join me on the Flag Bridge," she ordered. "I need to see the full picture before I start making any combat decisions."

CHAPTER 50

JANE STRODE ONTO MJOLNIR'S FLAG BRIDGE with as much determination and confidence as she could muster. She'd learned a trick, a long time earlier, of focusing on the magical fields around her. She could feel and see the energy flowing through the runes around her, the ones holding her feet to the deck and the rarer-but-still-present runes adding their own power to the ship's life support.

She could sense that power, and she was the only person on the starship with its ten-thousand-strong crew who could. That gave her the reminder that she was there by more than blood, by gift and talent and decades of hard work.

With an enemy fleet in the system, her staff didn't acknowledge her as she entered, their focus on their work. She waved O'Hannagain to a seat as she stepped up to the main hologram, studying the key locations.

The enemy fleet—designated Bandit One, she saw—was still exactly where the initial report had put it: twenty-seven million kilometers from Garuda, sorting out their own formations.

"Ops, report," she said, grimly aware that Chambers was on the surface.

"One hundred sixty-two contacts," a calmly sharp soprano answered her. Jane was surprised to have Mage-Commander Moran Miyajima on the Flag Bridge. She was the most junior of the three Ops shift leaders—and Jane wondered if she was there by luck of the draw or because her compatriots thought she was the best one to handle that part of the job.

"Masses are *not* a perfect match for previous types," Miyajima continued. "Vessels still fall into the same five categories, but roughly one-third of the larger vessels appear to be of a different variety." She paused. "They're uniformly *larger* than the ones we're used to, Admiral."

"The ships *Thorn* detected in Cozhan," Xiao suggested. "We knew that system was under Kazh control, but the vessels we scanned in Cozhan were larger than the ones present in the Nine."

"Possible," Jane conceded. "Commander Miyajima?"

"We're still pinning down exact masses, but the initial scans would match that hypothesis," the young Mage agreed instantly. "We have twelve Type Ones, eight of them seventy megatons and four of them eighty. Eighteen Type Twos, twelve fifty megatons and six larger ships we haven't locked in yet. Eighteen standard and twelve larger Type Threes, eighteen and twenty-four Type Twos. Sixty Type Fives; no clearly distinguished subgroups, but the Cozhan scan data suggests their escorts were comparably massed to those in the Nine."

"The presence of Cozhan ships may explain why they're earlier than we expected," Xiao told Jane. "If they were assembled and arrived in the Nine as a unit, they could have reduced the organizing timeline for a follow-up fleet significantly."

"We can worry about *how* they did it later," she replied. "Jundt, get me... Commodore Okorie and Mage-Captain Chambers."

She needed to know the status of Evac Convoy Two, and she needed to loop in her Operations Officer, even if that woman was on the ground and unlikely to be able to do much until they got her back into space.

From the speed the call opened, both Okorie and Chambers had been waiting for her. Chambers was only an avatar, a sign that she was taking the call audio-only through her wrist-comp. Okorie was a live video feed from *Saladin*, his expression as dark as his skin.

"Commodore, I need a timeline on loading," she said.

"We just started the first shuttle lift," Okorie replied. "They'll be aboard in five minutes, but it takes time to offload people and organize them. We can delay enough of our onboarding process to get the shuttles back into space ASAP, but—"

"A total time, Commodore," Jane interrupted. "I understand the complexity of the situation. Give me a number you can keep."

He was silent for longer than she'd like, clearly taking her words with the deadly seriousness they deserved.

"Twelve hours," he said flatly. "In twelve hours, we should be able to leave orbit. We're going to be loaded to the gills with civilians, Admiral. We can't go past one gee, and even with the Prometheans, we need to get at least two light-minutes clear of Garuda."

And a maximum velocity of a hundred kilometers per second. Jane didn't have the exact numbers, but she knew that would take well over a day.

"Thirty-three hours, total," Chambers interjected, her voice grim. "If they go for the evac floti—"

"There are options," a new voice interrupted. Two new figures appeared in the channel, virtual avatars flanking Okorie. Mikayla Spencer and William Connors were instantly recognizable to most of Second Fleet now, the anthropomorphic fox and the grizzled soldier serving as Okorie's right hands as well as *Saladin*'s Ship's Mages.

"We have been experimenting with what our computer links let us do," Spencer continued. "If the other ships download their jump parameters to us, we can calculate their jumps with a similar level of precision to our own.

"We won't know their Mages' limitations and abilities, but we understand the jump spell intimately, Admiral. We can reduce the safe jump radius by two-thi—"

"Half," Connors cut off his colleague. "We would be comfortable jumping the *Saladins* at thirty light-seconds, and it is *possible* we could manage the jumps for the others at forty to forty-five, but a full light-minute *will* be safe.

"There is no point to evacuating people only to vaporize them in a misjump because we were overconfident," the former First Legion Promethean reminded everyone. "That removes almost ten hours from the timeline that Admiral Alexander must buy us."

"We will do what we can," Jane promised.

"They may choose to send extreme-range fire at the flotilla when they realize what's happening," Chambers warned. "Defending the flotilla will be difficult."

"Let them try," Connors said flatly. "The *Saladins'* antimissile defenses are fully operational. It is a risk to expose us, but we can guard the rest of the flotilla—and they cannot guard us."

Spencer nodded firmly in agreement.

"Twelve hours to load, twenty-one to run," Okorie concluded. "We may carve a few minutes here and there out, Admiral, but that's the best I can guarantee."

"It will have to do. Get started, Commodore, Mages."

The three nodded with an eerie synchronicity, then vanished.

"You have to sortie now, sir," Chambers' voice told Alexander. "Once they start moving toward Garuda, they will be in position to fire on the convoy long before Okorie is ready to leave orbit."

"Our only option is to engage them as far forward as possible," Jane agreed. There was no reason to conceal capabilities now. Everyone was assuming that the Kazh force could take Second Fleet—but that meant that her objective was no longer *victory*.

Or, perhaps, simply that the definition of *victory* had changed.

"There's no time to collect anyone from the surface," she told Chambers. She was speaking generally, but they both knew what she meant. Her Operations Officer was going to be left behind, facing enemy invasion and occupation.

"There isn't," Chambers agreed, her voice admirably level. "But I'm in the Triangle. I can coordinate with Beck to find everyone who's still on the surface, and we have evacuation plans. I'll make certain we get our people to safety in the mountain bunkers."

Including herself, Jane hoped.

"You know your duty, Mage-Captain. As do I. Good luck."

"And to you, Admiral."

The channel dropped and Jane swallowed hard, once, before turning to face her crew.

"Jundt, Giannino," she said, pulling her Coms and Logistics Officers' attention. "Are *any* of our ships unable to move out right now?"

"All ships are at ninety-nine percent or higher on supplies, sir," Giannino replied crisply. "Munitions at one hundred percent across the board."

"No one has raised any concerns, sir," Jundt added. "All ships reporting green."

"All right."

Jane stepped back and took one final moment to take in the full scene. Her ships were in a high orbit of Garuda, a phalanx of seventy of the best ships the Royal Martian Navy could command.

Four extra cruisers were embedded with Evac Convoy Two, but she wasn't going to pull those out. They were *Honorific*-class ships, and she could spare their firepower. It wasn't like she was going to *win* this battle, after all.

"All ships will set course to intercept the enemy," Jane ordered. "Flank acceleration: fifteen gravities. They're expecting our trick from last time, but we're going to do it anyway—but this time, we're going to be the ones jumping away."

Every ship in her fleet had at least four Jump Mages aboard. That gave her options.

"Course laid in and transmitted to all ships, sir," Jundt told her a few seconds later.

"Execute," Jane ordered. She turned to her Ops Team and studied Moran Miyajima for a silent few seconds. The young Martian returned her gaze levelly and calmly, more than she'd expected from one of the more-junior officers on her bridge.

"Miyajima, get Rostami and Sharm into a conference and start hashing out details," she ordered. "You have two and a half hours. I want a full rundown of our options—where to jump in, when to jump out, what tricks we can pull on the bastards along the way.

"If you happen to find a way to win this fight, I'll take it—but what I *need* is a way to punch these fuckers in the nose and make them follow *us* instead of going for Garuda or the convoy."

"Yes, sir!"

Jane gave the young woman a firm nod, then surveyed her bridge. She felt *Mjolnir* shiver underneath her feet as the human-made mountain's engines lit up.

"Jundt, get me a direct link to Admiral Wang," she told her Coms Officer. "I'll take it in my office."

Wang looked like he'd aged another five years in the day since Jane had seen him last.

"Admiral Alexander," he said heavily. He was seated in his own office, both of them separated from their staff for a conversation they both knew was going to suck.

"Emerson, I think at this point you can call me Jane," she told him. "You know what I have to do."

"If nothing else, you're leaving my fleet behind, Jane," he said. "We can't match that acceleration, not even the gunships."

"I need to engage them as far away from Garuda as I can." She grimaced. "If I thought it would buy more time, I'd jump from where we are and bring you with us, but we need me to stretch this out."

"And you're intentionally leaving us behind."

Jane let that hang unchallenged. He wasn't wrong, not really.

"Evac Convoy Two can't pull more than one gravity, even once they're loaded," she told him quietly. "Your fleet can only pull three at extremes. Five ships won't make a difference to Second Fleet's fight... but they might make all the difference to Evac Convoy Two's survival."

"I will not abandon this system, Admiral. I am obliged to fight for Chimera, and I *will* do so. If nothing else, we can be a second string to the distraction keeping the bastards off the convoy. And who knows? We might find a miracle."

There were no miracles to be found. Jane knew that. Two-point-five billion tons of starships versus one-point-two billion tons. A hundred and sixty ships versus seventy. The Shining Shield of the Nine was every bit as paranoid as she'd anticipated—if she'd been reinforced by fifty percent or even had her strength *doubled*, this was still a battle she couldn't win.

"Emerson—"

He raised his hand, cutting her off.

"We have to fight, Jane. It's not a matter of honor or promises. This is our home. I could not order my people to run any more than I could walk away myself. It may not be the best choice, but we *have to fight.*"

She nodded slowly.

"I can understand that," she allowed. "There are three strategic targets in play here for the enemy. Second Fleet, Garuda and Evac Convoy Two. Without that miracle, I can't save Garuda."

"You have to act to preserve your fleet first and the evacuation convoy second," Wang said grimly. "I understand that."

"No." Jane met his gaze levelly. "Like you, there are things I *must* do. The Protectorate of the Kingdom of Mars swore that we would defend your people. We promised we would evacuate as many as we could and that we would return.

"I don't see an option that lets us prevent them from taking control of this system, Emerson, but I am not withdrawing from this system without a fight—nor, since I know you weren't actually suggesting that, am I going to preserve my fleet at all costs.

"We are getting the evacuation convoy out, Emerson." She smiled. "And the best option I see for that is to make the Shining Shield chase me."

"That's going to take some doing, but if anyone can manage it, your people can," Wang conceded. "Good luck."

"Cover the planet as best as you can," she told him. "I don't expect them to launch bombardments at range, but these are the people behind the Burning. We have no idea what their criteria for annihilating a world are."

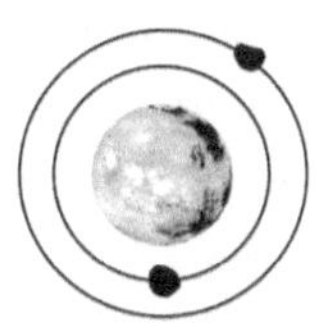

CHAPTER 51

THERE WAS, TO ROSLYN'S SURPRISE, an underground tramline between the Triangle's bunker and the Planetary Defense Command facility underneath the Legislature Building. It made sense, but it hadn't come up before.

The second surprise was that the moment the final numbers had come in, the Triangle had started evacuating. She and Kovalyow had stuck with General Badem, which had ended up with them on the tramline to the PDC.

"It's last call everywhere for the RCA," Badem told them, the Marine General having acquired a set of light body armor and a carbine somewhere. The trio of bodyguards leaning on the tram's three doors were more heavily armored and armed, though they still paled against the combat exosuits Roslyn knew were concealed across the planet.

"The Triangle, like the bases they designated decoys, is going to be an obvious target to the enemy. We expect them to hit it from orbit as they move in."

Roslyn shivered. She was one of the few living officers in the RMN to have ordered airburst munitions fired at her own position—modified for maximum EMP and minimum overall damage to deal with a nanotech weapon—and even *that* left her twitchy about the idea of being at ground zero of bombardment.

She knew the collateral damage that would be inflicted if the Triangle was hit.

"They're evacuating the residential areas inside several kilometers, but they also have to allow for the possibility that the enemy land," Badem said grimly. "A skeleton crew of volunteers is remaining on site. They're in the bunkers and there is an evac plan, but..."

"Brave troops," Kovalyow muttered.

"Exactly, Chief. At least if and when the reezh *land*, people can surrender."

They hoped. No one on Chimera really knew how the Reezh Kazh made war. The only signs they had were dead worlds.

The tram slid to a stop.

"There's a direct line from here to the continuity facility," one of the Marine bodyguards reminded the General. "Should we plan to get you moving, sir?"

"Soon, Sergeant," Badem promised. The other two guards were pointing their guns at the doors as they began to open. "First, though, I need to see the big picture before we lose it all."

She turned back to Chambers.

"Join me, Mage-Captain?"

If there was nothing else Roslyn had picked up from working as O'Hannagain's naval attaché, it was the ability to quickly summarize the position plot for the non-naval officers around her.

The PDC's central auditorium was busy, with more people than she was used to and all of them seeming to be doing three things at once. The central hologram still showed the tactical display of the area surrounding Garuda, with clear markers for the three major forces.

Four major forces, she corrected in her head. The CSN remained in orbit, separate from and higher up than Evac Convoy Two. Second Fleet was well on their way toward the enemy, but the Kazh force was burning inward at their own clear maximum thrust.

"Ministers," Badem greeted the Chimeran leaders as their tiny party joined the two politicians.

"General. Do you know where Generals David and Oronazh are?" Ojak asked.

"Both of them were headed for aircraft when I last spoke with them," Badem replied. "I don't know which bunker complexes are intended as their headquarters and I didn't ask."

"Good." The reezh Minister gestured to the display. "I am not skilled at reading this, despite my recent experience, but this seems to be our worst-case scenario."

The two Dyad Ministers both turned to Roslyn, she realized with a spark of both fear and amusement.

"It is, sirs," she confirmed quietly. "They arrived almost twenty-four hours before the earliest we calculated and with over twice Second Fleet's strength. We have used our magical capabilities and other surprises to balance out the odds before, but we have to assume that the enemy is aware of those tricks now.

"This may be more of a regular slugging match, and, well..." Roslyn looked at the screen and calculated mentally. "The enemy has forty thousand launchers to Admiral Alexander's eight thousand. They have greater range on their missiles and more-dangerous close-range weapons. Our only true advantage is that our Mages appear to be able to jump more flexibly and we have seen no sign of true amplifiers in the enemy warships."

"So, what can she do?" Hsieh asked.

Hsieh's question was about Second Fleet, but Roslyn saw that her gaze kept slipping back to the CSN formation in orbit of Garuda. Or perhaps to the evacuation flotilla and the shuttles dropping toward the planet at dangerous speeds.

They would lift more carefully, she hoped, but if there was a stage to take risks, it was while the shuttles only contained their crews.

"She can do a lot of things, Minister," Roslyn told the civilian. "She has five times their acceleration. While they have better range, we've established that their long-range accuracy isn't any better than ours. Alexander can control the engagement, set the terms of any given fight."

That was limited, of course, by the fact that the slowest missiles in play out-accelerated Second Fleet by a factor of six hundred or so. To truly control the fight, Alexander would have to use her Jump Mages.

"She's going to punch them in the nose and see if they follow her, isn't she?" Badem asked grimly.

"Likely, General," Roslyn confirmed. "Everything she is doing now is to buy time, Ministers. I suggest you use as much of it as you can."

"And the first use of it should be to get every single fucking one of you out of the biggest target on the planet."

Roslyn didn't know the voice and turned to see that the tall Warrant Gunnery Sergeant from the meeting had caught up. Unlike General Badem, *she'd* found an exosuit somewhere—and from the sounds around the room, a few friends with them too.

"Ministers, my keeper and the better half of my brain," General Badem said with a small wave. "Warranty Gunner Officer Yaroslava Matveyeva."

"Your flattery won't save you from missiles," Matveyeva told her boss. "If this planet is to have a chance, the Dyad Ministers need to move to the continuity facility. We need to blow that line *before* the Kazh makes orbit."

"That feels like surrendering already," Hsieh objected. "The first shots haven't even been fired."

As if summoned by Hsieh's words, green icons blazed out from Second Fleet. Samurai II missiles in extended-range mode, Roslyn presumed. Nothing else in the RMN arsenal had a chance of reaching the enemy at this range.

Of course, while the Samurai IIs could *reach* the invading fleet with their acceleration stepped down by fifty percent to double their flight time, their accuracy at over twenty million kilometers was going to be even worse than the Kazh's missiles at fourteen million.

"No transmissions, again," Ojak said. "I believe the Warrant Gunnery Sergeant is correct, Ai Ling. We can use this facility as a relay from the continuity bunkers for a while yet, but we will have to go dark to survive."

"Someone has to be here," Hsieh Ai Ling countered, glaring at her counterpart and then turning that baleful expression on the people around her.

There was something extra about the woman. Roslyn had sensed it when she first met the Minister, that je ne sais quoi that took an already-beautiful woman and made her one of the more attractive humans she'd ever met.

Right then, though, that extra presence was turned to the Minister's anger. "You know I'm right," she challenged.

Roslyn realized she was the only person meeting Hsieh's eyes, and the sheer burning anger behind the other woman's expression scared her.

"If a miracle happens, we need someone here to take advantage of it," she continued. "And if the worst comes to pass, someone has to be in this room to surrender. If they can't find someone with authority to stand everything down, they'll kill a lot of damn people."

"We're already looking at losing too many people, Hsieh," Ojak told her. "We need you."

The room was silent. Roslyn could have danced on the lines of tension in the air, and she had no idea what to suggest or even to say. Hsieh was right. Someone had to surrender the planet. It probably *did* need to be one the Dyad Ministers—and that would put the Minister in question in an extraordinarily dangerous position.

"This conversation is heartwarming and all," Matveyeva said drily, "but my people are running the numbers. In the worst-case scenario, we need the tram toward the mountains moving within fifteen minutes. We only have four cars here. We can move sixty people right now—exosuits will run behind—but we need to blow the tunnel and blow it soon."

"Go, Ojak," Hsieh ordered. "We have to—"

Roslyn had never even *heard* a weapon discharge like the one that echoed through the Planetary Defense Command information center, a burning-crackling sound that assaulted the ears and then fell to silence.

Hsieh Ai Ling crumpled like her strings had been cut, sparks of some electrical energy flickering off her dress for a moment. Matveyeva's exo-suited gauntlet moved faster than Roslyn could see or stop, lifting Izhaj Ojak off the ground.

The strangely bulbous weapon fell from his pebbly hands, and he stared down at the Marine NCO impassively.

"The weapon is nonlethal, Warrant Gunnery Sergeant," he said calm-ly—and Roslyn realized that Matveyeva had studied reezh anatomy well enough to be able to lift and disable the Minister with one gauntleted hand without seriously injuring the target.

"Ai Ling will awaken in forty-five minutes," the Minister concluded. "By which point you should have her well on the way to the continuity bunkers. Holding me up isn't going to help you much."

Roslyn knelt by Hsieh Ai Ling and checked her pulse. It was steady, as was her breathing.

"What *was* that?" she demanded.

"We have maintained certain of the old Reezh Ida technology, Mage-Captain," Ojak told her, still suspended in the air. "It is a neural-disruption beam. This one has been modified to have a setting for both human and reezh."

Badem had picked the weapon up. It wasn't designed for human hands, though a reezh grip wasn't *that* different. The switch was a clear addition and Badem toggled it to its other setting.

"So, if I shot you with it on this setting, you would be fine?" she asked flatly, pointing the emitter at Ojak.

"In about forty-five minutes, yes," Ojak confirmed. "It is even more reliable than your SmartDarts. That does not mean it is harmless, but if you feel that is required to be certain of Minister Hsieh's safety, please, fire."

Badem growled—but tucked the gun into her uniform jacket.

"Put him down, Gunny," she ordered. "What happens now, Minister?"

"Ai Ling is correct. A Dyad Minister must surrender our world. Another must survive to lead it. I am far older for my people than she is for hers. Take her to the mountains, General. Lead your soldiers and ours in the campaign to protect our people and our world until your Navy can return."

"And you will remain here?"

"I will remain. I will speak for all of Chimera, this one and only time," Ojak said calmly. "Your Warrant Gunnery Sergeant is clear on the timing. The faster you move, the better."

He turned to Roslyn.

"Mage-Captain Chambers, I place the Dyad in your care," he told her formally. "Take her to safety; guard over her. Promise me this."

"She will be safe," Roslyn confirmed. The Marines knew, probably better than Ojak did, what that meant. And all of them underestimated her. With the Rune of Power she concealed under her arm, she could be surprised, but no threat she saw coming could hurt her.

If only that was enough power to save a planet.

CHAPTER 52

"EITHER THAT'S MADE OUR POINT or been a complete waste of time," Jane told her staff. "Hold fire on the Samurais."

Second Fleet had launched ten salvos of the massive missiles, entirely from the two dreadnoughts and the *Salamander*-class cruisers.

Jane wasn't entirely sure she agreed with the assessment that the Samurais weren't cost-effective. She was going to miss the ability to throw missiles at an enemy twenty-odd million kilometers away when they'd given it up, she suspected—but the fact that the next-gen dreadnoughts had an extra fifty launchers by giving up the Samurais was a more-than-fair trade.

"No hits on the first salvo," Miyajima reported. "We've got some sensor drones in close enough to get a good scan of their defenses. They don't seem quite to know what to make of the Samurais, but that's been useful for us."

"They've overkilled on them?" Jane asked.

"Exactly," the Mage-Commander confirmed. "The Cozhan ships appear to have roughly the same active defenses as the ships from the Nine, relative to their larger mass. Slightly different beam wavelengths, though."

"Interesting." Jane turned to Xiao. "You're getting that data, Intel?"

"Not sure what I'm making of it yet, but I'm getting it," he confirmed. "Potentially the..." The dark-skinned Turkish-Chinese officer stopped in mid-thought.

"Care to explain for the class, Commodore?" Jane asked after a few seconds and the obliteration of their second salvo.

"Supply chains, sir," Xiao said. "We haven't seen anything in terms of logistics ships for any of these attacks. They've held them back, just in case. And then different wavelengths for ships from different systems—that means they're using different focusing crystals. From different sources."

"Would that make that much of a difference?" she countered. The RMN, at her last review, sourced lasing crystals for their warships from over a dozen star systems. Smaller ones, like in the RFLAMs, used artificially grown crystals—but the lasing mediums for capital-ship-grade lasers tended to be natural.

"It could," he confirmed. "If they're used to utilizing certain natural impurities to augment their beam weapons, the presence or lack of those in the supply available in one system could make a small but measurable change. It's not tactically significant, but it shows how limited their supply chains are."

"And yet they have hundreds of warships to throw at us."

"Because that's where the majority of their Mages and brain-engines are concentrated. Maintaining economic connections isn't in their mandate. Being ready to capture any Prime that stumbles is."

"Which means they're now pointing that invasion force at Chimera," Jane concluded. "Which does, at least, suggest a certain strategic fragility."

It felt like clawing at straws, but on the other hand, there'd been dozens of Type Ones, bigger than anything except her dreadnoughts, in the Nine. But the Kazh had only sent thirteen of the Nine's Type Ones to Chimera. The other four were from Cozhan.

"It doesn't help us today," she admitted aloud. "But I'll happily stick that in the notes for next year."

Assuming anyone in Second Fleet lived that long. Though, she supposed, *someone* was going to be prosecuting an all-out war against the reezh soon enough.

"Sir, we have some options for you," Miyajima told Jane quietly. "None of them require immediate action, but the sooner we make a decision, the better."

"All right, Mage-Commander. Lay them out."

Jane passed control of one of the repeater screens on her chair to the Ops station and watched as a series of icons and numbers took shape.

"We're designating all three plans *Horatio*," Miyajima noted. "Horatio-One is a near-duplicate of our maneuver against the last attack fleet. We jump at twenty light-seconds from Garuda to a new position twenty light-seconds from the enemy. Thirteen million kilometers, give or take. The default everyone is already calculating.

"We then accelerate toward the enemy at our full power, engaging as heavily as we can. We'll jump out when we assess we can't take more fire without losing key mission capabilities. Second jump is planned as a full light-minute. We'll be outside the Kazh's range but also outside of ours. We should be able to calculate the jump to shed most of our velocity, allowing us to come around into their trail, encouraging *them* to turn and engage us."

"Assuming we do enough damage that they see us as worth it," Jane said grimly.

"Exactly, sir. Horatio-One is a straightforward punch in the nose, maintaining Jump Mage capability as much as possible and giving us the opportunity to control both the beginning and the end of the engagement. It does, however, also rely on the enemy regarding Second Fleet as the main target in the system and being prepared to divert significantly in pursuit of us."

"I see." Horatio-One was acceptable—*straightforward*, as Miyajima had described it, but Jane wasn't sure that this situation could survive straightforward. Straightforward was *predictable*, and Horatio-One didn't bring any surprises to the table.

"Horatio-Two is, frankly, even more dependent on the enemy regarding Second Fleet as the main target on the board," the Mage-Commander continued briskly, before Jane could raise any commentary. "Like Horatio-One, it's a jump-in-jump-out scenario. We jump as per Horatio-One but jump out when the enemy missiles reach about fifty thousand klicks.

"We avoid any danger of taking significant damage, and given the Shield's demonstrated electronic-warfare capability, we honestly won't give up that much efficiency on our own missile strikes," Miyajima laid out. "We'd go to maximum rate of fire and unload at least four salvos before we jumped away. It's a theoretically risk-free scenario, but it again depends on the Kazh pursuing us of their own volition."

In Jane's opinion, the more damage they did to the enemy fleet, the more likely the invaders were to turn in their course and chase her. She could see adjustments to the plans to make them more effective—mostly, cutting the emergence point of the second jump so that they came out inside the enemy range.

Horatio-One and -Two were exactly what she would have expected from her staff. They were solid plans, reliable and dependable.

"You had three plans, you said," she noted carefully.

"Yeah. I told Sharm and Rostami that we weren't in a position to play things safe and that you were going to want something with more chutzpah."

Jane chuckled. That wasn't quite how she'd have described what she was looking for in a battle plan, but it wasn't wrong, either.

"Horatio-Three, then?" she asked.

"Horatio-Three is the *all cards on the table, kick the bastards in the nuts and insult their mothers* plan," Miyajima said. "I can't guarantee it will make the Shield turn after us, sir, but if anything will, it's Horatio-Three."

"Lay it out."

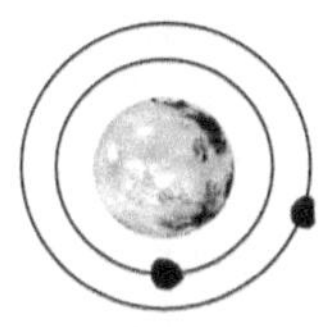

CHAPTER 53

CONNOR O'HANNAGAIN WAS A LOOSE THREAD.
There'd been no shuttle to take him back to the surface, which meant that however the next few hours played out, he'd broken his word to the people of Chimera.

He wasn't overly bothered by that. It wasn't his choice, and he'd certainly *intended* to remain on the planet, but one of the consequences of a career in politics and mediation based on keeping his word was that he knew when he had to break it.

Having a reputation for meaning his promises meant that the times he had to break them were mostly given a bit more slack—though he also knew that he had to keep a hundred or more promises for each one he broke.

And the one to remain on Chimera had been a big one. *Not overly bothered* didn't mean *not bothered*.

He'd returned to the conference room as Alexander took command of her fleet. She'd told him to come along, but he was a distraction her people didn't need. The meeting room had good display systems, and he had enough access to rig them up to give him some concept of what was going on.

That only left him missing Roslyn Chambers' ability to convert the iconography into useful explanations. Captain Beck hadn't been bad at it, but Chambers had been much better.

He hoped she was safe on the surface. She'd be with the military command, at least. That would be enough, he hoped.

The hatch slid open, and a familiar mustachioed Chief strode in at a speed one step short of outright charge.

"Ambassador! Are you all right?" Chief Zawisza asked.

"I am sitting in a secure conference room inside the most powerful warship humanity knows of," Connor said mildly. He gestured to the display above the table, showing the positions of Second Fleet and the enemy force.

"I even, in theory, have some idea of what's going on. Not that I can read more than *we're here* and *they're over there*," he admitted. "Do you need anything, Chief?"

"I was sent to make sure you were safe when the Admiral realized you'd left the Flag Bridge, sir," the Chief admitted. Zawisza paused, clearly reassessing the situation, then a mustachio twitched as he grinned.

"You seem to be doing fine, but I need to make sure you're kitted out, Ambassador," he noted. "I'm guessing that suit is armored, like the gentleman outside?"

Connor nodded, though he wasn't sure he wanted to know how Zawisza knew that Ansel's suit was armored.

"Might help against random bullets, but it won't keep you safe from vacuum. Come on. I'll get you and your bodyguard into vac-suits."

"Is that likely to be necessary?" Connor asked.

"It's war, sir," Sarvesh Ansel said flatly, stepping through the hatch after the Chief. "We're aboard the best-defended ship in the fleet, but that also means we're the biggest target. Am I right, Chief Zawisza?"

"You're right, Agent," the Chief agreed. "And back when I was a mere Petty Officer, I was on *Durendal*. If the Admiral doesn't put us right in the center of the firing line punching at the bad guys, she's lost what makes her *the* Admiral. And I haven't seen anything suggesting *that*, sir."

"Let's go find those vac-suits, Ambassador," Ansel insisted. "I don't know the Admiral's plan, but I suspect we have much less time than we expect."

The RMN issued all of their people with shipsuits that acted as the base layer of their uniform. They could be linked to external helmets but also had emergency helmets concealed in their collars. Without any additional equipment, a shipsuit could only keep its wearer alive for about thirty minutes, but there was emergency equipment in every space on a warship.

Those suits were, however, sized to the wearer. Connor assumed *Mjolnir* had the capacity to adjust the shipsuits—for that matter, he assumed the ship's workshops and fabricators could build them from raw materials—but they didn't have time to sort that out.

The emergency vac-suits were not so sleek and fitted. They had several adjustable straps and sections that allowed Chief Zawisza to adjust them to his two new charges. Once everything was in place, they fit decently, but Connor envied the spacer his form-fitted protection as he waved a bulky gloved hand around.

"Could be worse, I suppose," he said fatalistically. The helmet clipped onto a strap on his left shoulder, easy to access if an alert tore through their compartment.

"It has its advantages, sir," Zawisza pointed out. "Six-hour oxygen life, and it takes the same backup tanks as our shipsuits." He tapped an icon on the wall, a faded green O_2. "In an emergency, all of these will light up. Push them and the compartment opens."

He demonstrated, the symbol sliding in easily and allowing the Chief to move a panel up. That revealed a set of backup helmets that would fit either the shipsuits or the emergency vac-suits, and rows of oxygen bottles.

"All of these are supposed to be checked and filled, so you can grab one blindly if you're in a rush, but you're better off checking the bottom," Zawisza continued, pulling a bottle off the rack and showing it to them. The bottom appeared to be painted green.

"Green means ten hours, minimum," he told them. "If it's yellow, you're under ten hours. It will slowly get darker over those hours, turning red at one hour."

"Good to know," Connor said. "Is there somewhere I should be, Chief?"

"Well, we can go back to your little display in the conference room, but you've got the bona fides to go to the heart of the matter, don't you? Now you're safe, the Flag Bridge might be the best place to be, to know what's what."

Connor's professionalism had told him that the Flag Bridge was the last place for him to be. He was no spacer, no tactician, and if he jogged Jane Alexander's elbow, he couldn't even conceive of the consequences.

The rest of him, though, hadn't risen to becoming one of the best Arbitrators on the Commission and humanity's first interspecies Ambassador by wanting to stand aside. He'd tried to follow it from a conference room and failed.

Given the choice between waiting for the answers or being in the room where it happened...

"Lead on, Chief. Let's go see if we can find out what's happening."

Everyone on the Flag Bridge was even busier than they had been when they left. Connor still hoped to avoid getting in their way, which left him in something of a quandary once his credentials and security clearance had got them past the Marines outside the space.

Zawisza tugged at his sleeve and pointed toward a set of seats folded up onto one of the bulkheads. They seemed out of the way to Connor, probably intended for some kind of observer, like him.

He stayed carefully clear of people's paths as he stepped over to the seats, keeping one eye on the main display and trying to catch up on what was going on.

Thanks to the feed he'd been running in the conference room, he could see that nothing much had changed from the preceding two hours. Second Fleet was hurtling out toward the Shining Shield at fifteen gravities, and the Kazh were burning toward Garuda at three times their own homeworld's gravity—roughly two-point-eight-five Terran gees.

"We are approaching point Horatio-Alpha," someone reported.

"Time?" Alexander asked, something in her tone making Connor hurry finishing up folding the seat down and strapping himself in.

"Sixty seconds," the same person said. Connor didn't recognize the dark-skinned woman speaking. She wore the medallion of a Mage and the stripes of a full Commander, and from her reports, he guessed that she was filling in for Roslyn Chambers.

That would make her Mage-Commander Moran Miyajima, he decided, from what Chambers had told him of her new team.

"Make sure all ships have triple-confirmed their calculations," Alexander ordered. "We're too close to the planet and jumping too short for normal variances."

"Initiating check five, sir," Commodore Soból—who Connor *did* know—told Alexander, without a hint of sarcasm or irony in her voice.

"On all the jumps, if you please, Peta," Alexander noted.

"Yes, sir."

Connor wasn't sure how many jumps *all the jumps* was, which only drove home how out of his depth he was there. If the Reezh Kazh was sending demands, negotiations, threats, ultimatums... anything involving *talking* to them, he could handle. His experience on Chimera told him that while the reezh were alien, there were certain fundamental constants to being an oxygen-breathing sapient mammal he could lean on.

"All jumps confirmed on all ships," Soból finally said. "Ten-second countdown commencing... now."

To Connor's surprise, Alexander turned in her chair to meet his gaze across the room. There wasn't much between them, though the emergency seats were off from the main pathways through the room.

"If you are inclined to prayer, Ambassador, now would be the time," she told him.

"Then I wish you good luck, Mage-Admiral," he replied, pitching his voice clearly and confidently.

"Horatio-Alpha... *now*," Miyajima snapped.

Connor knew that some people—like Chambers—sensed something from a jump. He wasn't one of them. The only thing he registered was that the tactical display at the center of the room changed.

Instead of Second Fleet being six million kilometers from Garuda, suddenly they were over twenty million—and instead of being almost twenty million kilometers away from the Kazh, they were less than five!

Even *he* realized that was knife range in a space battle. The new icons and lines that appeared on the hologram as he thought that only proved the fear.

"Range is sixteen light-seconds," Miyajima reported. "All beams firing. All missiles firing. The count is twenty-nine, twenty-eight, twenty-seven..."

The Mage-Commander stopped counting aloud, but the countdown continued on the display in three-dimensional letters that had to be a meter high.

Connor resisted the urge to ask stupid questions. He could see that only one missile salvo had been launched and that Second Fleet was firing lasers like they were free, but he had no idea what the countdown was for.

All he knew was that the Kazh fleet didn't seem to be *responding* to their arrival—and that the tension in the command space was getting tighter by the second as the countdown ran toward zero.

"Horatio-Bravo... *now*," Miyajima declared.

The fact that Connor *didn't* sense anything made him figure they'd jumped—and the tactical display updated for that.

Except they hadn't jumped clear of the enemy fleet. They'd jumped in *even closer*.

"Range is *six* light-seconds," the Ops Officer reported. "Count is nine, eight..."

CHAPTER 54

IT WAS CALLED THE PICARD MANEUVER and Jane Alexander had never heard of anyone trying it with an entire fleet before. It had been used against the Royal Martian Navy by First Legion Awakened Prometheans—by, in fact, William Connors—to devastating effect.

By jumping from inside beam range to *still* inside beam range, the laser salvos coming from her ships after the jump were going in at the same time as the last salvos they'd fired from their more distant position. The Shining Shield was seeing her entire fleet duplicate, present in two places at once and *firing* from two places at once.

Equally, the *enemy's* particle weapons were only slightly slower than lightspeed. They had seen her fleet's arrival at Horatio-Alpha sixteen seconds after she'd arrived, and their return fire had reached Horatio-Alpha seventeen or so seconds later—about three seconds *after* they'd jumped forward to Horatio-Bravo.

The main difference between sixteen light-seconds and six was the amplifiers built into her ships. Not only lasers and missiles filled the space between the two fleets. The magical power that defined the Royal Martian Navy lashed out at her enemies, plasma and false lightning hammering into the reezh ships with astonishing power.

There was no time to even assess the impact of their fire. The light-speed loop that they were avoiding to taunt their enemies was the same one they'd use to assess the impact of even their initial hits. It was down to preplanning and estimates, and Jane felt a moment of surprise that everything was going according to plan.

At which point, of course, everything went to hell. A spike of pressure slammed into Jane's head, her sense of magic suddenly screaming that something was wrong. Then, with no other warning or preamble, *Excalibur* simply blew up.

One moment, a hundred-megaton dreadnought led the way toward the enemy, hurling beams and missiles and magic at the Kazh. The next, she was an expanding ball of fire along with ten thousand of Jane's people.

"What the *fuck*?" someone screamed.

A battleship ripped apart at the same time, and Jane *knew* the problem.

Amplified Mages could only *see* the same lightspeed data as anyone else, but their power could *affect* things instantaneously. The same power that was tearing in to the enemy's heaviest ship was being turned around on Second Fleet.

And despite everything, the Royal Martian Navy's counter-amplifier was still limited to *don't be there*.

There was no time for new orders. For four eternal seconds, Second Fleet took the magical fire of the Shining Shield, and then Horatio-Charlie hit.

Second Fleet jumped again.

"Damage report," Jane ordered, managing to keep her voice down from a shout by sheer force of will.

"We're collating," Soból told her grimly. "Not much *damage*, it looks like. The ships that got hit are just gone."

"That answers the question of whether the fuckers had amplifiers, I suppose," Miyajima noted. "We knew they had to; we'd just only seen ships with Engines of Sacred Sacrifice."

"And now we have seen them and we know they are just as powerful as ours," Jane said grimly. "Ops, get me details on the enemy status as quickly as you can."

"Already on it. First salvo is in space, sir," Miyajima added, almost as an afterthought.

Unlike an interstellar jump, an in-system jump didn't need the ship to match velocity with the local star. To manage multiple sequenced jumps the way they had, they hadn't been able to adjust *any* of the jumps after commencing the sequence—even if there had been time to react to the enemy counterattack, they hadn't been able to jump sooner.

Their third jump had been as carefully chosen as their first two. They were now ten million kilometers *past* the Kazh fleet and had lost about half their velocity to the jumps. They were shifting away from Garuda at over six hundred KPS—but they were inside their missile range of the enemy, and new missiles leapt into space.

"I have a handle on our losses," Soból reported grimly. "On your screen. *Excalibur*, *Pax India* and *Pax Eternal* are the worst, but we're down four cruisers and two destroyers as well."

Nine ships. Over a tenth of her fleet in a scheme whose sheer recklessness should have protected them from the worst of the enemy's responses.

A scheme that *had* protected her fleet from the worst of the enemy's power. That was the cruelest part.

"Sir, we're getting the lightspeed data from our strike now," Miyajima told her. "It is... a bit weird, watching the fight after the fact like this."

The urge to scream a warning at the ships that were still alive in the thirty-odd-second-old data was pointless, but Jane had lived through it a time or two herself. She knew what the Mage-Commander was dealing with.

"Tell me we hurt them, Ops," she said quietly.

"We hurt them bad, sir," Miyajima told her, a cold satisfaction in her voice. "Thirty-two ships in total destroyed, including four each of the Type Ones and Twos."

The numbers ran across Jane's screen. By any rational standard, Horatio-Three had been a crushing victory. She'd taken out a quarter of her enemies' tonnage and a fifth of their hulls in exchange for a tenth of her hulls... but over a fifth of her *own* tonnage and firepower.

She hated herself for being grateful that two of the cruisers and both destroyers lost had been older ships. Losing the one dreadnought was already more than she could afford if she wanted to prosecute this battle.

"Sir!" Miyajima's voice wasn't *excited*, not really—but that cold satisfaction was even more evident. "We appear to have made our point."

Jane knew what she *hoped* that meant, but she had to be sure. She focused her attention on the holoprojector, looking for the datacodes even before her Acting Operations Officer confirmed it.

"They're coming about and opening fire on us with every missile launcher they have, sir," the Mage-Commander concluded. "It seems they didn't like being punched in the nose after all."

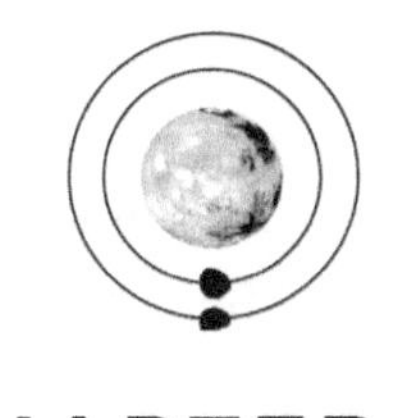

CHAPTER 55

"THEY SEEM TO HAVE FOUND some more acceleration somewhere, though I'm not sure I'd want to be them," one of Miyajima's Chiefs reported.

Jane nodded as the numbers percolated onto the display and her repeater screens. The Shining Shield fleet was up to thirty-seven meters per second squared, roughly three-point-eight gravities. Four times the pull of the Builder, their homeworld.

As the Chief said, that would be extremely unpleasant for the people aboard her. Presumably, the reezh ships had the same kind of accommodations as the Republic's ships had to allow the crew to function at three or four times their ordinary weight, but those could only do so much.

"Maintain our acceleration toward them at five gravities until our velocities equalize," Jane ordered.

That was going to take a while. She ran the numbers on the smaller screens on her chair and nodded to herself.

Just under three hours. Not long enough for her Mages to be ready to jump again—some of her Mages might be able to jump, she supposed, but getting that calculation wrong would kill them. There was a reason the RMN trained to and operated on fixed standards for that rest period.

It wasn't even a third of the time she still needed to buy. By the time they matched velocities, the Kazh would have lost almost all their closure toward Garuda.

The two fleets would be in each other's extreme missile range for that entire time, too, which raised other possibilities.

"Miyajima, Soból," she called the two women over to her. After a moment of thought, "Giannino, Xiao," she added.

The Logistics Officer was the odd man out of the quartet, his role in combat often limited.

"How many missiles do we have left?" Jane asked.

"Everyone except the dreadnoughts and the newest ships has twenty-five missiles per Phoenix launcher," Giannino said crisply. "Samurai launchers are only fifteen each."

"We've fired off eight salvos of Samurais and five of Phoenixes," Miyajima added. "That leaves us seven salvos of the heavy missiles and twenty of the standards."

"Are we firing Samurais right now?" Jane asked. She hadn't given orders either way, and she realized that was an oversight on her part.

"Commander Rostami pointed out that there would be a period as we approached velocity-matching that our regular missiles won't be able to reach the enemy with time on their drives, so we're holding them back for now," the Acting Ops Officer said.

And gave the credit to a senior officer who wasn't present, Jane noted. If she'd thought Miyajima was trying to hide behind Rostami, that would be something different, but the tone and presentation were the opposite.

"The *Victories*, *Virtues* and *Bards of Winter* all have forty missiles per launcher, as does *Mjolnir*," Giannino noted, checking his wrist-comp to confirm the numbers.

"That's only seven hundred launchers," Soból said. "We can't keep this battle going with seven hundred launchers."

"Agreed. Giannino—I'm pretty sure I know the answer, but is there any way the logistics group can rendezvous with us forty million klicks from Garuda to rearm?"

That number wasn't entirely arbitrary. She could change acceleration and get Second Fleet to that rendezvous point without letting the enemy think she was running away while still being out of range.

The Logistics Officer shook his head grimly.

"We could make the rendezvous, but the reloading capacity of our colliers is only about ten thousand missiles an hour. With the five of them, we're rated to be able to fully reequip the fleet in twenty hours, but..."

"But we'd only have a quarter-hour at most," Jane guessed. Enough to add two salvos back to her ships. It wasn't worth the risk.

"Pass the order to the logistics train, then. They're to move around to the opposite side of Garuda and fall back from the system. We'll rendezvous with them at fallback Romeo-Five."

She'd selected the point at random from a list of sixty possible locations, all of them two light-years from Chimera.

"Will do, sir," Giannino said calmly.

"Miyajima, we'll need to slow our fire," Jane continued, turning to the Mage-Commander. "If we keep a reserve of seven Phoenix salvos, that lets us launch every... ten minutes, if we're counting down to zero relative velocity, correct?"

"Roughly, sir," Miyajima confirmed. "I can set it up exactly. It will at least let us assess the impact of our shots before we fire the next ones."

"Make it work, Mage-Commander," Jane ordered.

The two junior officers slipped away to their tasks, leaving her with Soból and Xiao.

"We can't win this, sir," Soból murmured, her voice quiet to keep it between the three of them.

"We knew that going in. Right now, we're playing for time," Jane replied. "I'm realizing I should have kept our acceleration down before. Right now, they *know* we can run away from them faster than they're chasing. That means we have to keep maneuvering toward them like we want to close the range."

"What's our goal here, sir?" her Chief of Staff asked. "Run them out of missiles so they can't fire on the convoy?"

"I'm not going to turn that down if we can pull it off," she admitted. "But we're *just* playing for time, people. We need to watch how they react to the logistics train bugging out.

"Because in nine hours, Commodore Okorie is going to light off a series of fusion drives that make *this* fleet look like toy candles. We need to make sure that these bastards aren't in a position to fire on them."

"They're not going to buy us keeping our acceleration down for long, sir," Xiao warned. "Right now, they think we're trying to control the missile range. As time spins out and we all start running low on missiles, they're going to reconsider that."

"And whatever else happens, they can still make in-system jumps," Jane agreed grimly. "I want a one-light-minute emergency jump calculated on all ships—farther out from Garuda.

"I don't know if they have enough accuracy to drop into amplifier range of us like we did to them, but we've given them the idea. Unless their soldiers don't think like human soldiers at *all*, they're going to get impatient before this is over and try *something*.

"I want to be ready for whatever clever trick they think of."

The logistics train was less undefended than it looked at a distance, though there were no warships amongst the auxiliaries. If nothing else, after a great deal of hemming and hawing over the years, key ships in the collection had full amplifiers instead of mere jump matrices.

Jane, unlike almost everyone else in the Protectorate, was aware of the carefully concealed reality of the jump matrix: it *was* an amplifier but with additional runic structures added to prevent it being used for any spell except the teleport.

She knew partly because she was part of the Royal Family and that had been one of the first Desmond Alexander's tricks to maintain control of certain magics—and partly because she was a Rune Wright, and the nature of the matrix couldn't be concealed from a Rune Wright's ability to see magic.

That had almost given them a nasty headache when Damien Montgomery hadn't been identified as a Rune Wright yet. He'd worked out that secret and converted a freighter jump matrix into a fully functioning amplifier—and drawn all of the worst attention along the way.

If the now-Prince-Chancellor had been one iota less of a fundamentally honest person, he could have caused a massive nightmare, with a pirate ship that looked identical to every other merchant even *after* it had torn apart its prey.

Which was exactly the power of the concealed defenders amidst the logistics auxiliaries. Of the eighteen ships, six had amplifiers, and they were completely undistinguishable from the other twelve.

"Bandit One has definitely seen the auxiliaries move," Miyajima reported. "Blip in their acceleration. They've cut their thrust by seventy-five percent. Someone is making up their mind."

"They're still coming after us?" Jane asked.

"So far."

"Let me know the moment they change acceleration in either direction," she ordered.

Even as they spoke, more focused on the distant supply ships than on the immediate danger, a salvo of almost thirty thousand Kazh missiles was entering terminal acquisition. Commander Sharm in the Operations Center had the task of coordinating the defense—and at this range, the enemy's better seekers and jammers weren't enough to offset the loss of accuracy from a seventy-second-plus communication loop to their launching ships.

Commander Rostami, in turn, was handling their own missiles. The inverse was true for their missiles, of course. The Shining Shield's better jammers and decoys were adding to the drag of the communication loop, rendering their own missiles practically harmless.

Only one salvo had made it to the enemy so far, and they'd died far short of the Kazh's formation. If the numbers of missiles had been comparable, Jane would have been perfectly confident in her own people's ability to achieve the same.

The enemy missiles had almost ten thousand KPS less relative velocity than theirs, despite their better EW. There were just five times as many of them.

Mjolnir shook underneath her feet, the almost-incomprehensible mass of her hull jolting like a car slamming on the brakes.

"Miyajima, report," Jane said, as calmly as he could.

"Three—no, four near-misses on *Mjolnir*, sir," the Operations Officer replied, passing on information from Rostami. "We have a far better handle on their electronic warfare than we've ever had before, but they're throwing a *lot* of metal in our direction.

"Over two dozen missiles made it through," Miyajima concluded grimly. "They're still targeting the battleships and dreadnoughts. Mostly near-misses, but *Pax Excellence* took a solid strike.

"Captain Yakovlev says they've lost a laser but everything else is still functioning. She is *not* taking bets on the amount of duct tape involved."

"We can handle a few hits but not forever," Jane noted, her voice equally grim. "Even *Mjolnir* takes damage from antimatter explosions within a few kilometers."

"We're getting their number, sir, but there's only so much we can do," Miyajima admitted. Her voice was small, but like Roslyn Chambers, she didn't seem as young as she was to Jane. There were confidence and certainty in her tone.

"Do what you can."

"The enemy just increased their acceleration, sir," the same Chief—Carsten, Jane dragged out of the part of her brain that handled names—reported. "Back up to three-point-eight-five toward us."

"There aren't enough ships for them to decide it's worth more than us," Soból guessed. "It seems that the enemy agrees with Mage-Commander Miyajima's assessment from the exercises."

Jane gave her subordinate a questioning look.

"In any long-term sense, sir, Second Fleet is the only real strategic target in this system," the Commodore replied. "That was your assessment, correct, Mage-Commander?"

"In the isolation of a tactical exercise, yes," Miyajima confirmed carefully. "In this scenario, they have... three? Four?... major targets. But we're still the most important piece on the board *and* the one that hurt them."

"Us, the planet, the convoy and the Ifrit Accelerator," Xiao summarized, the Intelligence Officer clearly listening to the discussion. "And, somewhere farther down the list, the CSN, too."

"What is the status of the Accelerator?" Jane asked, a cold shiver running down her spine. So far, the only place the Reezh Kazh was using antimatter was in their weapon warheads. Neither branch of humanity could duplicate the efficiency and power of the fusion rockets the Shining Shield propelled their missiles with, but their access to magically created antimatter meant they could build overall better missiles.

A single accelerator ring had provided enough antimatter to the Republic of Faith and Reason for them to mass-produce antimatter-driven missiles *and* use antimatter as fuel for most of their key gunship deployments.

Added to whatever production the Kazh clearly had, it could dramatically change the threat level of the Shining Shield. The Ifrit Accelerator represented a massive effort, and she still found it hard to believe that they'd built it in the time they'd had. Jane hated that they had to destroy it.

"Final personnel are evacuating now," Jundt reported, the Coms Officer inevitably better informed about the events in the star system outside their battle than anyone else. "They are reporting that suicide charges have been deployed and set."

"Timers?" Jane asked. "We need to know that ring is going to go away before the Church of the Nine can use it, people."

She saw her subordinate tap several commands and talk into his headset, connected by Link to the Marines overseeing the evacuation.

His face turned white at the answer, and he looked back at Jane.

"Major Gniewek reports that... the Chimerans have set up proximity detonators," he said, swallowing in the middle of the sentence. "She has confirmed the sequences and has the final activator key. Once her shuttle is clear in the next few minutes, anyone approaching within a hundred kilometers of the ring will trigger the detonation sequence.

"She also reports that they used their last few days of antimatter production to upgrade the demo charges."

Jane whistled silently. That could be as much as a thousand tons of antimatter. The energy release of *that* reaction would be measured in *teratons* of TNT-equivalent.

"Gniewek is *certain* that the detonators will work?" she finally asked. "Tempting as that trap sounds, we cannot afford for that facility to fall into the hands of the Kazh."

"They're falling back to a dome colony on one of Ifrit's moons that supports the hydrogen scoops," Jundt reported. "Gniewek says that she has a backup manual detonator. The locals have a network of concealed sensors and narrow-band coms that she figures will give her overwatch on the ring.

"If she has any concerns whatsoever, she intends to hit the button."

It would have to do. Jane suspected that if she gave a hard order, the Marine officer would blow the station encircling Ifrit, but the possibilities inherent in what Gniewek and the Chimerans were trying to do were tempting.

The Kazh might never investigate Ifrit, and the ring would be intact when Jane came back to kick the bastards out of Chimera. That would save millions of worker-years of labor.

Far more likely, though, the Kazh would investigate the massive station with a major force. They would probably be careful enough that the explosion wouldn't take out an entire fleet, but every little bit was going to help over the next few months to years.

That was part of why she was glad to have Connor O'Hannagain on the bridge. It was never going to hurt to have one of the best negotiators in the Protectorate on the side of the Navy when pushing for the reality of the fight ahead of them.

New icons flared red on the main display, and Jane heard a very unprofessional curse cut short in the Ops Section.

She waited for the formal report, though the display told her what she needed to know.

"*Hope's Defender* just took multiple direct hits, sir," Miyajima said. "She's losing acceleration and I'm getting mixed reports on what weapons she still has online."

A *Guardian*-class battleship. Jane hated herself, but the number of *weapons* ran through her head before the people or names. Three hundred missile launchers and three hundred RFLAM turrets. Five thousand people.

"Get me a link to Mage-Captain Orenstein," Jane ordered. There was time. The Kazh were firing every nine minutes compared to the ten of her fleet, matching the full powered flight time of their missiles, but that still gave them time before the next salvo arrived.

Ernest Orenstein's image appeared on the repeater screen on the arm of her chair, Jundt judging that Jane didn't want this conversation shown to everyone on the bridge.

"Ernest, how bad is it?" she asked flatly.

"I don't know yet, which is an answer in itself," the Mage-Captain said. "I told Engineering to focus on making sure nothing blew up and fix anything non-critical after that. They... aren't through that phase yet."

"Can you jump?" The question was quite specific, really. There might be other Jump Mages aboard Orenstein's ship, but Orenstein could jump his own ship and was visibly at the simulacrum.

"Yes." His voice said he knew why she asked, and he was utterly torn. His duty was to stick with the fleet, help protect Garuda—but it was also to his crew, not to throw them or his ship away without a purpose.

"This is a delaying action, Mage-Captain. I'm not throwing away ships I don't have to. Fall back to Romeo-Five; rendezvous with the logistics train. Whatever else happens, get them safely to Exeter.

"That's an order, Orenstein."

"Yes, sir," he said heavily. "I'll get the auxiliaries home."

The channel cut, and a few seconds later, *Hope's Defender* vanished from the screen.

There was a grim silence as everyone stared at the gap in the formation—but Miyajima was already sending orders on Jane's behalf, tucking *Pax Excellence* and *Guardian of Freedom* closer together to fill the hole.

Defender wasn't the first ship they'd lost today. Jane knew damn well she wasn't going to be the last.

CHAPTER 56

CONNOR WANTED TO UNDERSTAND THE GAME being played around him. His life *depended* on the maneuvers and tricks that Jane Alexander was pulling, but after six hours and more ships lost than he could keep track of, he had to admit he didn't.

Half of the time needed for the evacuation ships to finish loading had passed. The two fleets were now tens of millions of kilometers from Garuda and heading away from the planet, exactly what they wanted.

"When... when have we pulled it off?" he muttered.

"When the evacuation ships have jumped," Zawisza told him, the Chief the only person close enough to hear him muttering. "Because those alien buggers can jump around the system just like us. Surprised they haven't tried it yet."

That thought hadn't occurred to Connor. He understood what Second Fleet had done to the enemy with their earlier series of jumps, but it hadn't clicked that the Kazh could do it to them too.

If he'd made a mistake like that in a negotiation, he'd probably have to retire in shame. But this wasn't his field, and he doubted that Jane Alexander would have made that mistake.

"It's a long damn day to be an observer," he muttered.

"Better than being one of the dead," Zawisza reminded him, the Chief's flat anger clear and excusable.

Connor didn't argue. Zawisza wasn't wrong—or angry at Connor, for that matter. The four ships that had managed to jump away were the lucky ones. Over a third of Second Fleet was gone now.

"Enemy is now almost ten minutes overdue for their next salvo," Miyajima reported. "I think they're holding fire."

"Then let's do the same," Alexander replied. "Hold the remaining Samurais. They're going to try to sucker-punch us, and I want a surprise for when they do."

"Range is starting to drop, sir," Soból reported.

Connor hadn't noticed, but as he looked at the displays, he was able to confirm that. The moment where the two fleets had the same velocity was past. Now Second Fleet's velocity away from Garuda was continuing to drop, while the Shining Shield's velocity was rising.

"Commodore Abbas, the Fleet will make turnover when the range is thirteen million kilometers," Alexander ordered, her tone level and cold, like she hadn't seen tens of thousands of her spacers killed over the last few hours. "We'll mark three gravities at that point."

"On it, sir."

Connor only knew that Captain Abbas was the Fleet Navigation Officer from the org chart. He had no idea who the man actually was, but he presumed it was the one answering the order.

New orders flickered out, though nothing changed immediately.

"Ninety minutes," Zawisza told Connor.

The Ambassador shook himself and glanced over at the Chief.

"We'll make that turnover in eighty-eight minutes, give or take," the spacer told him, clearly reading something off the parts of the displays that made no sense to Connor. "At three gees, they'll still be gaining on us.

"The Admiral's letting us get back into our missile range, then turning to hold the distance open. Gets us close to the final timeline we're dancing around."

Connor swallowed a sigh of frustration—and more than a little bit of fear.

"And is the convoy secure at that point?" he asked.

"So long as this 'Shining Shield' doesn't jump after them, probably," Zawisza confirmed. "But the only way to be sure of *that* would be to get them to burn up their jumps coming after *us*."

He was starting to wonder if staying behind and facing a planetary occupation might have been less stressful.

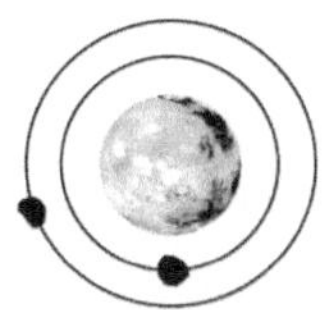

CHAPTER 57

BY THE END OF THE JOURNEY on the underground train, Roslyn fully understood why everyone had been so insistent that the key leadership cadre had to get moving right away.

Her time on Garuda had been spent either in Twin Sphinxes itself or in one of the two cities in the Duchy of the Blue River. One of those two cities, Blue Shores, was on the shore of Garuda's tempestuous seas. The other, at the far end of the duchy and near the headwaters of the titular Blue River, was Blue Rose—a mountainous city mostly anchoring ski resorts in the Blue Rose Mountain Range.

But Roslyn had never gone directly from Twin Sphinxes to either of the Duchy's cities. She'd gone up to a ship in between each time, which meant she had no real concept of the distance between them except as a number on the map.

The Blue Rose Range was seven hundred kilometers northeast of Twin Sphinxes and ran at a thirty-five degree northwest angle across most of the continent it sat on. The pass linking the Duchy of the Blue Rose to the road network leading to Twin Sphinxes was just over a thousand kilometers from the capital city.

The underground train ride had lasted over six hours before she finally got sick of sitting in silence while Hsieh Ai Ling fumed. The Dyad Minister hadn't said a single word to anyone since waking up, outside of a very pithy strip she'd torn off Gunny Matveyeva when the noncom had tried to check if the neural disruptor had done permanent damage.

Leaving the Minister under Matveyeva's watch, Roslyn stepped forward into the front car of the train. There were no windows anywhere in the vehicle, but there was a control station tucked away at the front. Two RCA troopers in unpowered armor and anonymizing helmets stood guard outside it.

"Can any of us help you, Mage-Captain?" a familiar voice asked.

Roslyn hadn't realized that Lieutenant General O'Neill was even aboard the train. She turned to see the buzz-cut officer leaning against the wall of the compartment, watching her idly.

"Stretching my legs and wondering about the universe," she told him. "Any news from outside?"

"Not as much as you'd think," he warned. "I know the Shining Shield hasn't made orbit yet, so I'm assuming the battle is ongoing, but this tunnel is completely sealed against electromagnetic emissions."

"How do you know the battle is ongoing?" she asked.

"There is a prearranged signal that will be sent using the power cables, mostly to warn us that we might lose power as they accelerated the demolition behind us."

Roslyn shivered, reminded that the plan called for the tunnel to be collapsed behind this train.

"*Accelerated,*" she echoed. "You mean it's already being collapsed?"

"By sections," he confirmed. "Demo is currently three hundred kilometers behind us and moving slightly slower than we are, so we're safe. If the enemy is close to entering orbit, they'll accelerate the work—and then the risk of something not getting disconnected in time goes up."

"And we, what, walk the rest of the way?" she asked.

"If necessary," O'Neill said, then chuckled at her face. "There are some pretty dense batteries in here with us, Mage-Captain. Not enough to make it the whole way, but enough to take the last few hundred klicks at a slower pace."

"How fast are we going?"

"A little over two-fifty klicks an hour." He shrugged. "The exact path of the train tunnel was kept pretty secret. I know the exact location of the facility we're heading to, but I couldn't tell you where we are right now.

"We've probably cleared enough of the tunnel behind us that the Kazh won't be able to trace it all this way, but we had to be sure. The plan is that the continuity facility doesn't open up again until your fleet comes back."

She hid a shiver. There was a lot riding on the presumption that the Protectorate would be able to rebuild, reorganize and come back to Chimera. She hadn't realized that the Chimeran government and parts of their key leadership were getting buried in a bunker and not leaving until the Navy returned.

"A lot of our people are down here too," she reminded O'Neill. "The Navy will be back."

"I know," he agreed calmly. "Has the Minister said anything else?"

"No. She is… extremely angry and I think she wants to avoid yelling at anyone who doesn't deserve it."

"One of them had to stay," the General noted. "I'll admit I didn't expect Ojak to go that far."

"And you knew him better than I did," Roslyn said. "I wish I'd been able to talk to our groundside team before I got hauled in here. I told the Admiral I'd coordinate that evac."

"I think you're going to be critical when we get to our destination, frankly," he told her. "But, if it helps, I went over those evacuation plans with Captain Beck yesterday. Your people are already out of Twin Sphinxes, Chambers. There weren't that many of you, and the plans were good."

She shook her head and glanced back at the sealed door to the control station.

"Even planning for it all, it's hard to swallow," she admitted. "Mars doesn't lose straight-up fights, General. We got taken by surprise at the start of the UnArcana Rebellions, but once we were on the right track, it was only a matter of time."

That was a vast simplification, she knew, but the sense was true. The Royal Martian Navy didn't think of itself as a force that lost battles, let alone had to concede systems—for all that it had happened in the UnArcana Rebellions, the culture of the Navy tended to regard that as all one defeat inflicted by treachery.

She supposed claiming their greatest defeat "didn't count" was particularly egotistical of the organization she served, but she also recognized the value of that culture.

After this, though, the RMN would have to reckon with the fact that they'd *known* they were going to have to abandon Chimera. That they'd evacuated almost eighty million people but hadn't saved the rest.

"You saw the same numbers I did, Chambers. Do you think this is a battle your Admiral Alexander can win?"

"No," Roslyn conceded. "She'll do what damage she can and she'll try to get the convoy out, but... she can't save Chimera."

"Then we'll dig in and wait for her to come back," O'Neill said firmly. A chime sounded through the train.

"That sounds like the ten-minute warning," he said. "We're almost there at last."

Stepping off into the Chimeran Continuity Citadel was like stepping into another world. Roslyn had known the tram was underground, but it had been moving at pace through a tunnel dug by a semi-automated process.

The C3 could not be more clearly underground than it was in the arrivals area. They exited the tram onto a platform carved from bare rock, where RCA troopers and Marines were waiting for them.

Their guides took the group through a tunnel, equally barren, to a hatch.

"Remember where the other side of this is," their lead guard instructed. "Only a small number of the Citadel's personnel are aware of this station. If you arrived via it, you are likely cleared to exit via it.

"Do not forget where it is."

Stepping through the hatch after the RCA soldier, Roslyn blinked against brilliantly harsh lighting. They were in some kind of storage space, vaulted ceilings hanging twenty meters above them.

Around them, resting like silent monuments in a tomb, were tanks. Republic-built Ericius-3 Heavy Main Battle Tanks, lined up in rows. A quick glance around the room gave Roslyn the estimate of a thousand tanks in this storage bunker alone.

Thankfully, the presence of the tanks also gave her "landmarks" to locate the stretch of wall holding the hatch back to the tram station.

"If the tunnel is being collapsed, what value is the station now?" General Badem asked, her voice curious.

"There is a second tunnel, sir," the trooper told her. "The tram can continue on along a further route along the mountain range. I don't know where it leads, honestly, beyond that it is a final escape route for the Dyad Minister if the C-Three is under threat."

"Good enough," Hsieh said, her voice calm and level—showing no sign of the anger she'd unleashed on the Gunny when Matveyeva had tried to check on her.

"Sergeant?" she continued, stepping up to the soldier.

"Yes, Minister?"

"Take me to the Information Center," Hsieh ordered. "My jiānzhà de tóngshì may have made the choice for me, but duty remains. I must know what's going on."

Roslyn wasn't quite sure what that Mandarin phrase meant.

She *was* sure she didn't want to know.

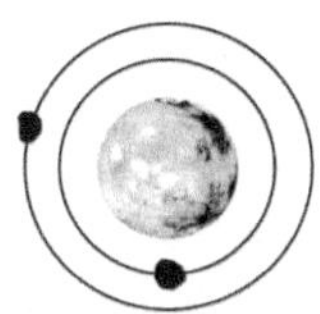

CHAPTER 58

THE CHIMERA CONTINUITY CITADEL'S main Information Center was the first place it became obvious that C3 was either brand-new or had been heavily refitted after the Royal Martian Marine Corps got involved. While the central hologram was identical to the one in Planetary Defense Command, the consoles around it were arranged based on Protectorate planetary-defense doctrine.

The consoles were a standard system shared by the Marines and the Navy, one that Roslyn could handle in her sleep. The main difference between this and the Operations Center on *Mjolnir* was sheer size.

Roslyn had an operations team of just under one hundred and ten human beings, including the ninety-six people assigned to the Operations Center and the twelve—including her—assigned to the Flag Bridge.

A quick count-and-multiply of the consoles she could see by the section divisions suggested that the Information Center held just over four hundred analysts, busily collating information coming in via hardline.

She followed Hsieh Ai Ling down to the central hologram. It was divided into a number of subsections, including overviews of both Garuda and the entire Chimera System; as well as the positions of the three fleets in the system and status reports on all three fleets plus Evac Convoy Two.

Long habit meant that Roslyn took in the status of the enemy first. The Shining Shield of the Nine had arrived in Chimera with over a hundred and sixty warships. Only a hundred and twenty remained after nine hours.

A third of the enemy numbers destroyed was less than thirty percent of their tonnage or firepower lost, she noted grimly. The smaller units had been hammered hard, but less than ten Type Ones or Twos were out of the fight.

Dreading what had to be the case, she checked on the CSN. Unsurprisingly, Wang's fleet was intact. Five capital ships and just over six hundred gunships waited in high orbit. A powerful force but not enough to hold against the tidal wave of steel heading their way.

Second Fleet's status report was a punch in the gut. Twenty-five of the seventy warships under Jane Alexander's command were gone. *Excalibur* was gone, and that loss alone hadn't been expected. The plan had been to keep the fight under control, using their acceleration to keep the Kazh at ranges where Second Fleet could dominate.

But the dreadnought's name was determinedly in the losses list, along with four battleships—*three* of them the newer *Peace*-class ships.

"The space battle continues," Hsieh growled. "That is better than we dared hope, I suppose, though it gives the lie to the urgency of our evacuation."

"The incoming fleet turned around to pursue the RMN, Minister," a CSN Commodore standing by the hologram said respectfully. His name tag said *CAMPBELL*, though Roslyn hadn't met him before. "If they had proceeded on their original course, they would have been in orbit hours ago.

"Second Fleet has taken grave risks to keep the Kazh distracted. The price has been high, but they remain in the fight."

"And what has that gained us?" Hsieh's tone was as harsh as her words. If Roslyn hadn't known what the Minister was angry about, she might have been insulted on Second Fleet's behalf.

As it was, she saw the blond Commodore start to inhale and met Campbell's gaze. He caught her attention—and the slight shake of her head.

The man sighed.

"At this moment, the Kazh fleet is farther from Garuda than their original emergence point," he told Hsieh. "Their velocity away from the planet is roughly three hundred KPS. It will take them over two hours just to lose that velocity, Minister, which means that the Martians have almost certainly bought enough time for the evac convoy to make it out."

Roslyn was studying the two fleet's current maneuvers and managed to not audibly argue, but she could see the problem immediately.

"Mage-Captain," Hsieh said sharply. She was apparently more perceptive than Roslyn would like. "You see something we don't."

"Commodore, I presume Second Fleet's maneuvers so far included in-system jumps?" she asked quietly.

"Three of them in sequence, Mage-Captain Chambers," Campbell confirmed. "Almost six hours ago now."

Three jumps. There was only one reason Roslyn could see to do that, which explained the damage to both fleets. If Alexander had successfully pulled off a Picard Maneuver, she'd have hammered the Kazh—but she wouldn't have been able to do it twice. Not until about then, in fact.

"Which means that Alexander's Mages are now ready to jump again," she noted aloud. "But that the enemy has also been shown our ability to jump around with tactical precision. It's not *easy* for us, Commodore, Minister. We spend a great deal of training to get to that level of precision—though my experience suggests that Awakened Prometheans can do it a bit more naturally."

"You think the enemy is considering a tactical jump?" Hsieh asked.

"I think Alexander is trying to provoke them into one," Roslyn said, gesturing at the maneuvers. "She *can* get out of their range, they know it, but both of them have fired off every missile they're willing to at this distance.

"If she can get them to jump her, she'll get hurt, but she can jump away," Roslyn concluded. "And by doing so, she burns their ability to jump on the Evac Convoy."

"Where the Kazh are holding back because they know she's intentionally letting them stay in range," Hsieh guessed, capturing the key point. The Minister might be a politician, not a soldier, but she understood how people thought.

"That's my assessment, Minister," Roslyn confirmed. "Right now, the range between the fleets is continuing to drop and they're content to spend the time. They may or may not realize what's going on in orbit, but they *know* Second Fleet are the major threat in the system."

"I see. Thank you, Mage-Captain," the Minister told her. "Commodore, what's the status of loading Evac Convoy Two?"

"We've had some trouble at the loading sites," he said grimly. "No casualties, thank God, but there are definitely people trying to squeeze onto the shuttles who aren't on the lists."

"For which we cannot blame them one bit," Hsieh conceded. "We always knew the final hours would be difficult. But where are we at?"

"Everyone involved has worked miracles, Minister. The final shuttle flights are landing now. Thirty, forty minutes to load everyone on. Another forty to make rendezvous with the transports.

"Okorie says they can maneuver with the shuttles still loaded, though they may need to ask people to stay on the small craft until they've made the first jump."

"Thirty hours, even once they move out," Roslyn said. The amount of time in play was terrifying.

"Twenty-one," the Commodore corrected. "It appears that the Prometheans have taken over jump calculations for the convoy and are confident they can all jump at one light-minute with one hundred KPS of velocity remaining."

Roslyn nodded slowly. She'd be comfortable doing that with a civilian jump matrix. She'd be *uncomfortable* jumping out of orbit in a warship, but she could do it. With the Prometheans running the numbers for everyone, sixty light-seconds should be safe.

"So, the Admiral merely needs to keep the enemy tied up for four times as long as she already has," Hsieh said grimly. "There has to be *something* we can do."

Roslyn shared a tired look with Commodore Campbell.

"There isn't, Minister," she told Hsieh. "At this point, it's about time and distance—and whether or not the Shining Shield can be convinced to use up whatever jump capability they have before the Convoy moves."

The C3's staff were coordinating the ground movement. Checks were being done on ground cables, making sure the Citadel was connected to the other bunkers and other facilities.

Maps were confirmed and double-confirmed. Units were contacted, tables of organization and equipment validated against the reality of what was at each of the dozens of underground bases. The Citadel had never been built with direct radio communication, but even the relays were shutting down as Roslyn watched. Their information was now entirely indirect, coming from other underground bases that were using disguised distant relays.

They could lose bases. They probably *would* lose bases, especially once the Reezh Kazh was in control on the ground. Roslyn assumed there were plans in place for if the Citadel was lost, but she suspected it would be a massive wrench in everyone's plans.

General Badem was at home in the heart of the organization. To Roslyn, it seemed like every time there was a spike of chaos or confusion, the Marine General was there, giving quiet encouragement or crisp orders as needed.

Through all of it, though, Roslyn could see that every person in the Information Center stopped to check the main display over and over again.

She wasn't looking away. After sitting in the tram for hours upon hours, she was content to stand at the edge of the main display, watching the numbers flicker across the screen.

"Has anyone informed Admiral Alexander of Okorie's new timeline?" she asked Campbell, a sudden horrible thought hitting her.

The CSN officer took longer to answer her than she liked.

"We didn't," he finally admitted. "Okorie is an RMN officer; we assumed he'd advise her himself."

"Make certain. This place has a Link, right?" she said.

"We do. It's disabled right now, though, until we have a chance to test to see if the enemy can detect its use."

Which made sense, she supposed, but was going to be a real problem until they'd run those tests.

"Then cable someone who has one we can use and *make certain*," she repeated. "There's less than an hour left until Evac Convoy Two moves, and that may well change Alexander's plans."

She knew she'd drafted plans for this scenario and those had used the departure time of the evacuation ships as a marker. None of her plans would have exactly fit, but she also hoped that her subordinates and superiors would use them for reference—to save time, if nothing else.

"I'll get on it," Campbell ordered.

"Good catch, Mage-Captain," Hsieh said quietly. "We can't assume anything right now. Even that our closest friends won't shoot us."

Roslyn swallowed a sigh and leveled her best Captain's Look on the Minister.

"With respect, I both was shot at by one of my closest friends and *shot* him, Minister Hsieh," she pointed out. "At the time, Matthias Beck was under the influence of hostile magic. If I hadn't stunned him, he would have done something we both would have regretted.

"Minister Ojak stunned you to save your life. And preempt an argument. He stole your agency, yes, but I don't know if I'd class what he did as a true betrayal."

There was a long moment, then Hsieh chuckled bitterly.

"One of us had to stay. It was my choice, and he robbed me of that. I understand why, but I'm going to hate him a little for it right now. I don't think I'm going to be able to later."

Roslyn shivered. She knew exactly what Hsieh meant: she wasn't going to be angry at Ojak when the reezh was dead.

And death was all too likely a fate for the visible leader of Chimera in the next few days.

"There's one more thing we need, Minister," she said quietly. In her mind, it was related to the conversation about Ojak, but she hoped that no one else was going to pick that up.

"The CSN isn't going to do much good once Second Fleet has been driven off," she warned. "But three of Admiral Wang's ships can still jump. Evac Convoy Two can use their antimissile defenses."

Sending those ships would also let Hsieh Ai Ling get Emerson Wang out of the suicidal last stand he was currently planning. The Minister had the authority to order him to run.

"It won't work, Roslyn."

She blinked, surprised at Hsieh's use of her first name, and turned to meet the other woman's gaze.

"I tried everything from giving him orders as his civilian commander to confessing my feelings and begging him to live for me," the other woman whispered. "But we gave him a home when he and his people had nothing left. He will not abandon us, even when it will achieve *nothing*."

That felt... very foolish to Roslyn. But then, she supposed she'd stand without question to guard Tau Ceti or Sol. Home was home.

"What do we do?" Roslyn asked.

"Well, frankly, my plan was to surrender the planet and probably be executed by the Kazh so I joined him in whatever afterlife exists," Hsieh Ai Ling told her, her whisper fading to near inaudibility. "Now... now I suppose we stand witness."

CHAPTER 59

"SIR, WE HAVE AN UPDATE FROM THE CHIMERANS," Jundt reported. "They wanted to confirm that Commodore Okorie has informed them that he expects to depart in roughly forty-five minutes."

"Have we received any reports from Okorie?" Jane asked. She could think of half a dozen reasons she'd get that information from Chimera—though she'd have expected to get an update from them on that a bit earlier.

"No, sir," Jundt confirmed. "We're actively in combat, so most of our people wouldn't attempt to contact us."

Which was a sensible policy ninety-nine percent of the time. Jane sighed.

"Ping Okorie and confirm an updated departure time," she ordered. "Abbas, get the helm crews on the line as well. Move the fleet to stand by for a maneuvering change."

At that moment, Second Fleet had sustained the same three gravities for far longer than Jane had originally planned on. So long as the Kazh were willing to chase her, she was willing to *let* them.

"Miyajima, Soból, to me," she ordered.

The two women were there before Jane had finished speaking.

"The Convoy is about to move," she told them. "They have a twenty-one-hour run to get to safe distance to jump."

They couldn't put the evacuees through multi-gravity acceleration, not for hours. They'd run at one gravity the entire way.

"We need a way to make sure the Kazh *cannot* attack them in that run. Pulling them this far away and out of position helps, but after ten hours, there's a decent chance that the Mages and Engines that got them *into* Chimera will be fully refreshed.

"Options, please."

"We have to assume they have a minimum of three jump-capable Mages or Engines per ship," Miyajima said. "That means we need to get them to jump three times to make the Convoy safe."

"We've been dragging our coats out here for hours and they haven't taken the bait," Soból said. "We can push to maximum accel and see if that draws them out."

"Or we can jump ourselves," Miyajima suggested. "If we hop, wait for them to arrive, and repeat, we can not only burn up their jump capability but potentially draw them even farther out of position."

Jane's own thinking had been closer to Miyajima's.

"If we repeated the Picard Maneuver, jumping early enough to avoid the amplifiers this time, that would draw them out," she noted. "Especially if we then went to hell and gone across the star system."

"Only four of the capital ships have more than four Mages, sir," Miyajima pointed out. "That's including *Mjolnir*, where the extra Jump Mages are you and me."

Jane nodded. That was true. A repeat of Horatio-Three would eat up three of her people's jump capacity and only get the Kazh to jump once.

"I think we still want to poke them in the nose," she noted. "But let's see what we can do."

She turned to the Fleet Navigator.

"Abbas, the fleet will adjust to fifteen gravities along our current vector," she ordered. "I'll have jump coordinates for all ships shortly.

"We've dragged our coats long enough. It's time to see if the Shining Shield is going to put up or shut up."

At fifteen gravities, it would only take them minutes to undo the velocity advantage the enemy had gained over hours. Jane figured the Kazh would let it run out for a bit, to see if this was some kind of sprint mode her ships couldn't sustain—though their earlier run to get clear of Garuda's gravity would suggest otherwise.

Possibilities and plans were still taking shape in her mind. One of those possibilities sent her diving back into a document she hadn't opened in years.

The Royal Martian Navy's counter-amplifier doctrine was entirely theoretical—out of *get out of range*, at least. But Second Fleet wasn't the first RMN force to ever engage an amplifier-equipped warship—and, more importantly for Jane's current search, *Mjolnir* wasn't the first to do so with a Rune Wright aboard.

Years ago, in the investigations that had revealed the Keepers and their Nemesis splinter faction to the Protectorate, Hand Damien Montgomery had collided with Hand Lawrence Octavian in the void between Tau Ceti and Sol.

Octavian had sworn his allegiance not only to the Keepers—and Jane Alexander had her suspicions about the interaction between the people sworn to keep her paranoid grandfather's secrets and the people sworn to directly serve his heirs—but to Nemesis itself.

The two Hands had dueled in the dark with their ship's amplifiers as their weapons. Octavian had lost because Montgomery was a Rune Wright. That meant he was the more powerful Mage... and also that he had senses the other Hand didn't.

The report filled in the gaps in her memory. Montgomery had been able to detect amplified spells forming and counter them. He'd even, though he had only realized it later, prevented Octavian's vessel from jumping.

A spike of guilt ran through Jane. Using her magical senses to sense and assess magic took a degree of focus, focus she chose not to spare in a battle. Only the massive blow of magic that had destroyed *Excalibur*—a ship that had been quite close, in deep space terms, to *Mjolnir*—had registered.

But if she'd remembered Montgomery's report and been paying attention, she could have countered some of those attacks. Could have saved her people.

She forced herself to put that aside.

"Abbas," she said calmly, onto a private channel. "When I give the word, I need the fleet to activate that one-light-minute jump we set up. No arguments, no discussions. We will need to jump *immediately*."

"Uh, yes, sir," he confirmed. Unspoken was that it would probably have happened anyway, but she needed him paying attention.

There wasn't going to be a lot of warning if she was right.

"They are maintaining their vector, sir," Miyajima reported. "No change in acceleration. Minor adjustment in vector to true up their line."

"What are you thinking?" Jane muttered to herself. She breathed out slowly, pulling on the focus she needed to fully access her gift. She could feel the ship around her, pulsing with power. Between emergency air-cleaning magics, the gravity runes, the amplifier matrix and a dozen other small and large runic matrices and ongoing magical efforts, *Mjolnir* was as much a creation of magic as technology.

More, in some ways, for all that she appeared purely technological on the surface. Even the materials that made up her immense multilayer armor were shaped and formed by magic. To a Rune Wright like Jane Alexander, her flagship *sang* with the magical power of the hundred or more Mages who'd worked on her construction and crewed her since.

She pushed her senses past that, sensing the distant song of the other ships of her fleet. Without the amplifier, there was a limit to the effect she could have by doing this, but the amplifier did nothing for this sense, the unique gift of the Rune Wrights and the Rune Wrights alone.

Past the other ships of her fleet was only the void. Empty space was no more actually empty to this sense than it was to anything else. Motes of loose power drifted between the stars, some coming off her fleet, some just the natural background thaumic nature of the universe.

And then she felt it. The same pressure in her skull as before—but with her eyes closed and her mind stretched out around her ships, she could locate it. Define it. *Know* that her sense of it was in real time, not delayed by the half dozen light-seconds from where the enemy was emerging.

"Abbas. *Jump*," she ordered.

With her senses still extended, she felt the flare of power as her Mage-Captains leapt to obey—and the matching flare of power as the Kazh fleet emerged from their own jump and their amplifiers lashed out.

Nothing connected. Second Fleet was gone.

"Clear. What... happened?" Abbas asked.

"Watch," Jane ordered. She was rolling the memory of the last few moments around in her mind, then nodded decisively.

"They have six amplifiers," she declared aloud. "Once we localize their jump emergences, I think I can identify which ones."

Everyone stared at her like she'd grown a second head and Jane Alexander smiled coldly.

"I am the daughter of a Mage-King of Mars," she reminded them all. "A Royal of the Mountain. We are only scratching the surface of what that means, but our enemy has *no idea*."

"There they are," Miyajima said, her voice soft with something approaching awe. "They emerged from jump... that can't be right."

"What can't, Mage-Commander?" Jane asked.

"They emerged from jump approximately one-point-six seconds before we jumped," the young woman reported. "They would have taken longer than that to get a new Mage on the simulacrum. Scans suggest amplified magic striking where we were."

"And that is why I am here, Mage-Commander," Jane told Miyajima. "Flick their final positions to my repeaters."

The younger woman obeyed, and Jane worked through the data. She kept her senses extended. The Kazh might still try to jump after them, but she suspected they were going to spend a few minutes working out precisely what her people had just done.

After a minute, Jane sighed.

"I can't narrow it down further than this," she said, flicking the data back to Miyajima with sixteen ships highlighted. All of the surviving Type Ones and six of the Type Twos. "There is definitely at least one amplifier on those Type Twos."

"You wouldn't tell me if I asked how, would you?" Miyajima asked slowly.

"Some things are need-to-know, Mage-Commander. You need to know the results, not the methodology. Those ships are target priority one." She considered for a moment. "The Type Twos especially. We can probably kill all of them with one beam pass, and removing an amplifier from the mix might be worth it."

"That *would* require a beam pass, sir," Soból pointed out. "Are we planning something risky?"

"You're finally getting to know me, Peta," Jane said, her grin expanding. "We can't drive these people off, but we can damn well make their life interesting.

"Abbas. I want a jump to sixteen light-seconds of the enemy. Same count as before—but our exit jump is to the edge of Longma's gravity zone."

She waited for her people to work through the math. Longma was Chimera-II, currently around eighteen light-minutes from Garuda and over twenty from their current position. It was a smaller planet, similar to Venus back in Sol, with nothing of sufficient value to draw the locals' attention.

Miners went on to the asteroid belt another half dozen light-minutes closer to the star. The hot gas giant of Ifrit had its own value—and issues from its proximity to Chimera itself—but at least didn't have the same depth of toxic atmosphere.

But it was far enough away to buy them time—and *not* so far away that the enemy wouldn't see them emerge before Evac Convoy Two got on their way.

"We're going to punch them in the nose again, then pull them away from the civilians," Jane concluded. "We'll be ready for them to try to close-range jump us again, but I suspect they'll be cautious on a twenty-plus-light-minute jump."

"We can do it, sir," Abbas confirmed, the Nav Officer's voice more confident than his eyes.

"I'll start laying in the firing patterns now," Miyajima said. "Targeting your designated Type Twos, correct?"

"Exactly."

Seconds counted but they needed to buy hours. Jane kept her attention expanded, trying to both maintain a presence on her Flag Bridge and have her senses spread out, watching for the magical signature of the enemy attempting to jump after them.

"Enemy has changed course, sir," Miyajima reported. "Their vector is now toward Garuda at point-nine-five gravities."

It seemed their enemy wasn't going to come after them. A light-minute was too much for them to try to cover in real space, but the maneuver didn't sit right to Jane, either.

"How far from Garuda are they now?" she asked.

"Thirty-nine million kilometers. One hundred and thirty light-seconds," her Ops Officer reported. "They lost about half their existing velocity vector in the jump, but at that acceleration, it will take them over five hours just to shed their velocity out-system. They're over forty hours from a zero-zero to Garudan orbit."

"They know they have time," Jane reflected. "And their crews must have been suffering under four times their usual gravity. After this long chasing us, they might be giving it up and heading back for the main objective while letting their crews rest."

"That would fit with them, say, only having one Mage or Engine per ship," Xiao noted. "Except that there is no way they made it here from the Nine and Cozhan since the last attack with that few jumpers."

"Someone is trying to be very clever," Jane told them all. "Abbas—I need that jump to Longma recalculated ASAP. I want every ship ready to move to Chimera-Two on my order."

"Yes, sir."

"They're prepping to try to surprise us again." Soból wasn't even asking a question. The Chief of Staff saw the exact same thing Jane did. "Can you... give us enough lead time to shoot back?"

"I can tell you that someone is jumping in, but direction and distance are too vague for targeting," Jane admitted. "No, if they try it again, we have to run."

"Even if they were heading to Garuda, they'd jump, wouldn't they?" Miyajima said. "If they're coming after us, sir... position to prep a missile spread set to self-targeting?"

"Do it," Jane ordered. Five thousand missiles wouldn't do much at maximum range, but coming at the enemy from close range when they weren't expected...

"Thirty minutes until Evac Convoy Two leaves," Soból warned. "If we want them to jump to Longma after us, we need to initiate that attack sequence inside the next five minutes or so."

"These bastards are *not* switching over to a leisurely course to Garuda after the last ten hours of bullshit," she growled. "We're not risking the nose-punch, Peta. I'd *rather* hit them, but unless I have misread things, there is *one* person in complete control over there and they're still pretty angry over the last time we poked the bear."

"If we jump to Longma and they're not pursuing us…"

"We might be wasting the time, yes," she agreed. "But risks are part of all of this. I think I have the measure of the brain on the other side, Peta, and if I—"

Pressure. She hadn't been paying enough attention to narrow it down at all, but she'd kept her senses spread out.

"Abbas, *jump*," she snapped.

The Kazh were too close. Her enemy had her measure almost as well as she had theirs, and they were coming out practically *on top* of Second Fleet.

She tried to cancel amplifier surges as she felt them, going off Montgomery's description of how he'd fought back against Octavian to protect *Duke of Magnificence*, but there were six Mages out there and only one of her.

They jumped at last—but with her magical senses spread as wide as she had them, she knew that not all of her ships made it.

CHAPTER 60

CONNOR UNDERSTOOD ENOUGH OF THE DISPLAY to follow the results of what had just happened. When Alexander had barked her order, forty-five warships had been burning for deep space, almost sixty million kilometers from Garuda.

Only forty green icons blazed next to Longma on the display.

"Report." Jane Alexander's voice didn't show a sign of the stress she had to be feeling.

"We lost..." Captain Jundt coughed, the Coms Officer clearly sick of being the bearer of bad news. "*Guardian of Faith*, *Defender of Earth*, *Victory at Midway*, *Tchaikovsky* and *Wagner*, sir."

"Two *Guardians*, a *Victory* and two *Bards of Winter*," Miyajima confirmed. The young Mage-Commander—she was Chambers' age, Connor judged, but something made her seem at least a few years younger—had the stress in her voice that her seniors didn't.

"Distance from the Kazh force now?" Alexander asked.

"Twenty-one light-minutes and change, sir," the Ops Officer confirmed. "They will see us at least five minutes before Commodore Okorie moves."

"Commodore Jundt, get us a sensor linkage from Garuda," the Admiral ordered, her voice still level and firm. "I want to know their status after that mess as soon as possible, not in twenty-odd minutes."

That was the advantage of the Link, Connor guessed. The ships and stations in Garudan orbit were only three light-minutes from the enemy fleet. They would know the result of the jump attack long before Second Fleet could see for themselves.

"Abbas, prep me two jumps for everyone," Alexander continued. "One will take us to the rough location of Evac Convoy Two, to help cover them out of the system. The other... will take us to fallback Romeo-Five."

Connor didn't like the sound of that. That would be leaving Chimera behind, conceding the battle as unwinnable—and, quite possibly, abandoning the Evac Convoy. He held his tongue for the moment, but he realized he needed to talk to the Admiral in private.

That was the kind of decision he needed to be involved in, not merely in the room where it happened.

"Xiao." She turned to her Intelligence Officer. "Assuming they left the Nine one week after the last attack, how many jumps per day were they managing?"

"At least ten," he said. "If they, for example, matched our standard for the civilian ships of nine light-years a day, they could have left four days later. That would be three Mages or four Engines of Sacred Sacrifice per ship."

That meant something to Alexander but nothing to Connor. He could see the wheels turning in her head and bit down a sigh. He tapped a quick message on his wrist-comp, hating to interrupt—but from what he understood, they had at least ten minutes.

Alexander paused, glancing down at one of her screens, then back at him.

He met her gaze levelly.

"Ambassador, my office," she told him. "Soból—if anything changes, tell me immediately. We'll be back before our light reaches the Kazh."

"You have about thirty seconds to explain what you need, O'Hannagain," Alexander growled the moment the hatch closed behind them. "In case you haven't been paying attention, I've lost almost *half* my fleet, including tens of thousands of people I was responsible for."

"I need to know what you're going to do, Admiral," he told her. "Because it's up to *me* to tell Chimera. If we're abandoning the Convoy—"

"We are *not* abandoning the Convoy," she snapped. "Not if we have a choice. But I need to have that jump worked up, O'Hannagain, because we might not have that choice. You might not have noticed, but we are badly outmatched here. So far, we've managed to outthink and outfight them, but attrition is not a game we're going to win.

"I am spending ships and *lives*, Ambassador, for no higher purpose than making the enemy jump after us in the hope that they won't be able to jump after the Evac Convoy. I don't know what more you think the Chimerans want from us, but I don't know if we can fucking *do it*."

Connor took the explosion for two reasons: first, that he'd asked a question he knew might trigger it—and second, because there was nobody else on the flagship that Jane Alexander *could* yell at.

"That's what I need to be able to tell the locals, Admiral," he said quietly. "How many jumps do we have left in us?"

"The destroyers and cruisers have three. I can send Miyajima to the main bridge and get the same out of *Mjolnir*, but the battleships only carry four Jump Mages," she told him. She was answering the question, but she was hardly calmer. "The *flagships* can jump five times, because both of my Vice Admirals are Jump Mages and can save their own ships, but the other four battleships and twenty-odd thousand people on them can't keep up."

"For another six hours," he guessed. "So, they can jump once, but then they *have* to go to the rendezvous point?"

"And without them, *Mjolnir* will be the target of every damn thing the bastards send at us," she told him. "We won't survive that for long, O'Hannagain. We are rapidly approaching the point where the only way I can buy Okorie time is to make the Kazh stop to kill us."

"Then we need to tell the Chimerans that," he said gently. "And that's not your job right now. Your job is to fight this battle and buy Evac Convoy Two as much time as you can. It's *my* job to tell the Chimerans that we're out of missiles and out of time."

She snorted.

"I guess so. Good luck with that."

"I'll take luck," he agreed. "I'll also borrow your office, if you'll let me. I don't think this is a call you want the crew listening in on."

"It's not. Use the space," she conceded. "Don't say anything stupid, all right?"

"This isn't the time for promises, Admiral," Connor told her. "This isn't even a time for negotiation. This is when we have to tell allies that we've run out of time and they are on their own."

Connor wasn't used to putting his own calls through anymore, but he'd made sure that he knew the processes to do so. The RMN systems were familiar to him, and he probably could have worked it out from scratch if necessary.

It was only as he was plugging in the code to connect to the Dyad Ministers that he realized he had no idea where Zahid Kootenay had ended up. Sarvesh Ansel and *some* of his Protectorate Secret Service detail were aboard *Mjolnir* somewhere—probably standing guard outside the Flag Bridge with the Marines—but his aide would be with the embassy staff.

The plans for the embassy staff were solid and clean, but he was still supposed to be with them. None of this had been the plan.

He sighed and sent a single text message to Kootenay.

I'm on Mjolnir. *Watch over our people for me. I know you can.*

Kootenay, after all, was MISS Counterintelligence. If anyone could keep the handful of bureaucrats that had made up their under-sized-in-hindsight delegation safe, it was him.

Connor's actual job was much less pleasant. He finished the connection code, using the Link to connect to Garuda's communications networks.

He was surprised to only have a single video feed pop up. The code he used connected to both Dyad Ministers, but only Ojak answered him.

The reezh Minister was seated at the desk in their office, the windows behind them turned as clear as possible to give an incredible view of the mixed architecture of Twin Sphinxes. There was no way to pretend, looking at that city, that it wasn't a syncretic mix of two cultures and species.

"Ambassador. I didn't expect to hear from you again."

"I didn't plan on being aboard *Mjolnir* when all of this went down," he admitted. "But I feel it necessary to give you an update. Where is Hsieh?"

"One of us must remain to treat with the Kazh. One of us must be free to lead our people," Ojak said levelly. "We discussed the matter, and she has been taken to safety."

Taken to safety suggested that Minister Hsieh had been less than on board with that division of labor.

"That will be necessary soon," Connor agreed. "Second Fleet has been heavily reduced, Minister, and Admiral Alexander is almost out of munitions. It is almost time for us to withdraw. She has one or two tricks left to protect the Convoy, but that is all that's left."

"How bad is it, Ambassador?"

"Assuming no survivors from the ships, Admiral Alexander has lost a hundred thousand spacers," he said flatly. "We have done all we can, Minister. If we are to relieve Chimera in the future, Second Fleet is spent."

"Then she should withdraw now," Ojak told him. "Admiral Wang will do his utmost to protect us all and to buy the last time the Convoy needs. Second Fleet must be intact enough to return, Ambassador."

"I... do not believe that is an order I have the authority to give the Admiral, Minister Ojak. Nor is it an order she would obey if I did. She has her plan to save as much as she can. I will not impede her."

"Wang is no better at obeying orders, but I will do what I can," Ojak replied, with the tilt to his four eyes that Connor had learned meant amusement.

"May your voyages be safe and bring you back to Garuda, Ambassador," they concluded. "I... fear I will not be here to meet you when you return.

"This, too, is duty. Admiral Alexander will understand."

"*I* understand, Minister," Connor told them. "And I swear to *you*, as Connor O'Hannagain, that I will see the Mountain's oath to your people kept. My Queen is unlikely to waver, but if she does, I will be there to remind her and our people of our promises.

"We are coming back, Izhaj Ojak. This I promise you."

CHAPTER 61

JANE RETURNED TO THE FLAG BRIDGE to find a positive surprise. She'd wanted the information on the Kazh attack on her fleet to compare to her magical senses of the action and see if there was any way she could improve for when the enemy came to them at Longma.

That information was being put together with a slow run-through of the sensor data on the main display—but next to it was a second set of analysis, marking their own kills.

"We managed to hit them?" she asked. "Not shabby, Ops. But... how?"

"We predeployed one salvo and fired a second on your jump order," Miyajima replied. "Ten thousand missiles made a bit of an impression, sir—but it helped that they were less than half a million klicks away."

Jane swallowed her whistle of shock.

"Was that accuracy or did they misjump?" she asked.

"No way to tell," Xiao replied. "Last time, they came in at a similar distance to our first Horatio jump, close enough for beams but too far for amplifiers. This time, they were definitely pushing for amplifier range and got it."

"The good news is that there was no way they switched Mages between the jump and the amplifier attacks," Abbas said grimly. "I doubt they lost any—and you'd know better than me—but I understand that those Mages are down for the count now."

"Works for me," Jane agreed coldly. The Mages in question had just killed thousands of her people. The thaumic burnout they'd subjected themselves to was the least punishment she could hope for.

"We got three of your potential amplifier battleships," Miyajima reported. "I don't know if we actually tagged the amplifier. They definitely had six when they started throwing magic at us, but they only hit five of our ships hard enough to take them out in the moments they had."

Jane took her seat and sipped at her lukewarm coffee. The tendency of coffee to cool in a battle was one of the real reasons she'd moved to drinking sweetened versions. Her latte was perfectly fine at just about any temperature, even chilled, though she did prefer it warm.

"How long until our friends see where we ended up?" she asked. "And what are they doing right now?"

Well, three and a half minutes or so earlier, given the lightspeed lag to Garuda and the small delay inherent in sending the information to her.

"They'll see the light of our emergence in about fifteen minutes," Soból told her. "About seven minutes before Okorie is expecting to start his burn. The last shuttles just took off."

Part of Jane wanted to declare that her fleet had done enough. They'd seen tens of thousands of their people die. They'd bought long enough for Evac Convoy Two to start running.

But they hadn't bought long enough for the Convoy to actually *run*. Civilian ships couldn't jump out of planetary orbit. Even the *Saladin*s and *Bushido*s, warship-adjacent as the troop transports were, weren't built to do that.

"So, we wait and see what our friend does," she said quietly. And hope that the Kazh only had one more jump in them.

The counters ticked down and Jane watched her enemies maneuver. They'd spread out after she'd jumped, directing their course back toward Garuda but also moving the ships apart to expand their sensor reach.

They were guessing that she was still in the system and making sure they saw where she emerged. She doubted they'd expected her to go as far as she had—part of her thought had been to convince them that there was something at Longma, fuel or munitions she could use to turn the tide of this battle.

She'd bled them but she couldn't destroy them. Even trying to bleed them now would take more than her people had left, she judged, but she didn't need to *fight*.

Just survive.

"Thirty seconds," someone reported.

Jane nodded and focused inward—and then back out, sending her network of magic out into the void around her, seeking the spark of her enemies' arrival. Hoping that, this time, she could pick them up early enough to keep her people safe.

A countdown hit zero with a soft chime. Every person on *Mjolnir*'s Flag Bridge fell silent. Conversation faded to nothing, even the reports hushed or sent electronically as her staff refused to distract her from her scanning.

She wanted to tell them not to bother. The silence was almost more distracting, her people desperately trying to help in any way they could—but they were trying to help and telling them off for it would be unfair.

"Sixty seconds past lightspeed lag," Miyajima reported quietly. "Should we tell Okorie to delay?"

"No," Jane said. "He's to leave the moment he has everyone aboard. We'll adjust if we have to."

That "adjustment" would almost certainly be a jump directly back to the Kazh to punch them in the nose again, probably sending the battleships on to Romeo-Five while *Mjolnir* and the escorts tried to draw the enemy away—

There. The pressure was clear in her mind now, and she wondered how she'd missed it in the past. She supposed she hadn't seen that many ships jumping within a few tens of light-seconds, not unless she was jumping with them.

Plus, how often were a hundred starships *ever* jumped in unison?

"We're clear; they're not in amplifier range," she said aloud. "Coming in oppositional to our approach to Longma. Estimate... six million klicks?"

Someone started a new countdown—the twenty seconds until they'd see the Shining Shield formation if it had emerged where Jane thought it had.

There was a tension released when the red icons finally blazed onto the display like a scattering of blood.

"Contacts at nineteen-point-five light-seconds," Miyajima said crisply. "Mass and signatures strongly suggest it's our Bandit One."

"Missile defenses free," Jane ordered. "If they fire, we may jump clear, but I want to have options."

"On it."

Second Fleet continued on their course through the dark. Jane figured the Kazh commander would see her plan: a gravity slingshot around the smaller planet that would send her hurtling back toward Garuda while using far less of her fuel.

If they wanted to think she was short on fuel, let them. As much as anything, she'd just needed a course that would convince the enemy she had a reason to be there, at a planet twenty light-minutes from the people she was actually trying to protect.

"Enemy missiles launching."

Jane registered the report, even as the shoals of red icons blazed into existence on her displays. Despite everything they had done, the enemy still had over twenty-five thousand missile launchers left.

"Any estimates on how many salvos they may have left?" she asked aloud, glancing over at Xiao.

"Best guess is that they kept the same seven in reserve that we did," he replied. "But it's not like we're getting through their defenses with what we have left."

"No." Jane turned to Miyajima. "Ops, how many salvos do we have left?"

"Used two of both Phoenixes and Samurais to trap them at the last jump, sir," the Mage-Commander told her. "That leaves us five full salvos. After that, five with the newer destroyers, *Mjolnir* and *Last Stand at the Alamo*. *Alamo* only has thirty missiles, so after that, we're down to just the destroyers and *Mjolnir*, for ten salvos of about eight hundred missiles."

"I think we're out of reasons to hold the missiles back, Commander Miyajima," Jane decided aloud. "Take a page from our Republican friends' book. Wonderwall defensive patterns. Use everything we have left."

"For how long, sir?" Soból asked.

"Until they run out of missiles, or we do, Commodore," Jane said softly. "Or I give new orders."

Mjolnir shivered as Second Fleet's weapons launched. Compared to the earlier salvos, the salvo of four thousand and change missiles was a paltry reminder of the initial power of the fleet. Jane wasn't even throwing them at her enemy, though she hoped it would take the Shining Shield commander a few rounds to realize that.

"Second enemy salvo in space. That was at their standard minimum cycle, sir."

Flight time of six minutes. Second Fleet was accelerating away from the Shining Shield, but the reezh ships were back up to four Builder gravities.

Jane leaned back in her seat. She'd done everything she could. Now there was one final decision in her hands: when they jumped to join the evac convoy.

The enemy missiles blazed in like suicidal meteors, and Miyajima's response went out to meet them. More missiles joined the chaos as the enemy kept launching. A third salvo. A fourth.

Then the Wonderwall missiles intercepted. The strategy had been designed to use a specific mode of the massive two-gigaton antimatter warheads used by the Republican Interstellar Navy, one that spread the antimatter over a larger volume even as it annihilated itself.

Any antimatter warhead created a radiation hash that degraded targeting through it. The RIN had managed to expand that space and used it as a defensive screen. Second Fleet's weapons didn't have that extra explosive charge, but they did well enough.

Not least because Miyajima waited long enough to have the explosions do double duty, blasting massive holes in the oncoming storm of missiles.

"They've launched five salvos, sir," Xiao reported as a second Wonderwall salvo detonated, and the enemy weapons screamed toward final acquisition.

"I think they have more, but they're holding them back," he concluded.

RFLAM beams lit up the void around Second Fleet, cutting down missiles by the dozens. Wonderwall had killed hundreds of missiles and left the rest half-blind. Shining Shield missiles were just... better than Martian ones, though, and half-blind was still going to be a problem in their thousands.

"Sir?" Soból murmured. "Okorie reports he's on his way. And I don't think we're going to stop enough of those missiles."

Jane took a deep breath, then nodded.

"Five salvos in exchange for time I wanted to spend anyway," she noted. "Let's do it. Abbas—the fleet jumps to Point Iceberg."

That was exactly halfway to the planned exit point of Evac Convoy Two. She didn't want to jump closer in to the planet than that, but that would put her fleet in position to threaten the Kazh if they went after the convoy.

But she'd been keeping track. They'd fired every full salvo they had left. The next fight would be down to a far-smaller base of fire.

As the jump spell tore through *Mjolnir*, she reflected that *threatening* might be all Second Fleet could do now.

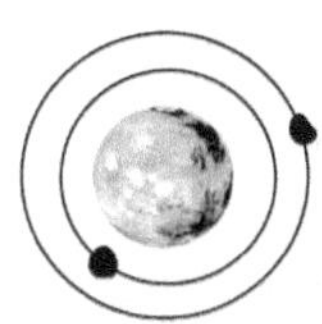

CHAPTER 62

NO ONE IN THE INFORMATION CENTER was running at one hundred percent. Roslyn knew that. She also knew that nobody in any of the fleets—including the Evac Convoy!—was running at one hundred percent either.

Everyone in charge of the ships and transports and people had been on since the Shining Shield had arrived in the system. The only saving grace was that Roslyn knew the Kazh officers, whatever structure the enemy used, had *also* been on for the same amount of time.

"Evac Convoy Two is moving!"

The shouted report brought a scattering of cheers and a sense of palpable relief. Roslyn knew that relief was foolish in many ways, almost a lie, even.

But it was real. So much thought and effort had been focused into getting those five hundred–plus ships and twenty-eight million people away that it felt like a victory, even there, among the people who weren't getting out.

"Their time to jump?" Hsieh asked.

"Should be twenty-one hours but... Wait," Commodore Campbell held up a hand as new numbers trickled in.

"Evac Convoy Two is running at one-point-five gravities," he reported. "Revised time to jump, seventeen hours, forty-three minutes."

Roslyn held her tongue. She'd have done the same, but she'd also sat on the Evacuation Commission meetings. The lottery had been weighted toward families. Not ridiculously so, but enough that, proportionally, there were a lot more children on the transports than anyone would allow for.

And while many claimed that children were made of rubber, she suspected that there were a lot of small humans on those ships who had no idea what was happening to them—and that there was a very real danger to the smallest of those children.

Not least because one-point-five *Earth* gravities was actually over two *Garudan* gravities.

"It's a risk," she finally whispered, close enough to Hsieh that she could be heard.

"I'd guessed. To the usual ones to suffer?"

"The small and the infirm," Roslyn confirmed.

"I would hate your Commodore Okorie for that, but I would have to do the same. It is risk some or lose all."

"I know. Wang isn't moving?"

"No." Hsieh stared blankly ahead for a long moment. "There might be almost thirty million on those ships, but there's still two billion here. He can't save either, dammit."

Roslyn nodded her understanding. There was nothing she could say.

"Wait—I have movement on our ships," Campbell said quietly. "*Ben-Hur* and *Scharnhorst* are moving, accelerating at two gees to catch up to the convoy."

She closed her eyes. She could see Wang's logic. She'd even bet a significant amount of money that one or both of *Chimera*'s Prometheans was now on *Scharnhorst*, transferred to get them out.

In fact...

"Commodore Campbell," she replied to the CSN officer, her voice just as quiet and level as his. "When were Cam and Ty transferred to *Scharnhorst*?"

The silence dropped the temperature several degrees as the Chimeran officer—a straw-haired local, maybe forty Terran years old—demonstrated that his rank didn't come with skill at lying.

"Commodore," Hsieh said firmly. "Answer the question."

"Both were transferred over to *Scharnhorst* while we were loading Evac Convoy One's second load, Mage-Captain, Minister," Campbell confirmed. "There are no Prometheans aboard *Chimera*, *Audacious* or *Acheron*."

Or the six hundred gunships formed up around those three ships. Wang had not been immune to the desire to save his people or the orders to help defend the convoy. He'd just chosen his own fate weeks earlier.

"We have no direct links to Orbital Command at this point, Minister," the Commodore warned. "Admiral Wang severed *all* links to the surface as soon as EC-Two started their burn."

He coughed.

"He also issued the order to destroy all Links in positions that could be seized by the enemy. That includes all systems in orbit or aboard CSN ships."

"That was part of the plan," Roslyn said. "The timing, of course, was always up to him."

"I am very sick, Mage-Captain Chambers," Hsieh Ai Ling said in a very flat voice, "of people deciding they are going to die for me, regardless of *my fucking opinion on it.*"

The words were addressed to Roslyn, but a lot of other people had to have heard them. They were just all pretending they hadn't.

"I am an officer of the Mage-Queen of Mars, Minister," she said carefully. "I am also a close personal friend of our Mage-Queen. If it came down to it, I would die for Kiera Alexander and her opinion of the matter wouldn't count for much."

She shrugged.

"That's the oath I swore, back before I'd met her in person. Before her aunt decided she owed me her life and I was therefore an adoptive cousin. It is my *job*. And whatever is between you and Emerson Wang, this is his job.

"To, if nothing else, convince the enemy that Chimera is defended."

"New contacts! Second Fleet just jumped in to Point Iceberg!"

Roslyn looked at the new contacts, praying that somehow there would be more than she'd seen before her friends had fled. The truth was what she'd anticipated: there were fewer.

Iceberg was thirty light-seconds out, around where the Convoy would have to make turnover to hit zero velocity at one light-minute. That put Second Fleet in missile range of the Convoy for its entire journey... if the Fleet had any missiles left, that was.

"Six warships in the Convoy," she muttered. "Three in orbit. Forty at Iceberg."

Hsieh glanced at her. "Counting hopes?" she asked.

"We'll see."

Roslyn didn't have it in her to shatter any illusions the Minister might still have. Second Fleet was almost certainly out of missiles. The four cruisers and two CSN ships in the Convoy were decently equipped to defend the refugee ships—especially backed by the *Saladins* and *Bushidos*, but against the scale of the enemy fleet...

"Do we still have a location on the Shining Shield?"

"We don't have the light from their emergence at Longma," Campbell admitted. "Our last number on them was via Link from Second Fleet before the Admiral shut down the FTL coms. We can relay through one of the other bases, but we were relying on the orbital stations to centralize telemetry data."

"We're blind," she said flatly. "Because we don't have those stations at all now."

"Our sensor feeds are... limited, yes."

Roslyn sighed.

"Once you have that relay, get me a channel to Second Fleet," she told them. "I'll get us data for as long as they're here."

Who knew how long *that* was going to be?

CHAPTER 63

JANE AND HER PEOPLE SPENT THE ENTIRE first hour on tenterhooks, just *waiting* for the end to come. There were a hundred warships twenty light-minutes away, and the moment they decided to move, it was going to be a final throw of the dice.

She could threaten the bastards, make them think she was a real danger. Miyajima had clever plans that Jane had approved, but all of it was smoke and mirrors.

If the Shining Shield jumped out and made a real push, they'd cut through everything she could do and capture or kill thirty million people.

But for a full hour, they did nothing. In fact, they appeared to be following *her* slingshot course around Longma, pulling their acceleration back down to point-nine-five gravities and using the planet to boost them toward Garuda.

Halfway into the second hour, Soból shook her head and stood back from the display, turning to look at Jane.

"That's it for at least a few hours, sir," she announced. "They're too deep into the planet's gravity well and moving too quickly for a safe jump of any kind."

The words hung in the bridge and Jane shook her head.

"They're safe from us trying to jump in on them too, aren't they?" she asked.

"We could pull something... but it would be riskier than I'm comfortable with."

"Whoever is in command over there has decided their people need time to breathe before they make their final push," Jane guessed. "What's the minimum time before they could complete the slingshot and be safe to jump?"

"A bit under three hours, sir."

She made a snap decision.

"Stand the fleet down to Condition One," Jane ordered. "Stand each shift down for an hour. They can eat, stretch, take a nap—whatever they think is best—but they're back on station to cover for the next shift after an hour."

"We'll make it happen, sir."

Jane didn't sleep, herself. She spent most of the next three hours in her office, being performatively unconcerned about the enemy.

Hard as Evac Convoy Two was pushing their passengers, the evacuation ships seemed to crawl across space. Even with the time the enemy was giving them, everything still hung in the balance of the next few hours and what the Shining Shield's commander chose.

In their place, *she'd* have let the convoy go. The Royal Martian Navy didn't make war on civilians. Chasing the evacuation ships down would leave her with a choice between being utterly ineffectual against them or committing a war crime.

One that even being the Mage-Queen's aunt wouldn't protect her from.

Still, the three hours passed in silence. So did the three *after* that, before Jane's patience finally ran out and she returned to the Flag Bridge.

The crew remained at two-thirds of full strength. Someone had decided, without asking her, to keep the crew at Condition One. Maybe they'd assumed that without an explicit order from her, that was where they should remain.

"Are they doing *anything*?" she demanded.

"They have completed their slingshot at a decent speed and are now heading directly toward Garuda at the same standard thrust," Soból told her. She was apparently mother-henning Operations again, with none of their shift leaders present on the Flag Bridge.

"They are *days* away on the course they've set, so I anticipate they're planning on jumping at some point. Probably once every ship in their fleet is ready to do so."

"Or they're playing games again," Jane countered. "If they only had three Promethean-equivalents aboard their ships, they couldn't have made it here after the last attack. If they had three Mages aboard, they'd have been ready to jump ten minutes ago."

"You're assuming they use the same intervals as our Navy Mages, sir," Soból said. "The Navy trains you all to jump every six hours, but civilian Mages limit themselves to every eight. I'm not clear on the reason why, but are we sure it applies to the Reezh Kazh?"

"The Navy selects the best Mages in the Protectorate," Jane told her subordinate. "A Mage who can't make a six-hour jump can't be a Navy Mage. They can try out for the Marines or even be a civilian Jump Mage, but they can't serve as a full Navy Mage."

There was also a group of Mages who were *employed* by the Navy but weren't Navy Mages, mostly working on auxiliaries and in logistics. While any Navy Mage was trained to do some complex transmutation, specialist Transmuters were better at it. There were a dozen of them aboard the logistics ships, critical to the operations of the Royal Martian Navy—but they weren't *Navy* Mages.

"But the Kazh don't have that many Mages," Xiao pointed out, the Intelligence Officer seeming to snap awake, for all that his eyes had been open. "That's why most of their fleet is using the Engines—because they don't *realize* the poor people they're murdering to fuel them are Mages.

"They may have more knowledge of magic than we do, more years of experience... but they don't have as broad a population to draw on. They can't meet the same recruiting standard we do."

"No. They can't," Jane agreed slowly. "So, if they're waiting for their Mages to rest, they're waiting *eight* hours."

And the trio that had gone from jump to amplified magic without resting were probably out for longer. The enemy would have two jumps in their back pocket for their Mage-powered ships—the ones she was certain were their command vessels.

"As much as two hours, then," she guessed aloud. "We'll keep our eyes open, but we'll bring the fleet back to battle stations in an hour.

"Let our people get what rest we can give them."

CHAPTER 64

JANE STRETCHED HER SENSES OUT ONCE MORE. She could feel the song of the fleet around her, something she'd never truly paid attention to before. In the distance, she could feel the song of the evacuation convoy, like a band playing halfway down the street.

There was an atonal sub-harmony to Evac Convoy Two's song, one she couldn't separate out at this distance, but one that felt both wrong and painfully familiar.

She could guess what it was. Even with the minds in it willing *now*, the Prometheus Interface and the Engine of Sacred Sacrifice were tools of murder, of twisting victims into forced servitude.

Jane hadn't noticed it in the enemy fleet, but she knew that was what was familiar about Evac Convoy Two. The subtly wrong magical harmony of a twisted hybrid of magic, technology, flesh and murder.

"As of twenty minutes ago, the enemy was continuing on course, no adjustments," Miyajima reported, sliding into her station as the rest of the Second Shift returned to their seats around Jane.

"Our assets?" Jane asked.

"*Chimera* and the two *Andreas*-class cruisers are still in Garudan orbit, supported by six hundred gunships. *Scharnhorst* and *Ben-Hur* are in with Evac Convoy Two, along with four of our *Honorific*-class cruisers.

"We have five missiles per launcher left on *Last Stand at the Alamo* and fifteen on the *Bards*, *Virtues* and *Mjolnir*," Miyajima continued. "That's only Phoenixes, of course. We fired off *Mjolnir*'s Samurais with the rest of them."

"Best guess is that the Kazh have either two or three missile salvos left," Xiao added. "Fifty to seventy thousand missiles."

More than enough, Jane suspected, to wipe Evac Convoy Two from the universe. Against any other enemy, she wouldn't have expected it. The human rule of war was that civilian ships were interned in orbit when the invading fleet arrived. Anything that got out of orbit before you reached missile range wasn't covered by that internment. They could be pursued and ordered to haul over, but neither the Republic nor the Protectorate had regularly fired on civilian ships.

The Republic had done a lot of things early in the war before the unspoken agreements had locked into place. They'd also, to Jane's surprise, actually executed several of their own officers as part of making those agreements real.

A rare moment of pragmatic justice from the men who'd broken humanity's unity.

"The convoy is currently in both our missile range and Admiral Wang's," Soból said. "If they try to jump in close to them, they're going to find themselves under fire from three directions. I think even their computers are going to have trouble with that."

Jane nodded, turning her focus to the void around them. She doubted she could sense far enough to detect the Shining Shield arriving at the distances she was expecting, but she could make sure they didn't jump her people at close range again.

The clock ticked, silent numbers changing on the screen. Eight hours since the enemy's last jump, and Jane caught herself starting to hold her breath.

"Contact," Miyajima reported. "Range… fourteen million kilometers from us. Ten million from Evac Convoy Two. About twelve from Garudan orbit."

A moment paused. The Kazh had cut their jump tight to the planet, but it had given them clear lines of fire on every force in the system.

"They have launched on the convoy, sir."

Jane shivered, the movement entirely involuntary. She'd prepared everything on the assumption that the enemy would attempt to destroy the civilian ships, but part of her hadn't truly believed it.

"All ships will launch missiles in defense mode," she ordered. "Cover the convoy."

Eight hundred missiles blazed out from her ships—and the icons on her screen lit up with more green dots. She had a Link connection with the *Honorifics* amidst EC-Two, and their own three hundred missiles showed on her display the moment they fired.

"Wang is maneuvering. All vessels in Garudan orbit just lit up their drives at three gravities, heading directly toward the Kazh," Miyajima reported. There was a pregnant pause. "The Shining Shield's course is for Garuda, sir. They are firing on the convoy, but they are not pursuing."

As the Mage-Commander spoke, a second shoal of red icons blazed onto the screen. Over fifty thousand missiles were now hurtling toward five hundred ships, all too few of which had any defenses at all.

"Commodore Okorie reports that the Prometheans are... executing Phalanx?" Jundt told her, confusion clear in his voice. "Do you know what that is, sir?"

Jane didn't *know*... but she had a suspicion.

"Get me a close up on the Convoy," she ordered.

The display adjusted, the green icons shifting around to match what she expected.

The fifteen *Saladins* and twenty *Bushidos* might carry over half of the evacuees, but they were also the only ships out of five hundred and thirty-eight that had *any* real defenses. The thirty-five transports had moved forward with the warships, forming a frail-seeming wall of their hulls and lasers against the oncoming storm.

"Third enemy salvo in space, sir," Miyajima said grimly. "No change in numbers or performance. Estimate five minutes to impact."

"Dump every missile we have into their path, Ops," Jane ordered. She knew they were already doing it, but giving the order made her feel slightly less hopeless.

"Sir! The Chimerans." Jane almost wrenched her neck, twisting to check out the section of the display showing Garuda. Then the display pulled back out, allowing her to see everything easily again—and to see the unimaginably immense salvo the orbital defenses had just launched.

"Estimate one hundred twenty thousand, repeat, one two zero zero zero zero missiles launched from Garuda's orbit," Miyajima said, filling in the context to her Chief's exclamation. "Even counting the gunships and stations, Wang only has six thousand launchers."

"I think the good Admiral decided that he had a pile of missiles in his storehouses and that, sometimes, a missile that's drifting in space is almost as good as one that gets launched," Jane replied. "It's not entirely true, but he *definitely* has their attention."

If the Shining Shield had any missiles left, they'd stopped firing them at EC-Two. They were probably still mothering them on their course toward the evacuees, but their focus seemed to be on the orbitals of Garuda.

After all, every missile Second Fleet and the ships with EC-Two were firing was in defensive mode. Hundreds of missiles self-destructed, taking hundreds of enemy weapons with them.

But thousands remained and two more salvos were behind them. Second Fleet couldn't calculate the jump to intercept them in time. They hadn't known the enemy's emergence point and so couldn't position themselves in the right place—she'd chosen a spot where she could fire at any salvos heading for the Convoy, not a place where she could block a few dozen of a potentially infinite number of attack vectors.

She wouldn't have guessed they'd come out where they had, focusing in on the planet while firing off their remaining missiles at the Convoy, almost out of spite.

With over a hundred thousand missiles heading their way, it might prove to be a mistake on the Kazh's part. Possibly even enough of one to turn the tide of the battle—something that might even make the loss of the Convoy worth it.

Jane still wasn't going to let that happen.

More missiles died to intercept salvos, and she watched in silence, part of her mind trying to run the calculations for the jump, knowing that there wasn't enough time.

Then they entered the outer defensive perimeter and she understood why the Prometheans had been prepared to risk their passengers. In a ship as large as any of their battleships and only a tithe smaller than their largest carriers, the Republic hadn't installed a single offensive weapon.

The primary value of the *Saladins* was their massive internal spaces, but that had left them with massive hulls that didn't have missile launchers or heavy lasers. Just RFLAM turrets.

And more RFLAM turrets.

And then more RFLAM turrets.

She'd seen the numbers. She hadn't quite conceived of just what six hundred of the Republic's one-gigawatt, eight-lasing-chamber antimissile turrets could do.

Fifteen *Saladins* fired nine thousand lasers at once. Twenty *Bushidos* added five thousand beams of their own. The actual warships shouldn't have felt like an afterthought, but they added a *mere* thousand more antimissile weapons.

And every one of those beams was cycling once a second. The best part of fifteen thousand defensive turrets tore into the incoming missiles, and Jane realized that the Evacuation Convoy probably didn't need Second Fleet's covering fire.

She wasn't going to stop sending it. Every missile her fire took down was one the turrets didn't need to worry about—and even a single hit could cause devastating casualties aboard a convoy packed full of civilians.

"Fire incoming on the Shining Shield," Miyajima reported. "Thirty seconds to impact. Estimate over a hundred thousand weapons still intact."

Handle that, you bastards.

Except that even as Jane thought it, she felt the pulse of pressure and knew what her enemy had decided.

"Enemy capital ships in Garudan orbit!" Miyajima exclaimed. "Multiple Type Ones engaging *Chimera*... *Chimera* is down."

The other ships didn't even get a mention. Five Shining Shield Type Ones, seventy-plus million tons apiece, were more than three ex-Republic warships could handle at point-blank range.

"Where are the rest of them?" Jane asked, wishing she had the time to mourn the people she knew had just died. All but two ships of the CSN had just been wiped from the universe, and their orbital defenses weren't lasting much longer—but only five of the enemy ships had Mages aboard, and *all* of them had vanished.

"We have no contacts, sir," Miyajima reported. "They jumped clear, but we have no idea where."

The Flag Bridge was silent.

"What do we do, sir?" Soból asked.

"Maneuver to rendezvous with the Evac Convoy," she ordered. "We cover them the rest of the way out."

She couldn't help but glare at the five red icons gleaming in orbit of Garuda.

"We can't go after them," Jane admitted. "But we can make absolutely certain they won't risk coming near the convoy."

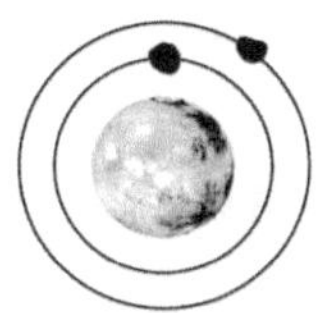

CHAPTER 65

"SHUT DOWN THE LINKS."

Roslyn didn't realize she'd used full command voice on a room full of people who weren't even part of her nation, let alone her service, until it was too late.

Her orders were necessary. The entire Information Center had frozen at the horrific speed with which the Fourth Battle of Chimera had come to an end. Where the Chimera Space Navy had held the orbitals a minute earlier, five massive warships from the Shining Shield of the Nine now hung alone.

The armed stations and forts died as quickly as *Chimera* and the cruisers. The enemy proton beams were utterly devastating at this range, single bolts vaporizing the central cores of stations a hundred meters across.

Thirty seconds after the Kazh arrived, there was a new debris cloud in orbit of Garuda, one that would pose a critical threat to the civilian infrastructure in orbit—and the enemy warships were in position to start scanning the surface.

"Links are down," Campbell confirmed, Roslyn having jarred him into action. "Thank you, Mage-Captain."

"The Royal Martian Navy spent years, Commodore, trying to find a way to detect the Links," she told him. "The Republic had us infiltrated six ways to Monday at the start of the war, with enough capacity that a large plurality of their agents had ready access to Link systems."

Some of them concealed aboard RMN warships. Hardly her Navy's most shining moment.

"We could never detect them, and they *should* be safe. But we have no idea what the Kazh can do, so your plan makes sense. It was better not forgotten."

She forced a wry smile. Most of the people she'd known in the CSN had been aboard *Chimera*.

"Without the Links, we're restricted to passive observatories in the mountains, cable-linked to the other bunkers," Badem warned, the Marine General stepping into the unofficial central command position by the main hologram.

Hsieh Ai Ling was gently ushered aside by Gunny Matveyeva, Roslyn saw, and she chose to leave the Minister to the NCO. If anyone in the room had a clue how to handle a woman who'd just lost the man she loved, it was a Marine Corps Gunnery Warrant Sergeant.

"Everyone," Badem said loudly, raising her voice to get the attention of the various people in the Citadel's Information Center. "Check your cables; check your connections with the other bases and bunkers.

"*They* all need to validate that they have shut down anything that might be emitting outside the surface. The next few hours are for all the cards, people. If they find even one bunker today, they won't stop hunting for more until long after it matters to us."

The shock gave way to the soft murmur of voices as the operators made their calls.

Badem shared a long look with Roslyn.

"You know Alexander," she murmured. "What will she do?"

"Form up on the Convoy and dare the Kazh to come at her, basically," Roslyn said. "Right now, there are a handful of ships with her that have missiles left—and those are the *only* ships with missiles in the star system. Not enough to be worth picking a fight with the Shield, but... enough to make them hesitate."

"She'll get the Convoy out, then," Badem guessed.

"I think so." Roslyn looked up at the hologram. She could see the markers declaring uncertainty zones. There was no more instant data, and even their lightspeed data was far more limited.

The icons for Second Fleet and Evac Convoy Two had merged. Both were heading outward at the same one-point-five gees Okorie had pushed the whole way out.

"What about the rest of the Shield fleet?" Campell asked.

"I'd guess those are the ships that don't have Mages aboard," Roslyn said. "They only have Engines of Sacred Sacrifice and weren't prepared for a clever stunt. They probably punched an emergency jump command to a present rendezvous point.

"How long until they're back depends on their communications and how far they jumped. If they jumped one light-minute, for example, they'd be back by now. If they jumped ten and whatever their FTL com tech is doesn't have tactical uses, they'll be back in around ten minutes."

Long enough for them to see what had happened with their other ships.

"Too unpredictable and almost certainly too soon for Alexander to try to chop the head off the snake," Badem concluded. "So, that's it, then."

"For the space battle, almost certainly," Roslyn confirmed.

Energy signatures blazed on the display, and she grimaced. The enemy ships were settling into very specific orbits, and their scans had clearly found something. Roslyn could pick out the energy signature of a proton beam on sight by now—but the information on the screen didn't add up for a moment.

"They fired on the surface," Campbell said, seeing the extra factor a second before Roslyn did. "Most of our ground-level intelligence and scanning are dependent on the satellite network. We weren't pulling from it to avoid signals."

"How many shots?"

"Dozens," a tech replied.

"Six targets, though," Roslyn said, gesturing at the concentration that the local specialist hadn't seen. "The decoy bases?"

"Can we confirm that?" Badem asked Campbell.

"We should be able to," he confirmed. He walked away to talk to one of the com specialists.

"Where the hell is O'Neill?" Badem muttered. "He's supposed to be the one actually running this place."

"I think he passed out a few hours ago," Roslyn said. "I doubt he's far, but I don't know where he is to wake him up."

Badem grunted.

"We should have planned better for that. I don't think the locals realized how long the battle was going to have to take."

Campbell rejoined them.

"We've confirmed it. They hit the decoy bases. Ground fire from energy weapons… that's not going to do good things to the weather, is it?"

"The RMN hasn't tested surface strikes for lasers in a while," Roslyn admitted. "We'll use them in upper atmosphere, but our beams lose a lot of power pushing through atmosphere. Proton beams… would have less of that issue but would still pump a lot of waste heat into the atmosphere."

"Plus, the impact effects themselves," Badem added. "We were planning for kinetic strikes. Those are messy, but the effects are relatively contained. This… We might be looking at firestorms."

"We have to leave that to local emergency services, Commodore," Roslyn told Campbell as he started to turn away. "There is *nothing* we can do right now."

He froze and she could see his shoulders slump.

"You're right, of course," he muttered.

"Sirs! Transmission from orbit. Wide beam, directed at the entire planetary surface," a tech reported.

The Kazh ships had finished their positioning, Roslyn saw. One ship hung above each pole and the other three were spread around the equator. All five were transmitting, making certain the entire planet got their message.

"After all of this, I suppose it is time for them to talk, isn't it?" Roslyn muttered grimly.

"Show us," Badem snapped. "And someone translate. I doubt these… people are speaking in English."

A new image was inserted into the hologram. For a moment, Roslyn thought the reezh at the center of the screen was suspended in space.

Then she realized it was the same illusion as a warship's simulacrum: thousands of high-fidelity fiberoptic cables bringing the light from outside the ship to its center.

The figure on the screen had their multi-jointed arms folded in front of them, a posture that looked painful to a human, and had lowered their head to focus all four of their eyes at the pickup around their armored frill.

They stood on what she realized was a transparent platform, surrounded by other platforms holding computer stations manned by other reezh, their images ever so slightly blurred.

Even across alien esthetics and technology, she recognized a Flag Bridge.

The reezh spoke. Roslyn could only begin to understand the reezh language, but it was clear that his speech was different. *Awkward* wasn't the right word, but it sounded more stilted. More... ornate?"

"I am Commandant-of-Forces Sword-of-Twilight," Campbell translated the alien words for them. "It is my honor to tell the children of Allosch that they are once more in the Light of the Nine.

"Those-Who-Speak have sought the People's lost children for hundreds of years, and we were disgusted to find you under the heel of an alien conqueror. We have now driven off these aliens, and we come to restore your faith and to reunite you with your people.

"Priests of the Nine will soon be among you. They will be guarded by our warriors. Others will see to the proper administration of Allosch. There is no need for violence. We are lost siblings, reunited in a single faith and as the People of the Nine."

The message ended and there was a cold silence in the Information Center.

"Hell of a demand for surrender," Badem observed. "Not a word until they've obliterated all resistance, then all *We have found you at last, our lost fellows.*"

"It is a lie and a grotesquery," a reezh officer growled. "Know that Commodore Campbell has... softened the Commandant's words. They mask enslavement in words of family."

"I'm not surprised," Badem noted. "There's nothing for us to do right now but keep our heads down." She sighed. "Not that I'm going anywhere."

"General, Minister Ojak is sending a message," the same com tech reported. "They are sending it on every media on the planet and beaming it into orbit, directed at all five ships."

"Show us," Badem said.

Ojak was seated at their desk, the city spreading out behind them as they faced their own camera.

"Commandant-of-Forces Sword-of-Twilight," he greeted the alien. Roslyn glanced at the hologram and saw the markers showing that it had been recorded in two languages. The tech was, thankfully, playing the English version.

"I am Minister Izhaj Ojak, elected by the people of... Allosch"—he corrected the name for the planet to the one Sword-of-Twilight had used—"to speak on their behalf. We have attempted to talk to you and your fleets before, only to be met with silence.

"The truth of your arrival is written across the skies of this world, in the broken ships and the debris of our space stations. It is written in the firestorms sweeping the plains to the north of this city, where you bombarded our world without a word.

"You claim siblinghood, but you have unleashed fire upon us, without any words or demands that we could yield to in order to spare our people. Only now, when we have lost tens of thousands of friends, siblings, parents, children, do you speak to us.

"For all your pretty words, you have brought fire and death to our world. And yet. And yet." Ojak closed their eyes for a long second.

Roslyn wasn't sure if they'd recorded in English and dubbed in reezh or vice versa. There might even be completely different recordings, though she suspected Ojak was capable of projecting their quite-real distress just as well if they had to repeat themselves.

"I have no choice. To prevent further loss of life, I offer the complete and unconditional surrender of the Dual Republics. I am ordering all of our remaining deployed troops to lay down their arms and go home.

"We... yield to the light of the Nine. We will learn of our lost siblings."

The message ended and Roslyn bit her lip. There was no choice—but she also noted that Ojak's orders were phrased to explicitly exclude the troops in the bunkers.

They weren't *deployed troops*. Not yet. Not until they sortied from their underground hiding places to retake Garuda for its people.

She only hoped there would be enough left of those people to save.

ABOUT THE AUTHOR

GLYNN STEWART is the author of Starship's Mage, a bestselling science fiction and fantasy series where faster-than-light travel is possible–but only because of magic. His other works include science fiction series Duchy of Terra, Castle Federation and Vigilante, as well as the urban fantasy series ONSET and Changeling Blood.

Writing managed to liberate Glynn from a bleak future as an accountant. With his personality and hope for a high-tech future intact, he lives in Canada with his partner, their cats, and an unstoppable writing habit.

CREDITS

The following people were involved in making this book:
Copyeditor: Richard Shealy
Cover Artist: Roman Chalyi
Faolan's Pen Publishing:
Jack Giesen

And a sincere thank you to Glynn's Patreon subscribers!

OTHER BOOKS BY GLYNN STEWART

For release announcements join the mailing list
or visit **GlynnStewart.com**

STARSHIP'S MAGE
Starship's Mage
Hand of Mars
Voice of Mars
Alien Arcana
Judgment of Mars
UnArcana Stars
Sword of Mars
Mountain of Mars
The Service of Mars
A Darker Magic
Mage-Commander
Beyond the Eyes of Mars
Nemesis of Mars
Chimera's Star
Ambassador for Mars
Chimera's Fall (*upcoming*)

Starship's Mage: Red Falcon
Interstellar Mage
Mage-Provocateur
Agents of Mars

Starship's Mage Novellas
Pulsar Race
Mage-Queen's Thief

DUCHY OF TERRA

The Terran Privateer
Duchess of Terra
Terra and Imperium
Darkness Beyond
Shield of Terra
Imperium Defiant
Relics of Eternity
Shadows of the Fall
Eyes of Tomorrow

SCATTERED STARS

Scattered Stars: Conviction

Conviction
Deception
Equilibrium
Fortitude
Huntress
Prodigal

Scattered Stars: Evasion

Evasion
Discretion
Absolution

PEACEKEEPERS OF SOL

Raven's Peace
The Peacekeeper Initiative
Raven's Course
Drifter's Folly
Remnant Faction
Raven's Flag
Wartorn Stars
Raven's Hope

Prequel Novella

Honor & Renown: A Peacekeepers of Sol Novella

HOUSE ADAMANT

The Exodus Gambit
The Old Guard
The Valkyrie Stratagem (*upcoming*)

EXILE

Exile
Refuge
Crusade
Ashen Stars: An Exile Novella

CASTLE FEDERATION

Space Carrier Avalon
Stellar Fox
Battle Group Avalon
Q-Ship Chameleon
Rimward Stars
Operation Medusa
A Question of Faith: A Castle Federation Novella

Dakotan Confederacy

Admiral's Oath
To Stand Defiant
Unbroken Faith

VIGILANTE

(WITH TERRY MIXON))
Heart of Vengeance
Oath of Vengeance

Bound By Stars: A Vigilante Series (With Terry Mixon)

Bound By Law
Bound by Honor
Bound by Blood

AETHER SPHERES

Nine Sailed Star

Void Spheres (*upcoming*)

TEER AND KARD

Wardtown

Blood Ward

Blood Adept

CHANGELING BLOOD

Changeling's Fealty

Hunter's Oath

Noble's Honor

Fae, Flames & Fedoras: A Changeling Blood Novella

ONSET

ONSET: To Serve and Protect

ONSET: My Enemy's Enemy

ONSET: Blood of the Innocent

ONSET: Stay of Execution

Murder by Magic: An ONSET Novella

STANDALONE NOVELS & NOVELLAS

Children of Prophecy

City in the Sky

Excalibur Lost: A Space Opera Novella

Balefire: A Dark Fantasy Novella

Icebreaker: A Fantasy Naval Thriller